Necro Sex Machine

Andre Duza

DEADITE PRESS
Tempe, Arizona

A BIZARRO NOVEL
www.bizarrocentral.com

DEADITE PRESS
AN ERASERHEAD PRESS COMPANY
WWW.ERASERHEADPRESS.COM

Deadite Press
5929 S. Juniper St.
Tempe, AZ 85283

ISBN: 1-933929-64-2

Copyright © 2008 by Andre Duza
Cover art copyright © 2008 by Fred Moore, colors by Juamar
Interior art copyright © 2008 by Fred Moore, Silverfish
Cover and interior design by: Carlton Mellick III
Copy-edited by: Geoff Baker
Proofreader: Brenda Wilkinson
Published by: Timothy Burkland and Deadite Press

Thanks to...
Brenda Wilkinson, Silverfish, Fred Moore, Juanmar, Wayne "Menz"
Simmons, Darin Basile, Camille, BombRog, Key, Razor and Blade

"She Swims With Corpses" first appeared in the chapbook *Dead Bitch Walking*, published by IndieGods Publishing.

All rights reserved. No part of this book may be reproduced or transmitted in any form or by any means, electronic or mechanical, including photo-copying, recording, or by any information storage and retrieval system, without the written consent of the publisher, except where permitted by law.

Printed in the USA

Contents

For Sergio Leone and Chang Cheh

We do what we want here; killing or raping…
- Lu Feng, *Masked Avengers*

Prologue

The Devil Has a Vagina

Testing... one, two... Testing... one, two... one, two...

The time is 10:35 pm, August 7, 2005.
My name is J. Günther Douglass-*J for Johnny, which*
I hate. Always have. *I'm a soldier with the Revenant Clan*
(or the Dead Bitch Army to all you haters), a member of Voo-
doo Posse. *I'm not really sure where* to start, or *how,* for that
matter. I couldn't even give you a clear answer as to *why* I'm
making these recordings, or *whom* I expect would listen to them.

I figured I'd just get something recorded to put myself
into some kind of a groove. So here goes....

The Revenant Clan consists of five main members...

CUT TO:

Close-up of what appears to be an extremely thin woman dressed
in sleek, protective body armor. The body armor is black and
made of a thick, durable Kevlar. A tube runs from a small, flat
backpack to the left side of her helmet. A blank white mask
makes up the front of the helmet. The woman is holding an ax
with a long wooden handle that curves downward at the butt. It is
her favorite weapon.

J. Günter Douglass (VO): Number one, the Queen, aka Bloody Mary, aka the Dead Bitch.

The camera does an abrupt, Shaw Brothers-style zoom to a wide shot. Mary is standing in a small room with blue walls and no windows, the axe resting casually against her shoulder. A sawed-off shotgun sits snugly in a holster on her hip. She is surrounded by human-shaped training dummies made of straw and bamboo. She lifts the fire axe and twirls it in her hand.

J. Günter Douglass (cont'd): Raised by the Ergeister Church, she was trained since childhood for the war. She is an expert with firearms, melee weapons, and hand-to-hand combat.

Mary hacks limbs from the dummies, swinging the axe in a stylized fashion. Old-school sound effects accompany her movements. The twirls, strikes, and poses suggest a polished fighting style executed with a primal intensity. Mary rests the axe against her shoulder and pulls the shotgun from her hip with her free hand. She fires upon a fresh set of intact dummies, instantly pulverizing them. She returns the gun to its holster.

The camera zooms in on her mask. She reaches up and opens her mask to reveal the nearly skeletal face beneath it.

J. Günter Douglass (cont'd): Few outside of the Queen's inner circle have actually seen her without her mask, but it is said that the sight of her face has been known to stop men's hearts.

Mary gnashes her teeth and hisses at the camera, but instead of her rasped voice, a ghastly cackle scores a quick zoom into the darkness of her hollow eye socket. The cackling continues to echo in the darkness.

CUT TO:

Close-up of a sturdy, angry-looking black man with long dreadlocks twisted into a single braid at the back of his head. His eyes are big and brown and mesmerizing. He is dressed in combat gear. He stands calmly with his hands clasped behind his back.

J. Günter Douglass (VO): Number two, General Elam, aka Griffen or Griff.

The camera zooms out to a wide shot. Griff is in a similar room with blue walls and no windows. Five anonymous men, who are armed with a table leg, baseball bats, a machete, and a handgun, surround him.

J. Günter Douglass (cont'd): Born with powerful psychokinetic and mind-control abilities, he was taken in by the Ergeister Church at a young age and trained alongside the Queen.

The anonymous men attack.

Griff thrusts his right hand at the man with the gun. A ripple of distortion travels outward from Griff's palm. The man with the gun suddenly turns his aim on the other men and shoots them one by one. The look on his face indicates that he is doing this against his will. He continues shooting until the gun clicks empty. He throws the gun down and stares at his hands, horrified. He turns to Griff. His eyes give away the rush of ideas that flood his brain. He charges.

Wild arms rain down on Griff. He blocks and evades them. He counters with a kick to the knee and a flurry of hands. The other

8

man staggers backward, punch-drunk. Griff hurls him into the rear wall without touching him. He bounces against the ceiling and from wall to wall, making impact with a crackle-smack. He hits the floor hard. His body is twisted into an awkward pose that suggests multiple shattered bones.

Griff straightens his clothing.

CUT TO:

A group of anonymous men are arranged in a pile in the middle of a room with blue walls and no windows. They repeatedly punch, kick, and stomp someone in the middle. Bodies suddenly fly apart. A bear of a man with a red beard and red hair pulled into a ponytail stands at the center of the bodies. He is wearing combat gear beneath a bloodstained lab coat.

J. Günter Douglass (VO): Number three, Professor Kagen, aka Dr. Kagen, aka Michelangelo the Butcher.

Invigorated by the ambush, Kagen balls his fists and flexes the muscles in his arms and torso. He squares off with the men as they encircle him. A few are still climbing to their feet.

Kagen: Come *on* you *fuckers!*

The men charge at him.

J. Günter Douglass (cont'd): Med-school dropout and self-styled artist, he made a name for himself as Michelangelo the Butcher, a brutal serial killer who was never caught by police, before crossing paths with the Queen and Griff in the early nine-

9

ties.

Kagen reaches out and snaps the first man's neck before the man can reach him. He tosses the second and third men into the rear wall. Bones shatter. He catches the fourth man, puts him in a headlock, and breaks his neck. He grabs the sixth man by the throat. The seventh man hits him from behind with a two-by-four. Kagen lifts the fifth man off his feet. He pulls the man close, takes a large bite out of his face, and throws the man into the wall. The seventh man continues to hit him with the two-by-four. Kagen turns and blocks the last strike with his forearm. He grabs the man and lifts him over his head. He slams the man's body down and breaks his back over his knee. He tosses the twitching body to the floor and rises into an antagonistic stance, ready for more. He bares teeth like a wild animal. His face is covered with blood.

CUT TO:

A pretty, young blond walks through a room with blue walls and no windows. She is wearing a tight biochemical suit that accentuates her curvaceous figure. "Badass" is stenciled over the left breast of her suit in bold letters. Her serpentine gait exudes confident sexuality. She walks past a small group of random hoodlums who are huddled together and talking, laughing, and smoking cigarettes. They "hoot and holler" as she passes. She ignores them.

J. Günter Douglass (VO): Number four, Rainah, aka Princess Rainah, aka Bloody Rainah, aka Hellcat, aka Lady Death, aka Lady Rain, aka Sexy Bitch, aka Blades, aka Badass.

Angered by her rejection, one of the men leans forward to grab her arm. Rainah turns and slashes at his neck. A metallic blur indicates something sharp in her hand. The man grabs his throat and begins to gag. Blood leaks out from between his fingers. He staggers and falls into his friends. He dies in their arms.

The other hoodlums attack Rainah.

J. Günter Douglass (cont'd): Kidnapped from her parents at a young age, she was raised by the Queen and trained to kill. Despite her playful demeanor, she is extremely ruthless, cunning, and deadly with a blade.

Rainah spins and slashes with balletic grace. Her movements fall into three categories: evade, parry, and strike. By the time she stops moving, the hoodlums lay dead and dying on the ground.

Rainah flips the large, serrated blade of her knife and slides it into a sheath on her forearm. She turns and lets out a dismissive "Humph!" before walking away.

CUT TO:

A young black man walks through a room with blue walls and no windows. He is wearing combat gear underneath a faded wool blazer. Two straps lined with bullets criss-cross his torso beneath the jacket. Suddenly, gunshots ring out from behind obstacles placed randomly around the room in front of him (parked cars, a garbage can, a mailbox, a fake-looking plastic tree, et cetera). The bullets miss him. The young man opens his coat to reveal antique revolvers holstered at each hip.

J. Günter Douglass (VO): Number six, Sergeant Derek Davies, aka Deadwood Derek, aka D & D.

Derek calmly snatches the antique revolvers from their holsters and fires a series of shots in different directions.

J. Günter Douglass (cont'd): A runaway who joined the group after murdering his parents as a teen, he is a direct descendant of black cowboy, Nat Love (aka Deadwood Dick), a heritage that he wears proudly.

Afterward, Derek twirls the revolvers and slides them back into their holsters.

There is a silent moment, and then... bodies fall from their hiding places (six altogether), each one the victim of a single, fatal gunshot.

_____

Forty percent of the Revenant Clan had enlisted simply because it was the best option if you lived in their part of the world-*was* being the operative word here.

You see, the thought process goes like this:

Hmmmm.

Moral dignity (life out in the wasteland): always hungry; moving from community to community; risking being robbed, raped, or killed just for trespassing on some whacked-out vigilante's property; starving to death, or at least coming damn close on a daily basis.

Versus...

Survival (linking up with one of the larger armies; in this case, the Revenant Clan): safety; security; peace of mind; three

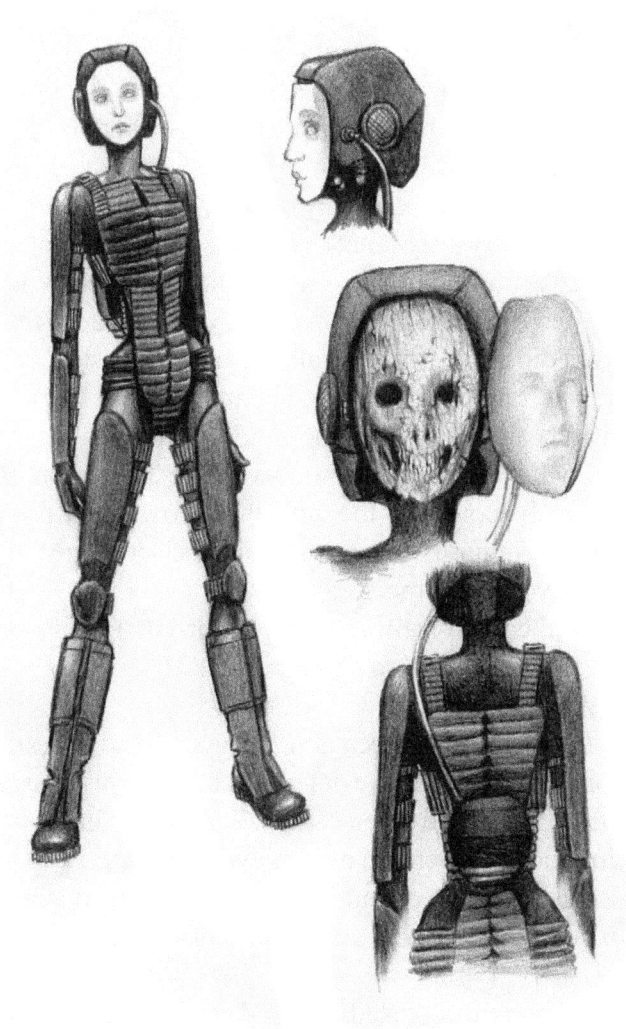

squares a day, plus you get to play with guns and tell people what to do.

The decision was easy for me.

You learn a few things about yourself when you've been dragged, kicking and screaming, to the precipice of death, as I had been on many occasions before I enlisted. I learned that I wanted to live... at all costs, and that I never wanted to feel like a victim again.

I used to be a decent guy back when the world was right. I try to remind myself of that as often as possible. Back then, I was the unassuming, slightly overweight horror geek you'd pass on the street or in a mall without noticing. I had a few good friends but did most of my socializing online, most of my movie watching at home (alone), and, as far as my sex life was concerned, all I can say is talk to the hand (chuckle).

Back then, guys like me... we were the new "normal."

I wish I could say the same thing now: that I'm a decent guy. After the things I've done... the things I let happen... I don't know what you'd call me.

G'ahead. It's all right. I've heard it all: cold-blooded killer, heartless bastard, coward, monster.

At least I'm alive (chuckle).

I'm writing this because I *do* have a heart. ~~Most... A lot of~~... Some of the things I've done have been for just reasons way down deep. As for the others... well, I try not to think about that stuff. Instead, I just remind myself over and over...

I used to be a decent guy. I used to be a decent guy. I used to be a decent guy. I used to be a decent guy....

When I first enlisted, I vowed that I would use this experience to make myself into the kind of person who would never take shit from anyone. I wasn't one of these Bloody Mary fanatics in search of some mythic zombie to take me on a romanticized

14

adventure across the wasteland. And I wasn't looking to become a disciple of the Ergeister Church.

I joined after the big separation. The Ergeister Church had been running one hell of a smear campaign against the Queen, and it was taking its toll on the troops. Many of them quit or deserted as a result. Membership was at an all-time low. The Ergeister communities that the Queen had helped to establish (back when we were a branch of the Ergeister Army) had turned on us. We couldn't even get within five miles of them before the shooting started.

You have to understand... the Queen... she's like a freakin' God to some-a-these people out here. Even without the church. And the church knows it. Plus, they're afraid that she'll eventually come after their asses. The Queen was raised in the church, and now they had abandoned her. From what I know of her past, she doesn't take that kind of thing lightly.

Between you and me, the Queen is just another megalo-maniacal freak in a long line of nutjobs fighting for control of what's left of this planet. She just happens to be one of the more successful ones. And, like I said, I was tired of being the victim. I wanted to learn how to fight, how to kill without conscience. I wanted to know what it felt like to be feared. I know it sounds grim, but you don't know what it's like out there. Or maybe you do. I don't know.

You're probably wondering if I've seen her. It's one of the first things people ask. Most of them want to know if it's true—if she's really dead like the legend says. 'Fraid I can't tell you that. What I can tell you is that *she* (the Queen) is a real person: real as in physically real. I've only seen her fully suited up and from afar.

There *are* things about the Queen that you notice right away. The way she moves, for instance... or... or the overbearing smell of bad perfume—supposedly to mask the rot. And to this day, I've never seen someone so goddamn thin. I can't imagine that you haven't seen the shaky video footage from the rave back in 2000 and the "massacre on South Broad" as it's become known. Both show her unmasked, and rotten, like a Romero zombie with attitude.

They have become perennial images in the smear campaign of the National News Network (formerly the New Philadelphia News Organization). That bitch Linda Ludlow runs the NNN. Remember her?

I always assumed that the footage was doctored. My uncle Jay had imparted unto me a good deal of skepticism. He was the black sheep of my family, the liberal conspiracy-theory nut.

If you've seen the footage, then you've seen about as much as most of us. We just have better seats.

I *have* seen the new body armor that Professor Kagen designed for her: an exoskeleton wrapped in black Kevlar flesh. The helmet has a section for interchangeable facemasks and a tube running from the left side to a compact Freon regulator on her back that, according to one of the mechanics I'm friendly with, pumps cold air through the suit to help preserve her. They made the thing from salvaged military parts.

Most of our artillery and vehicles (as well as our military-style designations) are "borrowed" from the traditional armed forces after they left them on the battlefield, if you didn't already know that. Calling our units "posses" was Colonel Davies' idea.

Small enclaves of military who are still loyal to what is left of the Federal Government remain engaged with their adversaries for dominance over their ever-shrinking territory. The Queen watches the attrition on the battlefield from a distance, waiting patiently for her opportunity to crush whatever forces remain on the disputed land.

In the suit, she looks like a post-apocalyptic dominatrix,

her face hidden behind a never-ending collection of masks. (The one I saw looked like the stoic face of a Greek goddess.) They say it's because she's falling apart—literally. That's why she's become so shy about showing herself these days, too. The exo-suit is supposed to protect her in battle and sustain her for as long as possible.

I'm not saying it ain't possible. A living dead woman ain't such a far stretch when you consider some of the toxic oddities that roam the wasteland. But I've always been a "show-me" kind-a-guy. It's sort of the way I felt about Jesus when I was a precocious kid. But you know what? I still went to church because, at the time, it was my best option.

So, naturally, I was fine with not knowing-*was*, again, being the operative word here.

You weren't going to catch me risking my ass to snap a picture of her without her mask. Do you know how many people have died trying to do that shit? Idiots.

J. Günther Douglass, SIGNING OFF

J. Günther, SIGNING ON
The time is 5:22 pm, August 18, 2005.

Growing up in the suburbs, I had this almost inborn fear of the city. All of my friends did. How could you blame us, with all the stories that we were raised on about big, angry black guys with knives and guns and giant penises and an insatiable lust for white women and chips on their shoulders for the man (*me*)?

Okay, so I went a little overboard, but the stories were always horribly exaggerated. Even *I* knew that, and back then, I didn't know shit. Thought I did, but we all know how that goes.

Philadelphia is a city of neighborhoods. It is... *was* one of the only places in the country where rich, poor, and middle-

17

class white, black, and everything in between could coexist peacefully (for the most part) all scrunched together—this according to the well-traveled members of Voodoo Posse.

I had told the guys that I used to come into Philly all the time: to go to the movies, hang out at bars, buy weed; basically, all the shit I wished I had done. They had already caught me in one lie. I originally said I was from Philly. It's what I told everybody for as long as I can remember. But when one of the guys from the city started asking me questions, I corrected myself.

"Well, actually, I'm from Drexel Hill, a suburb of Philly," I said.

It was the kind of lie that went mostly unnoticed, yet it still left me feeling rattled. Lying is something that the Revenant Clan doesn't tolerate.

When I found out that we were making a move on Center City (Philadelphia), I greeted the idea with a mixture of excitement and trepidation.

"Look who's got the guns now, niggers!!!"

That's how I pictured it. And I'm no racist, by the way. I've just had this irrational fear of them (black people) for so long that saying it felt… I don't know… liberating. And it helped me deal with the butterflies.

A lot of the guys were saying that they would go AWOL rather than risk exposure to such high levels of radiation. Most of us had seen a documentary or two about Chernobyl and the effects of radiation exposure back in the day.

You see, Philly is part of the Irradiated Zone. From its epicenter at the Three Mile Island Nuclear Generating Station in Dauphin County, Pennsylvania, the Zone includes all of Pennsylvania and parts of Upstate New York, New Jersey, Virginia, West Virginia, Ohio, Delaware, and Maryland.

18

It had been about six months since a missile fired during a battle between the warring Pennsylvania communities of Harrisburg and York tore through the containment building and cracked the nuclear reactor. The crack leaked radioactive gases, liquids, and debris into the already toxic atmosphere. Immediate casualties from contamination numbered in the hundreds. The New Philadelphia News Organization (which, at the time, was based in Philadelphia) broadcasted a special report advising the evacuation of all communities in the affected areas. The Ergeister headquarters in the Appalachians broadcasted a similar message to their members. They have since relocated to La-La Land. That's Los Angeles for all you dummies.

Radiation Sickness (RS), aka Radiation Poisoning or Acute Radiation Syndrome

Effects on Humans and Animals

Onset of signs and symptoms of radiation sickness depends on the level, duration, and the manner of exposure (ingestion, inhalation, or external contact) to radiation or radioactive materials.

Exposure to extremely high levels of radiation may result in severe skin damage, such as inflammation and radiodermatitis (skin burns). Symptoms also include nausea, vomiting, and severe diarrhea.

Extended effects of exposure include, but are not limited to, metastatic cancer, sterility, cataracts, bone marrow and gastrointestinal damage, and severe birth defects in pregnant women.

Exposure to extremely high levels of radiation during a singular event (ie, detonation of a nuclear bomb or a nuclear power plant explosion) will likely result in death within hours due to central nervous system trauma, severe anemia/hemorrhage, dehydration, and/or bone marrow necrosis.

For survivors of the initial event, early exposure symptoms (nausea, vomiting, diarrhea, etc.) may be dormant after initial expression. During this phase, which can last anywhere from 5 to 14 days depending on level, duration, and manner of exposure, patients often express a feeling of calm and well-being. Symptoms usually reappear, often resulting in death.

Standard biochem attire (for protection against chemical and biological contaminants) consists of a hooded gas mask and a body suit made of a charcoal substrate mixed with a very lightweight fabric that has carbon spheres affixed to it. They've got nicknames like gas-face, or bugsuit, or slee-stak. Most people I know call them bugsuits.

There are a couple variations of the official full-body bugsuit, but the differences basically boil down to baggy or snug (combat style).

Don't ask me how it works, but it does. Everyone looks the same on the streets these days because of their gas masks. Mine has a double filter. Some people like to dress them up with paint or jewelry. Some of the armies and security forces cover theirs with specific markings, like war paint.

They told us that standard bugsuits didn't work against prolonged exposure to radiation, so the mission would have to have to be carried out carefully. We would remain inside our vehicles in full gear throughout most of it. Short stints outside were okay, they said, as long as our suits protected us from head to toe.

The other guys didn't buy it, though. Plus, they had gotten themselves all worked up over the stories that some unknown faction that was immune to radiation inhabited the Zone, but that was just one of many rumors. Stories about the Zone were always laced with mutated animals and strange, forced unions of vastly different species lurking deep in the radioactive fog or in the contaminated lakes and rivers.

I was too curious to give in to irrational fear. I say "irrational" because most of the stories that we had heard were based on second- and third-hand accounts, so whatever truth there had been to the stories had long been lost to rumor and embellishment.

Without the Ergeister Church calling the shots from afar, the Queen's new objective was to build an empire by securing prime territories that haven't already been claimed by the church. Philly was her latest target. If we could get in and seal some of the buildings, we'd be set. We'd deal with trying to fix the reactor once we got settled in.

We were still riding high from the battle with General Sizemore's army in North Carolina when they broke the news about Philly. It took the steam right out of us… most of us, that is.

Sizemore had recently overthrown Aries and his army. Aries was one tough son-of-a-bitch, so defeating him was no small accomplishment. You can imagine what kind of animal Sizemore was to have pulled it off. Beating *him* was a real boost to our morale and collective ego.

There are others whom the Queen has her eye on: the Raggedy Men in the southwest, the Mortimer Tribe deep in the Everglades, and Reverend Link and his Aftermath Cult.

Reverend Link is a strange one. He can supposedly coax like General Elam, only he works more by suggestion. Coaxing, for those of you who don't know, is basically the name for the form of ESP that General Elam uses. It's sort of a cross between

21

telekinesis and mind control.

It would be interesting to see the two of them fight-Reverend Link and General Elam. We all had bets on who would win. My money (we used cigarettes, booze, weed, food, and water as surrogates) was on General Elam. I had seen what he could do first hand. Talk about a heartless bastard.

Our orders for the Philly mission were to take the area west of Broad Street block by block, starting on Washington Avenue in South Philly and traveling north through the neighborhoods to Lombard Street.

If there were any kind of army based in the city, they would most likely be situated in the old, high-rise office buildings and condos on Market Street and JFK Boulevard. The buildings stood pressed next to each other like jagged bars on a graph. Whole areas of downtown were on the brink of collapse a few years ago, so I can only imagine what the place looks like now.

We had heard that someone had been rebuilding Chestnut and Walnut Streets, where the old department stores, overpriced restaurants, designer boutiques, outdoor cafés, and coffee shops sat desecrated and vacant. The surrounding streets were always cluttered with trash and all-out devastation, just like the "bad parts of town" back in the day. There's no distinction now.

Like I said, I grew up in the suburbs, so if it sounds like I know my way around the city, it's only because the Friday before the raid (which was to go down the following Monday), I "borrowed" a scrapbook of pictures and newspaper clippings from Clark (the other guy from Philly) and looked it over while he was sleeping. He'd never let any of us lay a hand on his raggedy-ass books. Clark clung to those things like they were gold. They were his connection to the past. We all have something to remind us of the way things were. Mine is a T-shirt covered in my parent's blood. They died during the war. I was standing right next to them when it happened. I'm sure you'll understand if I'd rather not talk about it.

Along with Diesel, Wolfpack, and One-Shot Posses, we would secure locations in the east, west, north, and south, thus forming a perimeter around the highrises in the middle of the city. Then we'd sit tight and wait for the scouting parties to come back with reconnaissance reports before we gave the Queen the all-clear to roll in with Six-Eyes Posse. (The Six-Eyes Posse is the Queen's elite guard. Traditionally, they were called the Cerberus Posse, but they went through a couple variations of the name: from Cerberus Posse, to Three-Headed Dog Posse, and, finally, to Six-Eyes.)

It was supposed to be a cakewalk.
They told us that we might run into scavengers, if anything at all. No sweat.
"Starvation leads to fatigue, and fatigue makes pussies of us all," Colonel Davies said at the rallies, except the word he used was cowards: starvation makes *cowards* of us all. "The scavengers are far worse off than we are. Not only are they starving, the food that they *do* have is most likely toxic. They are outmanned, outgunned, and out of luck if they try to resist us."
That was the general tone of the bullshit that they fed us. And we lapped it up like good little drones. Most of the men still fall for the lies.
There are a few of us, however… maybe I shouldn't be talking about this.

Logic seemed to favor Colonel Davies' rhetoric in our minds. Everybody is starving these days. I mean e-v-e-r-y-b-o-d-y. Even we know how it feels to be hungry and what that hunger can do to your spirit… your will. And it was true that the scavengers are doing worse than us. A number of our troops are made up of former scavengers.

Speaking of which, it's chow time. Gotta go.

J. Günther Douglass, SIGNING OFF

J. Günther, SIGNING ON
The time is 8:07 pm, August 8, 2005.

I hadn't realized it was so close to evening chow when I started recording last time. Sorry about that. Chow time isn't something to miss. Not these days.

So, where were we? Oh, yeah…

We came in under the cover of night, crawling up from the Schuylkill River, a convoy of amphibious IFVs (Infantry Fighting Vehicles), teams of 10 in each, all suited up and ready to kick some ass if we had to. Our driver said that the Schuylkill was like marshland but with trash, clothes, wood, glass, and car parts instead of grass. We could hear stuff bumping against the outside of the IFV as we floated through it.

The posses split up and traveled down Washington Avenue to their designated starting points.

There were no women in Voodoo Posse, so we were riding on testosterone overload. It was the first run for a couple of the guys, like Tigger, who had lived as a scavenger before joining the Clan. The look in his eyes took me back to when I was as scared as he was. But Tigger had rage issues. He dealt with his fear by remaining on constant simmer, like he could erupt at any second. It was the kind of thing that made everyone around him tense. Tigger was big enough that having him rage out at the wrong time would be a serious problem.

"After a while, you become numb to it," I told him, in a show of support.

"I don't want to be numb," he growled at me, like I was trying to steal his food. "I *live* for this shit!"

Okay, whatever…

What I was going to tell him was that even when you're used to it, the fear is still there; only it's busy fueling something else.

It's a crapshoot, really, whether you get out alive. Heard a line from a song the other day: one of the brothas with their rap shit.

"No matter who you are, you can still catch a bullet scar."

How appropriate. The guy's name was Redman, I guess. Like I give a fuck.

My best friend Marco and I each had three runs apiece under our belts, so we thought we knew what to expect.

"Stay low, stay calm, stay crisp. Eyes like a hawk," we'd say to each other. I'd tease him about his pronunciation, or say something like "Fuck it. Eyes like Steve Austin." Then he'd say, "Who?" Aw man, that'd make me laugh, even with my gas mask on. Gas masks usually kept the humorous moments to a minimum.

So, we ran aground behind what used to be the Philadelphia Transfer and Recycling Station at the foot of the Grays Ferry Bridge. The communities that lived in the area before the atmosphere went radioactive used it to store and dispose of their dead. We got our first glimpse of those mutated animals we had heard about. They were chowing down on the mostly skeletal remains stacked to the ceiling of the massive, four-mouthed garage: a pile behind each open door. Looked like they used to be dogs.

We rolled past without incident. The FedEx Depot; the Dupont Laboratory; the Firehouse; the Post Office; the Shopping Plaza-all quiet.

Propaganda radiated from the loudspeakers atop the IFV

25

just in case there were people stupid enough to have remained in the area. It was the same old stuff that hooked me: "Submit to the Queen or die."

Then, suddenly, the sensors went berserk. The cameras pivoted in their orb-cases on all sides of the hull. The order came for us to be ready for anything. We were entering the neighborhoods.

Our eyes were glued to the monitor bank. The night-vision cameras colored everything green. There were traces of people ducking from sight and darting from shadow to shadow. They were dressed in ragged clothing and gas masks; women and children mostly. They were like ninjas, these fuckers, like ghosts, like… ghost-ninjas (laughs). Then I wondered what would make them stay. Someone suggested that maybe they were immune, like we had heard. It sent a chill down my spine.

"I'm definitely having a tickle-dick moment," I remember saying to Marco.

"More like an itch," he replied.

(A tickle- or flutter-dick moment is our way of describing how it feels when extreme fear is mixed with extreme exhilaration. Try to keep up.)

I was bracing myself for the jarring ping of tiny rounds bouncing off the IFV's hull. When that shit comes unexpected, it brings you crashing down into paranoid-survival mode, which is only fun when you're already "up-in-it," as the brothas would say.

All was still, as if the ghost-ninjas took the air with them when they scurried from sight. That usually meant that the shit was about to hit the fan. We knew we were being watched but, frankly, we were feeling too superior to worry about anything happening that we couldn't handle.

Once we hit Lombard Street, which is about six blocks

away from Market, we continued the rest of the way on foot. Those guys I mentioned, the ones who said that they'd rather go AWOL? They did, just before we left for the mission, so there were no freakouts or anything once the door of the IFV hissed open. That's not to say that we weren't aware of the radiation. It was on all of our minds, I'm sure.

Someone had indeed been restoring buildings as far down as Spruce Street, two blocks further south than we had expected. But none of them were finished.

Other than the recent construction, there was no sign of life.

Then... all of a sudden...

"Hey! Heads up."

It was Tigger. He had spotted an elderly couple in matching, loose-fitting bugsuits walking hand in hand. They had come down from Chestnut or Market. We watched them walk right up and try to pass us without saying a word.

Apparently, Tigger didn't like the way the old man looked at him. The rest of us were stuck somewhere between bewilderment and awe.

"Did you just roll your eyes at me?" Tigger said, standing face to face with the elderly man. "Don't you know who we are?"

"Tigger!" I said, as I looked to the sarge for support.

The sarge shook his head "no" and told me to leave him be.

The problem with Tigger was that he had gotten himself so psyched for battle that without it, he had nowhere to channel his bottled-up anticipation.

"Please, just let us pass," said the old man, trying to motion forward as he spoke.

"You'll pass when I *say* you can pass," Tigger growled.

"First, I think you owe me an apology for stepping on my shoe."

It was clear that the man hadn't touched Tigger's shoe.

It was at that point that I came crashing down into survival mode. I could just see the situation spiraling out of control. I could see in the eyes of the men that they were even tenser than before. Goddamn Tigger.

The sarge wasn't really much of a leader. He was a bit of a scatterbrain in my opinion, so having him there wasn't much comfort.

"Well... are you just going to stand there looking like you just shit your Depends, or are you going to apologize?" Tigger said. "If I were you..."

"Young man," the old woman interrupted. "We have no quarrel with you. We are just coming back from paying our initiation fee. We are Dorothy and Miles Hannah. You fellers can go ask for yourselves—maybe put in a good word for us."

None of us knew what she meant by "initiation fee," but I suspected it had to do with whoever was responsible for the renovations that we saw in passing. Thanks to Tigger's crazy ass, we never got around to discussing it.

"Ask?" Tigger said in a high-pitched voice. "Bitch, do you know who the fuck we are?"

Tigger pulled out his sidearm and pointed it at the old man's forehead. "You hear your old lady disrespect me like that? Now I *know* you better apologize."

"Tigger!" I called out again. I couldn't help myself. The sarge gave me a look.

I was helpless. Now, I'm no prude. I've killed plenty of people, but there was something about these two. With all that has happened in the world, here are two people who still have each other. I know it sounds like something a chick would say, but deep down, we all missed that sort of kinship with someone special.

I guess the old man was taking too long to apologize, because Tigger capped him, just like that. Like it was nothing.

"My love!" the old woman cried out as her husband's body fell straight back to the ground.

She ripped off her gas mask, knelt down beside him, held his head in her lap, and pressed her palm against the exit wound in the back of his head to stop the bleeding.

She took his gas mask off and peered deep into his eyes.

"Oh, please, no…" she wailed, rocking her husband back and forth, and stroking his thin, white hair. His eyelids fluttered. His hands flexed into claws, then relaxed, then flexed again. "Dear God, no!"

I know how she felt. I had been there before, with my parents.

If I wasn't wearing my mask, the others might've noticed that I was welling up.

I looked up and saw a few of the men handing off cigarettes as if they had lost a bet.

"Oh no you don't, lady," Tigger said, lifting the distraught woman by the armpits. He tried to make her kneel in front of him. "Kneeeel before Zod!"

That one got a healthy laugh from the men old enough to remember the reference.

The old woman was a mess. How can you blame her? I thought about walking up and putting her out of her misery, but I wasn't sure how Tigger or the sarge would react.

Each time Tigger would lift the old woman, she'd crumble to the ground and try to crawl over to her husband. Believe it or not, he was still clinging to life.

That, right there, is the kind of shit that gets under your skin.

Out of the blue, Tigger fired two shots into the old man's legs.

The pain seemed to yank the old man coherent long enough to acknowledge the pain with a wild twitch and a horribly moist groan.

"Leave him alone!" the old woman screamed, shielding her husband's body with her own.

"Oh, you want me to leave him alone?" Tigger said in a mocking tone. "Then get on your fucking knees."

Right then is when the sarge should've shot Tigger's ass for gross insubordination. Instead, he ordered the rest of us to fall back to Lombard Street. We were heading back to the IFV to wait for word from the rest of the posses.

"You're on your own," was all he said to Tigger.

"Don't wait up," Tigger responded. He clutched the old woman by her hair and forced her to kneel in front of him. "I don't know about you guys, but it's been a long time since I got my cock sucked."

"Are you fucking crazy? The radiation…" someone said as Tigger thumbed open a switchblade, cut a slit into the crotch of his uniform, and pulled his penis out.

"Gotta die someday, man," he replied, as he stroked the shaft to a rock-hard state. He was too caught up in his actions to understand their consequences.

"She's going to bite your shit off," someone else warned.

Tigger punched the woman in the mouth as hard as he could.

"Not if she doesn't have any teeth," he said.

I could hear the old woman gagging on Tigger's penis as we walked away. I don't know why I turned around and looked. He had his hands on the back of her head. He was using them to pull it toward him as he thrust violently at her face. The blood from her mouth had painted the shaft of his penis red.

I'd say it took about three minutes for him to reach orgasm. He let out a prolonged moan and ended it with a little whistle that I could barely hear over the old woman's gagging and crying.

When I looked around at the other guys, I was glad to see that I wasn't the only one disgusted by the whole thing.

We all figured Tigger would shoot her when he was done, but he just left her there, lying beside her husband's body. So, I told Marco to wait up for me, doubled back, and shot her in the head.

She told me that I would burn in hell.

"If there was a hell, you'd probably be right," I said.

Hell, I was working for the devil, right? That's what the graffiti scribbled on the old Ergeister Army recruitment posters said. We passed them on the way here, the ones with the Queen's likeness on them. "The Devil Has a Vagina," it says with an arrow pointing to the Queen. I thought that was kinda clever. I guess the graffiti artists got tired of writing the same-old "Fuck the Dead Bitch Army," and "Death to the Dead Bitch Army." We were instructed to tear them all down.

In this case, I thought I was doing the right thing by putting the old woman out of her misery. Like I said, some of the things I've done have been for just reasons.

"Don't you ever challenge my authority in front of the men like that, you hear?" the sarge said to me on the way back to Lombard.

"Challenge your authority?" I said. "You can't be serious!"

What about that shit Tigger just pulled? Why don't you act like a real fucking sergeant and reprimand his ass? What, does he get carte blanche because he's liable to take a swing at you for saying the wrong thing? What about the fact that half the men don't respect you? What about that, hunh?

I didn't actually say all that, but I wanted to. What I really wanted to do was beat the piss out of both the sarge and Tigger.

The sarge gave me some spiel about "the code" and how what happens in the theater of battle stays here.

Theater of battle? I thought. *More like theater of outright murder.*

"These boys need a release from time to time, especially a tightly wound sum-bitch like Tigger," he said. "I shouldn't have to tell you what lack of pussy can do to a strapping, young alpha male hankerin' to shoot his load on the world. I'm dying for a piece ma'self."

In a sense, the sarge was right. You have to understand the mentality of your average soldier. Once you find yourself aligned with a good army, your mind strays from perpetual survival mode. You start thinking about things like material possessions and women. Oftentimes, the lines between the two are blurred by the rampant desire for a piece-a-ass. I've never been big into drugs, but from what I know, I'd equate it to being addicted to some powerful shit.

The women out in the wasteland were usually infected, the victims of repeated rapes. I've known a few guys who've been desperate enough to dip their sticks in those cesspools. No thanks.

The communities kept their women hidden. Rape had become almost de rigeur. It was just something you did to relieve stress. All that pent-up testosterone ain't healthy. It can affect your performance on the battlefield... er... theatre of battle. I've seen it happen lots of times. Tigger was a good example of that.

I completely understood where the sarge was coming from, but all I kept thinking about was the elderly couple: the way the husband struggled to hold on as he lay dying; the ferocity with which Tigger face-fucked the wife; the noise she made as she gagged on his penis.

I couldn't stop thinking about how much the elderly couple reminded me of my parents.

"If I come across any old ladies, I'll be sure to send 'em your way," I said to the sarge. I forced a chuckle out after it just so he'd think I was joking.

It took him awhile to respond, like he was wondering whether or not I had just insulted him. Then he smiled. A part of me wished he didn't. But then, what the fuck was I going to do, really?

"No, thanks. I like mine young," the sarge replied as he walked away. "And preferably blonde."

Along with the rest of the posses, we set up fort on Lombard. Our posses covered the area from 24th to Front Street. We skipped over Broad, where the view from City Hall would've made us sitting ducks. Voodoo Posse settled on 22nd, which was a once-proud neighborhood of old brownstones.

Some of the guys were starting to complain about exposure, but the sarge said that we'd be fine in our uniforms as long as we didn't stay outside for more than two hours at a time. The trip up to Spruce and back took about forty minutes.

The men eventually retreated to the IFV. Me and Marco were already inside trying to catch a nap when they came in.

I couldn't sleep that night, so I decided to go for a walk. It was about 3:00 am, and the streets were as barren as they probably would've been before the war. I pretended that everything was normal again, but the pull of my M-201 rifle, which was strapped to my back, kept reminding me why I was here.

Marco's voice scared the piss outta me when it came across my earpiece. Apparently he couldn't sleep either.

"Where the fuck are you?" he said. I was touched that he

sounded so worried.

"Just going for a walk to clear my head," I replied. "That shit with Tigger… zgot-me-all…"

That's when I heard the voices. It sounded like a woman, or women, but I couldn't be sure. Poor Marco must've thought something happened to me because he kept yelling in my ear, "Günther! Günther! What's going on? Talk to me, Günther!"

In retrospect, I should've just given him the play-by-play, but I was on my toes, expecting the worst.

The voices were coming from the basement of an old church building with a crooked YMCA sign on the front. It was on the corner of Spruce and 17th. Yep, I had walked that far.

The windows were painted black, but there was a spot in one of them where a pinhole of light screamed through. In the pitch-black darkness, it was impossible to miss.

I turned off the night vision on my visor, praying that no one would hear me as I crept up to the window and peeked inside.

"What the fuck…" I said. It just rolled right out of my mouth at the sight of them.

"What? What is it, man?" Marco came back over my earpiece. "Talk to me, man! You're scaring me."

"Women," I said. "A whole roomful of 'em."

It seemed too good to be true, but there they were, showering completely naked and walking around in various degrees of undress. Got me so worked up that I didn't even think about the fact that they were walking around unprotected in a building that clearly wasn't sealed.

I knew that if the other guys found out about the women, it would be an all-out rapefest. After the shit with Tigger, that was the last thing I wanted. It bothered me so much that taking one of the women for myself hadn't even crossed my mind.

At the time, I didn't think about the crowd that had formed

around Marco as he called out to me on his communicator. If I had, I would've kept my big mouth shut.

Man, you should've seen how fast they came. My first instinct was to warn the women somehow, but it was too late, not to mention that that might've gotten us all killed.

Aside from Marco and me, there was one other man (John Diggs) who didn't participate in the mass rape. He stayed outside with us, keeping an eye out for... whatever. We had all taken our peeks, though.

The window was fogged with hot breath. It made the action inside bleed together, like a soup of naked flesh wriggling and writhing and thrusting like bunnies. Our men kept their gas masks on, but nothing else. They worked feverishly to minimize exposure time. I reminded the men that we were in the zone before they stormed the place. I told them that all bets are off once you take off your bugsuit. They mentioned how the girls were naked, yet showed no signs of radiation sickness. Said it meant that the building must be sealed.

I did my best to block out the women's muffled screaming by trading bad jokes with Marco, whom I could tell wanted to take part, but didn't because he was worried that it might affect my opinion of him.

Now, that's a real friend.

We thought John was coming to tell us about some lascivious sexual act that he'd just witnessed through a window on the other side or something when he came running around from the back of the church, pale as a ghost, with his eyes ready to jump out of their sockets.

"It's a trap!" he yelled. "Warn the men!"

From inside, a thunderous boom shook the ground and knocked all three of us off of our feet.

"You all right?" I said to Marco.

36

"Yeah... I think s..." he started to say when his head disappeared into a fine red mist. I watched in horror as Marco's headless body staggered toward me, arms reaching blindly in my direction before it plunked to the ground. Fucking awful, man. I still can't get the image outta my head. *Was he trying to reach me?* John Diggs, who was already on his feet, went down next, gurgling on his own blood. I didn't even hear a gunshot.

It was coming from the rooftops. I couldn't believe that they didn't hit me as I crawled on my stomach over to the wall of the church and pressed my back against it. It seemed like they spent a whole clip trying to hit me. I knew I had to think fast or I was dead. But first, I had to see what had happened inside. I just had to. There was a window not ten feet to my right. The explosion had blown out the glass, so the melee inside was loud and clear.

I crawled over to the window and looked in.

There were armed men dressed in red-and-black uniforms crawling out of the ground. Whoever they were, the bastards had caught us with our pants down. I could see through the hole in the floor that there were train tracks beneath the old church. But the tunnels didn't extend this far on any of the maps we'd seen.

It's something else, seeing the guys you served with come apart like they were made of wet cookie dough. The black-and-red soldiers let the women finish them off. Some of the women didn't even bother to get dressed before taking weapons from the soldiers and going to town. They were mostly using shrapnel guns—splitters, we called 'em. One pull could tear a body to shreds in seconds.

It was so fast that the body parts that remained hadn't yet realized what had happened to them.

I watched the sarge try to crawl away and save what was left of himself-a torso, badly burned from the explosion, with an arm and a stump. The soldiers (and a few of the women) stood around watching and laughing and cheering on their female comrades. I could've sworn that I saw some of the women's eyes flash yellow-red. Not sure what that meant or if it wasn't just my mind playing tricks.

Another group of black-and-red soldiers had Tigger off to the side. He was on his knees, crying. One of the soldiers—a big, beefy son of a bitch—stood directly in front of Tigger and snatched off his gas mask. The soldier pulled Tigger's face toward his crotch.

I turned away when I realized what was about to happen.

From the left, I could hear more of them coming. They were about a half a block away. The snipers on the roof had surely radioed to them and to the soldiers inside about me.

I took a deep breath, and I ran. After the first shot punched me in the left shoulder, I told my legs not to stop no matter how many bullets they put in me.

Thankfully, it was only five.

It wasn't until about ten hours later, when I awoke on a stretcher in the middle of a hallway thick with debris-mist and chunks of plaster and injured and dead soldiers, that I noticed the dried blood that covered my uniform. Marco's blood.

My meeting with General Elam is in two hours. I've been counting down the days since I first found out that he was coming here personally to speak with me. Common sense told me that wasn't a good thing.

Believe it or not, Tigger survived what the black-and-red soldiers did to him. I'm pretty sure that they meant for him to. A frightened-as-fuck traveling merchant dropped what was left of Tigger off at our temporary base in the old Atlantic City Convention Center. With my gun to his head, he said a man with no name, whose face he couldn't remember, paid him to deliver it.

The black-and-red soldiers had gouged Tigger's eyes out, cut off his arms and legs at the elbows and knees, and left him without any genitalia.

Frankly, I think I'd rather be dead.

The one thing that Tigger could do was talk. I was all ready to feel sorry for him until he told them that I was responsible for the massacre. *I* was the one who found the girls (while AWOL from the rest of the posse, I might add), and *I* was the one who suggested that the guys come and see the women for themselves. That simply wasn't true. Well, part of it was, but…

The mission was a failure on all fronts. It was as if the black-and-red soldiers were expecting us, which meant that it might have been an inside job. That took a little of the pressure off of me, or maybe it made it worse. Maybe General Elam would sense my growing disgust with the Revenant Clan as a sign of potential insurrection.

I'm well aware of General Elam's mind games: how he likes to probe for dirty little secrets when he engages you in conversation. He's been known to kill his own men for any hint of disloyalty. The General would keep his hands behind his back, his eyes looking straight ahead but seeing deep inside the minds of each person he passed as he reviewed the men standing at attention, side by side in über-erect poses. It would take just one mistake to be "relieved of duty," so to speak.

But I can understand why has always been my stance on that. There have been numerous attempts on the Queen's life. Better safe and crazy than sorry and dead.

In an hour and fifty-five minutes, I'm going to be sitting across a table from the man….

Part of the reason for these tapes is to vent my frustration, to clear my mind of it. If you don't hear from me again, then I guess it didn't work.

J. Günther Douglass, SIGNING OFF

Chapter 1

Atlantic City, New Jersey – September, 2005
Revenant Days: The Beachfront Massacre

"INCOMING!!!!"

The blast was preceded by a crackle, like distant thunder. The actual boom sounded out at a frequency that the human ear could not detect or apprehend. It was the phantom bass beneath the crunch of footsteps in snow.

The survivors—thirty-odd Revenant Clan soldiers from various posses—peered through the smoke over the bodies of their comrades: bugsuits torn apart to reveal emaciated bodies that appeared twice dead. Bug eyes examined, darting, staring out from the tinted goggles of their hooded gas masks, ready to take aim. C2 canisters protruded from their facemasks. Their skin-tight hoods gave them the appearance of bald, bug-eyed, humanoid creatures.

The men climbed drunkenly to their feet like zombie frogmen emerging from a swamp. Everyone was in shock. Minds played catch-up. The smoke began to dissipate and rise in curlicue patterns. Most of the men were still completely unaware that they had been physically displaced by hundreds of yards from the courtyard of the Oceanic Hotel, where they had been standing a moment ago.

Muffled ringing replaced the sounds of man-made thunderclaps, bullets chirping, buildings crumbling, and stifled voices barking from behind masks.

The blanket of fog that had crept up and settled over the jagged horizon of brick-and-mortar stalagmites yielded to reveal

41

the devastation. The beachfront metropolis, once an oasis among the borderless urban wastelands that surrounded it, had been reduced to rubble. An ocean stained red licked the ivory sands. The surface of the water was littered with cars, trucks, and city buses; furniture and clothing; and small and large appliances. Buildings surrendered themselves to the seas. People dead and soon dead clung to and slipped away from behemoth signs that read Bally's, Trump Taj Mahal, and Borgata as all was pulled downward toward the frothing dark that lay beneath the crimson surface.

Soldiers scrambled around, trying to make sense of it all, yelling that they had been hit, reacting in terror to the sight of their injuries and those of their comrades. Bulbous organs oozed and bubbled beneath mangled flesh casings, sliding through the shaking fingers that tried to hold them in place.

Some of the soldiers were pulling off their hoods to gasp for air. The ever-present fear of breathing in toxic fumes had given way to panic and sheer desperation.

"What are you doing?" yelled a sergeant in a heavy Irish brogue. His tall, angular frame stood out among the scrawny bodies of the troops. "Get your masks back on, lads, for feck's sake!"

But no one heard him, not even those who were standing within arms' reach. In fact, the sergeant couldn't hear his own voice. He couldn't hear anything over the ringing in his ears, which was beginning to pulsate.

The sergeant saw his men wandering about, looking wide-eyed and lost. Some were working feverishly to put themselves back together; others, with faces contorted and frozen, had given up the fight.

The sergeant conducted a self-check.

Everything seemed to be where it should. His hearing was fucked, or "fecked" as he'd say, but nothing was missing or leaking.

The soldiers were yelling at each other. Eyes flamed in urgency, but it was clear by the confused expressions all around that no one could hear.

The sergeant's eyes fell upon the Oceanic. The sight jogged his memory. Something important was inside. In the basement. Slowly, it came.

General Elam. He was inside with Mary and the Six-Eyes.

When he turned to alert the rest of the men, the sergeant was struck by the gesturing of one of the men. He was yelling directly at the sergeant and pointing east.

The sergeant turned slowly. Suddenly, he had a moment of clarity. They were being raided. It was, most likely, the army from Center City Philadelphia.

The Clan had been taken by surprise about an hour ago. An explosion caused them to evacuate their temporary headquarters in the former Atlantic City Convention Center. Whoever set it off had rigged the Clan's entire arsenal of stolen military vehicles.

Out of 225 soldiers, only 100 survived the explosion. They escaped to the Oceanic Hotel, which was being used by some of the men for quartering and "entertainment." Infected prostitutes from the wastelands plied their trade in what was one of the only buildings left standing in the area.

Griff had to be carried away from the wreckage on a stretcher. The explosion had left him unconscious and near death. Seeing him like that dealt a considerable blow to the resolve of the surviving troops. Griff was damn near godlike in their eyes. He was the last person they expected to see vulnerable and incapacitated.

By now, other soldiers had noticed the scene to the east. Reacting without hesitation, a few of them raised their weapons and fired. The others jumped about nervously, looking to the sergeant, who used a hand gesture to signal to the men to open fire.

From the east, a fleshtoned stampede approached with superhuman speed. There were dozens of them, running and leaping over each other like fleas as they pressed forward against the backdrop of jutting half-structures and overturned vehicles. The wall of naked bodies continued unabated despite the fierce resistance of the Revenant Clan soldiers (who were armed with a mixture of SR-47s, M-4s, M-16s and Shrike 5.56s).

A curtain of gunfire opened holes the size of tennis balls and tore limbs asunder, but the victims elicited little indication of pain. In some cases, grievous injuries made their hosts angrier and more determined. The ones who were rendered legless simply resorted to crawling at a faster pace than an average man could run. Their blood (if that was what it was that spit from their wounds) was the color of crude oil.

The sergeant tapped the side of his mask. His vision magnified.

His breath jumped out prematurely, causing him to immediately inhale. He tapped his mask again. His vision returned to normal. He looked around at the other men. They were waiting for his instruction.

The sergeant magnified his vision again, just to be sure.

Nope, he wasn't seeing things.

Physically, the naked (male and female) bodies appeared human, but they weren't altogether human. Their limbs were slightly elongated, and their upper-body muscles were swollen and grotesque. They wore expressions of exaggerated aggression. Curved fangs pointed down from their canines and up from their lateral incisors. Mouths snarled and fell open. Saliva bands stretched and popped, and broken strands blew away from their mouths as the exhaled.

Frowns tightened over glowing yellow eyes bordered in red. Their fingers ended in intimidating claws. Their ears were pointed. They carried no firearms but wielded mid-length blades that tapered in at the base where blade met pommel. The tips of the blades curved slightly, suggesting the instruments of a mad butcher. A second, more traditional-looking unit of soldiers, dressed in black-and-red uniforms, remained behind the ragged mass in the front, waiting to sweep in and pick off the scattered survivors. A caravan of modified trucks and bulky armored vehicles rumbled behind them.

What the fuck? Vampires?

The sergeant gestured for the Revenant Clan soldiers to lay down a suppressing fire and fall back to the hotel.

The first wave of vampires came in high, leaping over the front line of the Revenant Clan army. The soldiers fell to their backs and fired overhead, following the motion of their attackers.

The vampires alighted on a patch of land between the soldiers and the hotel and began hacking away with blinding speed, too furiously for the soldiers to react and defend themselves. It was a slaughter.

The attackers seemed invincible, but some of the vampires were felled by bullets to the head, a fact not lost on the desperate soldiers of the Revenant Clan. Forgetting that none of the soldiers could hear, they began to yell to each other to "Aim for the head!" The vampires took evasive action by darting in zigzag patterns. They moved laterally but ever forward in an insectoid blur, bouncing off obstacles and tumbling over each other like falling water. They overtook the soldiers, swinging wildly, clinging to their prey, and driving their blades downward with brutal efficiency.

Bones shattered like glass. Large men crumbled. Vampires climbed over pulverized bodies and continued to hack away

relentlessly at any sign of motion. The hyperkinetic movement of claws and slashes made them look like a single multi-armed machine. When the hacking was done, the vampires sunk their teeth into the soldiers' remains and sucked them dry. The taste of blood gave them a euphoric flutter that they acknowledged by yanking their heads from side to side as they fed. A few of them roared at the sky.

The sergeant snapped out of the paralysis that had gripped him as he watched the carnage unfold. He lifted his gun and squeezed the trigger. One of the smaller vampires rolled off a body and hissed at the sergeant. Its mouth was swathed in fresh blood. A steady, black stream poured from a bullet wound somewhere along its ribs. It found its feet and got set to pounce. The sergeant adjusted his aim and squeezed the trigger. The vampire's head exploded, and its headless body dropped and skidded forward, limbs flailing.

The sergeant swung left and picked off an unarmed vampire that was bearing down on him with outstretched claws, ready to mount and slash.

The first shot hit the vampire in the shoulder and interrupted its forward motion. The second shot blew its head to pieces.

The sergeant saw a vampire cocking its head back and stretching its mouth open to take a big bite out of one of his men, so he turned his gun on it and shot it in the head. The scared soldier thanked the sergeant with a nod. The sergeant nodded back.

If they hadn't already, the remaining soldiers began to adopt the sergeant's stun-then-killshot method. Eventually, they were able to clear a path to the Oceanic.

By the time the Revenant Clan soldiers reached the courtyard of the Oceanic Hotel, there were only eleven men standing with the sergeant, one seriously wounded. The vampires had suddenly stopped advancing and were fighting over body parts in the immediate distance.

The sergeant tried to stifle his awakening emotions so as not to let down his guard, even for a moment. Still, as the highest-ranking soldier present, he felt responsible for all the dead men out there. He worried selfishly that it would reflect badly on him when it came time to assign blame for what had happened. He'd heard what Griff had done to that Douglass kid who botched the Center City mission last month in what had been the Revenant Clan's biggest defeat. Combined, the Diesel, Wolfpack, One-Shot, and Voodoo Posses made up almost half of the remaining troops of the Revenant Clan (after the split with Ergeister), and now they were gone.

The vampires began dragging the bodies of their headless brethren off to the sides of the open-air arena. The sergeant tried to make sense of this. Were they going to bury their dead on an active battlefield? Or could it be that they weren't really dead? According to the legends (which he knew of through bad horror movies, mostly), vampires could regenerate. But even without a head?

From the corner of his eye, the sergeant noticed something moving. He turned and saw the seriously wounded soldier drop his gun and collapse. He could tell by the steely look in the soldier's eyes that he was dead before he hit the ground.

Yet another life that he was responsible for. But the guilt would have to wait, lest he risk allowing the remaining soldiers to dissolve into panic. Some of them were close to it.

The sergeant's hearing was slowly beginning to return. He could hear muffled hints of sound: most notably, a constant rumbling that traveled up from the ground.

"They're coming!" a soldier yelled from the far right.

The sergeant was pleasantly surprised to hear the sound of

the soldier's voice. But the celebration was bittersweet. In the distance, the second wave of armed black-and-red soldiers was making its way toward the Revenant Clan men. The bulky armored vehicles followed them. Judging by their slow approach, it seemed as if they expected the Revenant Clan soldiers to yield to them without any further resistance.

Ten men against a few hundred: those were bad odds. They wouldn't last more than a few seconds if they tried to stand their ground. The men pressed the sergeant for direction. They were in no condition to put up a good fight. Their weapons shook in their grasps. Tears streamed from the eyes of one or two of them.

The sergeant reluctantly considered surrendering, but that went against his instincts and, indeed, everything he stood for.

The black-and-red soldiers were gaining ground. The pressure to decide on a plan of action made the sergeant sick to his stomach, as did his ultimate decision.

The sergeant inhaled deeply and straightened his posture. He turned to the soldiers standing with him and met all their eyes with one roving, stalwart gaze. They seemed to know what he was about to say.

The sergeant raised his hand above his head. His fingers flexed straight. He let the tips hint at curling before balling his hand into a fist, which meant "Fire!"

At the last moment, a noise from behind caught the sergeant's attention. He spun around, dropped to one knee, and aimed his weapon. It was one of the Six-Eyes men. He had just exited the front door of the Oceanic. He was angling for the attention of the approaching troops by waving a white towel above his head as he made his way across the courtyard toward the sergeant.

"What the hell are you doing?" the sergeant protested.

"Step aside, Sergeant," the soldier replied. "Queen's orders."

Chapter 2

The Present...

Video: **The screen is black.**

Male Voice (Speaking through a gas-mask filter): "You know what? It don't even matter what happened to 'em... as long as they asses is gone."

FADE IN:

Open on a television screen broadcasting a montage of street interviews. The reception is terrible. The interviewees are dressed in varying styles of biochem attire (bugsuits). Their gas masks are painted and bejeweled. One mask sports a mane of feathers. A black-and-white photograph of another suit's wearer is layered over the surface of his mask. It's an unsettling combination. Another mask is covered with spikes.

The scenes cut from person to person. Their filtered voices are the only indication of gender in cases where the decorations are somewhat ambiguous.

Male: It was bound to happen. All the shit they done. Guessed they messed with the wrong people.

Male (intoxicated/high): Who knows, maaannnnnn... same thing that killed the dinosaurs, Idonknow....

Female: It's karma, plain and simple. You can't escape it.

Male: How do we know they're really gone? I mean, they could be just layin' low or something. I'll believe it when I see some bodies.

The street interviews end, and the scene cuts to an older woman (Linda Ludlow) sitting behind an anchor's desk in a thrown-to-gether studio that used to be a corporate office or a bank. Linda is sitting with her hands concealed in her lap as she faces the camera. Twisting lines and static frequently distort the image on the screen.

Linda: What happened to the Revenant Clan? Who or what was it that caused them to suddenly disappear? Is there any truth to the stories of an organized army from the Irradiated Zone, and how could they possibly survive prolonged exposure to such high levels of radiation? Two recent attempts at fly-overs were abandoned when a UH-60 Black Hawk Helicopter belonging to the military and one of our own National News choppers were fired upon while trying to collect aerial footage from the Zone.

Most of you know of my relationship with the Clan and with the city of Philadelphia, so it'll come as no surprise that I have a special interest in getting to the bottom of this story. You could even say that it has become a bit of an obsession for me. It's hard not to dwell on our... *relationship* when I'm reminded of it on a daily basis (looks down at her hands).

Linda pauses to compose herself.

Linda: Stay with us here at the National News for up-to-the-minute coverage as the story develops.

51

Rina, Ohio (formerly Green Hill, Ohio) – 2006

"You still awake back there, Rome?"

Rome's short for Roman Krychek, my real name. Most people around here know me by another name: Dr. Goodvibe. More on that later.

Chalk, the bartender, is one of the few people who still call me Rome or Roman. They call him Chalk because he's got psoriasis so bad that sometimes it looks like his skin is raining chalk-dust.

Chalk wouldn't know how to make a decent drink to save his life, but he had a way with words and a strange sense of humor that gave a lot of what he said a veneer of poignancy. Sometimes the sting wouldn't find you until it hit you a day later. Great guy. He used to be one of Mayor Knox's personal security guards, until he was reassigned. He told me about the whole thing once. He was part of a four-man team that was escorting Knox and a few members of City Council through the wasteland to a meeting up north somewhere—I forget the name of the community.

Somewhere along the way, they got ambushed. Scavengers, of course. Bastards took out two of the guards before they knew what hit 'em. The third guard (a Mexican-Indian fella by the name of Das Ramirez) was wounded bad. (I guess Ramirez and Chalk were pretty close. He talks about him every once and awhile. Calls him an ornery bastard, but funny as balls. "Ex merc, he was," Chalk would say. "This guy could take you apart and put you back together before you even knew what happened.")

The story goes like this: Chalk went back to help his buddy, who was still alive, but Knox stopped Chalk and ordered him to

52

leave Ramirez behind. I'm guessing Knox musta made some pretty serious threats, 'cause I can't see how Chalk would ever leave a buddy in trouble. Chalk is always vague about that part.

So, Chalk helps Knox and the City Council folks escape. When they got back, Knox tells Ramirez's wife that her husband had "sacrificed his life for the greater good."

It never sat right with Chalk. But he kept quiet until a few months later when Ramirez's wife ate a bullet.

He decides he's finally gonna confront Knox about it, and he announces it to the whole bar once he got stinkin' drunk. A couple days later, he's stripped of his elite guard status and threatened with serious jail time if he makes any trouble.

So, now he works "undercover" as a bartender. Knox put him here to protect my ass. That's the reason for the armed guard on either side of the entrance, too. Shows you where the mayor's priorities are, doesn't it?

"Rome, you awake?"

"Barely."

"Whaddya think?" he says, pointing at the TV screen on the wall with his eyes.

"You mean the Dead Bitch Army? Ehhh... gotta agree with the last guy. Show me some bodies. You?"

He thinks about it for a minute and says, "Whatever happened, it ain't enoughta make up for the hell they blazed."

We share a quiet moment to reflect on all the gruesome possibilities.

"You still fucking up the drinks?" I say to sort of steer the mood back to comfortable.

"You're still alive, ain't cha?" Chalk replies.

"Who's gonna make a move on me in this fortress?"

"You're thinking small-time, brother."

Whao! He's talking about Mayor Knox... I think...

"You know something I don't know?"
"Just tryin-na keep you on your toes."
See what I mean? Gotta love that bastard.

Chalk is referring to the latest round of RS casualties.
These days, RS is as common as AIDS was in the 1980s, maybe
even moreso. The off-campus cemetery (which used to be a
soccer field) is full of victims. It's a terrible way to go.

The off-campus folks are starting to complain about the
whole business: we're-not-your-dumping-ground kinda thing. But
City Council keeps 'em comin'.

Up here on Society Hill (the official name of the on-cam-
pus territory), some people refer to the off-campus streets as "the
'hood."

There've been a dozen or so RS deaths in the past couple
months. Five in April, I think, and seven in May. That number's
a little high, considering that we generally get three or four deaths
in a given month. Nothing to go nuts over, though. But, of course,
that's just what people around here are starting to do. It only
takes a few-a-them to get everyone sidetracked from the facts.
"Dramasauruses," I call them. Leave it to them to mix-and-match
and embellish the facts. There's usually a supernatural compo-
nent, too.

They've been trying their damnedest to tie the RS deaths
to whatever wiped out L'Aube Nouvelle (New Dawn) and Sunrise, two communities way east of here. Some people think the
Ergeister Church had something to do with it. Supposedly they
left the bodies of a couple of their fallen soldiers behind at both
places. That was a common yet unsubstantiated rumor. And, as
usual, the Church denied any involvement.

Uh... can you say 'radiation'? L'Aube Nouvelle and
Sunrise were situated right smack in the middle of the Zone. It's
likely that they just high-tailed it outta there.

Of course, things can never be that simple with those types. Oh no—it's gotta be aliens, or God, or the DBA, or this… "mysterious army" living in the Zone—which is probably just a group of wasteland flunkies who decided to organize.

The Christians believe that we're living in the Biblical Tribulation. You know, the seven-year period before the Rapture. They spend a lot of their time trying to force the events of our times to fit into the grim picture laid out in the Bible. For instance, "The rise of the false one-world religion"—to them, that's the Ergeister Church. Nice and convenient, huh?

The Dramasauruses had organized themselves into a group called the Concerned Citizens movement. You got 'em all right there: the invisible wives, the parent-Nazis, the cause-jumpers, the religious zealots…

Anyway, they claim that the past ten victims of RS were completely healthy days or even hours before they died, and their bodies had no discernible marks or wounds on them. The Concerned Citizens are pushing for an investigation into the deaths.

Investigation?

"Sorry about your losses, folks, but we're still trying to figure out how to keep our own asses alive out here." That's what I would've told 'em. Fuck it, right? Why beat around the bush?

Mayor Knox just gave 'em lip service. Like he thinks he's a real politician or something.

A few members of the Concerned Citizens are also active in that shit-fer-brains, "Drug-Free Rina" program. So, naturally, Chalk thinks *I* am their next logical target.

"I seen a few a-them pass through your office," he told me. "Won't be long before word gets out and your name starts coming up in-nem town-hall meetings."

Yeah, it's true that a few of the recent victims were customers of mine. But it's always been that way.

When Chalk isn't harping about that shit, he's warning me to stay away from the hookers who dance in the old storefront display windows off campus on Main. That two-block stretch of Main is set up like a poor man's Amsterdam. Some chucklehead referred to it as "the city's taint," and the name stuck. I think he meant it as an insult, though. Regardless, it's still Main Street to me. Just like off campus is off campus. I guess I do call campus "the Hill" sometimes.

The girls show off their moves behind the glass, and the suckers come a-callin'—myself included. They spend a lot of time standing around looking bored, actually. It's only when a vehicle or someone moving quickly on foot passes that the girls get-ta moving.

Sometimes I just like to watch them. I'll have whatever soldier is on driver detail that night swing down Main whenever I happen off campus, which isn't very often. Too much paperwork involved. I'll have 'em park a block or so away. I switch my goggles to "binocular mode," sit back, and leer like a dirty old man.

The newer drivers like to remind me that campus vehicles are for official use only. We haggle a bit. I find their price—they always have one. If they aren't a user, chances are they're looking for something medicinal, maybe for a friend or a loved one. Or they know someone who's willing to pay handsomely for something I've got. Anyway, I make a friend. Maybe someone I can count on in the future, that kind-a-thing.

Now that we're friends-n-all, some of the drivers'll comment real passive aggressive-like about how silly we look trying to hide in the big white Humvee with the official Rina seal plastered on both sides. "Especially with the streets so empty," they'll say, as if the streets' being empty is news to somebody.

By then, I'm already blessed out, lost in the sights, oblivious to their protests. Or I just outright ignore them.

The Dramasauruses complain that the Taint is too close to the nice part of College Road. The intersection of Main Street and College Road is considered, by most, to be the center of town.

It ain't like the old days, when people were just walking the streets, though. There're no midday family strolls. No nights out on the town. If you have to go outdoors at all, you go from point A to point B as quickly as possible. So I don't see what the problem is.

These days, the outdoors is bad for your health. Deadly even, depending on how long you're exposed to it. The sky is a perpetual shade of orange-red in the daytime. Blue skies, fresh air, and all that are all but extinct. I can't even remember what real air smells like or what the wind feels like against my bare skin. When I look outside now, I imagine it smells like New Jersey meets the perfume department at Macy's.

The United States Government did a good job of getting gas masks to the public at the beginning of the war, so most people still own one, but the average Joe doesn't have access to official biochem attire. Most people use layered clothing and blankets covered in lead paint and/or charcoal for protection and run from place to place at top speed to minimize exposure time. It sounds comical, but trust me, it ain't. Especially when the amplified Geiger counters are crackling up a storm from the tops of lampposts all over campus.

Except for the forlorn window displays, the buildings of the Taint (an old Gimble's Department Store, a True Value Hardware, a Blockbuster Video, and some old mom-and-pop used book shop) are vacant. The girls bed down with their johns in the dingy back rooms. VIPs get to take the girls home.

The girls like to sexualize their bugsuits to fit their manufactured streetwalker personae. You aren't supposed to wear anything that obscures the Rina logo stenciled on all official attire, but the girls get away with it.

Kat and Trixie prefer the teddy-and-garters look. Hardcore has her bugsuit painted to look exactly like her naked body. And DangerPussy likes crotchless leather chaps and a corset. She carries a fake rubber pistol with a penis-shaped barrel in a holster at her side. She appears to have a tail, but it's really just one of those whip-flogger things that she has attached to the back of her suit.

My latest crush is Desire. She works the Gimble's window with Hardcore. The store takes up an entire block, and the window runs almost the full length, divided by double doors in the front. Desire has one side. Hardcore has the other.

Layered over her combat-style bugsuit, Desire wears a black, waist-length leather jacket, a mini-skirt, and knee-high boots. Saying she is just another hooker is like calling a great white shark just another fish. It ain't right.

Desire is something special, like femininity manifested in a ghostly white hue. Long, slender legs that take an hour to climb. Winding curves. Jet-black hair that disappears behind broad, athletic shoulders. It's a dye-job, which I usually don't like. And I *do* find myself wondering how her natural color (whatever that may be) works with her complexion. But I can get past it in her case.

I wish I could explain exactly what it is Desire does to me; put it into words... I was struck from the moment I saw her teaser. (Teasers are short video promos set to stripper perennials like "Relax" by Frankie Goes to Hollywood, "I Touch Myself" by the Divinyls, or Motley Crue's "Girls, Girls, Girls." They run about 30 seconds—a clip of each girl slithering in and out of suggestive poses intercut with a "best of" montage of videotaped fuck scenes. All this is set against a background of psychedelic video effects.)

"Hi. I'm... Kat," they'll say in voiceover, for example. Kat's got a voice like a chain-smoking squirrel. Totally kills it for her.

Hardcore and Desire prefer to let their bodies do the talking. A disembodied voice whispers their name in conjunction with flashing letters that appear at the bottom of the screen at the end of their teasers. Hardcore's teaser is set to "Closer" by Nine Inch Nails. My girl Desire's is set to the Prodigy's "Firestarter."

I'm the troublestar-tah, punking instiga-TAH!

Sorry about that. It's one of those songs that get my blood going.

The girls run the teasers for potential customers to show them what they look like underneath their bugsuits. You walk up, talk into the speaker at the bottom of the window, and ask 'em if they wanna party. If they like you, they invite you backstage, so to speak. They flip open the little LCD screen on their camcorders and show you their teaser.

Sometimes a john'll ask the girls to remove their masks to make sure they're getting the same chick from the teaser. The girls don't like that, but they'll usually do it if you ask 'em nicely. And don't even think about pulling some shit, like robbing them or trying to take the pussy by force. They'll have your ass. Well, not all of 'em. I'd say Desire, Hardcore, and DangerPussy are the ones that you wouldn't wanna fuck with.

Generally, you have to proposition the girls to see their teasers. But it just so happens that one of the guys who films and edits the teasers is a customer of mine. I'll call him "Bob."

Bob works with the Robogeeks over at Channel 5. Channel 5 is the University's old closed-circuit channel. The Robogeeks handle the local news, which consists of the two of them running around filming shit with digital video cameras and airing the footage. Bob does the editing.

(I call 'em "Robogeeks" because of the way they look covered in all that video equipment. They've come up with interesting ways to attach as much gear as possible to their bugsuits. Looks kinda cool, actually…)

So I stuff a little extra in Bob's weekly quarter of weed, and he burns me a copy of whatever I want. That's how I got my hands on Desire's teaser.

Lately, I've been using it as therapy. I wish that were as funny as it sounds. Truth is I'm still hurtin' over Sabrina's death. It's been two years and, contrary to the old saying, time hasn't healed a goddamn thing.

Seeing her worked over like that… I never knew a memory could hurt so bad. It really did a number on my head. Turned me into a fucking retard with the ladies.

I've had a few, maybe three, since Sabrina. Moving from community to community… the rules are different, though. You tend to hook up right away when you meet someone. There's no bullshit period of ass-sniffing. No conversations about favorite movies, or songs, or places to fuck. No waiting by the phone. No ridiculous, puppy-love milestones.

Bottom line is the same as before, really. Nobody wants to be alone. Everybody wants to feel safe. It's all that shit just cranked up to the millionth power.

The planet is a much quieter place. Eerily quiet, if you ask me. Especially the night, which is… I don't know… blacker, or more uniform or something, and laced with sounds that you couldn't even imagine.

There are a few constants: the Geiger counter's crackle-crunch, for instance. Or, for the off-campus folks, the echoed madness that comes from the wasteland. Makes the guards hate working the borders.

Makes you wonder what kind of shit is brewing out there in the dark. All the more reason why, if you're a woman, you're

gonna be worried about protection.

Now, I've seen chicks who've turned themselves into fucking badasses. The hookers, for instance. But that kind of thing is the exception. Unless they're connected, most women are just looking for an alpha male who is not going to go apeshit on her over some minor disagreement. You see a lot of that these days, guys with no self-control, beating the shit outta their women. Rageaholics. A lotta chicks willing to put up with it, too. Moreso than before, I'm saying.

None of my relationships since Sabrina lasted more than two weeks, but they taught me that I was… er… that I *am* "one of those needy, super-overprotective types who can't stand to be without his woman." That's what one of the chicks said to me, verbatim. Well, she wrote it in a letter, actually, but same thing.

She's right, of course. No sense in denying it. Looking back, I could see that the others felt that way about me, too. They just didn't have the balls to tell me. Maybe they were afraid I was gonna drug them or something. That's another problem I run into once people find out what I do for a living.

Could've just come clean with 'em about Sabrina's death and the effect it had on me. At the time, I guess I felt like using Sabrina as an excuse disgraced her memory somehow. Even though her death *was* the reason for my… insecurities.

Until Desire came to town, I couldn't even remember what it felt like to be truly intoxicated by a woman, to feel her specific energy, to crave her scent when she's not around, even the smell of her pussy, and the warm valley deep inside the crack of her ass—assuming she's clean.

I thought I felt it with Kat, then with Trixie, then with Hardcore. But Desire is the real deal.

Everyone else says that I'm wasting my time. They say that I'm projecting Sabrina onto these girls. They say that I need to let it go.

Well, maybe they're right. I'm the one who still has nightmares so fucked up that you'd think I was certifiable if you knew my brain could produce such twisted bullshit—muscular, nonecked giants stomping through populated communities, snatching up their women and gulping them down whole or huge cockserpent things with circular mouthfuls of sharp teeth snapping open and shut, boring through landscapes of naked female bodies.

You would think after shit like that every night that I don't know how an event like Sabrina's rape and murder can play tricks on my mind. Well, I know. Trust me, I know.

But I wouldn't call what I do "stalking," for instance.

That's how City Council sees it. They say that I'm being a nuisance, that I... hinder the girls (Desire, this time) from doing their business. Desire only parties with Rina's VIPs and the alpha males who work security, so they especially don't like that I "monopolize" so much of her time. Their word, not mine.

It's not like I don't pay Desire for her time. The girls would even talk to me for free if I wanted, seeing as how it's my stuff that a few of them are getting high on. And there's no rule that says we can't just talk. And technically I *am* a VIP, so I don't see the problem.

I used to try to get to know the girls a little, but Kat, with her cigarette-butt rasp and her endless rants, put a stop to all that. I couldn't keep up the fantasy with her yapping away. Now I just like for them to listen. Desire is good at that. Can't say that I've ever even heard her voice. Hardcore was the same way.

Exactly two weeks ago, City Council banned me from seeing any of the girls. They kept bringing up the girls' "medicinal properties," let's say, with regard to Rina's male population. They mentioned how prevalent rape is in some of the other communities where prostitution is outlawed.

I understand where they're coming from, I really do. But

I just can't seem to stay away. Between you and me, I still have my drivers turn down Main just so I can steal a glance at her.

Desire…

My drug…

Chalk thinks I'm pressing my luck. He likes to lecture me about the power of pussy. "It can make men do crazy things," he'll say. "Sometimes even a whiff of pussy is enough."

As if I don't know that.

Look, I know how crazy all this sounds, but I assure you that I am in complete control. I have to be to do my job.

Here in Rina (which is short for *rinascita,* an Italian word that means "rebirth"), I'm the guy to see if you wanna know what's what. I'm also the guy to see if you've got a sweet tooth. By sweet tooth, I mean drug habit. It's not such a bad thing to admit to these days. Hell, you'd be in the majority.

If you need me, you can find me sitting in my "office" (booth number 12) in the back of the Rina Tavern.

Just ask for Dr. Goodvibes.

Chapter 3

September, 2005
Revenant Days: The Ride to Center City

There was a morbid beauty in the devastation. All it took was the right mindset and enough time to appreciate the scenery as more than just snapshots of the death of civilization. For the sixteen Revenant Clan soldiers (ten grunts, five Six-Eyes men, and Griff), it was the only respite from the pessimistic visualizations that had them predicting their possible fates and from the chaotic environment inside the livestock trailer that served as their mobile prison. The outer walls were made of vertical steel bars spaced inches apart and lined with a layer of flat steel with clusters of holes punched through for ventilation. The enormous tires kicked gravel up at the trailer's steel underbelly. The frame rattled with every bump. The prisoners bounced and slid.

The black-and-red soldiers called themselves the Sanguine Dawn. Their troops were made up of humans and vampires whose blood was black as oil. The human Sanguine Dawn soldiers referred to the vampires as "Alpha Dogs." The prisoners could glean no more information.

The Sanguine Dawn had confiscated the Revenant Clan's weapons, bugsuits, and gas masks, leaving them completely naked and exposed to the radioactive fumes that permeated the evening chill.

The endless fighting had bonded the Clan men, or at least

the men of equal rank. As such, their relationships with one another had become almost familial. All the archetypes were present and accounted for: the tough guy, the comedian, the sensitive momma's boy, the intellectual, the artist, et cetera. It was this bond that helped them to adjust to their present vulnerability.

The soldiers were situated on the cold steel floor in the back of the trailer where the spaces between the hole clusters looked out at the trailer's wire-tangled neck and the rear wall of the cab, which made up the trailer's head. A few of the grunts (including the sergeant) had regained their hearing to some extent, but it was hard for them to think straight, let alone hear what each other was saying over the grumble of the engine.

They were sitting in a horseshoe pattern, shivering and cupping their hands over their noses and mouths like improvised, fleshy gas masks. Some of them sat with their penises tucked between their thighs attempting to maintain some semblance of dignity.

An empty space separated the Six-Eyes men from the grunts. In the misery, old conflicts between the grunts and the Queen's personal guards simmered to the surface. The grunts felt that they did the brunt of the dirty work while the Six-Eyes men had it easy, especially with someone as powerful as Griff at their side. The Six-Eyes men tended to think that they had it the hardest because they had to deal with the Queen's volatile personality and the constant attempts on her life. The grunts countered with their extremely high casualty rate compared with the Six-Eyes' count. The Six-Eyes men shot back by pointing out Griff's regular spot-checks that could bring a death sentence to any man at any time. Sometimes, the slightest hint of a negative thought was all it took to wind up on his shit list. But he randomly scanned the grunts on occasion as well.

The basis of the tension was envy on the part of the grunts. Most of them longed for promotion into the Six-Eyes Posse. Even the sergeant held out hope that he would eventually be considered for promotion. Instead, he watched less qualified and able-bodied men (in his opinion) promoted over him. One day, he approached Griff about it.

"For the time being, I need someone with your talent to guide the men," Griff told him. "Be patient. Do your job, and your time will come."

So be it, he thought. There was nothing he could do, so the sergeant soldiered on. He tried not to let his disappointment fester into the kinds of thoughts that might get him into trouble.

The sergeant knelt in the middle of the horseshoe formation next to a Six-Eyes man (a medic) who was tending Griff's wounds. The medic looked annoyed by the sergeant's presence. He seemed to be using his body to block the sergeant's view of Griff's face.

The sergeant was clearly in the way, but he wasn't about to pass up an opportunity to land himself on Griff's good side should he pull through. That was why he crawled over from where he originally sat with the other grunts.

It wasn't looking good. Griff's entire left side was badly burned. His flesh was bloated and orange-red where the flames had burned away its elasticity and left it looking like glazed cheese that bubbled into blister patterns. Brittle flesh flaked to the touch, leaving deep, fibrous pits. His left eye was swollen shut.

The medic held one hand over his own nose and mouth while doing what he could to care for Griff with the other hand. The sergeant kept motioning to assist.

The soldiers shared the trailer with about a dozen other prisoners—a street merchant, two prostitutes, a few anonymous men, and a well-kept middle-aged woman who sat way in the front with her two pubescent daughters. With an arm around each one, she held them close in a way that concealed the bulk of their nudity and left only a side view. She buried her face between the tops of her daughter's heads and pressed their faces into her chest. The younger one occasionally broke out into hysterics. Taking a cue from the middle-aged woman, the street merchant sat sideways against the left wall with his knees held to his chest. The prostitutes huddled together next to him. The anonymous men curled into various protective shapes across from them.

The civilian prisoners followed the soldiers' lead and held a hand over their noses and mouths. They had been in the trailer longer than the soldiers, and most of them were trying (effectively) to conceal mild RS symptoms like itching and nausea. They had also been ruminating on the inevitable outcome of RS long enough to have reached some degree of acceptance of their fate.

They sat silently, feigning calm and perusing the gallery of unfamiliar faces. Unlike the soldiers, who had a shared ideology and a sense of valor to solidify their relationships with one another, the civilians were linked solely by their status as prisoners of the Sanguine Dawn. But, rather than acquaint themselves with names and personalities and the specifics of who each of them was back in the world and how they got here, they chose to maintain a certain disconnection. It was easier that way. Times of extreme tension made for fast (and sometimes deep) friendships. The people knew to keep their distance or set themselves up for heartbreak when one of those friendships is ended by an untimely death. It happened all the time.

Despite their best efforts to keep warm, the prisoners all fell victim to varying degrees of shivering punctuated by goose bumps the size of ball bearings. The frigid bite of the steel floor had them readjusting every couple of minutes.

They were traveling down the Atlantic City Expressway toward Philadelphia. Philadelphia sat on the northeast edge of Irradiated Zone. The Revenant Clan soldiers were discussing the layout of Philly based on intel from the failed Center City mission.

At some point, an anonymous grunt thought out loud,

"Well, at least we know what we're dealing with now."

"A lotta good that does us in here," another responded.

They spent a few moments discussing just how fucked they were. One of the grunts joked that "Maybe these Sanguine Dawn guys are hiring."

"Hey! I don't want to hear that kind of shite, soldier," the sergeant reprimanded.

"Yes, sir. Sorry, sir. Won't happen again."

And that was that.

Until a few moments ago, the prison-trailer had been positioned at the rear of a formation of APCs (armored personnel carriers) and modified trucks and buses. One of them, a city bus painted black, with dark, tinted windows carried the Alpha Dogs.

All but one of the vehicles (an APC) broke formation at Exit 53 and disappeared around the bend of the curved exit ramp. The bus carrying the Alpha Dogs pulled alongside the prison trailer before turning off. The trailer's reflection littered with eyes was cast in the bus's windows. A light switched on inside the bus and replaced the reflection with Alpha Dogs. The seats had been removed from the bus so they were just standing there glaring at the prisoners—a whole bus-load of them. One of them feigned a lunge.

The Revenant Clan soldiers shouted threats and profanities through the hole-clusters. A few of the other prisoners were screaming. The younger daughter was bawling. As the bus disappeared down the exit ramp the sergeant could see the Alpha Dogs laughing at them.

The ride from Atlantic City to Philadelphia usually took about an hour and a half. They were approximately 52 minutes into the journey. In that time, the sky faded lazily to blue-black and turned innocent shapes unsettling. Miscellaneous refused formed a lumpy surface layer. Rows of skeletal structures and half-facades where neighborhoods, and factories, and upscale housing developments used to be came off like rigid humps on the back of a large serpent skimming the surface of a junk sea. Up-rooted trees garnished the postcards of bizarro suburbia like giant, singed broccoli spears. Water towers leaned over the road like gargantuan spider-things angling for a closer look at what scurried beneath them. Severed water pipes reached up from underground like snaggle-toothed earthworms with an atomic-age makeover.

A few of the prisoners passed the time by spotting the unsettling shapes in the distance.

In between momentary inspections to monitor Griff's status, the sergeant dissected the events that led to their capture. The Intel from the Center City mission didn't mention anything about vampires. They could've prepared themselves had they known what they were up against.

Feelings conflicted. On one side the sergeant had his honor and his sworn loyalty to the queen. On the other was the missed opportunity to die with his dignity intact due to their surrender. For that he blamed the queen.

Whatever the Sanguine Dawn had in store for them, he knew it wouldn't be pretty. Butterfly wings fluttered against his stomach lining whenever he allowed his mind to skim the possibilities and rile his anxiety. His flesh ran hot, then immediately cold. The process left behind a damp layer that amplified the toxic breeze sifting through the hole-clusters.

The breeze smelled of sulfur. Due to all of the factories, the sulfur-smell had been a staple of the Atlantic City Turnpike before the war. These days it most likely meant that there were traces of sulfur mustard gas in the irradiated air. That's what the sergeant figured.

Mustard gas... Oh, it's only you? He thought. *Didn't*

you know? I'm radiation's bitch now.

He kept wondering which fate would be worse, a slow death as a result of infection or through torture at the hands of the Sanguine Dawn.

Probably the latter.

The sergeant overheard two Six-eyes men whispering earlier as the Sanguine Dawn soldiers herded them into the trailer at gunpoint. They were discussing the queen's escape route (through the basement of the Oceanic Hotel) and praying that the Sanguine Dawn soldiers took their word for it that she had perished in the original attack on the convention center. Apparently they did, but that didn't stop them from tearing through the Oceanic just in case.

The queen instructed the men to blast away a section of the wall to block off the entrance to the basement stairwell after she went down into the basement along with the rest of the Six-eyes Posse (including Rainah, Derek, and Kagen). The Oceanic connected to a layered parking garage across the street via an underground walkway that had only been partially completed before the war. So even if some of the Sanguine Dawn soldiers were familiar with the place, they might not have known about it.

Removing all the rubble was a daunting task. The Sanguine Dawn soldiers cleared a first layer, then a second, before finally giving up. A small survey team stayed behind to examine the area for possible inclusion into their expanding territory. The survey team filed in and out of a modified rock and roll tour bus with a giant airbrushed, half-naked woman with fangs, tiger stripes, and a wild mane of hair painted across both sides. She was on all fours in a pose that hinted at a cat-like forward slink. Apparently it used to belong to some retro-80s, hair-metal band.

Inside the trailer, the Revenant Clan soldiers were trying to come up with a list of things that were harmful to vampires. Someone mentioned that it was still daylight when the vampires attacked and how that "according to the rules," was impossible.

"Yeah, but it was overcast," one of the Six-eyes men pointed out in a tone that seemed to chastise the previous remark. "It's not daylight that kills them. It's sunlight."

"Well *excuse me*, Mr. Van-fuckin'-Helsing," a grunt responded.

"Actually, I think he was a doctor," commented another grunt.

"What?"

"Van Helsing... In the book, Dracula, I think he was supposed to be a doctor; right?"

"Man... so, what."

"Either way you're all gonna die," the street merchant blurted.

A few of the soldiers responded collectively, yelling at the merchant to "Shut up!"

Some of the other prisoners came to the merchant's defense. Many of them had experienced the Revenant Clan's wrath firsthand or lived through the Ergeister "occupations" back when the queen did the church's bidding. So they had nothing but contempt for the soldiers.

The prisoners argued.

One by one the voices faded until there was only the sound of the engine and the trailer creaking as the tires bounced over obstacles in the road. An outbreak of yawning befell the prisoners. They took turns nodding off. Heads bobbed and jolting awake. Languid eyes fluttered and rolled back. Rhythmic snore-sounds attempted to lure the others into sleep's comforting embrace.

Traces of moist crackling topped off with a slurp emanated from somewhere in the middle of the crowd.

"Now that's just sick," the street merchant blurted. "There

are children in here for God's sake."

"Awe shit, man!" yelled a Six-eyes man who had just woken up. He was leaning away from his posse-mate (who sat next to him) and staring down at the soldier's lap.

A dark colored mound with fibrous tentacles moved up and down over the soldier's crotch. He faced the ceiling, his head resting against the wall behind him. His eyes were rolled back. His mouth was wide open. From inside, pleasurable sounds (indecipherable tonnages riding heavy breathing) leaked out.

One of the prostitutes was fellating him. She had been cozying up to the soldier during the ride. It seemed innocent enough at first. The soldier next to him had seen her rest her head on his lap and close her eyes. At the time, he thought nothing of it.

The crowd collectively scolded the soldier.

The prostitute tried to pull away when she heard all the fuss, but the soldier was approaching climax, his body caught in the flux of sensations that took control of his will and forbade him from letting her stop until...

"Owwwww! FUCK!" the soldier cried out.

He shoved the prostitute away and thrust to his feet. He doubled over holding his throbbing penis in his hand. He coughed out a string of expletives and glared angrily at her.

The prostitute had fallen on her ass and hit her head against the opposite wall. She appeared to be in a daze. Moisture and curdled saliva decorated the corners of her wrinkled mouth. Her skin looked bloated and abrasive like cracked leather. Her eyes were sunken into their sockets. Her hair was long and stringy. She appeared to have a bald spot or two. She wore tight clothing that revealed every nook and cranny of her soggy physique.

The other prostitute leaned forward to console her, but the sergeant extended his arm and stopped her.

"Sit down, love," he ordered.

The second prostitute eyed him up and down and returned to her spot.

"Fucking bitch bit me," the soldier groaned and approached the first prostitute with his fist cocked.

The sergeant sprung forward and grabbed the soldier by the throat. He slammed the man against the wall of the trailer and leaned in face to face. They were standing over the prostitute, who seized the opportunity to grab the soldier's dangling scrotum and twist as hard as she could.

"Stupid motherfucker!" she growled.

The soldier screamed and jerked free from the sergeant's grip. The sergeant grabbed him by the shoulders and shoved him back into the wall. With his forearm held horizontally across the soldier's chest, the sergeant used his bodyweight to pin him there.

The other Six-Eyes men stood and motioned to intervene.

The grunts stood and motioned to defend the sergeant.

"Don't even think about it," one of the grunts warned.

"Hey now…. We're all on the same side, here," said another.

Without looking, the sergeant palmed the prostitute's face and shoved her away. He turned toward the looming Six-eyes men. He gave them a look that said, "Don't come any closer," and waited for them to back off.

A lithe, small-faced fellow who appeared to be the leader of the Six-eyes men motioned to the others to sit down. They complied.

The grunts followed suit.

The sergeant turned his attention to the soldier in his clutches.

The civilian prisoners watched. Disgusted. Afraid.

"You wanna tell all the lads we just lost that you were too busy get'n jiggy to help us come up with a way outta this mess? Eh? Do you?" the sergeant growled.

"What's the big deal? I mean we'll all be dead in a month or so," blurted one of the grunts. "And that's *if* these sharp-toothed ball-sacks let us live that long." He seemed surprised that the words came out of his mouth.

"I know it wasn't one of *our* lads who said that!" the sergeant scolded.

The grunt in question looked away. His posture shrunk.

"Okay, we got the point, Sergeant," said the Six-Eyes leader. "You can let him go now."

The sergeant hesitated. His eyes rolled from soldier to soldier. From their expressions he could tell that most of them agreed with the dude from Six-Eyes.

Reluctantly, the sergeant released his grip and pivoted to allow the soldier to pass.

The soldier nodded "thank you" to the Six-Eyes soldier and limped over to a spot across the trailer from where he originally sat on the floor. He sat down slowly, cupping his sore scrotum, and traded glares with the prostitutes. The one who bit him and grabbed his balls cursed him under her breath. With his other hand, the soldier massaged the inflamed area of his penis (just below the head) with his thumb. He developed an unintended erection. Embarrassed, he tucked his penis between his thighs.

The sergeant stared straight ahead through a hole-cluster out into the darkness. He wore a calm expression that, under the circumstances, suggested an impending meltdown.

The middle-aged woman in the back consoled her younger daughter, who had suddenly become hysterical again and was crying loudly.

The prostitutes and the Six-Eyes man with the sore penis were full-on arguing now.

"Shut... *the-feck*... up!" the sergeant demanded. "Everybody... shut! up!"

The arguing devolved into scornful stare-downs. Though

muffled by her mother's shoulder, the young girl's crying grew more intense.

The sergeant zeroed in on the muffled weeping. His eyes swirled with frustration.

"Listen girl," he said. "I don't care how, but you'd better shut that little whore up right now. I can't think straight with all-at bloody racket."

"Well, that's just too damn bad," the middle-aged woman replied, defensively.

Her response was followed by a series of gasps.

"Am I supposed to care that you can't think straight?" she added. "Fuck you! Fuck all of you! You're nothing but a bunch of murderers."

The sergeant made a move toward the woman.

"Stifle it, Sergeant!" yelled the Six-Eyes leader.

The sergeant froze. His eyes rolled over to where the street merchant had risen to a crouch. Apparently, he meant to "defend the honor" of the middle-aged woman.

"You again," the sergeant said as if the merchant's action offended him. "So you're the hero, eh?"

"You might wanna rethink your next move, mister," one of the grunts said to the street merchant.

"Better listen to him, lad," the sergeant added. "You're way outta your…"

"Oh, come off it," the middle-aged woman interrupted. "What are you gonna do, kill him? Why don't you just kill the rest of us too while you're at it? You'll be doing us a favor."

"Heeeyyy! Whoooa! Speak fer yourself, honey," came a muffled voice from among the prostitutes, and then "Amen to that."

The younger daughter continued to cry.

"Mommee, noooo. I don't want to die," she whimpered.

The older daughter began to well up, too.

"I'm sorry, babies. Mommy shouldn't have said that,"

the middle-aged woman whispered to her children before turning back to the soldiers. Her calm face turned, and she became enraged. "You cowards were all piss-'n'-vinegar when you had your Queen to protect you. I was there when your troops rolled through Buffalo. Do you have any idea how many people you killed... how many families you devastated? Do you even care? My sister was a beautiful person... and you bastards kidnapped her to work in your fucking brothels. Maybe you should go explain to her three children why their mother never came home."

The soldiers reacted in unison, hurling expletives at the woman.

"Your sister... what's her name, honey?" said one of the prostitutes.

"Yeah, maybe we know her."

The middle-aged woman shot an outraged look at the prostitutes, as if to suggest that her sister would never cavort with their kind. The prostitutes, who secretly enjoyed their conditions to some extent, maintained vacant expressions.

"It doesn't matter," the middle-aged woman replied. "She killed herself last month." She snapped her head toward the soldiers. "You hear that, huh? My sister killed herself rather than let you pieces-of-shit turn her into a sex slave."

"Mommee, please stop," the younger daughter interjected, wiping away tears. "You're scaring me."

"It's all right, baby," the woman cooed, cradling the girl to her bosom.

The older daughter reached over and caressed her younger sister's head.

"Who the feck *are* you?" the sergeant asked the middle-aged woman in an incredulous tone.

"I was wondering that myself," added the Six-Eyes leader.

"Whatdayou care?" the middle-aged woman replied.

"Just humor us," the sergeant said. "For curiosity's sake."

The woman hesitated.

"My name is Marianne Cross."

Silence.

"My husband was… *is* Jonathan Cross."

"The militia guy?" one of the soldiers blurted.

"He was a freedom fighter."

The soldiers gasped.

"Holy shit," one of them said. "And I thought *we* had it bad."

"Ironic, isn't it," said the middle-aged woman, "that you're riding in a prison trailer along with the wife of the man that even your precious Queen couldn't catch?"

"Watch it, lady," warned one of the grunts.

"No! *You* watch it," she responded defiantly.

Her response incited another argument, this time between the middle-aged woman and the soldiers.

It was the last thing the sergeant needed at the moment. He shook his head and balled his fists, ready to lash out at the nearest wall. He felt a sudden pressure at his wrist. He whipped his head down to find the Six-Eyes leader's hand wrapped around it.

The Six-Eyes leader lifted his index finger to his mouth and tilted his head summoning the sergeant closer.

The sergeant crouched to eye level with him.

"Listen, mate," the sergeant began, speaking softly. "Don't you think we should be coming up with some kind of plan instead of letting these boys give in to their urges? I mean…"

"I know, Sergeant, I know. That's what I wanted to speak to you about."

The sergeant detected confidence in the Six-Eyes leader's tone.

"You mean… there *is* a plan?"

The Six-Eyes leader looked around the trailer.

The soldiers were still arguing with the middle-aged woman. The rest of the prisoners followed the insults volley back and forth.

The Six-Eyes leader gave the sergeant a subtle nod.

"But we have to be careful," he whispered. "One of the people in here with us isn't who he appears to be."

The sergeant studied the Six-Eyes leader's expression. With his eyes, he directed the sergeant over to the anonymous men.

"You mean… a spy?"

The Six-Eyes leader nodded again.

"Which one?" the sergeant whispered.

"Just sit tight. You'll find out soon enough. For now, I need you to help me keep these men calm until we arrive at the Sanguine Dawn's base. Once we get there, watch for my signal. Okay?"

The sergeant nodded and returned to Griff's side. The news left him reinvigorated, as did the moment of kinship with the Six-Eyes soldier.

The soldier tending to Griff rolled his eyes as the sergeant returned.

"Everybody settle-the-fuck-down!" the Six-Eyes leader yelled.

The soldiers stopped arguing with the middle-aged woman. Their swollen postures began to deflate.

One of the grunts leaned over the sergeant's shoulder and asked him what he and the Six-Eyes leader were talking about.

The sergeant cleared his throat and searched for something clever to say to the curious kid. His eyes rolled around the room and stopped on Griff, who was looking up at him with his good (right) eye.

The sergeant was kneeling next to Griff's head. His back was facing the front of the trailer. The other prisoners (both Clan and civilian) couldn't see either of their faces.

Griff shook his head "no" and winked at the sergeant before closing his eye and continuing to feign being critically injured.

The sergeant turned to the grunt. "All in good time, soldier. All in good time."

Chapter 4

Rina, Ohio – 2006
Paging Dr. Goodvibes…
Dr. Goodvibes…

"Whoever said 'The meek shall inherit the Earth' needs to go spend some time out in the wasteland."

I still remember the way Sabrina's voice broke when she said it. There was a tremor in her tone that wasn't there ten minutes earlier, when we were going on and on about how much we missed each other like a couple-a lovesick teenagers.

We had met a year before. I was casing the Life-Threatening Injuries Wing at this joke-of-a-medical-facility in one of the independent communities down in New Mexico, looking for potential customers while attempting to soothe the serious skin-jones that was gnawing at me something awful.

You wouldn't think the sight of bare skin would be something worth jonesin' for. With everyone dressed in bugsuits or some improvised knock-off, showing bare skin in public has gone the way of green grass and deodorant.

Most "working" buildings are hermetically sealed and retrofitted with photovoltaic cells, which convert solar light into electricity. A series of batteries store the electricity for nighttime use. Some communities use the simpler stand-alone solar power stations instead.

By "working" buildings, I mean inhabited. They use air-filtration systems like the Hunter CBRN and the BioSafe® FA 300 HS to maintain clean environments. Protective clothing and gas masks aren't necessary once inside. There are folks who wear them anyway, though.

Our eyes met as soon as Sabrina turned the corner and started walking my way. I gave her the old "Hey babeh" stare.

She shot back a hungry look that all but said "I'll do anything for a fix."

Smack, I figured. Probably had something to do with the bony pincushions that peeked out from under the cuffs of her nurse's uniform. She had the sleeves hiked up to the swell of her forearm.

She had it bad. She was frazzled. Her eyes were bloodshot and bulging from their sockets, like she had been awake for days. She was trying to busy her time away with work, and it looked like it wasn't working.

Sabrina had the kind of look that I call "All-American Plain." She was the kind of chick with loads of potential who probably grew up in an environment that had little use for vanity. As a result, her beauty was vastly understated. On top of all that, the smack had her wearing an outer crust of ugly.

"Name's Roman," I said.

"You a patient here?" she asked.

I got the impression that she was about to scold me for being out of my room. Kinda turned me on.

"Ahhh, not exactly," I said. I could see that she was waiting for me to elaborate.

I told her that I dealt in pharmaceuticals. It was an old line I used with uptight folks. I figured she'd think that I was affiliated with the medical facility, that I was "safe." But a fiend might see in me an opportunity, like a golden ticket to get zooted off her ass on a regular basis.

She perked up and gave me an enthusiastic, "Oh… hi… I'm Sabrina."

The next morning, I kept giving her excuses whenever

she would mention getting high. She looked nervous and self-conscious. I wouldn't leave. She didn't want me to. But I wasn't going to let her out of my sight. Her heart sank as she realized what she would be forced to face.

I'd been around enough smackheads to know what withdrawal would be like. For Sabrina, I was willing to stick it out through the vomiting, the diarrhea, the muscle spasms and cramps, the shivering and chills, the panic—all of it.

When she would finally crawl out of the abyss, my face would be the first thing she would see. Even if she weren't genuinely into me, she would have to be grateful for my help and dedication. That would be my ticket in.

That was how our relationship began.

"Well, wha-did you think it was gonna be like when you decided to become a nurse?"

"I *didn't* think," she said. "That's the problem. The only reason I took the job was because of the access to drugs."

Ya don't say…

"The guy I was running with at the time had this big idea about selling them in one of the communities up north, where he was from."

"So, what happened?"

"He left me hanging is what happened. Friggin' loser. I finally got my hands on enough stuff to set us up real nice—Demerol, OxyContin, blue and yellow Vs, Dexedrine, some real hard-to-find stuff."

("Hard to find" is an understatement when it comes to legitimate pharmaceuticals. The old multinational corporations, the monopolies, the oligarchies are no more. The giants of the financial and entertainment industries have come to ruin. Once their protections were gone, they didn't last long. The drug companies were raided early on by looters who worked in organized groups. They would empty out the warehouses and unload the drugs on hospitals and medical facilities for some ridiculous price or in exchange for weapons, or vehicles, or residency privileges, or whatever was needed. That's how some of the smaller communities got their starts.)

"That night I dreamt about going on this huge shopping spree with all the money we were gonna make," Sabrina said. "I was buying jewelry'n furrsss'n designer clothes'n walking down red carpets, rubbing elbows with the rich and famous. So stupid.... Like it was gonna make the world all better or something. I woke up the next morning, and he was gone. Ceee-yaaa! I think I scared him away when I mentioned that I was having second thoughts about taking the stuff. I'd been working at the hospital for a month, and I sorta got to know some of the patients. My guilt level shot from zero to 60 when I realized that he had run off with the stuff. The patients were hurtin' bad—they still are. I had taken from them the one thing that gave them some kind of relief."

"I know guys who do that every day," I said. It jumped out before I could run it through my filter for inappropriate comments.

Sabrina's expression went dark. She gave me that look of hers that said "Are you finished?"

"If that makes you feel any better..." I added, trying to salvage the moment.

She hesitated and mulled over my comment like she was debating whether or not she should go on with her story.

I pretended to zip my lips.

She smiled... and continued. Thank God.

"I started out with this 'Well, they'll probably be dead soon anyway' sort of attitude," Sabrina said about the patients at the medical facility. "I mean, we had RS victims out the ass. We had people with huge, gaping holes in 'em... guts all hangin' out;

84

people with all four limbs blown or cut off; people covered from head to toe with third-degree burns. The *asshole* didn't get that far, though. They found his body the next day. They said he was beaten so badly that it took them a while to figure out whether the body was that of a man or woman. He was naked and lying face down in a dried-up creek bed about two miles outside the community border. I guess the scavengers got him. Serves him right. The best part is that they found his backpack with all the drugs in it. He must've hidden it when he realized he was in trouble."

The bitch could talk, that's for damn sure. One of my customers told me that I called Sabrina a bitch as a way of hiding my true feelings for her. I told him he was full-a-shit, but I knew he was probably right.

I can still picture the terror in Sabrina's eyes when that big beast of a man grabbed her from behind. He was shirtless, covered in blisters, and wearing a hooded gas mask. He had biceps the size of small planets and a chest like two large couch cushions slightly flattened from overuse. His eyes were big and freebasing on lust. They looked like they were about to pop out of his head and through the visor of his mask.

Sabrina and I were into each other hard, like dogs in heat, tradin' googly eyes and waxing poetic about our feelings when it happened. My guard was down... way down. Otherwise I would've noticed that we had wandered 100 yards or so outside the community border.

I went for my gun when another guy came up from behind and held a knife to my throat. Three more melted out of the shadows and held her down. Each of them was bigger than the last, but none of them came close to the first guy, who apparently was their leader.

They made me watch what they did to her. Sabrina was trying to hold her breath to keep the poison air out of her lungs. In situations like that, you forget that exposed skin is enough to do you in. I probably would've done the same thing, though.

Then they handed me a beating like you couldn't imagine. The guy with the knife to my throat kept making jokes about my mother and how good it felt to kick my ass.

"Why don't you put the knife down and fight me like a man," I said.

If you saw this guy, you'd realize exactly how foolish a remark that was. He was twice my size, at least, and the kind of shithead who lives on aggression. I knew it wouldn't make much difference if he were unarmed. But I'm a man. I had to say something.

He put down the knife and continued to pummel me barehanded. Me and my big fucking mouth...

It's hard to play dead when you've got a 250-pound meathead stomping and kicking the living shit outta you, but somehow I pulled it off. When I managed to lift my face out of the dirt, I saw them dragging Sabrina off into the night. I could barely see through the layer of caked dirt that covered my goggles, but I think she was still alive. Her eyes were blank until just before the darkness swallowed her. I was pretty sure that she frowned at me.

Does she blame me for this? I remember thinking.

That's what I get for caring, huh?

I went through all the usual shit associated with losing a loved one—depression, self-pity, denial, anger. I didn't care what happened to me. But, strangely, nothing did. I started to develop this ass-headed theory that this entire thing—the war, the wasteland, everything—was my punishment for all the bad shit I'd slung to the rich kids and the yuppies back in the '80s. I knew that most of them were in over their heads, but I kept on supplying their habits. At the time, I thought I was doing the world a favor. It was some personal beef I had against people with money. I remember saying to myself that it was bound to catch up with me at some point.

But that was then.

These days, I'm much more organized in the way I handle my business. And I must say I've done pretty well for myself as a result. I'd like to say that I'm more restrained emotionally when it comes to the ladies.

Used to be that I would fall hard.

Used to be... if I'm being honest here, than I guess I've probably got a little ways to go on that one.

My customers consist of the Rina hospital, Society Hill residents, traveling merchants, and supply-drivers from neighboring communities. I do business with the off-campus people (including the hookers) through the proper representatives.

I take cash only, except for the occasional trade. I don't discuss prices, but I'll tell you that my stuff ain't cheap. Regular customers pay a monthly fee at City Hall. It gets them two visits per month. No one-time deals. That's their rule, not mine, by the way. I'm not above making an exception to it here and there if I like someone.

I'm open to the general public (meaning Society Hill employees) on Tuesdays, Wednesdays, and Thursdays. Mondays and Fridays are set aside for the traveling merchants, supply-drivers, and the off-campus representatives. The marketplace and tavern are closed to Hill employees on those days. I guess Knox doesn't want 'em mixing with outsiders. A little paranoid, maybe, but I can dig it.

They come to the marketplace to barter for or buy food, weapons, clothing, tools, appliances, et cetera. You never know where the shit is coming from with the merchants and the supply-drivers. That's why I only eat the shit we grow here on the Hill.

They come to see me with their lists when they're done

with their "official" business. They have a drink or a bite to eat first, trying to be subtle, I guess. They slide me glances between swigs, or I get the nod from a food-stuffed mouth.

People still feel the need to tread lightly when it comes to drugs. Each comes with his own set of quirks and preconceived ideas about how "the deal" is supposed to go down. Some rubberneck and whisper. Some substitute the drug name with less conspicuous terms like "trees" for weed "baby powder" for coke. Some speak in bizarre riddles.

Idiots.

I can usually gauge the types of communities the supply-drivers come from based on the kinds of drugs their residents are into. Weed, coke, belladonna, calamus, 'shrooms, and henbane are markers of "normal" folk. What do I mean? Well, without sounding corny, I mean folks who lead productive lives within their respective communities. They care about the state of the world and actively do their part to help rebuild. They're just looking for something to ease the day-to-day pain of post-apocalyptic living, something to lift their minds above it.

Sometimes the lab rats come up with interesting chemical cocktails, usually for the Rina Hospital. All they've got aside from the "medicinal" shit that I sell them (weed and an assortment of natural hallucinogens, mostly) are expired, over-the-counter drugs like aspirin and ibuprofen and shit like rubbing alcohol. Knox originally wanted me to work out of the hospital, but I fought him on it. Been through my share of hospitals in my post-war travels, and I had no desire to be surrounded 24/7 by sickness, pain, and death. You get that no matter where you are these days, but the hospitals are like ground zero for that shit. All the stories about "Civil War-era" surgeries and slow, agonizing deaths: just thinking about it turns my stomach. You can even hear the patients screaming and begging the doctors to kill them from outside the building. Just go stand within 50 feet of the hospital, if you don't believe me. I dare you.

Some of these cocktails act as synthetic hallucinogens or super-stimulants. Taking any of that shit is like playing Russian roulette. Every now and again, I'll get a customer who's looking for that shit for recreational purposes. As a rule, I try to steer people away from it. Nine times outta 10, they don't listen: they want what they want, and they don't care about the risk. Sometimes they wind up dead.

Had this one knucklehead named Klimmick who thought he was invisible. Aura was the name of the synthetic. The shit had him running around naked and stalking chicks. He'd find out where they worked. Then he'd stand there naked, watching them through windows and jerking off in plain sight. Of course, he thought nobody could see him. Last I heard, he was locked up and dying from RS.

When the supply-drivers come asking about synthetics, I know that the people on the other end are troublemakers, instigators, adrenaline junkies, and impulsive folks who live for the moment. A community at the mercy of synthetics is on the brink of collapse.

Natural drugs are the intoxicants du jour. It all boils down to accessibility. Anything you can grow. My main supply is grown right here on the Hill in Weidner Hall. I supply the lab rats with seeds, hardwood, greenwood, and root cuttings and handle distribution. They do the rest.

Mayor Knox limits my off-campus customers to one item per visit. Hill residents and employees get two or sometimes three. And don't let on that you heard it from me, but Knox and the members of City Council are among my regulars.

Chapter 5

September 2005
Revenant Days: Center City

The last leg of the journey had been relatively quiet. Arguments came and went. The civilian prisoners grew less concerned with trying to conceal their RS symptoms, which had worsened.

The Revenant Clan's soldiers' symptoms were just starting to manifest.

In place of the tension of earlier, a strange campfire storytime vibe was attempting to settle in, thanks in large part to one of the prostitutes.

"So, if you knew yesterday where you would be right now, what would you have done differently?" she asked out of the blue. She had the whole group's attention.

Initially, her question drew jeers and remarks about her tact and her level of intelligence from some of the other prisoners.

The prostitute frowned and cleared her throat to respond. She was cut off by an anonymous Revenant Clan grunt who remarked, "We would've been ready for them pussies. I know that much."

"No… you can't do anything to change it," said the prostitute.

"Well, then, what's the point," said one of the grunts

Another said, "I don't know about you all, but I could go for a home-cooked meal. Steak-n-eggs. Spaghetti. A nice meatloaf. Anything."

"We could all use that, man," said a third. "I know I

could."

"And who you gonna get to make that for you, genius?" queried another. "Where you gonna get the uninfected meat?"

"Who knows, man? That wasn't the question."

The Revenant Clan soldiers seemed the most willing to share. The initial grip of their fear had relaxed, and they realized instinctively that they would have to maintain some mental fortitude during the final leg of the journey. No words could offer comfort now.

Eventually, some of the civilian prisoners warmed up to the discussion.

The street merchant sat up and smiled at a surfacing memory.

"The house I grew up in. It's a beautiful place right outside Sandusky, Ohio. Nice and peaceful. Green as far as the eye can see. I used to tell my wife that it was where I wanted to die. That's where I would go," he said.

"Is that where your wife is?" asked one of the prostitutes.

"Anthrax took her," he responded. "She passed last year."

"I'm sorry."

"I would look for my brother and sister," said the chubby man of ambiguous ethnicity. As a newcomer to the conversation, he seemed reluctant. "We... we got separated during the war. I would tell them that I love them."

The thin man next to him seemed startled by the sound of his voice. A few of the other prisoners reacted similarly.

A few minutes passed.

"Give me a good woman," quipped one of the grunts.

"Here. Here!" a voice responded.

"How you gonna keep it up when you're dying from RS?"

"I'll manage. Besides, who says I have to screw her? I'm talkin' 'bout companionship, man—someone to curl up with when it's cold outside. Laugh if you want, but a good woman'll

91

work wonders for your peace of mind. If I just wanted a piece-a-ass I could get that anywhere."

The grunt tilted his head in the direction of the prostitutes.

The prostitute who fellated the soldier earlier sucked her teeth and returned a twist-lipped glare.

"Ooo! I know what I would do," said the middle-aged woman's elder daughter. She had been lost in thought until now. The thoughts that started in her head had worked their way below her waist. "I want to have —!"

Her mother slapped a hand over her mouth and pulled her close.

"Not another word," she scolded. "You hear?"

The girl nodded.

"I have a question," said the chubby man to the soldiers. He hesitated before following up.

"Well?" a voice traveled out from the group of soldiers.

"The Queen…" he began. "Is she really…?"

"I can tell you what she is," the middle-aged woman interrupted. She had been doing her best to stifle her anger. She viewed the other prisoners' willingness to engage the soldiers on a somewhat friendly level as betrayal. "She's a fucking heartless bi…"

"Holy shit!" someone yelled. "We're here."

16ᵗʰ and Walnut Streets

The trailer moved slowly through the intersection, granting the prisoners a long look. Compared with the neighborhoods to the south, Walnut Street was relatively unmolested. Scaffolding was everywhere. Blue-collar types dressed in construction wear and hardhats with complicated tool belts dangling from their waists wandered about. The Sanguine Dawn soldiers who patrolled the block were the only ones around who were wearing gas masks.

There were a few damaged buildings, but for the most part, the street looked like a ritzy retail corridor undergoing heavy renovations. Large machinery moved chunks of rubble. Men with blowtorches worked on damaged façades. Light shined from inside a few of the buildings, suggesting that they were open for business or soon would be.

Workers set up tables with huge umbrellas sticking out of them outside of nearly completed eateries. Vendors scouted out prime locations and prepared booths. A sign on the front of one booth listed the items to be sold—brand new clothing for all occasions, flashlights, candles, batteries, portable gas/electric generators and more!!!

Everyone on the street paused to watch the trailer crawl past.

Chestnut Street

One block up, on Chestnut Street, the devastation was more prominent. Scaffolding. Blue-collar types navigated the scaffolding like children on monkey bars. As the bus crept closer toward Market Street and the old City Hall, where the headquarters of the Sanguine Dawn were located, bands of soldiers began to fill the streets and sidewalks.

The trailer stopped at the mouth of the intersection of 16th and Market. Industrial fencing stretched across 16th Street, separating Market from everything south of it. Across Market, another identical fence cut off the north side of the city. Razor-ribbon wire spiraled along the top of the fences.

Static hissed from an intercom box perched atop a four-and-a-half foot high steel post.

A voice leapt out.

"[Psssht] Bring the prisoners around to the west entrance. Dr. Lund will be there to meet you. [Psssht]"

The driver leaned out and craned his head down toward the intercom.

"Yes sir," he said.

The automatic slide gate shook to life and slid open with the shrieking sound of steel on steel.

The trailer drove through and turned right, onto Market.

Market Street

Formerly, Market Street was the corporate hub of Philadelphia. Glass towers stood shoulder to shoulder, locked in a permanent face-off with look-alike structures across the wide avenue.

More Sanguine Dawn soldiers in full gear and gas masks were positioned in front of the buildings from 16th to 15th.

As he watched through the hole-clusters in the trailer's skin, the sergeant began to formulate a theory about the inner workings of the Sanguine Dawn ranking system. It would seem that they used humans to do their grunt work. The vampire troops that attacked them earlier must be some type of Special Forces group. He relayed his theory to the men.

Outside, the Sanguine Dawn soldiers stood firm as the procession (the prison trailer, followed closely by an APC) rolled by. The vehicles' reflections bounced back and forth between the buildings' mirrored faces.

A few of the buildings had been gnarled down to serrated stumps. Looking up from the ground, the rough edges appeared to scratch the sky.

The fat moon had a bluish tint. From its place on high,

peering over the headless buildings, it quietly surveyed the events as they unfolded.

City Hall

Constructed of white marble and granite around a central public courtyard, the High Picturesque Eclecticism-style structure was poised with nobility in the center of the corporate diorama. Its design boasted turreted courtyard stair towers, a slate mansard roof with dormer windows, paired columns, and protruding corner pavilions. The windows were all hidden behind reinforced steel with horizontal slivers cut into them near the top. A small sliding door in the sliver could be opened and closed to illuminate the interior or serve as a sniper post.

Hundreds of sculptures representing historical, allegorical, and mythological subjects decorated its façade. A 548-foot tower extended up from the ground on the north side. Massive clocks were set near the top on all four sides. None of them worked anymore.

A 37-foot statue of William Penn was perched at the very top of the tower, his hand pointing northeast toward Shackamaxon, where he made a treaty with the Lenape Indians in 1682.

The courtyard in the middle was accessible via four arched portals that opened out onto the north, south, west, and east sides of the city. A circular island of pavement extended from the foot of the outer square of the building to a buffered ledge. The ledge hugged the inside of a wide, circular street that surrounded the building. The street branched off into four intersections that aligned with the arched portals. Back in the day, the street was perpetually gridlocked. The pavement island, with its small sitting areas and fountain mini-courtyards, was a haven for skateboarders, stoners, lunch-break zombies, and the homeless.

The Sanguine Dawn had made some changes since moving in.

They dug up the circular street surrounding City Hall and flooded the pipe-laden cavity with a stew of toxic liquids that could, it is told, dissolve an entire human body in a couple of minutes.

Dozens of 10-foot long metal pipes, sharpened to points, had been planted throughout the pavement island. Some of them were decorated with bodies slumped and dangling from the spots where the tips pierced their flesh and let loose their viscera. Smeared blood marked the downward journeys of the dead and dying bodies.

Standing proud, undamaged by the war, the castle-like edifice mocked the supposedly more advanced architecture that surrounded it. The sight of City Hall, sticking out of the fog bank that had settled in the forest of sharpened metal pipes, had a numbing effect on those who approached.

The trailer maintained a creeping pace down the middle of Market Street. Eyes peered out through hole-clusters and rolled around the small circumference of the holes to cover as much area as possible.

To the Sanguine Dawn soldiers who watched the procession, it looked like a twisted work of art—"Wall of eyes recessed in steel," maybe?

Exhaust pipes hissed. Brake pads squealed.

The trailer bounced to a stop. The APC behind it stopped and emptied its cargo of human Sanguine Dawn soldiers.

A single-file line marched up alongside the trailer (back to front) on both sides. At the same time, the soldiers stationed outside the buildings began marching forward toward the trailer.

From inside the trailer, it looked like a Fellini routine.

The soldiers marching back to front stopped at the front

of the trailer. A traveling wall of soldiers approached them and stopped five feet away. Turning sharply, the wall became a single-file line of men and formed a second, parallel row of soldiers on both sides of the trailer. There were 40 soldiers in all, 10 in each row. Standing at attention, the soldiers faced City Hall.

On both sides of the trailer, the first row of soldiers shifted their weight, heels clicking, as if to acknowledge the second row. The second row responded with the same shifting/heel-clicking motion. It marked the end of the barrage of echoed foot stomping that beat down the prisoners' resolve, as it was intended to do. It was followed by a quiet span laced with strange, vocal sounds that resonated from the distance and the hypnotic lapping sound of toxic waves snapping and licking the sides of the improvised moat.

A large door opened in the arched portal that faced west, where the trailer and the soldiers waited.

A dozen more Sanguine Dawn soldiers exited through the opened door. They walked in two single-file lines of six and flanked an older gentleman known as Dr. Lund.

Dr. Lund walked among the men, supporting his middle-aged, somewhat soft frame with a fancy-looking cane topped with a silver ball handle. He wore a dark-colored suit with huge shoulder pads that looked like football protective wear. A long, black cloak that swept the ground when he walked was draped over them.

The soldiers escorted Dr. Lund through the forest of metal pipes and up to a marble podium built into a ledge that looked down 10 feet into the toxic moat.

He walked up a small staircase to the podium and positioned himself behind the microphone. He choked the microphone's flexible neck, arched it downward in line with his mouth, and tapped the mesh-covered head. A deafening sonic thud echoed out from the marble-and-granite face of the building and bounced down Market Street.

Dr. Lund clasped his hands behind his back and shifted into an authoritative stance.

"What you've seen tonight as you passed through the streets of what was once known as Philadelphia is only the beginning of what will be a grand metropolis constructed in honor of a people whose history predates your own. For centuries since you stumbled upon us, we were forced to hide in the shadows, ashamed of our true identity, ashamed of our taste for the precious red liquid that sustains both our species, albeit in different ways. While you led your comfortable lives, *we* struggled for centuries to find a place amongst you. (Pause) Forget what you have heard about the Irradiated Zone. Set aside your human arrogance, and behold the new Sanguine Territories."

The Sanguine Dawn soldiers raised their guns and cheered. The sound was deafening.

"We are all survivors of the great war that has devastated this once beautiful planet. As such, I congratulate your determination to persevere in the face of such insurmountable odds, and I would ask that you display that same determination in the service of your new master, our supreme ruler, the great and magnificent Count Onyx."

The soldiers cheered again.

"As of this moment, your lives thus far are over. I urge you all to forget about your pasts. Your memories will only serve to distract you from your new lives of servitude and sacrifice as property of the Sanguine Dawn. As punishment for your crimes, some of you will give your lives in a public ceremony held here in the central courtyard. Your deaths will be an example to those who would choose to act against us. From this fate, there is no escape. Any attempt to resist will be met with swift and merciless action."

"He's talking about us, isn't he?" one of the Revenant

Clan grunts whined.

"I don't plan on sticking around long enough to find out."

"Got that right."

"You heard what he said about trying to escape?"

"Fuck what he said! I ain't about ta just lay down and take it up the ass. No, sir! Not without a fight."

"You men! Turn around and look sharp!" shouted the Six-Eyes leader. "All of you!"

The men snapped forward and sat perfectly erect.

The Six-Eyes leader turned back to the sergeant, with whom he was conversing.

Outside, Dr. Lund was still talking into the microphone. He was still talking five minutes later when an explosion shook the ground, interrupting his melodramatic presentation. It came from the south, and it was close.

A brief silence followed.

Heavy gunfire erupted. A second, smaller explosion momentarily drowned it out.

"They're here!" the sergeant whispered enthusiastically.

"Protect the south gate!" Dr. Lund yelled into the microphone.

Twenty of the Sanguine Dawn soldiers in the street scrambled toward the noise—gunfire, screaming, brake pads squealing, and heavy objects colliding. It sounded like it was coming from Locust or Spruce Street and was heading north toward them.

Inside the trailer, Griff sat up and shoved the sergeant out of the way. The glazed cheese blisters flexed and wrinkled. Griff winced at the pain. He held his left arm against his side to keep the wounded area from moving too much, took a deep breath, and trained his good eye on the thin man with the Spanish accent. The man was on his knees, peeking through a hole-cluster along with everyone else.

The thin man turned and met Griff's Cyclops glare as if he had been waiting for this moment all along. His posture tensed, threatening action.

The thin man flinched and seemed to simply appear standing up without going through the actual motion. His musculature had become inflated. His eyes swirled yellow-red. His face was longer, his cheekbones more prominent. His mouth had stretched slightly wider at the corners and was equipped with fangs. His penis was shriveled.

The naked vampire spread his arms and crouched into an aggressive stance.

Chapter 6

Rina, Ohio – 2006
The Doctor is in...

Monday

They tell me that the Concerned Citizens have linked up with the anti-drug chuckleheads over these latest RS casualties. Two more kicked it in the past three days, by the way. To hear people talk, it could've been anything from a manufactured virus, to—get this—some kind of radioactive ghost, possibly a creation of the Ergeister Church, that killed them. You heard me right—a ghost that irradiates its victims. Can you believe that crap? It all stems from footsteps that people in the victims' building claimed to have heard walking up walls and across rooftops. One little girl said that she saw a woman floating outside a window on the fifth floor.

But enough about that.

They're calling this new group the Citizens' Brigade.

They say they've got *me* in their sights. Ain't that a fucking bitch? Once they take me down, they'll be gunning for the hookers. That's Chalk's theory. He sounded so disappointed when he said it. Answered my question right there about his involvement with the hookers. Most decent people like to maintain some sort of discretion when it comes to their dealings with ladies of the night.

I, for one, would rather not know when it comes to

friends—the few I actually have. Makes it easier to maintain the friendship. Problem is once I find out, I start speculating about whether or not they've been with Desire. I get all jealous. My head starts whipping up overly sexualized scenarios worthy of late-night Cinemax flicks with "Fatal" in the title. It always leads to problems.

Speaking of which, I can hear the cooks gabbing in Spanish in the stairwell just beyond the front door. I can't see them from here, but I *can* see the guards who are standing about four feet away from them on either side of the door having their own conversation.

The Rina Tavern is located in the basement of the building, across the hall from a large open space similar to the one occupied by the market upstairs. It's currently being used for storage. Sometimes the guards like to take their little off-campus hookups there for secret rendezvous. And, of course, I get to hear about it in vivid detail.

Been trying not to listen to the guard on the right brag about his wild night with DangerPussy, Hardcore, and… I couldn't make out the last name he mentioned. I was busy humming to myself. It wasn't even a song or anything, just some vocal jibberish to block out the guards' voices when the cooks' conversation (which I was trying to use as a distraction) wasn't cutting it anymore. Maybe if I understood what they were saying… Whatever it is, it sounds like they're having a good ol' time while I sit back here in my office simultaneously listening and not listening for the guard on the right to mention a certain name.

I don't know why I get so jealous. It's not like I can stake any claim to Desire other than during the hour of her time that I pay her for… used to pay her for....

I exhale for the first time in what seems like 15 minutes when the guards finally move on to another subject. They're still bragging, though. This time it's about weapons: who's got the better arsenal, and all that. Not really my bag.

That's not to say that I don't carry. Well, not in here. Supposedly not in Society Hill at all. But fuck that. Except at the tavern, I carry a Colt Cobra .38 Special with me everywhere I go. It's small and easy to conceal. People like to razz me about it. Then comes the connection to my manhood. *Reeeal* original.

I tell them that I've never had the need to overcompensate for my shortcomings with cars and big guns. Just give me something practical that packs a wallop. Something that I can carry discreetly.

Now, out in the wasteland… That's a whole other story. Out there you *wanna* advertise. Let them scavengers know you ain't the one to fuck with. Because believe you me, if you're out there, they are out there watching you, sizing you up….

Chalk's got some brooding, bumpity bump-bump ambient shit on the overhead. I ask him what it is, and he mentions a Japanese name that I'd never heard before. Akira Yama-blahblah or something. I was going to tell him to turn it off until I started to dig it a little. I found myself strangely entranced by the haunting melody that oozed out between beats. Somehow it fit the lazy, meditative vibe that I've been feeling today. Been thinking a lot about the paths we choose in life, the unexpected turns they sometimes take, and all that….

When I was a kid, I used to have this dream of being a world-class journalist. I looked up to guys like Walter Cronkite and Dan Rather who did ballsy shit like reporting from the front line in Vietnam. My family would always bust my chops about staying in school, but my rebellious streak made me favor doing things my own way—still does. I used to tell them that I had enough random information swimming around my noggin to beat Ken Jennings in Jeopardy. I stand by that claim. I bullshitted my way to Segment Producer on a local news show called "Go Philly" on that miscellaneous information... and a little résumé embellishment.

I always hated that title, "Go Philly!" Sounds like some kinda second-rate, cable-access operation, doesn't it? Believe it or not, it was a pretty good show. We covered local politicians, businesses, and news personalities. Came on at seven in the evening—that kind of thing.

So what the hell happened, right? Well, it all started with a piece I was researching about the Philly drug culture. The politicians were saying it was just an inner-city phenomenon, but I had found that there were just as many affluent users, people with good careers and families. Prominent folks: doctors, lawyers, politicians, you name it. I was under a lotta stress at the time. I was the new "hotshot" on the show, so I had to bust my ass every time to live up to the title—at least I thought I did. On top of that, I was always worried that somebody was gonna check up on me and find out that my background was a sham. Shit had me on edge 24/7.

I guess I was in the right place at the right time. I was interviewing this doctor—neurologist, I think. Big shot from Rittenhouse Square. He offered me a line when the interview was over. Said I looked like I could use a "boost." I decided to do a little experimenting—for the sake of authenticity and all that....

Next thing I knew, I was rubbing elbows with Philly's movers and shakers. I went to all the best parties. I washed down pills with expensive wine and hors d'œuvres. I became addicted to the lifestyle... and to a smorgasbord drugs. I think it was the transient natural of it all. Every day was different, each one cast with interesting characters. I lived for that kind of... interaction, I guess you'd say.

These weren't lowlives I'm talkin' about. These were successful sons-a-bitches. Well-traveled folks. Folks who knew how to live.

I sorta let my job slip out from under me. I had made so many connections that people started calling *me* to find out who was holding and… well… you'd have to be pretty stupid not to see the potential in that situation. So to hell with my job. That's how I felt at the time. Truth is I couldn't handle the pressure. I'm big enough that I can admit that now.

It is what it is, right? At least I can't say that I've had a boring life.

As far as I can tell, Green Hill, Ohio was a typical small midwestern town before the war. It was the home of Green Hill State University, a school I'd never heard of.

Funny that it took a war to get me back here, in college, so to speak.

City Council is made up of friends and business associates of the mayor's from before the war. Back then, the name "William Knox" was synonymous with money.

That's right, William "Wild Bill" Knox, the billionaire real estate mogul with the laughable comb-over is the fucking mayor.

The members of City Council were all wildly successful in their own right back in the day. One was president of a Fortune 500 robotics company. One worked as a lawyer for the rich and famous. One designed security systems. One owned a million-dollar construction company. One was a high-ranking research scientist for the defense department. Trailing behind each of them is a small group of ass-kissers who compete like children for mommy or daddy's attention.

Knox grew up right outside of Green Hill in a little town called Mansfield. That's where he built his mansion after making it big. Beautiful place. I remember seeing it on some celebrity homes show—one of those "Look what I got" deals where the celebrity talks to the camera while guiding the audience on a tour. Not that I was into that kinda shit. I would watch whatever they had on at the old diner on 20th and Chestnut back in the day. The Midtown, it was called. The place was a grease stain, but they served the kinda crap that went down smooth at 2:00 am on a Friday night.

On the show, Knox walked the camera through a panic shelter he had built into the place. It looked like the bridge of a friggin' spaceship. There were walls lined with monitors and grids and expensive, high-backed office chairs tucked under desktops layered with keyboards and levers. There was a separate room for lounging and recreation, a lab/research area, and a large, dormitory-style bedroom.

When the shit hit the fan, Knox gathered all his successful friends and put them up in his shelter. He gave them (and us on occasion) this big speech about how he had foreseen the war in his dreams. He told them that he was giving them a chance to make history. They were going to help him rebuild. Make things better than before. Rules would be based on logic and reason instead of religious morality. Blah blah blah…

Eventually, survivors in the area started whispering things about Knox's place: how it was safe from the toxic air; how it still had electricity; how it was well stocked with food and water.

Knox and his millionaire squad barely made it out alive when the raids finally came. They ended up here, on the Hill, half a mile up at the top of Green Hill Mountain (which, technically, isn't a mountain). The old Green Hill State University campus looks like one of those old Carpathian mountaintop fortresses standing vigilant over the common folk in the town below that you'd see in the old black-and-white horror classics.

I understand that the students used to refer to it as Castle Frankenstein, or Transylvania U. The Hill is accessible by Green Hill Road, a winding, two-laned road cut into the bearded face of the mountain (which, again, isn't really a mountain).

You'll forgive me for repeating myself. I've gotten in the habit of following any mention of Green Hill Mountain with that little disclaimer thanks to all the outta-state folks who associate Ohio with flatlands and see fit to remind me of that whenever they ask where I'm from.

The campus' original gated stone archway still stands at the bottom of Green Hill Road; only now it's heavily guarded 'round the clock.

Here on the Hill, there's a medical facility, a security depot, a library, a state-of-the-art gym, dorms, access to computers, and endless laboratory space. All for the taking. Or, would it be "for the using?"

The god-fearing folks are pushing for a church. They want to use the old campus theater. Like that'll ever happen.

I'd say it's about 95% Christian here, broken down into three denominations—Catholic, Protestant, and Jehovah's Witness. And those folks can never seem to agree on anything. There's no way Knox is gonna give'm each a building, which is what they really want. As it is now, they meet at each other's homes to practice... er... worship... or fear... God. Or whatever they wanna call it.

During the war, the Red Cross used the campus as a medical facility/shelter for people in the area. You can still see the leaflets, posters, and equipment with their official seal hiding among the empty buildings and overgrown weeds on the west end of the Hill. A temporary wall made from highway construction barriers separates the west end from the rest of the Hill until Knox is ready to develop it.

The looters were good to the campus during the downtime between the departure of the Red Cross and our arrival. During that time, it sat vacant. They busted the place up a little, wrote on the walls, and stole furniture, tools, and appliances that they probably couldn't use, but that was about it. They were most likely looking for canned food. Everything else just happened along the way. That was usually the case.

Society Hill to Rina is basically what the National Mall is was to Washington, DC. Within the Hill itself, the hub is an area called Centre Square. Centre Square is composed of four buildings arranged in a tight square:

1. The administration office/security depot/jail = Rina City Hall
2. The student commons = Rina Marketplace & Rina Tavern
3. The campus infirmary = Rina Hospital
4. Weidner Hall (classrooms) = Rina Grow Facility, aka "the Greenhouse," & Rina Research Center

An outer layer of old high-rise dorms (one in each corner) hides the square from the rest of the Hill. Snipers occupy random floors in each building. The main sniper stations are located on the rooftops and are manned 24/7. And those bad boys don't fuck around.

Funny that they didn't report seeing any ghosts.

Knox, his cabinet, and Rina's "essential personnel" live in the southeast tower. The remaining Society Hill residents are spread out between the northeast and northwest towers.

I live by myself in the southwest tower. The building is still in the process of being renovated. I'd say it's about 60 percent complete. Knox offered to put me up in the southeast tower, but I couldn't see myself living so close to "the man," if ya know what I mean.

Security teams patrol the grounds in little golf-cart thingies with the old Green Hill State U. logo still plastered on the hoods. I guess they haven't gotten around to replacing 'em yet. Campus security is made up of volunteers—people with military or law-enforcement backgrounds, mostly. They work either for money or free housing, but not both. Money is still accepted in some places, like in the Federal and most of the Ergeister communities, to name a few. Some of the smaller communities (like this one) still accept it, but barter for commodities like food, weapons, supplies, services, or drugs is preferred to currency.

Some people accept money because they refuse to let go of this idea that things might one day get back to the way they were. They think that if they hoard as much cash as possible, they'll wind up sittin' pretty when that day comes. Knox thinks this way, too, but at least he's got the sense to plan for the alternative.

The mayor is currently working on converting the swimming pool in the campus recreation center into an improved graywater recycling system to replace the one that's already in use. They've been having problems with the old system from day one—mostly people getting sick because the recycled water wasn't treated properly. Until they perfect it, I'll continue to get my water elsewhere. Clean water ain't easy to come by these days. I struck a deal with one of the traveling merchants, a guy I've known for years. I give him blow; he gives me clean water. Done and done.

Outside of Society Hill, the rest of Rina's population of approximately 2,000 lives in the off-campus neighborhoods at the bottom of Green Hill Mountain (which isn't really… ah, to hell with it). Many of the off-campus homes have been ransacked by looting and gutted by fire. But, like in most places, there are habitable pockets.

The off-campus borders are protected by a multilayered system of blockades. The first layer consists of concrete road barriers. The second layer consists of automobile husks crushed and stacked on top of each other. The third barrier consists of a belt of land mines that reaches 50 feet in from its outer edge. Guards periodically patrol the borders in fortified Humvees.

The merchants, drivers, and reps aren't all that hungry today. They stop for a quick nibble and a glass of juice, but no one seems interested in an actual meal this morning. Could be that they're fed up with the liquid shitstorms—compliments of Rina's water supply. I noticed that some of them have been looking a little thinner lately. Or maybe they know of another community that's serving up something equally bland but much less expensive.

The prices here are outrageous by anyone's standards: $100 or barter of equal value for a meal. There isn't much of a selection: mostly canned fish, Spam, powdered foods that only require water (unsafe water), and dried fruits and vegetables.

A lot of people who remember the old ways act like you can't put together a good meal without beef, chicken, or fresh seafood, but you'd be surprised. If you've got 125 bucks (or equal barter), then I hear the solid white tuna platter or Portobello mushroom (one per customer) with baked potato and asparagus is pretty tasty.

To drink, it's (tainted) water, powdered juices (made with tainted water), very old and very flat soda, or the glorified moonshine that passes as alcohol nowadays. You have to have an iron stomach to drink that shit.

Chapter 7

September 2005
Revenant Days: The Second Battle

"Get outta the way!" Griff yelled.

The prisoners thrust away from the naked vampire. A shockwave of heat-distortion shoved the vampire back into the wall. The impact shook the trailer.

The vampire's engorged muscles flexed against the force that pressed him to the wall. His neck strained. His head thrashed from side to side. He was growling and carrying on like a desperate animal.

The prisoners ran to the other end of the trailer where the soldiers congregated around Griff. Their noses and gums were bleeding. Their bodies were swollen, their skin tender and irritated. Large, itchy rashes were forming all over their bodies.

Griff's nose was bleeding, too, either from radiation or from coaxing. At the moment, it didn't matter which. He was sitting Indian style, facing the vampire. He held his right hand out slightly. His palm faced up, fingers spread. Rippling heat-distortion traveled out from his palm. He acknowledged the pain in his left side by constantly arching his torso away from it, like he was working out a kink in his lower back.

The middle-aged woman's two daughters were hysterical.

The two prostitutes screamed into the street merchant's chest as they huddled in his protective embrace. Together they attempted to push their way further into the crowd.

The force from Griff's coaxing pinned the naked vampire to the wall of the trailer. The skin of his face was stretching taught against the bone structure underneath as if his skull was trying to push through. The back of his skull collapsed with a thud and brought his head closer to the wall. The vampire cried out and shook from the pain. The prisoners covered their ears to muffle his shrieking voice. His face ripped down the middle and snapped back on both sides like a bursting balloon, leaving a halo of blood around the vampire's head. The lightning-bolt seam continued down the rest of his naked body until his skin was completely gone. A muscle fiber/skeletal beast with fangs and bulging yellow-red eyes pushed its head outward and hissed before the force yanked it back to the wall. The vampire continued to thrash and shriek. His high-pitched voice carried through the prisoners' hands and hurt their ears.

The vampire's skeleton started to buckle. Its muscle fibers began to unravel.

Griff continued to push with his mind. The strain was making him light-headed. He was sweating badly. His skin was pale. He wasn't sure how much longer he could continue.

Outside, the 20 Sanguine Dawn soldiers who stayed with the trailer gathered around the drop-down door/ramp and raised their weapons. Two large sliding bolts held it secure. A soldier approached the door/ramp.

The top bolt slid open and startled the soldier. He hadn't even reached the lock yet. He was holding a ring of keys, but he had yet to single out the correct one. The background noise pressured him to act fast.

The second lock slid open. A second later, the door/ramp came down on top of the soldier with the keys and crushed him beneath it.

The other Sanguine Dawn soldiers ran over and lifted the ramp off the ground. The crushed soldier was stuck to the outside face. They had to shake the ramp to get him off.

A skeletal form crumbled to the floor at the mouth of the open trailer. It was the naked vampire.

"Secure the prisoners!" a gas-masked voice commanded.

The Sanguine Dawn soldiers shifted their aim up inside the trailer.

The Sanguine Dawn soldiers at the south gate formed a wall behind it. They braced for something large. One of them motioned to the soldiers manning the gate to open it.

The gate slid open.

A machine approached from the south.

"Shoot out the tires!" ordered one of the soldiers at the south gate.

A revving diesel engine bellowed. A deep horn sounded repeatedly.

On the other side of Market, the north gate slid open. Six more Sanguine Dawn soldiers exited and ran over to the south gate.

The Sanguine Dawn soldiers outside the prison trailer began acting peculiarly, as if they were suddenly overcome by a shared intoxicant. They swooned. Their bodies seized and became rigid. Their heads drooped as they lost consciousness. A second later, they appeared revitalized, but their movements were strangely robotic. Acting in unison, they turned their guns on their comrades at the north and south gates and opened fire.

The ambushed soldiers at the north and south gates arched and spun away from the bullets that punched through their protective gear. Wild reflexes made them fire their weapons as they lurched and stumbled. Friendly fire tore through the guards.

A few of them had only been wounded and were trying to adjust when a large, '80s hair-band tour bus barreled through the opened south gate and crushed them. The Sanguine Dawn soldiers who clung to the sides of the bus partially obstructed the airbrushed tigress that stretched its length on either side.

The bus swerved onto Market, leaning drastically as it turned. It traveled in an erratic pattern attempting to shake the soldiers off. As they fell, the coaxed Sanguine Dawn soldiers picked them off.

The bus raced toward the prison trailer, rolling over Sanguine Dawn soldiers along the way. By the time it skidded sideways 15 feet away from the trailer, there were only 20 coaxed Sanguine Dawn soldiers left standing in the street.

"Revenant Clan!" Griff yelled. The pain was evident in his voice and in the look on his face. "Fall in behind the Sanguine Dawn soldiers! We're gonna make a break for the tour bus. The rest of you are on your own."

Naked, swollen bodies poured out of the trailer. Many of them were covered in rashes.

Shots rained down from across the man-made moat behind them. Two of the 16 Revenant Clan soldiers were hit immediately.

The coaxed Sanguine Dawn soldiers spun around and opened fire on City Hall.

Bullets peppered the stone-and-marble face of the structure and chipped away at the podium until there was nothing left but the bullet-riddled body of one of Dr. Lund's escorts. The doctor had already retreated inside the building. The other escort was hit as he ran down a staircase that led to the forest of metal pipes. He swayed on his feet before falling headlong into the moat. He resurfaced, screaming and thrashing violently. Steam rose from his dissolving body.

The other Sanguine Dawn soldiers were situated further back from the podium. They crouched behind sculptures, pillars, and thick marble railings and struggled to return fire.

The coaxed Sanguine Dawn soldiers formed a protective circle around Griff and the remaining Revenant Clan soldiers. They continued firing at the west side of City Hall as they inched toward the tour bus.

The tour bus door hissed open. Rainah leaned out. There was no mistaking that form-fitting bugsuit with "Badass" stenciled over the left breast.

"Hurry!" she yelled through her gas mask.

The circular wall was halfway between the trailer and the tour bus when someone yelled, "RPG!"

Across the moat, a puff of smoke marked the position of the rocket launcher resting on a kneeling Sanguine Dawn soldier's shoulder. A projectile spiraled toward the circular wall.

Back at the trailer, the middle-aged woman was struggling to drag her younger daughter from inside. The girl had gone limp from fear and refused to budge. The older daughter had already jumped out, along with the other prisoners, who took off running in different directions as soon as their feet hit the ground. The street merchant and one of the prostitutes lay dead in the street, caught in the crossfire, as they tried to escape together.

The middle-aged woman's older daughter was attempting the climb back into the trailer to help her mother when the RPG struck it and exploded.

Shockwaves reached out from the blast and disrupted the circular wall of coaxed soldiers and its huddled nucleus of naked bodies.

Griff woke up seconds later, lying in the street. He shook away the hazy film that blurred the vision in his right eye. The left was so swollen that it felt like it was going to burst.

Someone was calling his name, a female. *Rainah...*

Thick arms snaked up under Griff's armpits. He was being lifted and dragged backward. Rainah jogged alongside the Revenant Clan soldier who carried Griff.

The sergeant and six anonymous grunts were the only other members of the Revenant Clan to survive of the blast.

Between the explosion and when Griff woke up, eight

armed Revenant Clan soldiers (led by Derek) had filed out of the bus to provide backup. They immediately took out the three surviving Sanguine Dawn soldiers.

"Take out the RPG!" Rainah yelled to someone out of Griff's view. She was pointing in the direction of City Hall.

Big guns bellowed all around them. The sound made the images in Griff's field of vision vibrate.

The prison trailer laid twisted and broken in two on its side. The front end was engulfed in flames. Derek and the armed Revenant Clan soldiers used the flames as cover from the Sanguine Dawn soldiers positioned along the west side of City Hall. From where they stood, the tour bus provided cover from the north and south gates, both of which were spitting out reinforcements.

"[psssht] Rainah… What's your status? [psssht]" Derek said into the microphone built into the mouthpiece of his mask.

"[Psssht] I'm inside. I've got Griff. The explosion shook him up, but he's okay. [Psssht]" Rainah's voice flowed directly into his ear.

Inside the bus, Griff and the seven other naked soldiers dressed themselves in the dead Sanguine Dawn survey team's clothing. Before slipping on the hooded gas mask, Griff bent over the sink and dowsed his face with cold water. The water soothed his inflamed skin and simultaneously stung his severe burns.

The faucet on the sink was shaped like a penis. The hot and cold knobs were shaped like a scrotum. Griff didn't notice them until he turned his face sideways and opened his mouth to let the water in.

More Revenant Clan soldiers crowded around Kagen, who sat in the driver's seat, and Mary, who stood over his shoulder, peering out through the tinted windshield. Using hand gestures, she ordered five more men outside to assist.

The soldiers filed out and hurried over to the spot between the trailer wreckage and the tour bus to help Derek and the others.

Bullets ricocheted off the tinted windows. Star-shaped sparks marked the bullets' impact. The first few caused Griff to duck.

"Bulletproof…" one of the half-naked, anonymous grunts blurted to no one in particular.

Underneath the layer of lab equipment, remnants of a decadent lifestyle peeked through: the smarmy color scheme, the gauche draperies, the phallic fixtures, the vibrating, heart-shaped bed in the back of the bus, and other accoutrements of late 20th Century playboy living.

Bullets continued to ricochet off the windows. Griff ducked behind the sink out of habit. He was still a little dizzy from the blast. The sergeant was crouching right next to him.

"What's your name, soldier?" Griff asked the sergeant.

"Simmons, sir," the sergeant responded. "But most folk call me Menz."

"You did well by keeping the men in line back in the trailer," he said.

"Aye. All for nothing, mind… " Menz responded in a melancholy tone.

"It ain't over 'til it's over, sergeant. Remember that."

"Please don't take this the wrong way, sir," Menz began. "But back in the trailer… why didn't you just kill that feckin' vampire before we got here?"

"It's not like we had some kind of contingency plan ready to deal with these mothafuckas. They caught us off guard. The plan sort of came together while we were on the road. I got banged up pretty bad back at the Convention Center. I wasn't even aware of it until I came to and coaxed to Mary. She filled me in. I informed Kurtwood (the Six-Eyes leader on the bus). Then you came over. At the time, I wasn't strong enough to deal with the vampire. Coaxing them is much more difficult than with people. The Sanguine Dawn had a spy on board to monitor us and send intelligence back to their base telepathically. Any move we made against him would've alerted the rest of their troops. I couldn't risk a full-on battle until I regained my strength."

"But we've all been exposed to the radiation with no protection whatsoever. Even you. Who knows how long we've got."

"Like I said, Sergeant: it ain't over til it's over. The Revenant Clan is bigger than you and me. While we're here, we've got to do what we can to ensure that it and the Queen live on."

Griff pulled the hooded gas mask over his head when he was done talking.

Outside, an alarm sounded. It was a haunting noise, like a primitive howl made by some biomechanical monstrosity. It echoed down from the City Hall Tower.

Floodlights mounted high on the corners of the buildings flickered on and cast roving beams of light into the night sky.

The remaining Sanguine Dawn soldiers suddenly stopped firing and began a slow retreat beyond the opened north and south gates. The soldiers positioned across the moat disappeared into the west portal.

Their actions confused the Revenant Clan soldiers.

Derek scanned his immediate surroundings and ordered the men to hold their positions.

The alarmed stopped. An eerie calm took its place.

The north and south gates grinded closed.

The bus-horn sounded. Derek and the 12 soldiers standing with him whipped toward the bus.

Derek tapped the side of his visor to magnify his vision. He could see Kagen sitting in the driver's seat behind the windshield. The large steering wheel extended up from between his legs. He was leaning over it and pointing up as if he was trying to tell Derek something.

"Revenant Clan! Get back to the bus! Now!" Rainah jumped out and yelled. She was looking up toward the sky.

Derek and the other soldiers slowly tracked their eyes up. Some of them took off running for the bus as soon as they saw it.

A line of shadowy figures standing side by side crowded the surrounding rooftops, 30 to 40 on each side of Market. They stood motionless, casting glowing yellow-red eyes down on the group. It was the Alpha Dogs.

One of the soldiers thought out loud, "Vampires!!!"

"C'mon, people!" Rainah yelled. "Let's go! Go! Go!"

Derek turned and high-tailed it toward the bus. The other soldiers were close behind him. Some of them were rubbernecking to the tops of the buildings and back as they ran.

A gravel-throated command sounded from high above.

"ATTACK!" The voice was almost godlike. It broke into two overlapping echoes as it bounced between the buildings on its way down to the street.

A thunderous stampede of feet swallowed the residual embers of the godlike tonnage. Battle cries voiced from bestial things rounded out the din.

As he drew closer to the bus, Derek could see the vampires' reflections in the large tinted windshield. Naked men and women with features painted demonic ran down the sides of the buildings armed with short, hacking blades.

They began leaping off at the third and second floors and continued the descent in corkscrewed, diving lunges.

Derek peeked over his shoulder as if to validate the reflection. The sight made him run faster. He turned back around and ran right into a group of 10 more Revenant Clan soldiers that had just exited the bus along with Mary, Rainah, and Griff, who was now armed with an SR-47. They fired their weapons at the sky all around them as they made their way toward Derek and the other soldiers.

"Get down!" someone yelled.

One of the soldiers tackled Derek.

Mary shoved her way to the front of the group. The stoic, white mask that covered her face contrasted the aggression with which she flung her arms.

One of the soldiers running behind Derek was suddenly snatched upward. He went kicking and screaming.

A blur came in horizontally—a vampire. The vampire collided at waist level with another soldier behind Derek. Bones shattered on impact. The soldier let out a painful cry that trailed off into the night as he was snatched sideways.

The rest of the retreating soldiers dived into the crowd of reinforcements.

A pair of clawed hands reached down, latched onto one of the men, and attempted to pull him up into the sky. The other soldiers grabbed onto his uniform as he ascended. A tug of war commenced between the soldiers and the vampire. It was five against one, yet the vampire (a female) was winning.

"Don't let 'er take me!" the soldier yelled down to his comrades.

Mary held her gun a foot away from the vampire's head and squeezed its trigger, but nothing happened. She threw it to the ground and raised her right arm. Holding her hand in a fist, she aimed at the vampire. A small metal arrow launched from the top of her wrist and struck the vampire in its eye.

The vampire let go of the soldier and shot up 10 feet into the air. The soldiers stumbled backwards and fell. The soldier who they were fighting to save fell on top of them.

The vampire reached up to snatch the arrow from her eye. The arrow exploded. The vampire's head and right forearm exploded along with it.

Black blood rained down on the soldiers. The vampire's body hit the ground like a bag of sticks and wet mud.

The air overhead was buzzing with angry humanoid shapes wielding blades. Vampires whizzed by, zigzagging and crisscrossing each other to throw off the soldiers' aim. Bullet-riddled bodies fell from the sky and thrashed violently at the soldiers' feet as they retreated back to the bus.

"I'm out!" a soldier yelled, his gun clicking empty.

"Me too."

"Yep."

Vampires landed all around the soldiers and began closing in. They held their blades cocked or down by their sides.

"We're not gonna make it!"

Griff and Rainah took up the rear of the retreating group. They picked their shots carefully, aiming at the vampires who appeared overly eager.

Griff's gun clicked empty. He threw it down and started tossing one vampire after another aside without making physical contact. His hands were moving fast, like a boxer throwing open-handed combinations at the air.

Rainah continued firing.

Mary stepped between Griff and Rainah and raised her right arm. Moving in a semi-circular arc, she fired arrows into the ground at the feet of the approaching crowd. The arrows exploded in succession and momentarily stunned the vampires standing closest to them.

"C'mon!" Griff yelled to Mary and Rainah.

Together they ran back to the bus.

"Go!" Griff yelled to Kagen once they were all inside.

Kagen stomped on the gas. The engine roared. The bus plowed backward. Fallen bodies rocked its hull like speed bumps. Its massive tires squeezed them like toothpaste tubes until they popped and left chunky red or black designs in the street.

Vampires leaped at the bus. They slammed into its long, black hull and dug in with their claws. They hung on as the bus barreled into the lobby of the building behind it. It was one of those buildings where you could see into the main floor through a thick glass wall that extended 25 feet up to the first floor.

Vampires came flying off of the bus. They hit the glass wall like bugs on a windshield.

The soldiers inside the bus toppled over each other.

"Hey!"

"What the fuck!"

"Anybody who thinks they can do a better job is welcome to come up here and try," Kagen yelled over his shoulder.

"Just go!" Griff ordered.

Kagen shifted gears and stepped on the gas. The bus bucked against the fresh wound in the building, struggling to free itself. The tires spun. Hot rubber kicked up steam.

The vampires piled on. By the time the bus worked itself free from the building, it was completely covered in bodies.

"North! North!" Griff yelled.

The bus charged north.

Vampires shrieked and hissed through the glass and pressed their faces against it. They were too busy holding on to use their weapons just yet.

The soldiers stood back-to-back or knelt in the aisle, waiting for the vampires to break through the windows. They had their guns drawn. Empty or not, they held them ready. If they weren't out of ammunition, they were running low.

Kagen was having a hard time seeing through the bodies that crawled all over the windshield. He chased openings in the ever-shifting layer and peeked through. Sometimes, he only had seconds to look.

"Better grab holda somethin'," Kagen yelled over the shrieking, growling, and hissing and the deep timber of the bus's diesel engine.

It was a wonder that anyone heard him.

The bus crashed through the north gate and tore the sliding door from its post. The rest of the gate flexed and flapped. The sliding door stuck to the front of the bus and sandwiched vampires against it. Eventually it fell down and was gobbled up by the large tires. A number of vampires were sucked underneath the bus along with it.

"What are we working with, people?" Griff yelled to the soldiers.

The soldiers responded accordingly. All told, only 12 (out of more than 30 soldiers on the bus) had any ammo left. Out of those 12, seven of them were down to less than half of a clip.

"Rainah?" Griff yelled.

"A little more than half a clip," she replied.

"Derek?"

"Good to go," Derek responded.

Griff scanned the crowd, his eyes seeing beyond the surface layer of fake courage and into the well of anxiety and fear that was on the way to overflowing in many of them.

He addressed the entire group.

"I know the situation seems grim. I know you're afraid. But right now, I need you to channel that fear. Dig deep. If it takes every last ounce of your strength, reach down into the depths of your soul and make that fear your bitch. You tell it that that you ain't taking no applications for cowardice. Not today. You are true, badass, Revenant Clan mothafuckas. And true badass Revenant Clan mothafuckas don't back down just because the odds might not be stacked in their favor. They fight to the bitter end. Now, I told all of you when you enlisted that it wasn't always going to be easy. Well, now's the time to show me what you're really made of. When those bloodsuckers come through those windows, I need you to stay focused and choose your shots carefully. I want all of you to form a barrier around the Queen and, until this mess is over, make her safety the most important thing in your lives."

The soldiers positioned themselves in a defensive shield around Mary.

Griff turned to Kagen and ordered him, "Use the buildings to knock them off!"

The vampires were banging their weapons against the windows now. The windows shattered. The left side first, then the right.

"Remember, choose your shots carefully!" Griff reiterated.

Vampires poured in the bus and began planting sharp blades deep into soft human frames.

The soldiers fired in short bursts, but the vampires kept coming. They were crawling on the walls and the ceiling now. Their hip joints opened differently than those of a human, which allowed them to slink on all fours like lizards.

They reached down and tossed soldiers out through the broken windows and into the street. Anything that landed was swarmed upon and hacked to pieces.

"The Queen!" a random soldier yelled as Mary sailed backward and out one of the windows.

Griff spun in her direction and thrust his arms out in front of him. His palms flew open. A pair of clawed hands clamped around his wrists and attempted to yank him up toward the ceiling.

"Kagen! Brake!" Rainah yelled.

"What!" Kagen said over his shoulder.

"I said, brake! Now!"

Kagen stomped on the brakes. The forced snatched Griff out of the vampire's icy grasp. He landed on the floor on top of a pile of soldiers who were uprooted by the sudden stop.

In addition to freeing Griff, it had separated the humans (who fell to the floor) from the vampires (who were still stuck to walls and the ceiling).

Griff jumped to his feet. He was angry. Damn angry. His face tightened. His fingers curled into claws. Heat waves wafted from his eyes.

"Everybody, down!" he ordered.

Using both arms, Griff made a large, outward (horizontal) sweeping motion. A violent ripple of distortion thundered down both sides of the bus. The fiberglass and steel frame rippled like liquid. The forced flung the vampires off of the outside of the bus.

Griff made a second (vertical) sweeping motion aimed at the vampires crawling around inside the bus. Another ripple traveled front to back. It peeled the vampires off the walls and the ceiling and crushed their bodies against the back wall of the bus. The wall buckled and crumbled outward sending flattened bodies hurling sloppily through the air.

"Go, Kagen! Go!" Griff ordered.

The bus yanked forward.

Many of the vampires were still running on the walls of the building when they turned the corner from Market. Half of them went after Mary. The other half followed the bus.

"They're going after Mary," Rainah yelled, as she watched the shrinking scene through the broken window.

Griff spun toward the window and leaned forward to shorten the distance. His eyes registered concern. He closed them and inhaled deeply.

Mary was able to hold off the first few vampires through sheer brute force, but they quickly overwhelmed her. They came at her all at once and began piling on.

She was down on one knee, struggling to maintain the weight of bodies piled on top of her. They clawed and scratched and knocked her around a bit. She pushed a button on her left wrist. An electric current surged through her suit and jolted the vampires off. They went flying in all directions.

Mary climbed to her feet. An electrified glow peeked through the edges of her uniform's padded surface layer. The glow indicated that "current mode" had been activated.

She stood in a calculated pose, radiating confidence... and an electric hum. Her shoulders arched backward. Her chest heaved. She looked the skittering vampires over in a way that seemed almost dismissive. Maybe it was the blank mask. Maybe it was just the way Mary carried herself in the moment. Her body language seemed to say, "I'm the Queen, bitches! Who the hell are you?"

Vampires leaped at Mary left and right. The current stung them and sent them bouncing away. They landed sloppily, dazed by the electric jolt. They righted themselves and assumed aggressive poses. They clawed and lunged and threatened to strike, but none of them dared touch Mary, who walked with a self-assured stride, scanning the bloodthirsty crowd for an opening to exploit.

A swell of intense heat warmed her left shoulder. It had been incubating there for the past few minutes, but she hadn't realized it until now. It was the first physical sensation that Mary had felt in decades. It hit her like an orgasm.

Mary looked down at her shoulder. There were four puncture marks. She had been bitten. Her uniform was made of Kevlar with a padded outer shell made of fiberglass and a rubber lining. It would've taken one hell of a bite to pierce all of that.

A voice interrupted her thoughts. At the moment, her thoughts consisted of strategic scenarios.

It was Griff. "The subway," he coaxed. "There's an access doorway in the basement of the building up ahead. Try to get inside without their seeing you."

Mary headed toward the building. The bite would have to wait until later when she had time to ponder its implications.

The vampires followed.

Running the uniform in current mode was a heavy drain on the battery. The same battery powered the Freon backpack that helped to preserve her. Without the threat of an electrified wallop to ward them off, the vampires would be all over Mary. She would have to come up with an alternative to hold them off.

Chapter 8

Rina, Ohio – 2006
The Doctor is in

Still Monday

I keep coming back to Graham's story about the Revenant Clan. Graham is a supply-driver from a tiny little community outside of Cleveland called Revival Springs—Revival for short. He had replaced Saffron Dawson, the old driver, after Saffron up and went missing one day. That was around six months ago. Graham says the crime was never solved. That kind of thing happens every day, so people pay it little mind.

Graham does his business in the market and comes in for his fix like everyone else. Real bad shit, though. Synthetic, of course. The lab rats call it Supernova. Graham just doesn't seem like the type to fuck around with that kinda shit. He's too cool for that.

I promised to stop giving Graham such a hard time about it last time he was here. He said some shit about Supernova and how it speaks to his soul. Now that's deep.

Guys like Graham are like crack to an interaction junkie like me. This guy is the embodiment of cool… like an old blues legend with 1970s ghetto crime-boss swagger… He has an intangible presence that makes him pleasant to be around and a voice that knocks you over the head with its colorfully weathered, self-assured drawl. I remember joking about how they must hand out voices like his to black men once they reach a certain age. I'm guessing that Graham is in his 70s even though he doesn't look a day older than 55. You know how it is with old black guys. I could just ask him, but that would ruin the mystery.

Graham laughed real big at the crack about his voice. Told me that it was just how their music sounded.

"We each have our own, son," he added.

If Graham had a theme song, it would be something like Muddy Waters' "Mannish Boy" covered by Hendrix. He wears a tan fedora and a trench coat over his combat-style bugsuit and double-vented mask with tinted goggles. He did this thing where he'd sit down and talk for a while before taking his mask off. Always thought that was strange.

Graham's face is chocolate-smooth with deep, noble creases. If you heard his voice before you saw him, it's just what you'd expect him to look like. It's all these factors that make Graham's stories so fucking entertaining.

"I'm like an old book-a-songs that never closes," he said when I mentioned how he's always got a story.

I look forward to Graham's visits. They put the cherry on my day.

Chalk had the National News playing in the background during Graham's last visit. When Linda Ludlow started talking about the Clan, Graham mentioned that he had heard what happened to them. I gave him my "What the fuck?!" face and said something like, "And you're just now telling me this?"

"You didn't ask," Graham responded.

I was looking for a scoop, something worthy of my reputation as Rina's go-to guy for general information and gossip. Instead, I got vampires. I had to stop Graham and ask to make sure I heard it right.

"Did you just say… vampires??" I said.

"Yep... fangs, yellow eyes—the whole shebang," Graham replied.

"Where'd you say you heard this?"

"A buddy-a-mine who works border security back in Revival."

Well, your buddy is full of shit, I wanted to say. He could've said just about anything else: mutants or cannibals, or... or... I'd even accept monsters, given the wide range of pragmatic, non-supernatural definitions. Or maybe if he were speaking figuratively, like, "These guys were bloodthirsty, like a pack of vampires," or something... I don't know. But honest-to-goodness, sharp-toothed, blood-sucking, Dracula offspring? I don't think so.

I remember looking at Graham differently when he said it—like he had suddenly become a gullible old man to me. It was only for a moment before his coolness shined through. In that moment, I was reminded of all that Bloody Mary zombie nonsense that the Ergeister people tried to push on everybody back in the nineties.

I was one of the few people who didn't fall for that snow job. For one thing, I didn't own a television at the time, so their access to my mind was limited to newspapers and the occasional conversation that I'd overhear on the street. Sounded like a militia disguised as a cult disguised as a religion to me. And I moved on.

I used to know a guy who lived in one of the communities the Clan overtook for the Ergeister Church. He would tell me about the things they did—twisted shit that you wouldn't believe.

I liked Graham too much to rain on his parade like I wanted to, so I just let him talk.

The time...

I glance at my watch—an old Timex that had taken a

licking and kept on ticking, just like the old commercial. The old-school digital window flashed "11:45 am" in red numbers and letters. I snatch my two-way (Motorola SX 800 R) from its belt clip and glance at the LCD screen for a second opinion. Same.

"Where the hell are they?" I whine out loud.

The shipment should've been here by now. On top of worrying that something might have happened to my guys (the mayor's guys, actually) on the way here, I was concerned that Artemus would show up any second now to pick up Knox's order. He said he'd be here first thing last I spoke to him. Last thing I needed was Artemus' adding to my stress when he finds out that the shipment is late.

What's so special about the shipment? One word: morphine. Not sure what Knox wants with it. He's typically a weed/blow kinda guy.

Artemus Collins is Mayor Knox's personal assistant. He's one of these guys who always seem a few steps away from a nervous breakdown. And he has a strange ability to suck you into his weird, irrational paranoia. I can just imagine having to endure his pessimistic bullshit while we're waiting for my guys.

The morphine is coming from my man Charlie Knuckles in Detroit. According to Charlie, his boys came across it when one of them plugged some kind of mutated hyena that attacked them out in the wasteland. It happened up near the Irradiated Zone just outside of Pittsburgh. They figured that it most likely came from the old Pittsburgh Zoo.

They found 18 vials of morphine stuffed in a zipped fannypack when they cut the thing's stomach open. Wasteland animals will eat just about anything. You never know what you might find in their bellies.

Charlie and me are part of a network of mid-level drug dealers left over from the old days. There are five of us.

1. Me, in Ohio

2. Charlie, in Michigan
3. Alfonzo, in Houston
4. Jeff the Baker, in Colorado
5. Locke Medusa (the albino Rastafarian), in California

I knew Jeff the Baker before the war. We reconnected back in '03, when we ran into each other at a community down south. He kept jawing about putting together a network of dealers. Said he was sittin' on some serious stash—brand-name pharmaceuticals, even. "We can make out like bandits," he said.

After a while, it started to sound like a good idea, so we recruited the others from the various communities where they were slinging. The plan was to spread out across the country and hook up with good independent communities.

These days, you'd be hard pressed to find an independent community that ain't jonesin' for a dope man. Drugs are still illegal in some communities. Chalk thinks that Rina might follow suit, and soon. I don't think Knox'll ever go for it, though. Doesn't mean I ain't a little concerned over this shit with the Citizens' Brigade trying to pin the RS deaths on me. At this point, I'm trying not to dwell on it, but acceptance is tapping me on the shoulder.

You can usually tell right away whether or not you're in a drug-friendly community. The anti-drug communities produce a certain type of person. Like the Citizens' Brigade folks. But a whole city of 'em.

They still cling to their God and to their weird ideas about morality. It makes their postures rigid, their asses squeezed tight. They walk upright in the truest sense of the word. Full of nervous energy. Always hurried. Always worried about what someone else is doing, even if it doesn't affect them. There's an immediate air of suspicion when it comes to outsiders. People stare and point. You get that sort of thing in any community to some extent, but the vibe in the morality-based communities is like,

"Whothefuckareyou-whyareyouheregetthefuckout!"

It hits you as soon as you reach the entrance security checkpoint.

The smart communities (like Rina) supply us dealers with the resources and the space to grow whatever we need. Me and Charlie have our own little side deal, a grow facility in his community of New Detroit. It's a secret place located in the basement of an old tenement. We set it up as a safeguard against… whatever.

The days of the roving armies seem to be winding down, but you never know. I feel better knowing that I wouldn't be completely outta business if someone decided to hit Rina with a raid.

If you lived through the cold war, like me, then you probably have this idea of a completely decimated planet remaining in the aftermath a global showdown between superpowers. There are places that come pretty close to that, but much of the world was left fairly intact.

There was plenty of traditional fighting, plenty of missiles with poison tips lobbed back and forth. Most of the civilian casualties (in America at least) were due to sleeper cells—unassuming folk with unassuming jobs living below the radar, waiting for the word to act. They were strategically placed in all the major cities: agents disguised as average white men and armed with chemical and biological bombs hidden in briefcases and backpacks.

People were dropping like flies. People in the cities evacuated, the toxic fog hot on their heels. Gridlock dominated for miles. Missiles touched down in the distance and rocked the terrain. F-16s and -18s buzzed overhead, flying in formation. Panic set in and itself took a couple thousand lives. Symptoms began to surface—symptoms of poisoning with anthrax and sarin nerve gas. Together, they took thousands more. Desperation led to infighting, with its own grisly outcomes.

Traveling inland from the coasts, the refugees sought shelter in the Midwest. But they weren't always welcomed with open arms. Worn out and jaded from the journey, some of the refugees were content to meet violence with violence if that was what it took to secure new homes.

The United States Government struggled to maintain some sense of order, but they were stretched thin as it was, dealing with the military, civilian unrest, and the intricacies of war from their classified safety facilities in Maryland, Virginia, and the foothills of the Allegheny Mountains. The armed forces saw their numbers reduced exponentially every day. It soon became evident that there would be no true winners of this war; that mankind itself was about to take a big, throbbing, non-lubricated, toxic fist up the ass. That's when the men started deserting.

The actual fighting was over fairly quickly. The toxic layer that staked its claim on the Earth's atmosphere had scared them into hiding.

Gas masks and protective clothing became the new fashion trend. Those without access to them either died out or became shut-ins.

Curious individuals arose from the war-torn landscape. Free from the societal constraints that pressured their behavior in the past, they traveled the desolate terrain robbing, raping, and committing all kinds of terrible acts.

After a while, people began to reclaim the cities. That old bat Linda Ludlow started her New Philadelphia News Organization, the precursor to her National News. The kids call her "Lobster Claws" because of her three-pronged metallic prostheses. They mimic the robotic fashion in which the prongs open and close whenever they see her picture. They mock her from afar in public. Little punks make sure to wait until her bodyguard, Mizz P. (stands for Phoenix, supposedly), ain't looking.

Mizz P.—she's a little thing with a big swagger. She stands

about five-and-a-half feet tall, dressed in a weird-looking black bugsuit that's decked out with handguns, a machete, and a big ol' hole puncher strapped to her back. The suit has extra padding around the shoulder, elbow, and knee joints. Each of the pads has a metal hinge on one side. Not sure what the purpose of the hinges is, but they sure do look cool.

I catch myself wishing that someone would make a move whenever there's footage of Linda in public just so I can see Mizz P. live up to all the stories.

"Rome..."

I look up. Chalk directs me toward the front door with a nod. The guards are patting Graham down. One of them finds a utility knife in Graham's pocket and gives him shit about it. "No weapons what-so-ever on Campus," I see the guard tell him as he confiscates the knife.

Graham plays it cool.

I immediately check my watch. 12:25 pm and still no sign of my guys or Artemus.

Shit!

"He's cool," I yell to the guards, and they let Graham in.

Graham stops at the bar, orders a drink (something called a Gut Punch), and chats briefly with Chalk before heading back to my office. I use the time to reign in my anxiety. I'm not in the mood to explain everything to Graham.

It occurs to me that even at his age, Graham could've been with one of the hookers. It always occurs to me when I see him. Something about his energy makes it seem entirely possible for young women to find him attractive. Don't know what that has to do with the hookers, but...

"Tony Rommmme...," Graham sings affectionately. He said it was the name of a Frank Sinatra flick from way back. I was never a fan of Ol' Blue Eyes, so I wouldn't know.

"Gramps," I reply, trying to sound as happy to see him as I would have been without all the stress in my life. He and his vampires are at the bottom of the list of shit to worry about, so I let it slide for now.

Graham sits down across the table from me and falls back against the cushion.

"You'd think I had ma shitkicker with me, the way them boys wuz acting," he says.

Graham is referring to his AA12 Automatic Shotgun.

"Don't pay them any mind," I say. "They don't get to exert their authority too often on tavern detail. They tend to get carried away over little things as a result."

"These old bones are worn out, son," Graham says, shifting the subject away from the guards. "Beautiful day, though."

A chuckle-breath jumps out of my mouth. I follow it with a "Wha-choo-talkin'-'bout-Willis?" expression.

"I'd hate to see what your idea of a *bad* day looks like."

"It's all whatchu make of it, son. Some people see death and destruction... a society in ruins. I see a new beginning. New possibilities."

I guess...

"So, how're things in the wasteland?" I ask.

"Survival of the fittest. Same-iz always."

"You run into some trouble?"

Graham takes off his mask and scrunches his face to work out the tightness. He sets it down beside him on the bench and takes a sip from his glass. He works the hot poison down like it's nothing.

I imagine that it burns. My face shows it. You'd think I took a sip.

How can you drink that shit? I'd ask Graham again if I hadn't already asked him so many times. His answer is always the same. "Works out the kinks," he says.

137

"Nothing this ol' man can't handle," Graham says about the trouble in the wasteland.

"Scavengers?" I almost said "vampires" as a joke.

"Unh-huh…. Some fools playin' that ol' victimized-couple routine. Their kid got kilt. Wife got gang-raped. I's waitin' for them to tell me that she was pregnant, too. I guess they see an ol' man like me and think it's gonna be all smiles and foggy memories."

"What about your guards?"

The successful communities assign armed guards to travel with all of their vehicles. Sometimes they're worse than the scavengers.

"They were lappin' that shit up like a coupla wasteland dogs. The wife had'er tits-'n'-ass all hangin' out, actin' like she was tryin'a cover up and all this nonsense."

Chalk's line about pussy making men do crazy things comes to mind.

"Anything worth mentioning?"

Graham pauses, confused.

"The wife with the tits and ass…" I say.

"Nah, this girlie was waaaay past her prime."

"Says a lot about yer guards."

"Yeah, man. A twat is a twat to some of these trifling bastards out here. Don't matter what's goin' on upstairs."

"So wha'dyoudo?"

"I pulled out my shitkicker and sent them to meet their maker. You shoulda seen the guards' faces. They were eyein' me up like I was crazy until I had them check the bodies."

"Strapped?"

"To the hilt. You wouldn't think a person could find so many places to hide a weapon. *Shifty muthafuckas…*"

Graham says "Shifty muthafuckas" in a way that indicates to me that something balls-to-the-wall went down. Ol' Graham

with his fucking hat and trench coat… I can't imagine him gettin' down like that. I mean, I see it in his eyes sometimes… that deep-seeded anger that a lot of black guys have. I ain't saying nothin' about nothin'. Just an observation.

"Before I forget…" I say, as I slide Graham's order of Supernova across the table.

"Thankya kindly," he replies, putting it in his pocket without looking. Most people take a moment to inspect the product.

"So, what's the word in Rina-town?" Graham says.

"Bugsuits and bad water," I reply.

"Same as everywhere, son."

"Same as everywhere.…"

I can tell that he's waiting for me to elaborate. I'm sure he's heard about the RS deaths and the growing unrest.

I feel eyes on me all of a sudden. I look to my right, expecting to see Artemus standing there. Nope. It's only Ned, a traveling merchant, sitting at a booth up front.

Ned looks away when our eyes meet and tries to act like he's checking out a menu.

I check my watch once again. 12:47 pm, and still no sign of my guys or Artemus.

What the fuck, man?

Ned must've come in while Graham and I were talking. As usual, he's dressed as post-apocalyptic Elvis—the hair, the sideburns, the glasses, the sequins along the piping of his bugsuit. And as usual, I shake my head.

Graham is sitting with his back to Ned. The look on my face catches his attention.

"What'zat?" Graham says and turns to see what I'm looking at.

I want to tell him not to make it so obvious, but it's too late.

"It's just Ned," I say.

"Is *that* his name?"

"You know him?"

"Just in passing. We see each other in the market."

Graham waves to Ned while mumbling under his breath, "Somebody needs to have a talk with that poor brotha."

I try to stifle my smile as I wave.

Ned waves back. He follows it with a "Hey, Doc…"

"Must be a pain in the ass to maintain that shit all the time, huh?" I say to Graham. Like Graham, I speak softly.

"Prolly wears all that nonsense to sleep. Layin' up-in-tha bed in one-a-them bullshit karate poses Elvis liked to do. That's how they buried him, you know."

"Get the fuck outta here," I say, half-jokingly.

Graham just looks at me with a straight face.

I hit him with a skeptical squint. "You're serious?"

"Of course not," he says after a long pause. "Don't be so gullible."

We share a laugh.

A few moments pass. I can sense that Ned is getting impatient.

"I'm gonna to have to deal with this," I tell Graham.

"Not a problem," he replies. He glances over his shoulder at Chalk behind the bar thumbing through a CD carrying case. He finishes his drink in one deep swig and says, "I'll be at the bar until you're done."

"Oh, you're coming back?" It comes out in an unusually high pitch.

Graham gives me a strange look. It's not unusual for him to stay awhile. I think I just said what I said out of nervousness, which Graham seemed to pick up on. I really want him to leave. Nothing against Graham. I'm just a little preoccupied about the morphine, and Artemus.

I pull one outta my ass. "I just thought you might wanna

get home and… you know… decompress after that thing with the couple."

"My being an old man and all…" Graham jokes.

"You know that's not what I meant."

"Just another day in the wasteland, son," Graham says over his shoulder as he turns and walks away.

Chapter 9

September 2005
Revenant Days: Club Adonis (Mary)

The place was easy to miss. There was no flashing neon sign, no ironic mascot painted in comical strokes, no decorative letters that spelled out "Adonis" in a way that hinted at the feel of the place. There was only a small wooden sign that read "1221 Sansom Street." It was set up that way to throw off the hatemongers disguised as politicians and the church-folk back in the day when Club Adonis was a gay bathhouse.

Like most other places in the Sanguine Territories (aka Sanguine City, or the slang variant, Red City), Club Adonis was in the process of being renovated to fit the specific tastes of the new clientele. A group of ladders lay on their sides in the back of the room. Canvas dropcloths covered some of the furniture. Other than that, the first floor looked and smelled of cigarettes, like any other bar. Black leather and red crushed velvet adorned sections of the walls. There were tables and booths and tall metal barstools with cracked leather seat-pads. Cracks in the walls and ceiling revealed years of neglect. Zigzagging puddles of dark red liquid pooled at the edges of the cracks on the ceiling. Save for the droplets that fell into half-full buckets placed strategically on the floor, the liquid seemed to defy gravity.

A bartender filled glass after glass with bloody cocktails topped off with decorative umbrellas and cherries impaled on tiny plastic swords.

Club Adonis was a place where the clientele could let their fangs down, so to speak. Here they wore their vampirism on their sleeves. Most of them, anyway. There were always a few who preferred to sport a human disguise.

There was a theory for that kind of mindset. The theory blamed all the racist imagery produced by human film and literature in the past for certain vampires' discomfort with their heritage. The community at large frowned upon those types. They called them names like "sellout," and "pseudo-vamp."

At the bar, patrons (construction workers, mostly) listened intently to a ham radio broadcast of the aftermath of the "Showdown on Market Street." A reporter-type relayed the details and urged citizens to be on the lookout for members of the Revenant Clan and their Queen, Bloody Mary. They had been on the loose for two hours and by now could be anywhere within the city limits, the reporter said.

A man in a tight black shirt that showed off his sculpted physique pulled a hand truck into a room to the right of the bar. He hoisted an empty keg like a rag doll and leaned it against the door to hold it open. He walked over to the freezer in the back of the room and opened the door. Frozen human bodies were stacked in a pile in the middle of the floor.

He walked in.

Two staircases (one in the front, one in the back) led up to the second floor.

The main room on the second floor was made to look like a Roman bathhouse, with faux marble walls and pillars and an Olympic-sized pool (filled with human blood) built into the floor in the middle of the room. Naked men and women lined the sides of the shallow end of the pool. They divided their attention between the static-filled voice pouring out of the speakers and the other patrons.

The men and women in the shallow end of the pool leaned against the walls and rested their elbows on the tile lip. They were submerged up to various points along their torsos depending on their height. They scoffed at the more spirited folk who frolicked out in the deep end. The spirited folk returned their scorn.

Some people lounged in sitting areas stocked with plump, body-sized leather pillows. A pair of braided iron candleholders flanked the pillows. Lit candles sat on top of them. A small marble table sat low to the ground in the middle of each area. Three sitting areas spanned the length of the pool on either side.

A 12-foot walkway separated the sitting areas from the pool. More naked men and women walked back and forth around the rectangular circumference. There was no shame, no bashful awkwardness, regardless of body type. There were all kinds here.

Toward the middle of the room, on the right side, a hallway led back to the viewing rooms, where blood-spattered women sporting fangs simulated sexual acts alone or with partners.

In one of the sitting areas, a black man of high repute reclined on a surface of pillows, watching the other patrons. He was aware of the judging eyes that rolled his way when he wasn't looking.

A sleeping feminine shape clung to him from the chest down. She was petite and olive-skinned, with long black hair.

The black man was well muscled, but not big. His skin was medium brown and smooth as silk. He had a spiked Mohawk and light-colored eyes. He had a tattoo on his left pectoral muscle that spelled out the word "Bully" in cursive strokes. There was another tattoo on the right side of his head—two rows of humanoid silhouettes standing side by side. A line had been drawn through each one. There were 12 all together, eight in the top row and four in the bottom.

It was hard to think of anything other than sex with so many tits and asses floating to the surface of the pool like fleshy dorsal fins in some perverted nightmare, but the black man found himself dwelling on food. The heavy-duty stank of vanilla (from the candles) had his stomach growling.

In the back of his mind, he worried that one of his on-again, off-again fuck-buddies might happen by the club and throw some jealousy his way. Vampires were typically polyamorous, but the women were jealous of the occasional seductions of their men by their human counterparts. They considered themselves above them in every way.

The black man didn't really care what people thought of him. He was spent from a marathon fuck session with the petite girl and definitely not in the mood for drama. He had put everything he had into her. He suspected that he might have injured her, but no matter. She'd be all right once he turned her.

If not for his status as a retired Alpha-Dog Commander, he would've been barred access to the club for bringing the petite girl with him. He referred to her as "new blood" that he personally had recruited. She was to be turned in the morning, and he was just showing her around, he said. He knew of the risk when he brought her here, but it was a chance to show off his new piece.

The problem was that everyone knew each other intimately in Red City. Seeing the same faces, the same naked bodies twisted and arched into the same old positions left him wanting more. And he wasn't the only one who felt that way. Most vampires adhered to the Cardinal rule: Don't mix with humans.

Once they were turned, that's a different story, but membership into the bloodline was a long process that few humans completed. With few exceptions, turning humans without committee approval was forbidden.

The black man banked on his status to circumvent the process with his new find. He simply couldn't wait for this one to go through the normal channels. Her overall presentation rivaled the city's most notorious beauties. She was soft and demure yet wrapped in a voluptuous package that she had yet to master. Her face was arranged differently, in a way that some might find unappealing. To those who understood and appreciated the arrangement, it was like sex-magic.

The black man knew as soon as he laid eyes on the girl that she would be his. She was standing at the back of a processing line with the rest of the prisoners from the Aube Nouvelle raid. Or maybe it was the raid on Sunrise? He wasn't sure which. The black man convinced one of the grunts to give her to him in exchange for mentioning the grunt's name to Count Onyx for a possible promotion. Of course he never did.

"I'm hungry. You?" the black man whispered to the sleeping beauty. He half-expected that she'd be too incapacitated to respond.

"Hmmmm?" she replied.

Apparently she was okay. Her face was buried in his chest, which caused her voice to travel inward and vibrate his flesh to a bumpy texture. It was a pleasant sound, like he had stirred her out of a great dream. It made him feel like pumping his fist in the air in honor of his conquest. But it was nothing special. Human sexuality was vastly inferior to vampires'.

"I said do you want a bite to eat?"

"Hmmmm???" The petite girl's voice traveled inward the same as before. This time, there were no goose bumps.

The longer he sat there caressing her soft skin, the more intense the bloodlust became. The sedative qualities of the multiple orgasms he had experienced moments ago were wearing off. He could either fuck her again or sink his teeth into her soft, delectable flesh and get it over with. There would be some explaining to do if he turned her now, but he wasn't too worried about that at the moment.

Every once and a while, someone would trickle in, giving

the black man pause. Then they'd spot him with the petite girl and stare. He could tell that some of them wanted her for themselves. He could see their mouths watering, their fangs growing longer as they sized her up. When they noticed the black man watching them, they turned away. One or two of them were of equally high repute as he was. That could be a problem.

Time to go.

The black man got up and carried the sleeping beauty to the back staircase. He could have easily bitten her upstairs in front of everyone, but he was beginning to suspect that someone might try to challenge him.

He didn't make it all the way to the first floor. The scent of the petite girl's blood had him fiending for it by the bottom of the first landing. His eyes swirled with wanting as he focused on the meat of her thighs and buttocks. Despite her small stature, she had a plump little bottom—not big at all, just well rounded and tight, with just the right buoyancy. Its bounce intoxicated him as he jogged down the steps, cradling her in his arms.

He placed the petite girl down on the landing. It wasn't exactly a secluded spot. Anyone looking over this way could see him from the chest up if he stood. It would only take a minute or so to bite her. As long as he kept low to the ground he'd be fine though, unless someone happened over this way. But most of the other patrons probably figured that he had left.

The black man spread the petite girl's legs and looked longingly at her deflated labia, down to the succulent under-bubble of her ass, and over to her inner thigh. His teeth were primed to pierce the soft skin of her upper thigh and interrupt the flow of her femoral artery. Some vampires preferred the jugular vein, some the radial artery, but the femoral was his favorite spot from which to draw blood. Aside from its proximity to the "goodies," or maybe because of it, femoral blood had an especially sweet aftertaste.

There was someone else on the landing with them. The black man hadn't seen the pair of legs jutting out from the darkness over in the corner until he was just about to dig in. It both startled and agitated him.

"Who's there?" he growled, brandishing teeth, yellow-red eyes glowing beneath a pronounced frown.

He didn't think it would actually come to this, but he was ready to defend his catch.

There was movement from the corner (a slight, afflicted shuffle) but no response.

The black man placed the petite girl down softly and rose to a hunch, clawed hands upturned.

He recognized the shape in the corner as a naked woman, and as he stepped closer, his head tilted and craned forward and down, he began to recognize the rhythm of her shuffle.

A feeling of relief washed over him and persuaded his tense muscles to relax. It made him forget that he was angry.

"First time, huh?" he said to the female shape. "Don't fight it. I know it hurts right now, but just give it a while. Trust me. It's the best high you'll ever experience."

As far as he knew, a member of the club had bitten her, which meant that he wasn't the only one trying to circumvent the system for his own special someone to turn. But why had they left her alone? Or had they?

The black man checked every inch of the darkness. They were definitely alone on the landing.

Hmmmm...

Though he couldn't tell yet, she was probably quite beautiful, like the petite girl. He was all kinds of curious to know what she looked like.

The first time was always a pinnacle experience. Most described it as the high that never subsided. It started with severe abdominal cramping, then as the hot sensation migrated to every inch of the body, severe nausea set in. Eventually the pain of the virgin metamorphosis (blood boiling, teeth sliding down, fingers stretching into long, bony claws, facial bones restructuring) gave way to euphoria, as heightened senses, strength, and the trademark thirst set in. Culturally, it was known as the "virgin metamorgasm."

Dominant personalities and those with an inborn propensity toward violence experienced a nitro-kick to the libido, an animalistic surge that took them over completely. It sent them on an aggression-frenzy that lasted up to a week. It was the basis of the popular myths of murderous bloodsuckers.

If the woman in the corner was as attractive as her aura let on, then she was most likely a dominant personality—confident, and used to getting her way based on her looks. Thus, she would probably be looking for someone with whom to quench her amplified lust when the metamorphosis was complete.

The black man checked over his shoulder to make sure that the petite girl was still asleep. She was completely out.

The woman in the corner was standing when he turned back around. His eyes pierced the outer level of darkness that engulfed the woman from the waist up.

She was tall and incredibly thin. Her flesh was shriveled and horribly rotten. Her right arm and leg were held together by thick twine threaded through her flesh at the shoulder and hip joints. Her breasts sagged. Her ribcage jutted out through a large wound on her right side. Bleached bone peeked through various gaps in the expanse of stale flesh throughout her body.

"Holy shit!!!!" the black man said. "What the hell happened to you?"

He certainly didn't expect to see what amounted to a beautiful zombie. As grotesque a sight as it was, he didn't find her condition especially unusual. He himself had been shot, stabbed, drowned, pushed off a cliff, decapitated, and burned over 90 percent of his body in the past. He'd known vampires who had been blown to pieces. Being blown up was especially worrisome, as the pieces were known to merge with surrounding debris or other blown-up bodies upon regeneration. Regeneration rarely took longer than a week.

The woman was definitely *feelin' it.* The black man could tell by the way she swayed on her feet and stumbled backward into the wall.

She righted herself and shook off the dizziness. A wave of sexualized euphoria traveled up from her feet and caused her to buck. She braced herself with her hands, pressing her palms against the wall behind her, and let her head fall back. Her long, straight hair dangled and swished against the wall like worn bristles on a giant paintbrush.

The black man knew better than to interfere with the process. Standing back, he watched and waited. He chased down the origins of every little sound that resonated near him, fearing that the vampire responsible for biting this woman might return and react angrily to his curiosity. His eyes passed right over the petite girl who was still sleeping on the floor. At the moment, she might as well have been dead.

Mary Jane Mezerak walked out of the darkness; her skeletal smile was topped off with curved fangs that dripped saliva. Her cheekbones were more pronounced and jutting out through her brittle flesh on the right. The sway of her hips was like music the way it spoke directly to the black man's libido. Her aural cadence screamed "vixen on the prowl."

It had been a while since anyone had seen Mary out of her uniform. The black man didn't recognize her.

A window was completely broken out at the bottom of the second flight of stairs. The black man noticed it out the corner of his eye as Mary walked toward him. Security was tight outside Club Adonis, especially with the Revenant Clan running loose in the city. There was no way someone was getting in who wasn't invited, not even through a seemingly forgotten old window in the back of the building. Whoever had broken it mangled the steel security bars as well. That would've taken a considerable amount of time and effort, as they were reinforced to hold against 20 men or your average vampire.

*   *   *

"I know he's here," the girl with chunky dreadlocks dyed blond and a septum ring remarked to her needy, shorthaired friend. "I can *smell* him."

Chunky dreads stood about 10 feet from the deep end of the blood-filled pool, scanning the clusters of naked bodies and honing in on specific voices (like reverse echolocation) for the one she knew better than her own.

The shorthaired girl stood to her direct left. "Yeah, I smell it too," she replied.

"You see, I told you. I *told you* he'd be here."

Chunky dreads crept forward, leading with her head. Her neck slithered in pursuit of a familiar scent. It led her to an empty sitting area on the left side of the pool.

The shorthaired girl walked over to the nearest cluster of naked bodies on the right side of the pool-three women pawing and petting each other in one of the sitting areas.

Their arms intertwined like a warm pretzel (thick on one side and thin on the other); two of the women embraced. They writhed on top of a third woman, one riding the strap-on she wore like underwear, one positioned over her face. Through the opening in the pulsating triangle, the shorthaired girl crouched, waiting for the women to acknowledge her.

The chubby side of the triangle whipped around startled and climaxed a moment later. Her eyes glowed yellow-red. Small, curved fangs pointed down and up inside her strangely shaped mouth.

With her thumb, the shorthaired girl pointed at Chunky Dreads and addressed them all, "You know the dude she comes here with: black guy, Mohawk, tattoos, calls himself 'Bully?'"

They shook their heads "no." The chubby one took several seconds to respond.

The shorthaired girl moved on to the next cluster (a heterosexual couple) and the next (a large group of men and women sleeping in a pile).

"He was with some dark-haired girl," one of the men mumbled in an agitated tone. "A human."

The shorthaired girl grinned from ear to ear. She couldn't wait to tell her friend.

The look on the face of Chunky Dreads said that she already knew. She was leaning over the pillows in the empty sitting area, her eyes studying them as if she were trying to see the past. Her head bounced and pivoted and jerked like an insect. She could certainly smell it… and *him*. Bully. *The fucker!!!!*

There was a sudden commotion from the back stairs.

Chunky Dreads focused on the unlit corridor that carried the stairs down to the first landing. Something dark and fibrous had just broken the surface of the top step and quickly submerged. It happened again… and again. It looked like hair flopping.

The shorthaired girl hurried over to Chunky Dreads, who stomped around the pool toward the staircase.

Together, they looked over the edge, down into the darkness, at the landing below.

There were two people—a zombified woman sitting with her back to them on top of a man. The woman cupped her hand beneath her naked left breast and explored its mashed, saggy contour. Her long, wispy hair hung forward and hid her face as she hunched over her victim.

The woman moved like a literal necro sex machine. She was digging in with her hips, moving them in small circles, pushing forward and down and isolating her pelvic region. Cocking her ass and pausing, she thrust and clamped her inner thighs.

Chunky Dreads saw every last move. The woman's body spoke a language that she understood. She spoke it as well. The fact that Bully would stoop to fucking someone in the shape that this woman appeared to be in made Chunky Dreads embarrassed for him; if those were indeed Bully's legs that jutted out from beneath the woman's bony ass. They were about the right hue, thickness, and length.

"Bully! You lying sack of shit!!!!" Chunky Dreads roared.

Mary took her time to acknowledge the voice from behind. When she finally got up and turned around, there were large fangs hanging from her upper jaw like curved, ivory stalactites stained red. Smaller fangs pointed up from her lower jaw. Loose meat dangled from them. On her face, she wore a beauty-mask made of thick black blood painted on sloppily.

Beneath her, Bully's body bucked and kicked. His eyes were rolled back, his neck ripped open. The wound in his neck wheezed air in large and small bubbles like mangled lips oozing thick, black spittle. Flayed skin, stretched and pulled jagged at the edges, decorated the wound's western border, forming a star-shaped design.

"Oh... oh my God," Chunky Dreads whimpered loudly. "Yyy you... killed... hhhim."

"Oh, this bitch is so dead," the shorthaired girl added, half-serious and half-posturing to impress her friend with her loyalty.

She whipped her fingers straight at her sides. Each one was tipped with razor sharp claws that weren't there before. They extended at least an inch from her fingertips and curled under slightly.

Both girls sported fangs and yellow-red eyes. Chunky Dreads's teeth were longer, and sharper than the shorthaired girl's. Her eyes gave off a more vibrant glow, too-signs of one who was born with the bloodlust as opposed to being turned.

The girls hissed angrily at Mary. Their voices, bouncing from wall to wall, came off like a warning to the other members: the shit was about to hit the fan.

Mary's desiccated brow crunched to a frown. Hollow eyes squinting like slits emitted beams of tangible darkness. Exaggerated cheekbones pushed against brittle flesh. She opened her mouth wide and roared like a predatory beast confronting challengers to its kill. Her voice was dry and rasped, but it got the point across.

The petite girl on the floor woke up and thrust herself into a seated position. She turned to her right and stopped on the zombie… vampire… thing that had just turned and looked at her.

Mary looked the petite girl up and down and turned back to Chunky Dreads and the shorthaired girl, who now stood at the top of the steps. Until now, they hadn't even noticed that the petite girl was lying there.

The petite girl screamed.

Behind Chunky Dreads and her shorthaired friend, a crowd of naked people sporting fangs, yellow-red eyes, and features exaggerated in a specific way (each face with its own unique twist) turned and glared at Mary.

As if led by an invisible conductor, they hissed at her simultaneously.

"Whatcha gonna do now, bitch!" the shorthaired girl growled at Mary. Her voice sank lower with each word. She prepared to lunge.

Chapter 10

Rina, Ohio – 2006
The Doctor is in...

The days having been slipping by under my nose since Artemus' visit on Monday. I was expecting him to grill me about the shipment, so you can imagine my surprise when he said that he already picked it up. Apparently he had the guards stop my guys at the front gate "for a routine inspection," he said. That's why they were late that day.

Can you believe that shit?

Then I find out that Knox has been having his people inspect my supply in the greenhouse. They told the lab rats that the inspection was just a precautionary measure. City Council was under pressure from the Citizens' Brigade. They were able to blow them off at first. But the RS deaths keep mounting. The voices of protest grew louder and more confident with each new death.

There've been two more deaths since Monday. Guys I knew this time. I had just spoken to one of them (Latin guy named Ellis Santos) on Saturday. Big fucker. So was the other guy, in fact. Both worked as guards.

Doesn't change my theory, though. What it did do was to put a face on this... outbreak. And it made me feel more vulnerable to it all of a sudden.

As usual, they were buried right away in the off-campus cemetery. Knox put a few guards on patrol to make sure nobody tried to fuck with the bodies. Word is that the off-campus folks were threatening to do just that if that's what it took to get the bottom of this.

I guess I should mention that Santos' neighbors claimed to have heard footsteps walking up the side of their building the night before his death. And the Robogeeks have been running interviews with folks who're saying that they've seen this "ghostly woman" floating outside bedroom windows, "like she's searching for victims." Except they're thinking she might be a vampire instead.

Makes me think I should be selling whatever it is that they're on.

Being the inquisitive chucklehead that I am, I figured the time was right for an informal investigation of my own. So I asked my ace-in-the-hole to look into it. "And while you're at it, see if you can't find out what Knox wants with the morphine," I told him.

I call him Ace, but that's not his real name. He works security on the Hill. He'll do just about anything I ask as long as I supply him with weed. We do the old handshake transfer at some arbitrary spot on campus whenever I go out for a walk, which I haven't done in a while. I've been getting a lot of weird stares lately. A lot of people eyeing me up for the figurative kill from behind office windows and such.

That's all you need to know about that.

Now I've got Chalk calling me Dr. Scapegoat and hitting me with "I told you so" every chance he gets. I can't get mad at him, though. He's only looking out for my best interests.

Chalk would probably have a fit if he knew that I had been to see Desire. I know, I know…. But I couldn't help it. I needed something to calm my nerves after the shit with Artemus and City Council.

I hid from all the stares by lying across the back seat of the Humvee as we drove through Society Hill. My reason for taking out an official vehicle was to check on my supply at the greenhouse. I really did want to make sure City Council hadn't done anything to harm it. Afterward, I asked the driver (a new guy) to take me off campus. Told him that I wanted to see the sights. He didn't suspect a thing. The guards at the front gate seemed cagey when they saw me, though, like maybe they were buyin' all the hoopla from the Citizens' Brigade.

Great. And, to top it all off, Desire was too busy negotiating with some beefy fucker to notice me when we cruised by. Either that or she was deliberately ignoring me. God, I hope not.

The driver pegged the beefy fucker as some kinda shot-caller for the off-campus folks.

Hmm... Didn't know they were giving VIP status to off-campus folks now. But that's cool....

I would've had the driver stop, but being that he was new, I was a little worried that he might rat me out. Plus, the shot-caller was eyein' us up like we just stole his steroids. So I thought it best that we get back to the Hill. The vibe out there was... different. It definitely left me feeling uneasy.

The next time I remember to pay attention to the time, it's...

Thursday

"You're a lifesaver, Doc," says the big-eared kid. He stands and stuffs the baggie of weed into his fannypack with a juvenile giddiness that seems to posses 95 percent of my customers on their way outta here. Unless, of course I don't have what they want. Then their reaction is much different, although equally juvenile.

The kid told me his name more than once but I couldn't

remember it for the life of me. I just know him as the big-eared kid who works maintenance on the Hill. He stops by for weed maybe once a month, sometimes twice.

"Make sure you tell your *friend* what I said," I remind him.

"My sister's friend," he responds.

"Whatever."

It's funny how people feel obligated to give me their full attention when they're sitting across the table from me, at least until they get what they came for. The big-eared kid was asking about an Ergeister community in Colorado. I guess his "sister's friend" was thinking about leaving the community he was in (some tiny independent about an hour west of here, he said) and joining up with them.

My advice is always the same when it comes to communities. A good independent community is your best bet. You wanna make sure it's well fortified with food, weapons, and semi-decent people, and that they have access to solar power, clean water, and working Geiger counters.

The Federal communities tried to monopolize the solar technology in the beginning, but their security forces (made up of the military and volunteers) were down to scraps. It made them prime targets for a bust-up.

The raids came hard and fast. They rolled over the Virginia and Maryland Federal communities with ease. I think it was Reverend Link and his people. Or maybe it was General Sizemore. It's hard to remember anymore.

The independents generally take a more utilitarian approach to living without the complicated rules and religious edicts of, say, a Christian or an Ergeister community. It's true that you have to take the ideology of the people in power into account with the independents. And there are some *scaaaary* fuckers out there, let me tell you.

It's been my experience, though, that most organized communities have the same basic wants—uninfected food and water and a safe place to live. Some discriminate more than others when it comes to whom they allow to reside within their borders. I can't say I've had too much trouble fitting in to the places I've been. But I see where someone might have a problem based on… the way they look, let's say.

Anyway, if you already belong to a community that fulfills those basic requirements (uninfected food and water and a safe place to live), then, by all means, stay there.

Looking at it from a 'safety-in-numbers' standpoint, I can see how someone with a family to protect might wanna link up with Ergeister. They're probably the largest and best-fortified organization around. They have their own TV station, too. They run it out of the old Paramount Studio in Hollyweird. That's how they pipe the propaganda out to their communities. Not sure I'd want my family around the clothing-optional ceremonies and the general vibe of promiscuity, though. Might be different for a single person.

On the downside, you've got all the religious nonsense. Plus, they're tough as balls on their criminals. *Aaaand* they've got the death penalty. Word is they give you options. You can go out the regular way (firing squad, I think) or as part of some kind of ritual sacrifice.

Ergeisterites remind me of the Scientologists back in the day. Remember them? The way their members walked around like they had all the answers and the rest of us were just a bunch of Neanderthal retards… "smug" is the word I'm looking for. That kind of attitude breeds contempt, especially considering their history.

Ergeister's list of enemies seems to be growing by the month. If it ain't the rumors about their being behind the fallen communities in their secret quest for world domination, then it's some failed initiate or former member calling bullshit on their way of life. Of course, they always have to drudge up Ergeister's relationship with the Dead Bitch Army as part of their argument.

Last I heard, McLaughlin City was calling them out. Something about the mayor's wife running off to become an Ergeisterite.

I did my best to talk the big-eared kid (er, I mean his sister's friend, through him) out of going Ergeister. Even had help from Linda Ludlow when Chalk turned up the TV while me and the kid were talking.

I can see Chalk looking at me like he's got something important to say. I wait until the kid looks away for a minute and I glance over at him.

Chalk points to the screen. The words "Exclusive Footage" dare me to look away from it. Ludlow comes on and starts talking about a raid. My heart jumps. I don't know why exactly. Just nerves I guess. With everything that's going on, I wasn't sure what to expect.

Somehow, Ludlow's words make it through the kid's machine-gun dialogue. At first, I thought he was waiting for me to turn back around when he stopped talking. When I did, I saw that his eyes were glued to the screen.

VIDEO (Helmet-Cam):

It is nighttime. The aftermath of a large-scale battle materializes via a shaky camera view enhanced by night-vision technology, which adds a haunting green tint. Wasteland fixtures populate the background. In the foreground, a pair of soldiers clothed in desert-colored bugsuits survey the damage. Their mechanized breathing scores the incredulous moment. Similar voices can be heard just off camera. They are commenting on the scene.

Bodies are everywhere, stripped naked and wearing open-faced wounds made by large-caliber rounds. Steaming viscera spills out of one body. The bodies are stained a chalky hue. Faces are frozen in terror. Eyes are clouded over and desiccated.

The shaky-cam moves from body to body and zooms in briefly on each one. Most of them appear to be large, strapping men. The official Ergeister seal (a circle made of intermingling branches) is stitched into the upper arms of the dead men's uniforms. The cameraman comments under his breath.

Cameraman (off-camera): Hoo-leee sheee-yyyit!

At some point, the shaky-cam whips around and reveals at least 20 more soldiers dressed the same as the first two. They are reacting similarly to the scene. Behind them, an armored tractor-trailer sits idle.

The camera returns to the first two soldiers.

Soldier 1: Scavengers?

Soldier 2: Takin' out an entire Ergeister regiment? Not likely.

Anonymous soldier (off-camera): Then who?

Soldier 2: Had to be another army. Scavengers wouldn't dare move on professional soldiers like this.

Anonymous soldier (hand enters the frame, pointing): Look

162

at this guy, here… and that one…

Soldier 1: Look like bite marks.

Soldier 2: The animals out here prolly been having a field day on the remains.

Anonymous soldier (off-camera): Listen up, men.

The camera spins and stops on a soldier who is standing on the hood of an automobile husk. His bugsuit is slightly different from the others. He is their leader.

Lead soldier: We are just passing through. What happened here is not our concern. I want you all to search the area for supplies, weapons, and/or gear and double back to the transport ASAP. Something ain't right here, and I don't wanna be hanging around any longer'n we have to. Understood?

All soldiers: Yes, sir!

The soldiers split up and scan the area around the bodies. They find a few personal effects. A short time later, the leader orders them to "fall in." The soldiers congregate around the trailer. Many conversations can be heard.
A sliding door opens on the side of the trailer. The walls inside are lined with gear and weapons. A metal bench extends the entire length of the trailer on both sides.
The shaky-cam stays with the crowd.

Anonymous soldier: Shit! The bodies…. Where'd they go?

The camera spins around. On its way, it captures the soldiers' heads whipping toward the scene. The bodies are gone.

Lead soldier: Everybody inside NOW!

The soldiers begin climbing into the trailer. Strange animal sounds leap out of the darkness all around them. The soldiers freeze. A few of the men raise their weapons.

The shaky-cam catches hints of movement in the darkness.

Lead soldier: We're under attack!

The soldiers fire their weapons into the darkness. They yell to each other, "Where? Which way?" The camera moves without direction as the cameraman hustles for cover behind one of the trailer's large tires.

Anonymous soldier (to cameraman): Heads up!

The shaky-cam follows the cameraman's movement as he looks up and captures a dubious image. It looks like a body coming down at him in a squat-like pose.

Static.

CUT TO:

Linda Ludlow sitting behind her anchor's desk. A green-screen filled with static fades to black behind her.

Linda: Representatives from the Ergeister Headquarters in Los Angeles are vehemently denying any involvement in the ambush on a group of 40 soldiers from a small, independent community from the Wichita, Kansas, area known as McLaughlin City. D. Michael McLaughlin, founder and mayor of McLaughlin City, denounced the attack in a press conference held earlier today, calling the Ergeister Army's actions "cheap, Hollywood theatrics," stopping just short of declaring all-out war on the Ergeister Church. Ergeister representatives are calling for a meeting between leaders to discuss the incident. Mr. McLaughlin had this to say in response to the invitation:

CUT TO:

A robust gentleman (D. Michael McLaughlin) stands behind a podium addressing an auditorium full of rowdy spectators. His anger is palpable.

McLaughlin: Right. So they can pull another ambush on us? No, thank you. How's that saying go? "Fool me once… shame on you. Fool me twice…" eh… (struggling to remember) you just can't be fooled! (Pause) And I am fully aware of what the numbers… what their numbers are. So I don't want to hear anything else about numbers. The fact is that I am *not* prepared to sit back and let this… this… cowardly… despicable act of barbarism go unanswered. No, sir. It seems that our friends in the Ergeister organization have yet to learn their lesson from their past dealings with the Revenant Clan. Apparently, living in Hollywood has warped their perception of reality to the point where they feel they can throw their weight around with reckless abandon. After watching that footage, you have to wonder what these people will stoop to next. I say it's about time that someone held them accountable.

Cheers can be heard from the crowd.

McLaughlin: I am currently in discussions with officials from Renaissance, New Eastborough, and the New Comanche Territories about forming a coalition of communities to handle this situation and any others like it that might arise in the future.

CUT TO:

Linda Ludlow sitting behind her anchor's desk.

Linda: Tough words from an understandably embittered McLaughlin. If we are to believe the church's assertion that they are not behind the attack, then who or what exactly are we dealing with? The answers vary depending on whom you ask. One scenario holds the Revenant Clan responsible. According to this scenario, the Clan staged their own downfall to take some of the heat off of them as a result of their public divorce from the Ergeister Church and to use the downtime to reinvigorate their forces. While I find this scenario to be improbable, I must admit being reminded of Griffen Elam's visions as I watched the footage.

Stay tuned for more details as the story develops.

I expected the big-eared kid to hit me up with a million questions like I knew more than he did about what had happened, but instead he blew it off like it was old news. Had me thinking he didn't trust me anymore because of the Citizens' Brigade.
"You're not even the slightest bit curious?" I ask him.
"About the ambush?" he says. "Heard about it yester-

day, just like everybody else around here."

Everyone except for yours truly.

"What? You didn't know?"

I shake my head "no."

"I thought you were supposed to be the man with all the answers."

The way he chuckles out his response makes me want to grab the kid by his big fucking ears and slam his face into the table. The kid's got his "got-some-weed" muscles on so he's being a bit more liberal with his tone. And our positioning in relation to each other (me sitting, the big-eared kid standing and looking down) is making him feel dominant. Gotta figure that the news about me is playing a role as well. You come to sense these kinds of things when you deal with people as much as I do.

"I thought so, too," I say, and I leave it at that.

It might seem like small potatoes to you, but when you put it in perspective, Artemus' stopping my guys; City Council's shifty antics; the Citizens' Brigade's belly-aching; and the fact that business has been slower than usual lately... Something as seemingly insignificant as being out of the loop could be a sign of worse things to come.

"What about your sister's friend?" I say. "You don't want him getting caught up in all that nonsense."

"You don't really believe that Ergeister is behind that mess? What would they have to gain by attacking a nice little mom-and-pop community like McLaughlin?"

"It does seem a little too... convenient. Plus, I can't imagine the Ergeister people would be so careless. Allowing themselves to be caught on video-'n'-all... I suppose it coulda been payback for all the shit McLaughlin gave 'em over his wife. The guy's been nipping at their heels ever since she ran off."

"Dude, do you know how many people's wives... *and* husbands for that matter, have run off for the same reason? What?

You expect the church to go after every pissed-off spouse who's got something negative to say about them?"

He's right about that.

"Gotta be those freaks from the Zone," the kid says. "They're saying they got themselves an army and everything. Real nice and organized. But here's the weird part. One-ah my co-workers said they overheard Councilman Hewitt saying that they was…"

"Please don't say 'vampires.'"

"Oh, you heard?"

"Are people really buyin' that shit?"

"Why wouldn't they? I figure if Bloody Mary were real, then why not?"

Well, therein lies yer problem, kid. I would've been sitting here debating the subject all morning if I had actually said that. So I keep it to myself.

As much as I don't like the Ergeister Church, I think it's safe to assume that this whole thing was probably some kind of frame-job. As far as who's behind it… well, your guess is as good as mine. Fucking with Ergeister like that? They've definitely got themselves a pair, whoever it is.

Gotta say that my boundaries are relaxing a bit on this one. As I watched the footage, I kept thinking that it might just be this army from the Zone. Then, when Linda Ludlow mentioned Griff and his coaxing crap, I immediately thought of Graham's story about the Clan's disappearance. It was like the pieces suddenly fit into place. Maybe the Clan had used the vampire mythos to throw people off. If that were the case, then what is the likelihood that they're behind these vampire stories coming from the Zone, or even that they and this Zone army are one in the same? For the record, I never said that they (the Clan) didn't exist, only that I didn't believe all the supernatural nonsense that people associate with them.

I decided, for the time being, to file this new "theory" away until I can back it up with something more than wild speculation.

Linking up with Ergeister just seems like more trouble than it's worth. I told the kid how, just the other day, I saw some "new frontier" chucklehead on the news bitching about how his family was murdered by wasteland scavengers.

Well... *nooo* shit...

The new frontier is what the Ergeister people are calling the wasteland now. They've got their people buyin' into this idea of a new enlightened society rising out of the ashes—some rainbow, candyland utopia where every race under the sun can sing songs about how much they love each other... as long as they pledge their undying loyalty to the Ergeister Church.

The kid just shrugs it off. "I guess it's what you make of it," he says.

I've been hearing that a lot these days.

You'll wish you had listened to me when you find yourself staring down the barrel of gun while some Revenant Clan flunky kills everyone you care about... then eats them.

I could never say anything so cliché, so I kept it on the tip of my tongue while I watched the kid walk away. You really should see the ears on this kid.

Ah, well, I tried. Doubt the kid'll relay my message with the same conviction if it turns out that this sister's friend thing isn't just a cover.

Chapter 11

September 2005
Revenant Days: Next Stop – Hollywood

By now, Rainah's ass was numb. She adjusted her weight against the merciless wooden planks on the old park bench and settled in for another five or so minutes until she felt she was able to continue. She had been on the run since the '80s hair-band tour bus flipped onto its side and skidded 50 feet on the Ben Franklin Parkway and stopped about a quarter of a mile from the old Philadelphia Art Museum.

The crash took out a few more Revenant Clan soldiers. On Griff's orders, 18 of the surviving grunts positioned themselves around the wreckage and prepared to engage the approaching vampires. Griff was struggling to coax the bus upright when he ordered a small group of them (Derek, Rainah, Menz, and a few grunts) to "Go! Now! We'll hold these mothafuckas off."

Rainah and Derek had tried unsuccessfully to pull Kagen (who was unconscious) from the wreckage before Griff climbed out and took over.

The vampires were running and leaping toward the wall of grunts as Griff worked to get the bus on its feet.

"Split up and find someplace to lay low. I'll coax to you when I can," he yelled to them as they ran.

They had split up at some point. Rainah was running so fast that she didn't even realize it until Derek didn't answer her when she (thinking that he was right behind her) called out to him. She stopped in front of the museum stairs and wasted a moment or two trying to decide whether to look for the rest of the group.

Standing in front of the iconic staircase, she couldn't help thinking of Rocky's running up the steps in his trademark grey sweatsuit.

When she looked behind her, Rainah saw a humanoid shape leave the ground and disappear into the dead trees that lined the parkway. The trees begin to sway as if accommodating extra weight. The swaying drew closer. A shape slinked from tree to tree. Or maybe not.

Rainah took off running. She ducked into the woods behind the museum and hid beneath a mound of loose dirt, trash, and dead tree limbs. She lay there listening for the telltale signs of approach—twigs crunching under foot, trees swaying, voices, heavy breathing. After an hour or so (it seemed), Rainah rose, living-dead style, from beneath the detritus and started to make her way back to the bus. The wooden park bench beckoned to her fatigued body to take a load off when she passed it, so she did.

Though tired and wary, her adrenaline still simmered. It kept her blood warm. Her pores flexed open and vomited beads of sweat. Her bugsuit was an excellent insulator of heat. Mixed with the suffocating backdraft of her own hot breath, it left her feeling anxious and slightly claustrophobic, like she was sitting in a sauna custom-built to fit her body. She wanted to rip the damn thing off and let her skin breathe. It was a dilemma that was shared by many in this day and age. It drove some people to stop wearing biochem attire all together. Some people... but not Rainah.

Fuck that.

The dirt was a son-of-a-bitch to get out of the crevices of her gas mask. She used the sleeve of her uniform to wipe the smears from the lens.

She assumed, as she had the entire time she hid, that Griff's voice would suddenly pop into her head, telling her that everything was all right. As time went on, she began to fear the worst.

171

Rainah sat on the bench with her face (mask) buried in her hands. She was wondering how it all came to this when she heard a voice.

"Hey, blondie..."

From its timbre, she surmised that the voice belonged to a young man. It came from somewhere behind her where the short, bulky shrubs were tightly packed. Although there were no leaves, the twigs and branches intertwined in a way that made it equally hard to see through them.

Rainah thrust to her feet and spun toward the voice. Her fingertips caressed the knife-handle that peeked out from its sheath that was strapped to her thigh. It was her only remaining weapon.

Nothing.

Something told her to turn around. She spun again and completed the invisible circle.

There was a young man standing about 10 feet from her.

The first thing Rainah noticed was that he wasn't wearing a bugsuit.

The young man looked somewhere between 18 and 20 years old, probably around 5'10" or 5'11", with an athletic build and dirty-blond hair styled in a short buzz with tapered sides. He was that all-American type, so much so that it almost bordered on Casper Van Dien-ish parody. He looked like he hadn't slept in days, and the last time he *did* sleep, it was in the faded, '80s-style denim-jacket-and-jeans ensemble that he was wearing.

"Want some company?" the young man said with a grin that he probably used to charm the panties off all the ladies.

The guy didn't strike Rainah as a vampire, but he had to be if he was walking around in the Zone without protective gear. That's what logic told her.

Her intuition told her that vampire or not, he was up to no good. As much as her tired muscles would allow, she prepared herself to do battle. She had taken down bigger, more capable men in the past. At the time, she had the inner confidence to act without fear. But things were different now, so different that she found herself feeling insecure about her chances against this... this... kid.

Just go away. Shut up! Rainah thought in reference to the voice of self-doubt that whispered in her brain.

"Who are you?" Rainah inquired. "Are you... one of *them*?"

"One of... *them*?" the young man replied.

"Don't play with me, kid. If you're from around here, then you definitely know what I'm talking about."

"I am. And I don't. Honestly? I was just out lookin' for a good time. And here you are, all alone. Don't *badasses* need love, too?"

Rainah glanced down at the stencil over her left breast. *Cute.* She tried to read the young man's responses. He was being coy, which meant to her that he knew something more than he was letting on. She didn't want to have to actually say "vampire," but it was looking like she had no other choice. As she prepared to respond, she suddenly remembered... *He called me blondie... How did he know what color my hair is beneath the mask?*

Rainah tensed up.

Time to strike, girl, her inner voice suggested. Running was another option, and based on what she'd seen of the vampires' fighting prowess, it was the one she preferred. She probably wouldn't get far, though. Not unless she somehow wounded him first. That wouldn't be easy, even if she weren't tired.

Opting for the diplomatic approach, Rainah tried one last time to reason with the kid. Sure, the "blondie" comment was a dead giveaway, but she was pessimistic about the outcome should they come to blows. Maybe if she had a little more time to think, she could come up with a feasible plan of attack.

173

"Do me a favor kid, and…"

"Call me Hollywood."

There was a scratching sound, like someone dragging a needle across a record.

Everything (the trees, the background noise, the night itself) paused as if to react to the ridiculous name.

"Hollywood!?!" Rainah scoffed. She would've laughed in his face if she were in a better mood.

Hollywood struck a pose, presenting himself with open arms.

"Don't I look like a star?" He flashed the straightest, whitest smile that Rainah had ever seen. A sparkle of light gleamed across his teeth. It was accompanied by a twinkling sound.

"Do me a favor, *Hollywood*, and go home to your family."

"Don't have a family," he responded before she finished her sentence. "And even if I did, I have a feeling that I'd still rather be out here with you."

"Look, Goddammit. I'm going to tell you one more time…"

"And I'm tellin' *you* that I'm staying right here. Am I really that bad that you'd rather sit here all by yourself? I mean… look at me."

He turned his profile to her and posed.

Rainah didn't say another word. Her scattershot mind had birthed a strategy. She would have to get uncomfortably close to him to pull it off, though.

She channeled a "naughty-girl" affect and approached him.

"You see something you like and you just have to have it, huh?" she said.

Hollywood didn't know what to make of Rainah's sudden change of heart. His little head told him to go with the flow, but his big head said that she was up to something. He knew now

174

that she knew what he was. Was she simply giving in to an unwinnable situation or playing him like a fool?

Only about a half an hour ago, Hollywood was sitting in a hotel room listening to the radio broadcast of the Market Street showdown as he decompressed from a double shift of construction work. They mentioned a hefty reward for the capture of any Revenant Clan soldiers. He didn't go out looking, though. His intention was to hang upside down from the trees and think, which he liked to do from time to time.

Hollywood laid back in his stance and watched Rainah approach. Her curves screamed through her uniform. He salivated at the possibilities.

He lifted his arms to accept her, cautiously at first.

Rainah reached out, cupped Hollywood's groin in her hand and begin to fondle the area. They were close, closer than Rainah had been to a man in this context in some time. He was staring down at her with intense brown eyes. His breathing was beginning to flutter. She had him.

Eventually, Hollywood relinquished his caution to the moment. He cocked his head back and closed his eyes. It was just the opportunity that Rainah was waiting for.

Rainah snatched the knife from her thigh and swung it horizontally at eye level. Using all of her remaining strength, she applied pressure as the serrated blade struck its target and slid through. Friction caused it to stutter on its way across his eyes and the bridge of his nose. One of his eyeballs (the left) bobbed and bounced on the blade, then popped out its socket and dangled against his cheek. The other one split open like a hard-boiled egg.

Hollywood groaned. His features shot vampiric. He spun away from Rainah and threw his hands up over his face. The dangling eyeball spun with him.

"You fucking bitch! Fucking... human... *CUNT*!"

Rainah followed Hollywood as he stumbled, directionless. She began stabbing at his body wherever she saw an opening. She stabbed and stabbed and stabbed (it seemed like a hundred times, at least) until he swung his arm blindly, knocking her on her ass.

Rainah was back on her feet in an instant. She was standing further away from Hollywood than before; maybe 25 feet separated them. It was then that she realized how bad the blow that knocked her back hurt. His arm caught her right across the chest. Had she not been so energized, she would've realized that it winded her.

Rainah felt nothing when Hollywood collapsed: no euphoria, no speedball of adrenaline, no erogenous sting, not a damn thing. It made taking a life seem rather ugly. The black blood that poured from his wounds and stained his clothing reminded her that he wasn't human—and that he most likely wasn't dead.

She took off running deeper into the woods.

Clutching her knife in a firm grip, Rainah moved through the woods like a pro. She took long steps and pushed off of trees for extra thrust or to enable her to continue forward at an impossible angle when needed.

She was traveling along a hilltop one layer deep in the brush. She had a good view of the neighborhoods below. They looked pretty much the same as anywhere else, with rows and rows of devastation sprinkled with pockets of buildings left undamaged. And construction. Pinpoints of blowtorch light flickered on distant façades like connect-the-dots. Interior light gleamed from windows here and there. Down in the street that separated the hillside from the neighborhoods, traffic buzzed.

There was something different, a zest for life that was missing from any of the other communities, except maybe for the Ergeister Capital in LA. It was as if these people weren't aware that the planet had become a toxic cesspool. Either that or they just didn't give a fuck.

Rainah maintained her focus in split-screen. On the left, she navigated a course through the obstacles that impeded her—cock-eyed trees with their wooden tentacles reaching everywhere, chubby roots that poked and knuckled up from the dirt, vines that tried to choke or trip her, and the sudden changes in the ground's texture, from soft to smooth to lumpy. On the right, she scoped out the neighborhoods.

She ran until her beleaguered lungs forced her to stop and replenish her breath. She picked a secluded spot behind two trees that merged at the waist.

"Blonnndiiieeee, where arrreee yooouuuu?" A spectral voice called out in surround-sound, coming from near and far.

Hollywood!!!

Rainah spun herself off balance trying to identify its source. Suddenly the trees seemed to crowd her with their stalwart presence, the lower shrubs closing in with their bare, pointed fingers.

"I know you're out there, blondie…. I can *smell* your blood."

This time, the voice came from right over her shoulder.

Rainah slashed at the darkness behind her. It was a blind strike delivered with an upward arc starting at where she assumed Hollywood's stomach might be. But there were only the merging trees, and shrubs and darkness.

Rainah ran away from the talking air.

"Where ya goin', blondie?" Hollywood's voice bounced along the trees echoing after Rainah as she huffed and willed her legs to move.

It came from the right…

"You think because I can't see that I won't find you?"

From the left…

"Don't you know anything?"

From the front…

"You can't get away from me, girl."

…and from the rear…

"Not with that sweet, sweet blood of yours."

Rainah was eyeing a clearing in the tangle of dead bushes that bordered the hilltop. It was coming up on her right, about 30 feet away. As she came closer, she could see that someone… some*thing* was hiding in those bushes. Whatever it was had caused them to rustle.

Rainah flipped her knife blade-side down and held it ready. She was going through that clearing one way or another.

The bushes growled the next time they shook. It was deep and angry, like the howl of a ghettoized pit bull.

The growling grew more ferocious as Rainah closed the distance. The bushes shook faster, harder. By the time she was 10 feet from the clearing, it sounded as if the dog were going to jump out and attack.

But it didn't.

"I wouldn't go that way if I were you, blondie…."

The voice swooped down on her, coming from every-where, from everything at the same time—trees, rocks, empty space. The many different manifestations overlapped and drowned each other out. The growling crept underneath it all, ferocious as can be. Now *it* was directionless, too.

The voice… the growling… and now laughter… goofy laughter…

Rainah stopped, put her hands up to the sides of her mask (where her ears would be), and did a twisting, lunatic dance. Covering the sides of her mask did nothing to mute the noise. It was merely an instinctive move, enacted without thought.

Rainah stepped erratically. It appeared that she had lost it, or that she was stepping in awkward circles away from and toward the noise.

Without warning, Rainah planted her feet and tightened her stance. She yanked her arms down from the sides of her mask. Hot breath inflated her trunk. It was intense.

"UrrrghcccCome out here and show yourself, Goddammit! RIGHT-FUCKING-NOW!" she roared, her frustration spilling over.

Dead silence.

"YOU WANT ME SO BAD? WELL, HERE I AM!" She wasn't even sure whom she was talking to at this point, but she kept it coming. "WHAT? YOU AFRAID OF A GIRL?"

Nothing.

Rainah stood there cycling deep breaths and waited for a response. She waited long enough for her fiery enthusiasm to wither. She was about to yell again when the stocky bushes to her right chuckled and shook.

Hollywood stood from behind the bushes and smiled. He made a "Ta-da!" motion with his arms. An asterisk of light gleamed from a point on his perfect smile. It was accompanied by a twinkling sound. Black blood streamed from his eye sockets like mascara moistened by tears. His left eyeball dangled from squishy black strands.

"Awww, man," he laughed as he parted the bushes with his hand and stepped over them. "I wish I could see the look on your face."

Rainah was too worked up to respond with words. Instead, she flipped the knife in her hand and charged. She feigned left, then came at him from the right, swinging her weapon in practiced patterns.

Hollywood didn't even try to lean away, or duck, or to grab for the metallic blur like most people instinctively attempted. Rainah was sure she had him until he vanished into thin air and reappeared a few feet away, standing casually with his arms folded across his chest. He was humming and acting as if he had been

waiting on her for long time.

Rainah adjusted to the real-time edit and closed the distance in seconds.

Hollywood let her get dangerously close before vanishing again. This time, he reappeared sitting down with his legs crossed, whistling.

Rainah stutter-stepped, changed directions, and attacked.

Hollywood vanished and reappeared. He was standing right next to her, sticking out his tongue like a precocious child. His thumbs were in his ears, fingers spread and wiggling.

The next time he was lying on his side, chilling.

After that, he appeared in a wobbly, single-legged crane stance (like in "The Karate Kid") and made faces at her.

The next time, he was standing again, his right arm raised over his head and dropping in exaggerated stabbing motions accompanied by his very own vocal rendition of the shower scene music from "Psycho." "Drink! Drink! Drink! Drink! Drink!" he joked in a high-pitch.

Hollywood was always just out of Rainah's reach as she tried to adapt to his unorthodox strategy. Until…

He appeared behind her and went in for a bite. His mouth stretched open wide enough to swallow her entire head.

Rainah spun around and plunged her knife deep into his chest. She looked pleasantly surprised that the blade found its mark.

She grabbed the handle with both hands and forced the blade in deeper. Sliding closer as the blade sunk, their bodies touched. Rainah could smell Hollywood's breath as he wheezed at the mercy of his pierced lung. There were no words to describe the stench.

Rainah hadn't felt a body as hard as Hollywood's was since… since forever, it seemed. He was streamlined and cut like a male gymnast.

Hollywood grabbed the top of Rainah's head and dug his claws into the fabric of her hooded mask. His fist closed around a jumble of torn fabric and matted, dirty-blond hair. He twisted to secure a hold, his bony knuckles digging in "super-noogies," and lifted her off her feet.

Rainah shrieked. By the time she reacted (grabbing Hollywood's wrist and pulling up to take the slack off her hair), she was already dangling. Her scalp was on fire. She could feel every last strand fighting to stay planted in her flesh. Some of them let go.

Hollywood held Rainah at arm's length out in front of him. She watched his teeth grow longer before her eyes. He curled his lips back to give her a good view.

"I shoulda just turned you in, bitch," Hollywood said.

He used a single fingernail to slice Rainah's bugsuit from her collar down to her navel. The thick, durable fabric curled away from her skin. She was naked underneath. A moist sheen sparkled in the moonlight.

Rainah wriggled and kicked at Hollywood's knees and shins to no effect. She couldn't use her hands unless she wanted her hair to rip out of her scalp.

Hollywood pointed his nose at her and sniffed. That left eye of his was hanging lower than before and swinging to follow his movement. It swung right at Rainah a few times. Droplets of black blood dotted her bare chest.

"Mmmmm... I bet they look as good as you smell."

Rainah had always been proud of her breasts. They weren't all that big, but they were firm, nicely rounded, and topped off with button nipples and understated areolas.

Hollywood kneaded her breasts in his hand.

"You'd better kill me," Rainah warned. Pain turned her voice coarse and husky. She gnashed her teeth between words. "You hear me, *fucker*? I swear it..."

She dug deep down into her throat and hocked a glob of phlegm at Hollywood's face.

He licked it from the corner of his mouth and pulled Rainah closer to him.

"Nah, I think I'll collect that reward… let Onyx do what he wants with you. But not before I have a piece-a-that *fine-ass pussy*. He'll probably end up having all you assholes tortured and executed in the courtyard anyway, so I doubt he'll mind."

Rainah absolutely hated weak women. She had no time for them and the way they whimpered, whined, and crumbled without a fight nine times out of 10. She hated the way those types tried to talk while they were crying. She hated when they tried to appeal to her or Griff/Derek/Kagen's good side. With Mary, they usually just stared in awe.

As much as she hated it, Rainah was contemplating going the damsel-in-distress route just this one time. If it worked, then why not? Griff was always saying to "do what you gotta do to get the job done." She knew she'd never forgive herself, though.

An idea came to her out of left field. It was something so simple that her inner voice commented, *Oh yeah…*

Rainah reestablished her grip around Hollywood's wrist and thrust her knee up into his groin.

Hollywood gasped like a woman. It was just the pitch that Rainah was looking for. He shoved her backwards and fell to his knees. His entire face tightened as if he were about to cry.

Rainah skidded down the damp, grassy slope that led to the street below. Hollywood must've thrown her a good 40 feet.

She landed in the lane traveling east. She was dizzy from her trip down the hill but too determined to survive to let it stop her. There was sporadic traffic in both lanes, enough that Rainah had to time her sprint across. Her bugsuit hung open in the front where Hollywood sliced it to have a look at her breasts. They bounced as she ran. A messy, bloodstained loop of dirty-blond hair bobbed on top of her head.

Horns blared.

Somewhere along the way, Rainah saw a shape leap out into the open at the top of the hill. It looked like the woods just spit it out. It was Hollywood. His feet were nowhere near the ground. His knees were bent, his torso hunched forward in a sort of flying squat launched from a running start. His head moved jerkily, like an insect's, as he searched for her.

Rainah collapsed to her knees on the other side of the road. She thought about kissing the ground.

More horns scolded her. A few people insulted her.

She thrust herself upright and checked the hill. Hollywood was already in the street and coming right for her.

Cars skidded to avoid him. People yelled profanities out their windows. He paid them no mind. He was focused on finding Rainah.

Hollywood searched for her with his nose, sticking it out and bobbing for a scent. It didn't take long for him to find it.

He followed it forward, brandishing fangs like ivory daggers. He swung his arms out in front of him to check for obstacles. Other than that, he didn't seem terribly encumbered by the temporary loss of his sight.

The traffic had stopped.

People were standing outside of their cars, looking and speculating. They aimed suspecting stares at Rainah. Some were cursing at her.

Every last one of them had yellow-red eyes.

Rainah held the front of her uniform together as she ran into the parking lot of a decayed stripmall that lay on the outer edge of the Red City expansion. The expansion was on its way to taking over all of Philadelphia.

A half-operating grocery store sat at the head of the strip.

It was small and sparsely stocked. There were people inside, walking around, shopping, and acting like everything was all right with the world. At the same time, store employees walked about, inspecting damaged areas and jotting things down on clipboards that they all carried.

There weren't too many people in the parking lot, but there were some.

Rainah ran behind a delivery truck and planted her back against it. She stayed there for a minute or so before moving on to the next large vehicle... and the next. The cars were spaced quite far apart, which made staying out of sight more difficult. She tried to keep herself low as she ran, but there was no question that people had seen her.

Moving from back to front, Rainah inched along the side of a minivan. When she reached the driver's side window, she peeked through it and saw a small crowd coming in her general direction from the front of the lot. She saw Hollywood, too. He was approaching from the side entrance.

Rainah turned and ran right into a young woman who had just finished loading bags into the back of her car.

The collision knocked Rainah back. She stumbled and shot upright to catch her balance.

It was strange. The young woman was much smaller than Rainah and about as far from the athletic type as you could get. It didn't make sense that she didn't even budge.

"She's over here!" the young woman yelled.

Standing out in the open, Rainah looked around the lot. The crowd had her locked in their sights now. Hollywood was only a few cars away.

Rainah ran away from the woman. She spotted a small, unlit road that snaked off into the night at the rear of the lot. She could hear Hollywood gaining on her. Soon he would be close enough to reach out and...

Rainah stopped and turned, defiant. It was obvious that she couldn't get away. If she was going out, it wasn't going to be running from some *boy*, vampire or not.

She dug her feet in to meet Hollywood's momentum.

"Come on, you mother*fucker*!" she said.

Hollywood was less than 10 feet away when a black Chrysler came out of nowhere, slammed into his side, and snatched him from Rainah's sight-path. It made a horrible crackle-thud sound. Hollywood cried out, but his voice was immediately slapped down by the second phase of the collision. The first was when the car made initial contact; the second was when his torso folded over the hood and he smacked it face first.

The Chrysler's bulk laid into its thick tires as it slid to a stop. Through the driver's side window, Rainah saw Griff behind the wheel. Derek was beside him in the passenger's seat.

The back door swung open by itself.

"Griff?!?" Rainah huffed.

"Get in!" Griff responded.

Rainah dived in. The door closed behind her.

Hollywood's body laid twisted and broken 100 feet in front of the car.

Griff backed away from it, turned, and peeled off toward the unlit road at the back of the lot.

Rainah sat up and took a deep, liberating breath.

"Please tell me you've heard from Mary" were the first words out of her mouth.

Griff paused. He seemed genuinely concerned. "She's been bitten. I sensed a burning sensation… caught a vision of her tearing her suit off."

"She's turning," Derek added.

"She's making her way east, toward Delaware Avenue," Griff said. "That's where we're going."

Rainah pondered for a moment.

"What about Kagen?"

Silence.

Rainah lowered her head. It seemed like she was just going over the events in her mind, but after awhile Derek and Griff heard sobbing.

In the rearview, a four-legged, spider-thing (Hollywood) stepped drunkenly, on unfamiliar appendages, and eventually fell. Its joints were in weird places along its four legs—two short and two long.

Using his arms and legs, Hollywood pushed against the cold asphalt and lifted himself. His back was to the ground. The shattered bones between his shoulder girdle and pelvis caused that section of his body to droop. His head drooped, too. There was nothing but flesh and muscle keeping it attached to his shoulders.

There was no way he would catch the Chrysler in that condition. That was what he was trying to do.

A crowd had formed around him. They were watching the Chrysler speed away. Their yellow-red eyes burned holes in the darkness.

Derek and Rainah spent the next few minutes trying to avoid each other's fleeting glances via the rearview mirror. Rainah sat in the very corner, holding the front of her bugsuit together and feeling around her bloodied scalp where her hood was torn away. She felt violated, ashamed—words that the kind of women she hated would use.

There was a shared sense of defeat, a shared feeling of "How could this have possibly happened?" Not too long ago, they were going to take over the world.

"Wha… what happened?" Rainah asked, almost as if she didn't want to hear the answer.

Derek looked over at Griff, then turned and rested his

arm on the headrest of his seat to anchor his torso.

"After we got split up, me and the grunts made it to the neighborhoods up north. The vamps cornered us in an abandoned house. We were holed up in the basement. There musta been 30 or 40 of 'em. They had the place surrounded. Some official-sounding dude tried to talk us out all hostage-negotiator-like: 'Come out now and maybe we'll let you live,' and alladat kind-a-bullshit."

"Dr. Lund... He's sorta like their mouthpiece," Griff added. The words seeped out the side of his face.

Derek picked up where he left off.

"It was either go out blazin' or sit there while they bumrushed the place. Between the six of us, we only had three M4s with less than half a clip each, but fuck it. We were gonna have to work with what we had. I gotta give it up to Menz. He was the first one out the door."

"Who?" Rainah said.

"One of the grunts. A sergeant. Good man. He didn't make it far before... before they took him apart. The rest of us were right behind him. I thought it was the end, man. And I was ready, boy... ready like a mug. Then here comes the bus rolling up the street. Vamps hangin' all over it-n-shit, just like before. Man... they were everywhere. I was like, 'There's no way we're gonna be able to get on that thing.' Then Griff coaxes to us. Tells us to get back inside the house."

"I got Kagen out while the men held off the vamps," Griff interjected. "I dragged him behind some cars sittin' dead on the parkway and went back to help. We held 'em off for a while, but the men were low on ammo, and there were more vamps comin' down the parkway, so I took cover and scoped out both your situations. That's when I coaxed the bus in Derek's direction. The vamps assumed that more of us were on board so they followed it. I knew those muthafuckas would take the bait."

"What about the men?" Rainah questioned.

"Soldiers are replaceable, Rainah."

Silence.

"So there's three of us left," Derek said. "We make it back inside the house just before the bus reaches the crowd and goes up big. We made a break while they were dealing with that shit. Then this big... black... ugly... *thing* comes flying at us. I mean this jawn was fuckin' huge. Griff saw it."

"Their leader... Calls himself Count Onyx," Griff said.

"So Griff is coaxing his position to me. I'm heading toward him. The grunts are following my lead. Count-fucking-Chocula is coming after us. I could hear his clothes snapping in the wind over our heads. We're diving behind cars and lightposts-n-shit, and running in and out of abandoned buildings trying to get away from this dude. But he's picking us off one by one.... The next thing I know, I'm the only one left. Dude's right on top of me. I go for my gun, thinkin' this is it *again,* when I hear a loud crash. I look up and see dude's legs sticking out from under a car that's flying backwards on its side. They both go slamming into the side of a building. I look down and see Griff standing there. He and this guy go at it. Griff is throwing cars, garbage cans, phone booths, and whatever he could coax at this dude. He tags him a few times, but dude was quick, man. He would like... disappear and reappear over here (demonstrates with hands) before he even vanished."

Rainah perked up. "I've seen it," she said.

"Then, for some reason, dude just stops coming. We thought we had him hurt. So we're heading back to get Kagen."

"I left him in the lobby of an abandoned apartment building on Fairmount Street while I looked for a car," Griff said.

"When we got there..." Derek paused. "When we got there, that Onyx motherfucker was carrying his body up the side of the building."

"Kagen? He was carrying Kagen's body?" Rainah asked. Derek shook his head "yes." "He got away," he added.

Rainah suddenly felt nauseous. She leaned forward away from the back of her seat. The back of Derek's seat leaned in and planted kisses on her knee. A bump in the road bounced her into the right door. A hard left turn sent her sliding into the left one.

She reached behind her head and unzipped her mask. Her hands were shaking as she peeled it off.

"What the hell are you…" Derek started to say before the sight of Rainah's face affected him. It was like seeing an old friend again, one who he had never seen look so sad.

A single stream of blood rolled away from Rainah's hairline and down the right side of her face. She did nothing to stop it.

Derek turned around and settled into his seat. After a few moments of introspection, he unzipped his mask and peeled it off.

Griff drove along for a while, pretending not to notice. Eventually, he let go of the steering wheel and coaxed the car along. He reached up and unzipped his mask.

Rainah's mask looked up at her from her lap. She was staring down at it and clutching the front of her uniform. Tears streamed from her eyes and immediately became lost in the layer of sweat that covered her face. It matted her hair to sides of her face and made her skin glow. When she looked up, she almost didn't recognize the two men sitting in front of her. They looked different—older maybe, more self-assured, something…. Each of them experienced it. On top of that, Griff's left eye had swelled to the size of a golf ball.

Trading long, meaningful stares, they expressed their feelings for each other.

Griff, who said the least, spoke mainly through the rearview mirror when he addressed Rainah. He spoke to Derek in a quarter-turn.

"It wasn't supposed to happen like this!" Rainah cried out and threw down her mask. "It's not supposed to happen like this! We... we can't lose.... Don't they know... don't they know who they're fucking with? Tell 'em, Griff. Tell 'em that they can't do this to us!"

"You schitzin', Rai," Derek said. "'Best to close that window, girl... let it blow on by.... Isn't that what *you* are always telling *me*?"

"Oh, so *now* you're all good and everything, right? Mister 'What if the church was wrong? What if it's all a load of bullshit?' Mister 'I'm sick of their treating Kagen and me like we're just peripheral characters. We're just as important as the rest of you.'"

"Goddammit, Rai! That was years ago!" Derek replied. "Neither of us knew what we were in for. So I was fucking scared! Now, c'mon girl... focus. This ain't like you."

"He's right, Rainah," Griff said. "No matter how bad it is, you've gotta put it past you and get with the program. Mary's alive.... As long as that fact holds true, the game is on. Now, you wanna start comin' apart at the seams, then I'll kindly pull this car over, and you can take that shit somewhere else."

Griff's brown eye hovered in the rear-view, waiting....

Rainah's shoulders were slumped. Her face was buried in her right hand. She knew that Griff's eye was there. She could sense the wavelength of its shine.

"And you *should* know that you ain't alone in this," Griff added. "So stop feeling sorry for yourself."

Despite how she really felt, Rainah was eventually able to maintain a calm exterior. Her eyes rolled up and stopped on the back of Griff's head.

"I'm sorry," she said.

Griff turned to the side and...

A clawed fist punched through the roof of the car. It

191

came down at an angle and clocked Griff in the side of the head, knocking him unconscious. The hand retracted and peeled a jagged section of the roof clean off.

A vampire straddled the car's frame and snarled down on them. It was Kagen.

Rainah almost smiled. But this Kagen had a look in his yellow-red eyes that was completely foreign to the Kagen she knew… and loved. Plus, he was looking at them like he didn't know who they were, like they were little more than food.

Kagen dug his claws into Griff's shoulders, yanked him out of his seat, and tossed him straight up into the air. Another vampire hovered 50 feet up, waiting to catch Griff's flailing body. The airborne vampire snatched Griff sideways and vanished traveling east. A dark smear lingered where it hovered above the car.

Kagen was still straddling the frame. He reached down and cranked the steering wheel to the right.

The car swerved sideways. The tires stuck. The car flipped and began to roll.

Rainah was tossed from the back seat. She landed in an overgrown field.

Finger-blades of grass caressed her face and probed her nostrils and mouth when she rolled over.

Some time passed. She wasn't exactly sure how long: maybe 10 minutes, maybe 15….

There was a sound, like rubber snapping and liquid squirting from pressurized tubes.

Rainah lifted her head and sat up. Her breasts peeked from behind the dangling fabric of her bugsuit. She did nothing to hide them.

She saw the Chrysler. It was upside down in the middle of the road and on fire.

She saw Kagen. He was kneeling over a body with its arms and legs sprawled out. They flinched whenever Kagen leaned over and took a bite. A bridge of elastic flesh and venous tubing extended from his mouth to the body.

"Derek?" Rainah cried out in a way that felt as if her mouth was moving in slow motion. She didn't believe it at first. She couldn't. "No... DEREK!"

Kagen whipped around and spotted her. He looked so angry. The Kagen she knew would never look at her that way. Not in a million years. He was drooling blood. It left the bottom half of his face heavily stained. His beard was dripping wet. Something solid slid down the side of his face and fell from his hairy chin.

"I was wonderin' when you were gonna wake up," Kagen said, as he rose to his feet.

Rainah could see Derek now that Kagen wasn't blocking her view. He was looking at her. His eyes were plump with fear. He was gasping for air and trying to communicate to her to "get away" or something. His abdomen had been ripped open.

Kagen was walking toward her now. His penis was erect. She could see the impression in his pants.

"If you knew the kinds of things I dreamt of doin' to you, darlin'," Kagen said as he approached. "I... I never thought it was really my place to make an honest effort for your affections, but... suddenly, I feel so uninhibited... so... free to express myself. I wish I could make you understand."

"Derek was family, K!" Rainah screamed. "He was family, and you killed him!"

"I got a new family now, Rai. It's... it's like nothing you could ever imagine. If you let me, I'll make you a member, too. You would love it, Rai. Trust me."

Rainah kept shaking her head "no."

Kagen was a few feet away when someone jumped on him from behind and wrapped his arms and legs around him.

It was Derek. He held a grenade in his left hand.

He thumbed the pin out and winked to Rainah.

"See you on the other side, old friend," he said to Kagen.

Rainah rolled back onto her stomach and buried her face in her arms. She felt the moist earth against her naked breasts.

Kagen reached up and attempted to throw Derek off.

The grenade exploded.

There were two main plops, followed by a shower of small splat sounds that rained down all around Rainah soon after. She lay there until the rain subsided.

"Look at that," boomed a thunderous voice somewhere above and behind her. "The humans go to pieces over this one. I guess there's no accounting for taste."

Laughter.

Rainah lifted her head and turned around groggily. Tears poured from her eyes.

The laughter stopped.

A crowd of vampires brandishing curved blades (Alpha Dogs) stood in the middle of the road, glaring silently. Standing front and center, a 7-foot-tall, bald, shiny man-thing painted oil-black smiled down at her.

Rainah immediately recalled Derek's story and the name that Griff rattled off: Count Onyx.

His eyes were completely white with no eyeballs. Along with his smile, they stood out against his skin, which was more or less the absence of light made manifest. His fangs were curved like those of the vampires that stood on either side of him, only his upper set was twice the size of theirs.

Despite the demonic features, he had a pretty face for a man. His clothing (a blazer left unbuttoned and slacks) was the same color as his skin.

He was shirtless underneath the blazer, standing barefoot. His body was naturally toned. He wore a silver crucifix around his neck as a "fuck you" to humankind. His hands and feet were huge. The backs of them were lumpy with crisscrossing veins. Long, bony fingers and toes ended in razor-sharp claws. Something resembling a dewclaw protruded from the back of his ankles.

The others had it, too.

Onyx clasped his hands behind his back and stepped forward.

"Save those tears for later, baby," he said. "The worst is yet to come."

Chapter 12

Rina, Ohio – 2006
Friday

I should've known it would be a bad day when I woke up this morning to a call from Artemus on my two-way radio. I keep it on the nightstand next to my bed in case of emergencies.

It was 8:32 in the fucking morning, and I wasn't due in 'til 10:00. The shithead had the audacity to act surprised when I told him that. No "Hello. How are you doing today?" No "Sorry for waking you, but…"

Instead I got "What time are you coming in?" like I owed it to him to make some kind of exception in his case. Well… in a way I guess I do, but I was half-awake and pissed. You know how it is.

My first instinct (after checking the clock) was to tell Artemus to lose my fucking number and throw the two-way across the room. Of course that wouldn't have been very productive. I knew that Artemus was only speaking for Mayor Knox, which meant that I had no choice but to come in early.

I expected Artemus to be waiting for me when I came in, but the bastard didn't show up until 9:51. And here I was, all stressin' because the guard that Knox just appointed to escort me from my building to the tavern was 10 minutes late showing up.

It's a short walk that seems to take forever these days. Feels like one of those scenes in the old cartoons where the main character is surrounded by hundreds of eyes leering from the darkness all around. I try to make small talk with the guard to pass the time.

I was having breakfast with Graham (more like watching him eat), who had just come off an early run when Artemus finally arrived. I would've welcomed the interruption had it been anyone else.

Artemus was one of the few people that the guards didn't frisk. Usually that gave me a moment or two to prepare for whoever had just come in.

Artemus was shaking like an epileptic smackhead in withdrawal when he walked up and interrupted our conversation. Again there was no apology, no "Excuse me for interrupting." Not even a "Good morning, gentlemen." He just walked right up and stood there like he had to pee until I asked Graham to move to another booth while I handled this.

"First of all, my client really enjoyed that special shipment that came in last time," Artemus says, as he slides behind the table.

Well, you can tell Mayor Knox that he could at least show me a little gratitude by not having his lackey call me at 8:32 in the morning.

Artemus... what a fucking idiot. This guy has his nose so far up Knox's ass that he can probably smell what the man is thinking. Everything about the guy rubs me the wrong way.

"I aim to please," I say.

"He... my client was wondering if he could possibly acquire more."

"Sorry. Like I told him... er... *you* last week (*after you cock-blocked the shipment*), that was a one-time deal."

The fucker doesn't believe me. I can tell by the way he shifts in his seat. He keeps fidgeting and looking around like he's expecting someone to walk in the door and yell, "This is a raid!"

I put my hand on his and tell him to "Relax," but he flinches and pulls away like I'm a leper or something. He tries to play it off like he had flung off an insect when he realizes it was just my hand.

I can see that he's mulling over something important, something that it seems like he doesn't want to say. So, I figured I'd let him off the hook.

"What?" I say. "Lemme guess. You think I'm holding out?"

"Ah... well... not me personally, but my client, you see.... He seems to think that you may have saved some for yourself."

"Now, ain't that a motherfucker."

"Perhaps you intend to use it for medicinal purposes...?"
Perhaps...

"Excuse me if I'm mistaken, but you *did* confiscate the entire shipment at the gate, right?"

"Half of that went to the hospital. Besides, I'm sure you have other avenues of acquiring your goods."

"What? Like a transporter?"

Artemus gives me this look that says "That'll be enougha that, young man." Even though I'm pleasantly surprised that he caught the reference to *Star Trek*, that look of his makes me wanna smack it right off his sweaty face.

"Look, it ain't like I just walked outta the wasteland last week," I say. "And *your client* should know the way the system that *he* set up works by now. It ain't like before the war, when I could get my hands on just about anything under the sun."

"Ssssssssh! Keep your voice down!" Artemus rasps.

He's holding his finger to his lips like we're in grade school or something, so I reach across the table and snap it back like a chicken bone.

Well... that's what happened in my head anyway. The scene was colored by thunderous musical cues and bombastic, flashing colors to illustrate the way I felt. It wasn't pure anger, but more like a mixture of it and frustration. It reminded me of the way I felt when I tried to use logic in an argument with a chick.

"You *do* realize that most-a-the people in this town don't give a fuck that *your client* uses, right?"

He raises his eyebrows, as if to say, "Ah... have you been paying attention to what's going on around here?"

"Aw, ta hell with those idiots," I say. Then I yell to Graham, who's sitting three tables away, "You give a fuck about his client?"

"Don't make me no nevamind," Graham replies and swallows a mouthful of food.

"What about you, Chalk?"

"Nope."

"You guys?" I yell to the guards.

The guard on the right smiles and shakes his head "no." The guard on the left waits for the other guard to respond before signaling accordingly.

Pussy.

Artemus is trying to reel me in the whole time. He's leaning forward and reaching across the table and hissing my name over and over. But my little blow-up is a long time in coming, and I'm ready to go the distance.

"Hell, 80 percent of this place would probably suck my cock for a fix if it came down to it," I say, talking over Artemus' attempts to shut me up. "Drugs are the only things helping them get by out there. I'm talking everybody: from security, to officials, to doctors, to scientists, to regular day-to-day folks, even some-a-those hypocrites in the friggin' Brigade. Even our boss, the head fucking Don Corleone/Tony Montana of this whole operation. And *this* is how you thank me? By accusing me of lying? And speaking of this business with the Brigade... you people could at least show some loyalty. Get these fuckers off my back. Shit's got folks acting like fools. Some-a-my most loyal customers are afraid to admit they use. Business is drying up. Maybe if *your client* was up front about his usage, or if he just put his goddamn foot down and stopped trying to please everyone, we wouldn't be in this mess. You and I both know those deaths don't have a *damn* thing to do with..."

"This is not the *time,* nor the *place,* for this discussion, Mr. Krychek," he says. Now, I'm going to ask again that you keep your voice down."

"Or what? You gonna call the DEA on me? Call the president, for all I care. He's probably in that bunker-a-his, gettin' zooted with the rest of his cabinet."

I expected a quick retort, but instead Artemus just sits there, looking down at the table and shaking his head. I glance over at Graham. He looks up from his plate as if he knew my eyes were on their way. We trade gestures.

Mine says, "Thisssss fucking guy...."

I take Graham's as a warning: "Be careful."

It's obvious that Artemus isn't used to being stood up to by anyone other than the mayor. He's one of these people who would prefer to avoid confrontation. Now that he's faced with it, he isn't sure how to act. I can see his mind working. I imagine old, wooden cogs struggling to turn. I wonder how hard you must have to think to break a sweat from it the way he had.

Artemus sits there for so long that I start to feel sorry for him. I was about to let him off the hook again when he finally looks up. His rampant fidgeting suddenly stops. He seems to be channeling some inner-strength bullshit, the way his face jumps relaxed.

"I had hoped it wouldn't come to this, but as we seem to be at a crossroads here, you leave me little choice," he says.

Uh-oh...

"What's that supposed to mean?" I ask.

"It *meanzzz* that my client is aware of your visits to Main Street even after you were told to stay away from the girls."

Shit! Fucking rookie driver!

Artemus catches me off guard. My eyes shoot over to Graham who looks away just as they land on him. I'm not sure if Chalk overheard. If he did, he'll be itching to throw another "I told you so" my way, so I avoid looking at him.

My fluster-fuck turns to anger.

"Now, hold on a fuckin' minute here!" I say, but Artemus simply raises his voice and keeps on going. *Funny how quickly the tables turn*, I thought.

"He knows that you've been trying to talk to Desire."

"First of all, that's none of your business."

"But as the mayor's personal assistant, it *is* my business when someone breaks the rules," he says. "We *were* willing to overlook it. But since you want to give me a hard time..."

The bastard is beginning to find his stride, relaxing into his role as my superior. It's nice to see for a change, but I had to bring him down. Bring him down hard...

"Get out! Get tha-fuck outta my office right fucking now!" *Pretty original, huh?*

Maybe I shouldn't have gotten so angry, but Artemus had gone too far. In his defense, it was probably Knox's idea to bring Desire into this. I try to remind myself of that, but my mind is busy jumping to conclusions... bad conclusions.

The guards head toward us with their game faces on. My heart starts to race. I'm not sure what's about to happen.

I glance over at Graham. His face is buried in his plate.

I look at Chalk, but it's like he deliberately causes the skin-flake cloud to thicken around his head to hide his face from me. Either that or he's just having an especially cloudy day like he does from time to time. Poor guy.

Artemus turns to the guards and raises his hand. "It's okay," he says.

The guards back off.

Whew. I had gotten to know a few of the guards on that

man-level where dirty jokes and pussy talk live. I thought they had my back, but friends don't look at friends the way those two were looking at me just now. I shoulda known. Maybe this job *is* making me too trusting—another one of Chalk's concerns.

"You tell *your client* to remember whom he's dealing with the next time he wants to start making threats." All right, now this next part, I really shouldn't have said: "If you wanna get down to it, he's just another addict. Does he really wanna fuck with his only connection? You ask him nat."

Now, what is the likelihood that this will come back to bite me in the ass? I ask myself, as I watch Artemus storm out. *Pretty fucking likely…*

"Sweet Dreams" by the Eurythmics crawls out of the overhead while I sit there going over the incident with Artemus in my head. I was already wishing that I could take it all back.

Suddenly…

Graham's voice jumps out of thin air. I didn't even notice that he had come back over. When I turn around, he's sitting across the table from me like he'd never left. He starts talking about the off-campus folk, saying how he sensed "funny vibes" while driving through the streets on his way here today.

"Folks seem on edge, combative… like somethin's about to go down," he says.

"It's because of the RS deaths," I say. "The Brigade ain't just made up of Society Hill residents, you know."

I ponder the situation and shake my head.

"This thing is really getting outta hand," I say under my breath.

I think of the girls. I think of Desire—how I long to be in her presence and all that.

Graham keeps on talking, and I keep on listening, just enough to respond with a nod or an "uh huh." Then, out of the blue, he says, "Didn't yo momma ever tell you ta stay away from *de ladies ov de night*?" He puts on an old-school Dracula affect for the latter part of his comment.

My brain slams on the brakes. The sudden stop makes me lightheaded. I blurt out a quick response—too quick, "Wha...?" It comes out sounding slightly perturbed, so I remind myself that Graham was only joking.

"Artemus' crack about Main Street," Graham says. "He was talking about the Taint, huh?"

I fumble for an excuse, trying to keep it playful: "Uh... well, you know.... Look, it's a long story."

"It usually is with women, son. What'chu gotchorself caught up in? No shame in it. Happens to the best of us."

"No, it's not like that..."

Graham puts his hands up and says, "None-a-my business." He says it in a way that implies... I don't know what the hell it implies, but I don't like it. Seems a little condescending, I guess, like he's saying I can't handle my feelings for Desire or something.

Until further notice, the doctor will no longer be seeing patients...

Tuesday... or Wednesday...

Remember the shit I said about the days bleeding together? Well, that was nothing compared with this.

I'm on suspension from my job and restricted to campus like a fucking prisoner until Saturday, when I'm supposed to meet with Knox in his office, of all places. That's two days... no, *three* days away.

Word came down last Friday evening. They had some snot-nosed peon deliver it to my door. He was hiding behind two guards when he handed me the letter and said something like "Make sure you show up on time."

Knox rarely, if ever, invites people to his office. That was the next thing that went through my mind after I thought about reaching between those two guards and choking the life outta that peon.

"Maybe Charlie Knuckles has some extra." That's what I told the peon to tell Knox.

I wasn't really gonna ask Charlie because he had already made it clear that what he gave me last time was the most he could spare. You have to understand how guys like Charlie think. In his mind, I'd be calling him a liar. That's enough to provoke a hot-lead beatdown in our little world of insecurity and mistrust.

But I had to say something.

Next, I put in a call to the lab rats over at the greenhouse. I wanted to know if they had anything that I might be able to use as a substitute for morphine. Apparently, Knox had gotten to them already because they wouldn't even take my call.

I called Graham and told him that I've got a case and a half of Supernova left over from the last batch that the lab rats made up for me. I've also got a few vials of codeine, a couple baggies of 'shrooms, and four Zs of weed. But you didn't hear that from me.

I don't usually go out of my way like that for people, but Graham is a friend (at a time when friends are hard to come by), and the lab rats were going to toss all the remaining vials of Supernova because Artemus refuses to sell the homemade stuff except to the hospital for emergencies. I told Graham that I could just give him the whole thing if he wanted. That way it would save him a stop with the new restrictions and all.

Graham joked that I was trying to avoid him. I took it as his way of saying he liked our hang-out time as much as I did. Technically, he was supposed to get his drugs from Artemus now; because, like I said, Artemus refuses to sell the homemade stuff, we would be breaking the law—twice.

"Then I guess we'll hafta be extra careful then, won't we?" Graham said when I told him all that.

"Extra careful doesn't allow for much hang-out time, though."

"Ain't always about the quantity, son. Sometimes it's the little moments that last the longest."

I told Graham that I was gonna have to have Ace get it to him, at least until the heat on me dies down a bit. Just to be safe. We'd have to have our hang-out time over the two-way until then. He agreed that it was probably a good idea.

The two-way has only a 16-mile maximum range in optimum conditions, so I have to plan the calls around his weekly visits.

They might as well've confined me to my room. It's getting so bad around here that people are ignoring the Geiger counters' warnings just so they can gather in rowdy groups and snarl and bark at the guards on the other side of the police barriers that Knox had put up outside City Hall and the tavern. They want blood. No way I'm steppin' into that quicksand.

Ace stopped by and told me that they're shoveling all kinds of shit with my name on it to keep the crowds at bay. Won't be long before they find their way over to my building. Artemus denied my request to have guards posted outside my door. Gave me some short answer about limited resources and priorities. I pushed the subject, and he told me how he really felt.

"I wouldn't even waste those guards in the lobby on your sorry ass if it were up to me," he said.

Well, that's nice to know.

I guess they're saying that the bodies of these latest RS victims had weird, "puncture-like" marks on 'em. "Like from a needle," Ace said. He went on to say that the bodies were buried right away. No ceremony or nothing.

"On whose word?" I asked.

"City Hall's," he said. Then he nodded at my reaction, as if to acknowledge the implications. "They're twisting it to sound like *you* ordered it, though."

"What makes them think I've got the authority to pull off something like that?" I asked.

"Beats me, man. But they're thinkin' it."

Dr. Scapegoat, I thought. I pictured Chalk with a big grin on his face, peeking at me through the skin-flake cloud. *How appropriate…*

At least I *thought* I thought it, but I must've said it out loud, because Ace said, "There's another theory going around, and this one's got nothing to do with you," in a way that suggested (to me anyway) that he was trying to console me. Whatever it was, I was betting on it to be the "bottom of it" that we were trying to get to.

Know what he told me? He said that people were saying that the puncture wounds in the RS victims' bodies were caused by fangs.

"Like from a snake?" I asked, just to give him the benefit of the doubt.

"Vampires, believe it or not," he said.

I could tell by the way he shook his head that he didn't believe it either. So much so that it embarrassed him to have to say it. That counted for something, at least.

"I guess Bigfoot and Nessie are passé anymore, huh?" I said jokingly.

He didn't laugh.

"So, what do *you* think it is? What's killing 'em, I mean?"

206

I asked.

Personally, I'm leaning toward a serial killer—probably a woman. I know what I said before about some new kind of toxin, but just hear me out. I say it's a woman because of the fact that the bodies had no visible marks, no signs of struggle or of being restrained, or anything. She was probably able to get close enough to her victims to inject them with something. That might explain the puncture marks. They used to call those kinds of killers "Black Widows."

I was all ready to have an interesting dialogue about all that when Ace said, "Wratha God, man. You know what they say about the Tribulation."

Really? I mean... *really*?

I would've never pegged Ace for a God-head. Ah, well, I didn't sweat it. Blaming God isn't as ridiculous as some of these other theories. I mean it is, but it isn't.

I thought about Ace's expression when mentioned the vampires. He probably thinks they're demons instead. In that case, it *is* just as ridiculous.

"Some people are talking about questioning the hook-ers," Ace said. "They're saying they had contact with some of the victims. Not sure if that's true or not, but..."

I can see how people might suspect the hookers (especially considering my new theory), but that's just too easy. Besides, I know plenty of their customers who're still walking around—myself included.

I know: former customer... But I *was* still seeing 'em when these recent RS deaths started.

"What happened to this... ghost... or vampire... or whatever: the one who likes to hover outside people's windows?" I asked in a dismissive tone.

"Haven't heard much about that lately. Oh... wait... I guess I *did* hear that somebody said they saw her wandering around the cemetery down in the 'hood. But that's about it."

"How serious are they about the hookers?" I asked.

"Serious."

"What the fuck, man?" I said in an exasperated tone. I was thinking of Desire's safety.

"Nothing yet on Knox and the morphine," Ace added. "But I'm on it."

I gave him a short list that included a request for an official guard-style Rina bugsuit (preferably size medium), instructions on getting the Supernova to Graham, and a message for Charlie Knuckles that read as follows:

Knuckles,

City Hall's putting the squeeze on me. Might need your help. Keep your ears on. More later.

-Goodvibe

I realized how much I was asking, so I told Ace that if he did this for me, I'd get him whatever he wanted when I get back on my feet. I stressed the importance of finding out what Knox wants with the morphine, too. Didn't tell him why, but I'm sure he has a good idea that I'm looking for something to use as leverage. Good thing Ace is such a fiend for the green stuff.

I wonder what Knox is really up to, what he's trying to hide. I keep trying to make the pieces fit: puncture wounds, rushed burials, morphine....

I find myself obsessing over Desire as sort of an escape. Knowing what I know now, I can't help worrying about her, though.

At a time like this, I could really use a trip to Main Street to lay my eyes on her. One look and my problems would seem like a minor inconvenience. The idea of glomming off her aura, touching her, or just trying to see those seductive green eyes through her tinted goggles gives me an itch that I can never seem to pin down. It reminds of withdrawal; Desire is my addiction. The only way to stop it (barring a visit to the Main) is to rub one out. But sometimes you just don't feel like going through all the preparatory shit, or dealing with the shame that comes on the heels of a busted nut.

I know what you're thinking: that I brought all this on myself for causing a scene with Artemus. The guy had it coming. From what I hear, he's been fucking up orders left and right. Prolly figured my job was easy, that it was all about moving product as quickly as possible.

Couldn't be more wrong. You have to know how to talk to the customers, how to make them feel at ease. I coulda told him that when he asked me if there was anything he should know, but I was thinking strategically. Now I got him calling me all the time with stupid questions.

I've been making it a point to keep myself busy—well, except for the first few hours, which I spent wallowing in self-pity and racking my brain for a way off campus without being seen. Got myself so worked up that I punched a hole in my wall…. Okay, three holes…. Okay, five.

There are a thousand things to do around my apartment, things that I've been meaning to take care of but never got around to, for whatever reason. Today is the day I set aside to tackle all that stuff, so I put on some Zeppelin and got to work.

I did laundry. I straightened up and vacuumed. I rearranged furniture. I did more laundry. I straightened up some more. I re-rearranged furniture. I tried to lose myself in the repetition (and the music), but I kept getting interrupted by random banging, jackhammer tremors, and the two-way doing a cheesy ringtone version of Wagner's "Ride of the Valkyries." The ringtone was just loud enough that I could hear it creeping beneath the music coming from the stereo.

I checked the number on the LCD screen. Fucking Artemus... most likely with another stupid question, too. I stood in complete limbo, trying to decide whether or not I should answer.

A knock at the door, I think... it scared a fart outta me. Now I was all heated. Well, maybe "heated" is too strong of a word, but you know that feeling when something mundane startles you, and you feel silly for reacting like that once you realize what it is? I guess "annoyed" would be a better word.

I was not quite convinced that it wasn't just in my mind, so I stood there listening with my ear tilted toward the...

There it was again. Definitely a knock.

"Who is it?" I called out, wondering if whoever it is could hear my voice over Robert Plant's sexualized wailing.

"Ah, it's building security, sir," a stern (almost too stern) male voice said.

Sir??? That's a first.

"There's... been an emergency. We might require your assistance out here."

Emergency?

I made sure to stand beside the door and lean as I look through the peephole. I've seen far too many movies where some chucklehead gets shot through the door.

Sonofa...

I recognized the guy right away. It's one of my customers. Some dude named Felix, a family man who likes the nose candy. I think he's a desk jockey in City Hall or something equally insignificant.

Talk about customer loyalty. Apparently, he had gotten desperate enough to find my address and sneak past the guards in the lobby. Bastard's taking a serious risk coming here. Society Hill resident or not, the guards'll shoot his ass in a heartbeat for trespassing.

He apologized for deceiving me and asked if he can come in. I ignored the apology, and the question, and demanded that he speak his piece through the door.

He said that Artemus has some guard doing the orders for him and that the guy mixed up his order with some kind of synthetic that he had set aside for his own personal use. As a result, Felix's wife went into convulsions and had to be rushed to the emergency room.

A name comes to mind: Cowell, Sergeant Cowell to be precise. He's in charge of the front-gate patrol, and he's a real junkie for the synthetics.

"I was so angry that I was seriously considering offing the shithead," Felix says. "But where would that get me, right?"

"I feel your pain, brother," I told him, "and I wish I could help you, but I'm on thin ice as it is. Sorry."

He didn't leave right away. I could hear him cursing me through the door even after I turned the volume up on the stereo.

Felix wasn't the last customer to find his way to my door. Well, I assumed they were all customers. I stopped answering the door after the second one came knocking with some bullshit about a fire downstairs.

The constant interruptions eventually pulled me out of my domestic busywork coma. I did a little window gazing. I flipped through a few old magazines that I keep as reminders of the way things used to be.

Yeah, so I've got a sentimental side. So what?

Nothing seemed to be working. The two-way kept ringing. The construction. The fucking Geiger counters going nuts outside. I couldn't concentrate with all that crunchy static.

At some point, the knocking stopped. A good 15 minutes had gone by with no knocking on my door. The construction noises stopped soon after. The Geiger counters were still going strong, though. And I could hear something else… like distant

211

voices. Coming from outside.

I went over to the window and followed the voices down to the courtyard in front of my building. I saw people standing around like something bad just went down. They were staring at the building and pointing. I tried, but I couldn't see what they're looking at. Frustrated, I hurried over to the couch, scooped up the remote, and switched on the television.

Channel 5

Commotion. Screaming. Voices stepping over each other. They jumped out at me from the television as I waited for the screen to adjust. Wait a minute... I recognize that voice. That one, too...

Guards were everywhere. A few of them are customers of mine. I recognized the markings on their bugsuits. It took a moment to register that the footage is from the lobby of my building. Right downstairs...

I had a "Holy shit!" moment, and then I leaned in closer to the screen "on pins and needles," as my mother used to say.

Looked like one of the Robogeeks was right outside in the courtyard, filming the scene through the glass walls that surround the lobby. One of the giant panes had been shot out. The guards inside were yelling at one another. I couldn't tell if they're angry or just trying to talk over all the noise. Broken glass was everywhere. There were bullet holes in the walls... and bodies... two of them, sprawled out on the floor. Felix?

Fucking jackhammer musta drowned out the gunfire.

I felt a lump in my chest. My pores widened. I struggled to keep my thoughts from dwelling on how Knox and City Council could (and would) manipulate the shootings to justify my ousting from Rina if it came down to that. Exile is my worst-case scenario.

Anxiety traveled down from my brain in the form of a muscle spasm, goose bumps in its wake. It reached my arms, my hands, and my fingers. It caused my thumb to press down on the channel button.

My head got away from me as I flipped through the working stations—all six of them, and all news-related. The working stations are all spread out (5, 19, 36, 60, 84, and 109), with endless static-filled channels between them. I guess I could just use the television's "Add channel" feature to program them in, but I don't want to risk possibly missing something. New stations come and go all the time.

Then I remembered the National News. Today is the day of Linda Ludlow's Ergeister interview.

Shit! Did I miss it?

I punched in…

Channel 36

Now, I'm not usually one to get all jazzed about a TV program. I was just curious to see how all this unfolds between Ergeister and McLaughlin City.

The interview was already underway by the time I tuned in. Linda was sitting across from some refined hippie-type who had salt-and-pepper half-hair (halfway between long and short), a shaggy, gray beard, and an earring in his left ear. He kept running his hand through his hair (front to back) to keep it out of his face. He was dressed in a daddy sweater and khakis. The ensemble seemed forced, like something he wouldn't normally be caught dead wearing. A strategic move, no doubt. The caption on the bottom of the screen read "Larson P. Hemmings, High

213

Priest-Elect, Church of Earthbound Flesh, an Ergeister Church."
I gave an internal smirk to the ridiculously complicated title and to
how uncomfortable he looked as Linda repeatedly smacked him
upside the head with questions. The interview was intercut with
video footage of daily life in an Ergeister community.

They live almost exclusively indoors. Clean streets and
glossed-over destruction exist on the outside. Entire neighborhoods have been completely rebuilt and connected by enclosed
corridors, some as wide as a four-lane street. The walls of the
corridors are decorated with posters and mini-billboards for local
businesses and for the Ergeister Church. An attempt has been
made to create a feeling of space, more like a city street and less
like a glorified subway concourse. High-tech equipment and vehicles and surveillance cameras are everywhere. Security out the
ass.

Crowds travel back and forth through the corridors, families and regular folks going about their lives. All are armed—men,
women, and children. They don't even try to conceal their weapons. I see all kinds of weapons: handguns, shotguns, hunting knives,
and machetes. They seem to have adopted a general uniform that
everyone wears—a variety of earth-toned jumpsuits with hidden
pockets galore and hooded, blazer-style jackets over top. The
jackets are shorter and tapered at the waist for women. No one
is wearing a mask. Small backpacks have been built into their
jackets. The backpacks contain emergency "save your ass from
radiation" kits that include a gas mask, a hypodermic, and a couple
vials of pentetate zinc trisodium and pentetate calcium trisodium.
I own a kit myself. Got it from one of my customers as barter for
two keys of blow.

Brief testimonials from random folks followed. They smile
and wave for the camera. Life is good. A woman holding a baby
in her arms talks to the camera about how it took such a tragedy
as the war to give her the family she always wanted.

The camera cut to the Larson Hemmings' pleased reaction.

I wonder if he's really that stupid that he doesn't smell the set-up.

Apparently so…

The sucker-punch came in the form of footage of rarely seen Ergeister ceremonies. It started out mundane, with shots of various Ergeister communities involved in similar rituals and large crowds gathered around totems and flaming effigies of Ergeister deities.

Hemmings tried to speak, but Linda kept him bobbling syllables with what might just be the longest accusatory question on record. She has taken the kitchen-sink approach, using clever methods to incorporate everything into one comprehensive outburst. The McLaughlin incident. Aube Nouvelle and Sunrise. The claims of cultism. The strange, clothing-optional ceremonies. Human sacrifices and cannibalism. The outright murder of their own members—"Ceremonial or not," she adds.

It's a dangerous game she's playing. Exciting, but dangerous.

The images continued to come and go as she talked. Strange, theatrical church services are displayed. Spooky-looking statues loom over lavish altars. One popular figure looks sorta clownish with a touch of those gray alien things that supposedly couldn't keep their hands offa people in the '70s and '80s.

None-a-this stuff is news to anyone, by the way. It's just the first time most folks outside the Ergeister communities are seeing it with their own eyes. Kinda takes away some of the mystery, if you ask me. Doesn't mean I ain't gonna look, though.

The footage got around to the clothing-optional ceremonies.

I leaned closer to the TV.

Sex—ceremonial sex, but naked bodies thrusting and

writhing just the same.

Closer…

Orgies…

Closer…

Sacrifices…

Whoa! I leaned away, startled by the images and mildly disgusted, yet curious… maybe even fascinated.

Shots of lethal obstacle courses claiming victims… some guy gets impaled on a trap made of spiked branches. Another guy activates a tripwire and sets an elaborate booby-trap in motion. The look in his eyes while he watches this happen is… *whew!*

Seeing it coming like that must be awful. I turned away and listened. I heard a whirling sound and a springing, like flung metal. Something sharp cut through the air. Impact. I heard the poor guy cough and choke. He's trying to speak.

These are members of the church dying like this. There's something extra-fucked about an organization that does that kind of shit to its own people.

The Geiger counters sneaked through a quiet moment. Angry voices swimming in the crunchy static.

The lobby!!!

I hit the quick-view button.

Channel 5

A crowd has formed outside the lobby of my building. Looks like friends or coworkers of the dead guys in the lobby standing in front. They're yelling at the guards that rally around their colleagues inside. The crowd outside was made up of looky-loos and busybodies. Some of them happened to be members of

216

the Citizens' Brigade who made their way over from the tavern. They're easy to pick out from the others because they're carrying signs with photos of recent RS victims on them. I recognized some of the folks in the photographs.

Waitaminute…

One of the Brigade's rejects mentioned my name. "And that goes for Mayor Knox, City Council, *and* that glorified pharmacist who calls himself Dr. Goodvibes," were the guy's exact words. Not sure what he said before that, but it gave me the icy fingers just the same.

Man, this is *sooo* fucked.

The guards were yelling at the crowd to "Stay back!" I heard people calling the guards "cowards" and "murderers," and repeating over and over that they (the guards) "didn't hafta shoot 'em."

I hit the quick-view.

Channel 36

Larson Hemmings had that look on his face that politicians get when some reporter lobs a comment about an embarrassing, personal indiscretion out of left field. Sort of a calm scowl, I guess you'd call it.

His lips curled away from his teeth on certain words. I could tell that he wanted to lean forward and pop Linda Ludlow across the mouth. She's been a thorn in the Church's side from the beginning. I'd pay to see that just so we could finally get a glimpse of Mizz P. in action.

I couldn't help but develop a sudden respect for the old bat. Her spunk reminded me of Cronkite and Rather in the '60s and '70s. As good as I suspect she might be, Mizz P. can't beat an entire army. Hemmings could have his people disappear both of their asses in the blink of an eye, but that doesn't stop Linda from going for the gusto with that jerkoff. Of course, they'd be stupid to try anything like that. Linda's got the most popular show in what's left of the country, maybe even the world. And she's a resident of a Federal community. The American Government might not be the powerhouse that it once was, but they still have the technology and the numbers to pose a threat.

"You call your organization a safe haven... a 'beacon of light in dark times,' to quote your literature. I'm just trying to understand how an organization that stresses peace and oneness with the Earth explains the outright murder of its own members," Linda said.

"You're glib... you're being glib," Hemmings replied. "You're passing judgment on things that you know nothing about."

"Oh, c'mon, Mr. Hemmings..."

"'High Priest-Elect' or 'Priest Hemmings' will be fine, thank you."

"Lest you think the rest of the world is naïve regarding your organization's questionable ideals and the things that go on in your communities, let me assure you that..."

"There you go again, trying to twist and turn and manipulate the rituals and practices that we hold sacred into something you can sink your teeth into."

"That's not at all what I'm trying to..."

"The prisoners that we use..."

"No, you've misunderstood me..." Linda says.

"The *PRISONERS*... that we use in our hunts have all been convicted of capital crimes—and I understood you perfectly, by the way. Each of the prisoners in that footage chose his fate over a quicker, more humane death as a ceremonial sacrifice. We have been training to survive these very times that are upon us since before either of us were born, Ms. Ludlow. *Each* and *every* one of our members is a dedicated child of Ergeister and, as such, a fearless soldier in the Ergeister Army, willing to lay down his or her life to ensure the survival of our way of life. You've seen what it's like out there, out in the wasteland.... Violence and death. And that's if you're lucky. We educate our members... our *soldiers*... about the dangers that lurk beyond the borders of our communities. We pull no punches in training to prepare them to face those dangers. To give one's life in the courses is to become one with the spirit of the hunt: a spirit-guide, if you will, for all those who come after them."

"You make it sound so nice and neat... as if you were talking about summer camp or something."

Hemmings' patience is wearing thin.

"Perhaps you should take a lesson from the rest of the country, Ms Ludlow, and let Mary Mezerak and her kin rest in the hell they created for themselves in *this* life," he said. "I fail to comprehend why someone who is so revered by so many as a symbol of strength and superior intellect would continue to allow her unresolved issues with that unfortunate period to color her views."

Linda gave Hemmings a look that said, "You can't hurt me with your childish kung fu skills."

Well, maybe she wouldn't have used those exact words, but that kind of vibe... ya know?

She leaned closer to him, like a teacher would in the face of a troublesome student.

"Young man, do you really think that there's anything you could pull out of that manipulative little head of yours that I haven't seen or heard before? Look, I understand the demands of running a successful campaign, how they can overwhelm you, make you say and do things that might go against your better judgment, make you forget who you are for the sake of the greater good. Believe me. I've interviewed quite a few politicians in my time. Men much bigger than you."

"Is there a point to all this?"

"Absolutely, there is. A very simple point that I think you'll find useful if you'd just listen."

Hemmings looked like he's gonna blow, sittin' there with this face stuck on bottled tension, like he's performing an internal countdown.

Mizz P. was standing closer to Linda than before. Arms crossed same as before.

I didn't even see her move.

"Ms. Ludlow, it's not my intention to have this interview deteriorate into a verbal sparring match."

"Nor is it mine. Now, if you'd just listen for a moment, you might learn something."

"I'm not going to sit here and…"

"My point is…"

"…ALLOW YOU to speak to me as if I were some…"

"MY POINT IS… that you should choose your battles wisely."

That got his attention.

"Now you're making threats?" he said. "Do you realize where you are?"

Mizz P.'s arms dropped to her sides. She stepped closer. Linda waves Mizz P. off without looking. Sometimes you forget about her hands until you see 'em. Kinda fucks with your perspective.

"You didn't let me finish," she says. "I was going to elaborate that while you might see the Revenant Clan as a minor blemish on your glorious record, there are people out there, *families* out there who are still reeling from the things they did to their loved ones. There are entire communities—Ergeister communities—that were established through violence and death by *Mary Mezerak and her kin*, as you call them. You think that you can just wash over that kind of resentment with religious proverbs and a couple coats of paint... and tunnels? Don't be fooled by the tranquil atmosphere that you-all have created for yourselves here. The world is a volatile place, Mr. Hemmings. People aren't going to wait for concrete proof before deciding to act on what they see as injustice. The fact is that people *do* associate you with the Clan, and it only helps to solidify their mistrust when your organization pops up again in association with some senseless act."

"You're referring to the McLaughlin incident, I presume?"

"Primarily, yes. Unless there's something else you'd like to confess."

"It's exactly that kind of attitude—which lends itself to biased reporting—that continues to cast our organization in a negative light. If you were truly interested in fair and balanced reporting, you would've mentioned our meeting with the McLaughlin folks, during which we resolved this whole misunderstanding."

"*Misunderstanding*? Interesting choice of words."

"My point exactly. You're going to believe what you're going to believe, no matter what I say. I'm not going to waste anymore time trying to convince you otherwise. And to put a period on this Mary Mezerak business, yes, it's true that Mary and her associate Griffen Elam were raised in the church. Her father, Joshua, was a High Priest of the Church of 1000 Earthly Deities, a somewhat aggressive, shall we say, branch of Ergeister that was located in Huntingdon, Pennsylvania. Her father had high hopes for Mary to lead the flock after the Great Awakening, although I doubt his vision depicted her as the... undead *thing* she ultimately became. And the assertion that *we* as a collective body somehow created that monster couldn't be further from the truth. Yes, she was trained in the ways of survival, just like every other member. Sometimes that means taking a life to defend your own. But we don't teach murder for murder's sake. And if you're looking for an explanation for why she was the way she was, believe it or not, even we don't know. There is one theory that it was her father's doing, that he put a curse on her as he lay dying, stabbed to death by his own daughter because he wouldn't let her leave the Church. Like I said, that's only a theory; one that we weren't ever able to prove or else we would've acted earlier to exile her and her associate from the Church."

Linda tried to act like that little bit of information didn't totally knock her on her ass.

"Was anyone ever charged with the father's murder?"

"Joshua Ray had an explosive personality. Brilliant man… but he ran very hot and cold. It wasn't unusual for him to disappear for a few days to clear his head. As far as we knew, he had gone off somewhere to do just that. His body was never found, and Mary ended up staying with the Church, so the outcomes put that theory to rest, in my opinion."

WHOA-leee sheeyittt!!!

An explosion… It sounded close, so close that the shockwaves shook my feet out from under me. I landed on my ass and rolled onto my stomach. I kissed the carpet and waited for the windows to shatter, but it never happened.

Instead, I heard screaming. I heard what sounded like… like… chunks raining down—big chunks of concrete and glass and metal.

I still hear it.

I traced the sounds to estimate the distance of the explosion. Coulda been the tavern… or the hospital… or the greenhouse…. Could've even been City Hall. That would be something, wouldn't it? The thought of it got my heart racing.

I measured my distance from the window (about eight feet) as I contemplated crawling over to it, paratrooper-style, and looking out. But then my mind suggested a safer alternative. The TV.

Duh…

I literally slithered over to the couch and up onto the cushions. I kept my arms down by my sides and did it like the cartoons do when they're being sneaky. Don't ask me how I pulled it off. It just happened that way.

I fished for the remote. Remotes, along with inkpens, loose change, and various pieces of stationery, appear to be parts of a balanced diet for couches. My fingers probed the deep creases and valleys. In the background, I heard Linda Ludlow and Larson Hemmings going at it again on the TV. I tried to piece together the conversation as I heard it (peripherally) since the explosion. I think it all stemmed from a smartass remark Linda made in response to Hemmings' story about Mary and her father. Some crack about Ergeister having a spell to find missing persons.

I forgot about all that when my fingertips grazed a familiar configuration of soft, raised buttons. My hand lunged, snakelike, and clamped around the remote. I yanked it from between the cushions and pressed quick-view….

Channel 5

Channel 5 showed a split-screen of the crowd outside my building on one side and a wide shot of Center Square on the other. The crowd outside my building was looking up, all "It's a bird, it's a plane, it's Superman" like.

Ohhh *man*, it *was* City Hall. Looked like the fifth or maybe the sixth floor. Maybe both. Knox's office is on five.

Oh man…

On the ground, there was debris everywhere. People were kneeling over screaming bodies, dragging the wounded out of harm's way, walking around in a daze, cursing whoever set off the explosion. Guards milled around anxiously, not knowing whether to help or to prepare to defend themselves.

The majority of the crowd from the tavern and City Hall stood back a good 100 feet from the temporary barricades, looking up with their mouths hanging open, like their whole world just got rocked. The windows on the two sides of the building that I could see were completely blown out, exposing City Hall's guts.

The scene cut to a replay of the explosion. One of the Robogeeks was positioned behind the crowd outside the tavern, shooting over the tops of their heads.

Ohhh mannnn...

It was huge. There was a bright white flash, immediately followed by a rush of red-orange smoke that billowed out in all directions before the sound of the explosion reached the crowd. The sound came seconds later and seemed to take everyone by surprise. The camera shook. Screaming and panic. The picture went berserk, then froze on the crowd ducking for cover and running scared.

The picture returned. The camera angled up to the fifth floor of City Hall and zoomed abruptly. Smoke-trails fell like spider legs from the main cloud that engulfed the face of the building. Debris rained down and took out a few slowpokes.

Ohhh mannnn...

Chapter 13

Rina, Ohio – 2006
The Plan...

Figures Artemus would be one of the two survivors of the explosion. They say Councilman Sam Hewitt (the other one) might pull through, but it's a longshot. Until then, Artemus is mayor by default. It was just the push I needed to get my ass outta here.

Some good people here in Rina. For their sakes, I hope Hewitt makes it. I'd hate to see what this place'll become under Artemus' leadership. People think it's bad now.

Sorry to break it to ya, folks, but these past two weeks—lockdown, the door-to-door searches, all that—has only been a taste of the chaos that shit-fer-brains'll bring down on this place.

The plan is simple enough. I'm going to stay at Graham's place in Revival—for a while at least. Feel things out. Maybe even set up shop. Graham tells me they're looking. That's one of those things I've gotta see for myself, though.

I was surprised when he volunteered his place. Staying with Graham was a thought that had never even crossed my mind—not because of anything wrong with him. It just hadn't. Guys his age are usually set in their ways. I wouldn't have thought he'd have the tolerance for a couple with our kind of... baggage.

That would be Desire and me, in case you were wondering. Of course, she doesn't know about it yet. I know she'll say yes once she weighs her options, though. The girls haven't done any business since the explosion. They're prisoners in their own homes, just like everyone else. And it's only gonna get worse. How could anyone in her right mind turn down my offer?

I've got my presentation polished to perfection. I'm gonna roll right up to her place and hit her with my "A" game.

"We'd be helping each other," Graham said when I told him that I didn't want to burden him with my… situation. "I could do with the company—and the sights… if you don't mind my sayin'."

It hit me late. He was talking about Desire. I remember thinking, *Should I be worried about that?*

I had originally planned to do it during the funeral tomorrow (Saturday), but Artemus is shutting the city down completely, and I wouldn't be able to move around without being noticed. Instead, it's going down this coming Monday morning while Artemus is busy with the daily announcements. The "daily announcements" is something new he instituted to remind everyone of exactly who wears the pants around here now. The guards are the only people allowed to roam during the announcements, so I'm gonna use the bugsuit that Ace swiped for me to blend in with 'em and make my way to the campus garage. Ace will be waiting for me there.

Come to find out he's running too. He'd made plans to shack up with some chick he'd met only a couple times while working security for the Rina supply-drivers. And she was from one of these Christian communities, too—some place deep in the heartland. The sucker was already calling her his girl.

But who am I to criticize? That soft heart of his made him more sympathetic to my situation with Desire. As far as he knows, she's *my* girl, and we've been keeping our relationship under the radar. I remember how he reacted when I first told him that. He looked at me like he thought I was getting in over my head or something.

I'm sure he's heard stories, I thought at the time. *Maybe he's even been with her.*

I had to stop myself from getting caught up in it. I reminded myself that Desire is a hooker. *That's her job. At least until I take her away from all this.* Back then, I didn't have a plan, though. It was more or less just wishful thinking.

We're gonna make the trip in one of the two official Humvees equipped for wasteland travel. Ace had fake delivery forms made up to show his buddies at the gate and at the off-campus checkpoint. "By the time they realize what happened, we'll be long gone," he said.

Not very godly of him, huh?

Ace's girl's place is on the way to Revival, so he's willing to drop me off. His price is whatever weed I've got left. Done. And done.

Then here comes Graham with his own plan. He said he'd been sittin' on a souped-up '95 Mercedes S-Class that used to belong to the son of one of the old Medellín Cartel bigshots. He went down the list of features like he was trying to sell me the damn thing.

Bulletproof.

Hood-mounted machine guns.

Rear-firing rocket launchers.

Oil slick.

"Did you say 'oil slick?'" I asked.

"Yeah, brotha. It's a trip," Graham said. "This ol' girl was wasteland equipped before there was a wasteland. Real James Bond shit."

Did you notice how I've been upgraded from "son" to "brother" now that we would be living together? I certainly did.

"She'll do zero-ta-60 in five and a half seconds, easy. And let me tell you, brotha, speed is the key out in the shit. Fuck all-lat armor-plating, slowin' you down."

Drivers and their theories. Speed is the key. Stealth is the key. Weaponry is the key. Strength in numbers. Sometimes I forget that Graham is one of them.

"You should see ma-truck," he says. "Ol' heffa moves like molasses when I'm haulin' a full load. S'why it pays to know your routes, brotha. No use take'n shortcuts when they have you ride'n right into an ambush."

"So the right route is the key?" I said like a smartass. I think Graham thought I was serious.

"It is if you wanna come back from your run in one piece."

Graham wanted to meet up at the old Becker Auto Removal and Salvage Yard at the intersection of Adkins and Main off campus. Apparently, the drivers liked to meet there to swap goodies and war stories before officially signing in on the Hill to unload their haul. Graham made sure to point out that the shop was only two-and-a-half blocks from the Taint.

"You can have your girl hook up with us there," he added.

Graham, like Ace, is under the impression that Desire knows she's coming with us. I couldn't imagine why….

That was a joke, by the way.

I felt bad for turning down Graham's offer. I understood where the gesture had come from and what it said about his opinion of me as a friend. But let's be serious: Graham ain't exactly in his prime, and there were just too many variables involved for his plan to work. Maybe I could've overlooked one or two things, but making it from my building all the way to Becker Auto on my own was unlikely.

We're talking one straight shot with Ace, and in an official Humvee to boot.

"No offense," I said to Graham, "but I'd rather be sitting behind a couple sheets of armor-plating when the ugly shit comes out there. Besides… I've ridden in those babies lots-a-times, and they're fast enough for me. I'm sure you understand."

I could sense that Graham was disappointed. He didn't actually say anything or speak in any kind of tone that would indicate that, but I could tell. In the end, we agreed that the important thing was that I make it to his place safely.

The Funeral

The entire city was on lockdown. The "terrorists" (as Artemus was calling them) who were responsible for the explosion that killed Mayor William "Wild Bill" Knox and all but one of the members of City Council had yet to be apprehended. They were in a meeting when the bomb went off. C4 and M1 military dynamite. Councilman Sam Hewitt, the only survivor, was laid up critical in the hospital.

Artemus believed that *he* might be next in line for a sneak attack. His first act as interim mayor was to round up every last member of the Citizens' Brigade and have them interrogated. When that failed to turn up any clues, he went after private citizens— rebellious types, troublemakers, and anyone else he saw fit to have brought in for questioning. If anyone protested, he threatened to have him arrested.

For safety reasons, the funeral was restricted to colleagues and associates. It was no coincidence that many of them were on Artemus' long list of suspects. He threatened to arrest anyone on his invite list who didn't show.

You could see the anxiety in the faces of the people who'd taken off their gas masks and in the uncomfortable body language of the people who kept theirs on. All of them together like this. It was the perfect opportunity for these "terrorists" to wipe out Rina's remaining VIPs in one shot. That's what was on their minds.

Standing somewhat numb, the audience faced forward, looking past the present, past the five white-oak coffins that lay side by side in the center of the altar. A framed 8" x 10" photograph of the occupant rested at a slant on top of each coffin. This might be the end of yet another community. For some of them, it would be their third or fourth time.

Guards, who were posted every 25 feet from the triple-bolted doors to the altar on the opposite side of the room, cradled large guns in large, beefy arms as they surveyed the crowd. They stood across from each other—two at the door, two in the middle of the room, and two on the altar (where Artemus stood, eulogizing the deceased).

Although there were still renovations to complete, the ceremony marked the official christening of the No-Frills Church. The campus theatre hadn't been used since the university held its last performance of *Death of a Salesman* there back in early '99, yet there were still framed posters touting the "Green Hill Players" and overdone theatre mainstays like *Of Mice and Men*, *Fences*, and *A Streetcar Named Desire*. The windows had been bricked up and painted over with faux stained-glass murals. The painted scenes depicted ordinary people overcoming hardship— the war, the aftermath, et cetera.

A skeletal grimace with faux stained-glass eyes and coffin teeth loomed over Artemus' head and shoulders as he rambled, primarily about William Knox, "the misunderstood visionary," into the microphone. He kept pausing when the music from the overhead speakers would reach a crescendo, looking all kinds of impatient as he awaited the end of another pipe-organ beatdown. He had asked for something "churchy" to play during the funeral. The closest they had was Bach's Toccata and Fugue in D minor.

Beethoven, Bach: It was all the same to Artemus.

"Who else among us would have had the wherewithal to turn a dead college campus into a bustling mini-metropolis?" Artemus posed, his eyes scrolling for hints of disapproval as he spoke.

The audience wasn't taking the bait. Half of them were only present in a physical sense; the rest were preoccupied with getting home safely and living through another day. The bombing and Artemus' "investigation" produced a climate of fear that made the days in Rina seem darker and the nights likely to gobble up anyone dumb enough to venture out and spit him out in pieces.

"Yes, we've made mistakes, but…"

A groan from the rear-left…

Artemus slid his eyes to the left and turned slightly. Unsure.

Artemus looked over his shoulder at the guard standing behind him. The guard's arms were folded across his chest. At this range (about 10 feet), the guy's gun looked a lot bigger than the others'. The barrel was partially wrapped in twine. A pair of feathers—one red, one white—plucked from a fairly large bird dangled from the end of the wrapped section.

The guard nodded.

Artemus nodded back, thinking, *Musta been hearing things.*

He cleared his throat and slid his eyes down to the sheet of paper where his speech (in Arial font and double-spaced, just as he demanded) was printed to find his spot. He was self-conscious. Had the audience seen his little moment with the guard with the feathered gun? *They're going to think you're weak if they did. Can't let them think you're weak. No, it was just a short pause… a look (a funny look?)… a nod. Coulda meant anything. Plus, why would they even care at a time like this? Shoulda wore your bugsuit, but noooo… you had to be Mr. Connect-With-the-People-on-a-More-Intimate-Level. Now look where it got you: your big, stupid face, hovering right where everybody can see it. And the cameras, too. Flippin' Horace.*

Horace Banks was Artemus' assistant. He had instructed Horace to have the Robogeeks film the funeral from the altar so as not to see his face the whole time, but they sat down in the audience, instead, their cameras pointing up at him.

After this crap, he's gone. Yep, definitely gotta go...

On the surface, Artemus seemed to have pulled himself together. He continued his speech where he left off.

"...mistakes that we have every intention of rectifying when..."

"A little late for that, amigo, don't you think?"

He heard the voice clearly this time, spoken through a gas-mask filter. It had come from the same place and resonated with the same cadence as the voice that produced the groan. It was a familiar voice, but he couldn't place it. Must have been the guard. No question it was the guard. But he was a big fucker with a big fucking gun.

Artemus knew that the audience most likely didn't hear it so he kept on talking until he could think of something.

"Bill, of course, wouldn't call them 'mistakes,'" Artemus said. "He would call them 'learning experiences.'"

But he was thinking: *What's this about? Is this a coup? I've only been in charge for a flippin' week, for crying out loud. Doesn't matter. Doesn't matter. Gotta be strong. Gotta show them you're strong. Gotta take control of the situation. Gotta take charge. Oh, and wipe that look off your face, dipshit. Remember: They can see you.*

"Bill would say that we could and *should* use those learning experiences to help us become better as a society," Artemus continued.

"Well, Bill ain't sayin' Jack-*shit* now... 'cause he's fucking *dead*!"

The voice was loud this time, loud enough that most of the audience heard it. It sounded so delighted to be saying such a horrible thing.

A collective gasp. An undertone of grumbling and the gas-mask tinniness sounded like a swarm of giant insects.

Artemus whipped around. His anger empowered him. "What is your name, soldier!" he growled.

The guard with the feathered gun looked right to left, channeling levity. He flexed his fingers and, with his wrist hanging limp, touched the tips to his chest in a manner that seemed to say, "Moi?"

Artemus turned to the guard on the other side of the altar. He pointed at Feathered Gun across the way and ordered, "Arrest this man!"

"Don't waste your time, amigo," Feathered Gun said. "He's with me."

Feathered Gun walked over and stuck his gun in Artemus' face. Artemus threw his hands up and cowered from the barrel's open-mouthed kiss. He went to scream, but the audience's horrified reactions drowned out his own. Guards from other areas of the room moved to handle the situation.

Feathered Gun snatched Artemus by the arm and pressed the tip of the barrel against his crotch. Using Artemus as a shield, he addressed the other guards.

"Take another step and I'll blow off his…" He changed his mind and tilted the barrel up. He pressed the tip against Artemus' temple. "Or I'll blow off his fucking head!"

The approaching guards held their positions.

Feathered Gun tilted his head down and whispered to Artemus, "Doubt you even know what balls are, amigo."

He ordered the guards to drop their weapons and instructed his accomplice to retrieve them and put them in a pile on the stage. He made one of the guards use the keypad on the doorframe to lock and alarm it. "That alarm goes off, and somebody's getting shot," he threatened.

"Who are you?" Artemus pleaded, his voice trembling. "Are you the one responsible for…"

"For blowin' your founding fathers to kingdom come? And what if I am, amigo? What are *you* prepared to do about it, huh? What are any of you gonna do about it?"

Feathered Gun spun Artemus into a single-handed choke and pulled him close. He snapped his gun-arm erect and swung it around to the audience. The audience began to panic, scattering and diving away from the pointed weapon.

"I got this," said the accomplice.

He had taken one of the guards' guns from the pile and was now going double-strapped to hold down the audience. He held the butts in his armpits to take the slack off of his biceps, forearms, and hands. Something about having a gun in each hand made men like the accomplice feel invincible, even if the weapons were entirely impractical, like these big hole-punchers.

"I'll tell you what you're gonna do, amigo," Feathered Gun said to Artemus. "You're gonna do the same thing you did for me when I lay dying out there in the shit. The same thing you did for my wife when she came to you looking for the truth about what happened to me. Nothing. Not a goddamned thing."

"Rah-mirez?" Artemus strained.

Ramirez reached up and peeled off his mask.

Artemus recognized that face even before the mask came all the way off. That deep, sienna complexion, the permanent five o'clock shadow: Das Ramirez was one of the very last people that Artemus ever expected to see again.

He had all the right components of a handsome man (squared jaw; sharp, cat-like features; and thick, wavy hair pulled into a tight ponytail), but they were arranged in a way that made him look almost alien.

Ramirez let his mask fall to the floor. He looked down and smiled at Artemus.

"That's right, amigo," he responded.

"But wait! I... I had nothing to do with..." Artemus began.

"Don't give me that bullshit. You were *there* in the truck

with the others. You were *there*! You coulda done something. You coulda told that *rulacho* to wait. You coulda told my Delilah the truth. Helped her through it. Done something. Anything. But you didn't, and she killed herself. You and your precious boss... and all your little hermanos in City Council—you-all might as well have pulled the trigger as far as I'm concerned."

Ramirez craned his arm down until Artemus appeared at the other end of the barrel. He was dug into the crevice where the podium stand met the floor, brandishing limbs, like a turtle on its back.

"No! Please!" Artemus begged. "I'll give you whatever you want."

"Really? Can you bring back my Delilah? Can you do that, amigo?"

Artemus didn't respond.

"I didn't think so. Now... what was it you were saying about your beloved Bill? That he would say to use an experience like this as a lesson, right? Isn't that what you said, amigo?"

Ramirez unsheathed a large hunting knife from his hip and nodded at his accomplice.

The accomplice nodded back. He let one of his two guns dangle by the strap and made a ready motion with his empty hand.

Ramirez pinched the blade and tossed the knife underhand.

The accomplice caught it by the butt and flipped it blade down. He walked over to the coffin with Mayor Knox's photograph on top. He swept aside the flowers and the photograph and worked the lid open.

The sight of Knox's charred corpse caused a swell in the background noise. He was decked out in his favorite ensemble—blazer, slacks, and a high-end casual tee.

A woman fainted, then another.

The accomplice turned to see what was going on. He

could see that the audience was wondering what would happen next. He glanced over at Ramirez, who nodded when their eyes met.

"Wh… whatever you have in mind, I'm begging you to reconsider…" Artemus whimpered.

"And I'm telling you to shut your fucking mouth and take your punishment like a man."

The accomplice was hunched over Knox's coffin, his arms reaching inside. His right arm worked vigorously in a sawing motion. He let out a grunt or two.

The accomplice put the knife down, rested his forearms on the lip of the coffin, and took a moment to slow his breathing.

"Let's go!" Ramirez scolded.

The accomplice jumped into gear. He reached back into the coffin and placed a hand on either side of Knox's head. He looked away and twisted to loosen the brittle bones and yanked on it (twice) until Knox's severed head snapped from his body. He tossed the head to Ramirez, who caught it like a football between his arm and his ribcage. The other hand was still holding his gun on the audience. He worked his hand around to the top of Knox's head and clutched a patch of singed hair. He walked the width of the stage and back with the head held out to the audience.

The accomplice stood back and covered him. He had a gun in each hand again, butts tucked in his armpits.

The pipe organ attacked.

The background vocals peaked—loud sighs and crying. Faces were frozen at "What the fuck!?"

There were no discernable features left on the bad side of Knox's face. It looked like the worst friction burn you could imagine, as if he turned his head away from the explosion and his features were smoothed over by hot wind traveling at maddening speed and replaced with blackened crust with a sort of sphincter-crescent where the corner of his mouth should've been. The good side retained some of Knox's former pigment, but it was bloated and decorated with freckle-lacerations and charred skidmarks. His only eye was rolled up and desiccated. His brow was frozen mid-wince. There was a recognizable mouth on this side. It was hanging open. Gums were red and black. Teeth were clenched.

"Some of you here today will be called upon to take on leadership roles if Rina is to survive the events that thisss... man and his people have brought upon this town. Let this be a lesson to all of you. *This*... is what can happen when you take the lives of others for granted, when you treat people differently based on their value to you and your colleagues in positions of power. I have shown you the fury that such arrogance can bring about. I urge you not to make the same mistakes."

Ramirez tilted his head down and ordered Artemus to get up.

Artemus sat there for a moment, wondering what to do. He played it off by acting like he didn't hear Ramirez' command and paid for it with a jab to the face with the barrel of the feathered gun.

"Oww!" Artemus cried out.

"Well, get your ass up then."

Artemus climbed to his feet like he was a novice at standing. He peered back toward the audience once his head cleared the podium. He was beyond worrying about how utterly useless he must have looked to everyone in attendance.

"Listen..." Artemus began. "If you'd just listen to me, I know that there's something..."

"I told you before, amigo: Unless you can bring my Delilah back, then you ain't got nothing to say ta-me. Understood?"

Artemus gave a tentative nod. The motion shook loose a tear or two.

Ramirez signaled the accomplice over. He handed Knox's

head to him.

"Hold it out so they can see it," he instructed. "Grab the patch of hair here…."

Ramirez pulled Artemus to the center of the stage by his arm.

Artemus was beginning to sense the end. He started to weep uncontrollably. Unintelligible sounds leapt out between breaths.

"No! Wait!" Artemus cried out. "Just… just let me explain…."

Slight physical resistance turned to panic. He tugged feverishly at Ramirez' sure grip, which clamped tighter around his bony forearm in response. Artemus was certain it was going to break. He almost welcomed the pain as a possible anesthetic for the soul-stirring terror that had turned his bones to liquid. He went limp in Ramirez' grasp.

"Have it your way," Ramirez said, as he let go and watched Artemus crumble to the floor.

Ramirez trained his gun on him and prepared to address the audience. He was suddenly overcome by a hot sensation. He could feel himself starting to perspire. This would finally be closure for him. It was a moment that he had been building up in his head since he decided that he was going to live despite the multiple bullet wounds and all the blood that he had lost as he lay there looking up at the sky after his buddy Chalk left him for dead.

"I'm aware that many of you had some knowledge of my situation," Ramirez said to the audience. "Knowledge that you coulda passed on to my wife when she came looking."

Roving glances and fidgeting outed the guilty. Ramirez took pleasure in their anxiety.

"Relax. Relax, amigos…" he said. "Today I am only interested in *this* man (pointing at Artemus). When I am finished here, you will never see… or hear from me again. Do not try to follow me. I have survived the worst barrios in East Los Angeles, walked the wasteland on the strength of my own two hands… I have killed men more capable than anyone you could think of sending against me. Many men. And I promise you: If you come looking, I will take you to a level of hell that'll make you question everything you thought you knew about violence and savagery."

Ramirez gave his words a moment to sink in and then shifted his focus to Artemus.

"Artemus Collins: You are hereby charged as complicit in the events that led to my being left behind to die in the wasteland; to the two months I spent hiding out in an old schoolbus shell, recovering from my injuries; to the additional month I spent out in that scavenger- and mutant-infested hell, ducking in and out of any dark space I could find at the slightest hint of danger as I made my way back here; and, ultimately, to the death…" He began to choke up. "To the lonely… pitiful death… of Delilah Ramirez… my wife."

Ramirez fought back his emotions. He cleared his throat and asked Artemus, "How do you plead?"

Artemus responded with sobbing and unintelligible sounds.

"Don't make me ask you again," Ramirez warned.

"What does it matter?" Artemus yelled. "You're going to kill me regardless of what I say."

Ramirez nodded, "You're right, there. But I wanna hear you accept responsibility for your part in…"

Suddenly, commotion in the audience began to build. Ramirez looked up and saw a gallery of holy-shit expressions. His accomplice hadn't seen it yet, but the head that Ramirez was holding (William "Wild Bill" Knox's head) had sprung to life, sprouting fangs. Knox's disembodied visage morphed through stages of confusion. His jaw opened and closed, testing its flexion. His one good eye had gone yellow-red. It rolled around a bit, then to the corner, as if to see what was behind him, restricting his movement.

The accomplice was wondering why the audience had suddenly stopped ducking the barrel of his gun as he swept it back and forth in a semi-playful manner. He felt something move in his hand, not directly up against it, but more like weight shifting slightly and causing the head to sway. He made a quick visual pass around the room and landed on Ramirez, who was looking at him and pointing. Then he heard a scream.

He turned Knox's head around to face him.

Knox looked as horrified as everyone else when his eye met the accomplice's bugged-out goggles. He opened the good side of his mouth and screamed and was startled by the shrieking hiss that came out.

The accomplice made a strange yelping sound and flung Knox's head away. He lifted his gun and chased it with a steady stream of gunfire, screaming, "Ahhhhhh! It's alive! Motherfucker's alive!"

Bullets tore into the far wall and sent bits of plaster, wood, and asbestos flying.

Knox's head hit the floor and bounced toward Ramirez. He was yelling to his accomplice to "Stop fucking firing," when the head... and then the bullets came at him.

"Shit!" Ramirez yelled and dived out of the way.

The audience went for the door in trample mode, kicking, screaming, and shoving their way through. The guards downstage ducked beneath the crowd and skulked toward the right side of the stage where their weapons were stacked.

The pipe organ bellowed. The door alarm sounded but the doors remained closed.

The accomplice's gun clicked empty. The sound snatched him out of panic-kill mode. In one smooth motion, he let the weapon dangle and replaced it in his grip with the other one.

"You all right?" He leaned toward Ramirez (who had rolled onto his stomach) and inquired with genuine concern.

Artemus woke up on his stomach, face to face with the floor, blood painted across his teeth. His tongue probed the lining of his mouth in search of the source: a laceration just inside his lower lip. He felt dampness against his inner thigh. He had soiled himself.

The last thing Artemus remembered was Ramirez' shouting at him about taking responsibility. He thought that maybe Ramirez had shot him and this was what it was like to wake up on the other side. The screaming and commotion were merely the audience's reaction to his death. Their level of distress was almost flattering.

Artemus lifted his face from the floor, half-expecting to see a tunnel with a bright light at the end. Instead, he saw Knox's head rolling toward him. It came to rest a few feet from his face, lying on its bad side. Knox's good eye opened and rolled around confused before focusing straight ahead. There was a spark of recognition. Artemus shook his head "no."

"Hellllpp mm…" Knox began with a coarse, bubbly accent. His mouth opened wide to compensate for the fangs and the rigid sphincter-crescent that impeded his speech.

Artemus panicked and batted the head away.

Ramirez rolled onto his side and tossed his accomplice the evil eye. Behind him, one of the other guards was creeping toward the pile of weapons.

"Heads up!" Ramirez yelled to the accomplice, who took the command literally and pointed his gun at Knox's head as it sailed through the air and down into the crowd. "No! Behind you!"

The accomplice shifted his aim and…

Ramirez sat up, snatched his gun into position, and fired

at the guard by the pile. The gun jammed, but not before a few rounds leaped out at the guard. Ramirez saw the man drop but couldn't be sure if he was hit.

A thunderous sound, like a giant foot stomping, resonated from center stage, pausing the commotion. Startled gazes traced the sound to the coffins. Whatever it was had knocked the framed photographs off of them.

Then, suddenly, Knox's coffin bounced. The same thunderous sound jumped out from underneath and caused the audience to cry out almost in unison.

Ramirez spotted another guard trying for the pile of weapons. He had climbed up the middle of the stage and was close enough to tackle him.

Ramirez sprung forward toward the man.

The accomplice sidestepped away from the coffin, whipping his head from it to the approaching guard, and fired. He hadn't accounted for Ramirez's sudden lunge, though.

The guard did a kind of football move where he motioned right and then dove left.

Large, messy bullet holes tracked up Ramirez' side from his waist to his armpit. Flayed skin flapped on blowback. Ramirez hit the floor like a bag of defective limbs.

The accomplice expected some kind of protest, something to indicate that Ramirez was angry with him but otherwise all right. He had seen the bullets punch through his side, but his mind was racing and taking wild, oafish strides that overstepped the obvious. Then it hit him.

"No," he whimpered, like a child learning of a pet's death.

He adjusted his aim and took out the guard who knelt beside Ramirez and was tossing guns to his colleagues offstage.

"Look what you made me do!"

The accomplice was in tears, walking forward, bullets diving out of starbursts at the tip of his weapon. He fired until the gun was empty. The guard's hole-punched body twitched and twitched. He was lying on his side. His leg was sliding and scraping the floor, bending at the knee and straightening, as if he were trying to take a step.

"Look what you made me do!" the accomplice continued to scream. His anger was so focused and passionate that he didn't think about the other guards offstage; he thought only of payback.

The accomplice lurched sideways, as if someone had come up from behind and punched him in the hip. He didn't realize that he had been shot until he looked down and saw the hole in his mangled bugsuit, bone jutting through. His left leg gave out and sent him stumbling. He was looking for a place to fall when he locked bug-eyes with the guard who shot him. The guard was standing just offstage, holding his gun like he was waiting for the accomplice to notice him.

The accomplice was already in mid-fall. He tried to swing his aim around to the guard. A bright flash smacked him square in the face. It was the last thing he would ever see.

Inside the coffin, Knox's headless body flailed and bucked until the coffin tipped over and rolled on top of him. The weight pinned him there momentarily. Onlookers recoiled when the body twitched, then bucked again. The coffin went flying and came down with a noiseless thud. The hall was now filled with the shrill screaming coming from the severed head that was being kicked around the stampede like a soccer ball. People in shock were standing on the pews, holding each other and screaming, their focus split between the floor and the headless body that had staggered to its feet and was loping drunkenly into pews, people, and anything else in its crooked path.

The pipe organ. The alarm...

A small group was crowded by the front door, fighting against the locks and punching numbers into the keypad until it

243

flashed, "System Malfunction! Contact Security Personnel!"

Muffled voices from the other side of the door kept instructing them to "Step away from the door!" But they were too frightened to listen, too flustered to understand that the voices meant to shoot the lock and free them.

Knox's head was trying to guide his body to it, but it never stayed in one place for more than a few seconds.

The three remaining guards were huddled by the stage. One of the guards lifted his gun and prepared to shoot the headless, flailing corpse. The guard standing next to him placed his hand on the barrel and guided it back down to his side.

"You're liable to hit one of them," the guard added, chin-checking toward the panicked audience. "Just hold tight. I'll get it when it comes this way. Better yet, you two go handle that (nodding toward the crowd) before they kill each other."

"I never would've believed it if I hadn't seen it with my own eyes," one of them said.

"Just go!"

Knox's headless body flailed to the rhythm of the pipe organ's maniacal ascent. It kept falling over people and things, getting back up, and blindly chasing the crowd from one side of the room to the other. He would occasionally close in on his head, only to have it kicked away at the last minute again and again.

The two guards ran up and tried to get the audience's attention. One of them fired his weapon at the ceiling. The audience jolted stiff and tracked their eyes up to the chips and plaster dust that rained down.

"Nobody move!" said the guard. Then he spread his arms and pushed with his body to herd the crowd toward the door.

The other guard went for the keypad. By then, it was hanging by multicolored wires from the doorframe.

The guard near the stage stood poised and watched the headless body with hawk eyes. Eventually, the form danced its way to the center aisle and followed the rolling, sliding head toward the stage. The guard squeezed the trigger. The bullet struck Knox's body in the chest, causing it to stagger. He squeezed the trigger again and again. The body staggered with each high-velocity blow but kept its balance. Black blood encircled the wounds.

The crowd got low in reaction to the gunshots.

The guard at the door heard the voices coming from the other side. They were his colleagues. They were discussing whether or not they should blow the doors.

With his ear turned to the door, the guard signaled to the other one, who was herding the crowd, to move into the pews and get down. Then he turned his mouth to the door and yelled into it, "All clear on this side! Gahead and blow the doors!"

He waited for a response.

"Stand back!" the muffled voice yelled.

The guard by the stage had lowered his aim to look for bright ideas. One came suddenly. He scanned the floor for Knox's head and found it lying motionless on its side beneath a pew. He couldn't tell if it was dead or just trying to hide. He lifted his gun and took careful aim. He could see Knox's body coming into his peripheral vision, stumbling with its hands out like a blind Frankenstein. Ol' Wild Bill Boris Karloff seemed to know where his head was now.

"Owa here… qh-wickly!" Knox's head commanded.

The muffled voice on the other side of the door shouted another warning.

"Fire in the hole!"

The guard ran and dived between the pews with the other folks. On his way, he repeated the muffled voice's warning:

"Fire in the hole!"

The guard by the stage watched Knox's body walk up

and stand over its head before squatting down and feeling around the floor until its fingers made contact. Knox grabbed his head in both hands and stood. Holding it at around chest level, Knox turned his head to one side and saw the crowd (plus one guard) curled up on the floor, hiding behind pews. They were covering their ears and burying their faces in their hands. He turned it to the other side and...

The guard by the stage squeezed the trigger. Knox's head (and most of his right hand) popped like a meat balloon and painted the floor, the walls, the pews, and a few of the people with black, chunky polka dots.

Knox's headless, one-handed body jumped erect. Even its remaining fingers and toes (which were slightly clawed) were flexed. It began to convulse right there in the aisle.

The front door exploded inward. Another group of guards ran in, waving big guns. The crowd ran out screaming from behind the pews. Sunlight made a beeline down the middle aisle and hit the headless, one-handed, convulsing body of William "Wild Bill" Knox like a strong gust of wind. He threw his back into a painful arch. His remaining fingers curled into rigid claws. Smoke billowed from beneath the cuffs of his sleeves and pant-legs. His skin appeared to be microscopic grains of ash held together in the shape of a body. A network of cracks started at his fingertips and raced up underneath the cuffs of his shirt. The convulsions suddenly stopped.

The headless, one-handed body rose from the floor as if lifted by invisible wires and was suddenly snatched backward into nothingness. It was accompanied by a loud suction. Only his clothing remained, empty and gliding to the ground like laundry blown from an outdoor clothesline.

A prolonged silence...

"Somebody mind explaining to me what the fuck just happened?" said one of the guards who had just run in.

The guard by the stage stood there, wondering if he had done the right thing.

"You there," said a voice from the stage behind him. It was Artemus. He was standing over Ramirez, who was still barely alive.

The guard turned slowly, like he didn't want to look away from the spot where the mayor's headless body was standing only moments ago.

"Your weapon. Give it to me," Artemus ordered.

The guard lifted the strap over his head and tossed his gun to Artemus, who bobbled it before gaining a secure hold. He was brimming with nervous aggression, his eyes swollen from crying, clothing disheveled. He wiped the lingering glaze of sweat, tears, and snot from his face and pointed the weapon down at Ramirez.

Ramirez coughed out a painful grunt and ran his fingers over the trail of jagged, circular wounds that traveled up his side. There was a moist sensation amidst the throbbing heat. It was blood, his blood. At this point, Artemus' presence was a nominal factor.

Artemus stood shaking, waiting for the right words to materialize. He hoped they would come before Ramirez looked up at him. Only one word came to mind when he finally did.

"Guilty," Artemus said as he pulled the trigger over and over. "Guilty! Guilty! Guilty! Guilty!"

Chapter 14

Rina, Ohio – 2006

Doesn't mean there's a God...

I don't know why, but it was one of the first thoughts to scroll through my mind after watching the footage from the funeral. So why then am I sitting here, trying to fit his existence into my logic? Guess it's better than worrying about what to say when Desire comes out of the bathroom.

I remind myself that I'm a man. *So act like one.* Probably told you this before, but Desire has a way of bringing out the 14-year-old, pizza-faced social retard in me. My tongue twists into knots. My palms sweat. She has that effect on me.

Not to bang my own drum, but I've partied with models and celebrities. I was the guy who could strike up a conversation with anyone, and here I am, rendered speechless by... by a hooker. As much as I don't like referring to Desire by that designation, that's what she is, right?

Maybe she *is* a vampire. Aren't they supposed to be able to seduce folks with their sheer presence?

That was a joke.

Becker Auto Removal and Salvage Yard is a nasty place. The apartment above the main office smells like sloppy, fat sex and open butt cheeks.

"Somebody's been doin' an awful lotta fuckin' up-n-*hee-auh*," Graham joked during the initial walkthrough.

"Either that or this place was built on some kind of Indian burial ground for sex addicts."

"Not funny," Kat said in that fucking voice of hers. We had only been together for about 20 minutes, and I already wanted to shove something in her mouth to keep her annoying ass quiet.

"Rome's jokes never are," Graham said with that genial arrogance of his.

"It's a talent," I added.

The place had been ransacked like 40 times over. There was shit everywhere.

"You guys use this place?" I asked Graham.

"Yeah, man," he responded.

"I've seen worse." Of course Kat had to throw in her two cents.

"I bet you have."

I intended the remark as a slight to her, but she didn't respond.

The walls on the first floor were covered with pictures of hotrods and half-naked women. A large corkboard on the wall outside the main office was crowded with missing-persons fliers pinned on top of scheduling grids with names and hours worked scribbled in ink. The office itself was relatively clean. Empty boxes of various sizes were situated in a semi-neat pile in the back.

Out in the main area, someone had cleared a path through the furniture chunks, paper, cardboard, plastic, and splintered wood that were piled waist deep. The path started at the front door and forked toward the garage (which led to the junkyard), the main office, and the staircase.

We made our way to the second floor and dug in. There were two efficiency-style rooms connected by a small bathroom. I'm guessing they used to rent them out to students. There was no furniture, aside from a gaudy old lamp in the shape of a 1930s burlesque chick, a cassette deck, and two dirty mattresses stacked on top of each other on the floor. Trash was everywhere. The walls were painted an awful shade of brown, as if the former owner's intention was to make this place look like the setting for some underground fetish video. Desire and I took the room on the right, and Graham and Kat took the other one.

We had a few close calls on the way here, so Graham thought it best that we lay low "for a minute," he said, until the rioting in the streets died down a bit.

"Suppose it doesn't?" I asked. "Suppose they come looking?"

"They won't come in here," Graham responded in a confident tone, like he knew something that I didn't. No follow-up. No explanation. But somehow he convinced me that hunkering down for a while was the right thing to do.

I was thinking all kinds-a-things: *Maybe he's got a stash of weapons around here. Or maybe there's a secret tunnel...*

I would've asked, but I was focusing on Desire's desires: moving shit outta her way and helping her over the shit that I couldn't lift by myself, like the soda machine that was tipped on its side in the hallway at the top of the stairs.

Getting here didn't quite work out the way I expected.

"Man makes a plan and God laughs" was Graham's conclusion.

It was his comment, in fact, that got me started on this whole "is-he-or-isn't-he" thing. Two seconds later, I'm scolding myself for being so gullible as to even entertain the thought. Then I reminded myself of the feeling I got when I found out that Ace was a believer. I wouldn't want somebody feelin' that way about me.

It is what it is, right? Just shut up and accept it, right? Well, it ain't that simple. A thing like that... like finding out vampires exist? I mean, *vampires* for Christ's sake! S'like a kid finding out the truth about Santa Claus... only in reverse or something.

It opens up a whole new can-a-worms for a guy like me, Mr. Logical Explanation. Mr. Science. I don't think science has all the answers, but I am down with the basic concepts—big bang theory, evolution, out of Africa, and all that. Doesn't leave much room for fanged, bloodsucking people (or whatever you call them) who can survive despite being blown to bits and decapitated.

The crowd was chasing Kat and Desire when we found them. They had just turned the corner from Main onto East Merry Avenue (where we were) and literally ran right into our car. You could hear the crowd growling in the distance. They got close enough that I could see the huge shadow on the side of the buildings across the intersection—a big mass of heads and shoulders with like 20 arms sticking out the front. Hands curled into claws and fists. Some were holding weapons, guns even. They fired a few shots in the girls' direction when they came around the corner.

Kat told us that an angry mob of residents came to each of the girls' places and forced them to come outside at gunpoint. They rounded them up in the middle of the street and demanded that they take off their gas masks. Kat and Trixie weren't wearing theirs. Kat said that Trixie was a mess. She was begging them not to make her come outside without it, but the residents didn't care.

Kat just held her breath, thinking, like an idiot, that that would protect her.

She said that the residents had some woman and a little girl with them who had supposedly seen "the floating woman." They pushed them to the front and asked them if any of the girls looked like her. The woman kept claiming that she was standing too far away from "the floating woman" to get a good look, so she couldn't be sure. The little girl, however, turned white as a ghost when she saw Desire's face. They were going to shoot Desire right there, but the other girls jumped to her defense. Then, Hardcore pulled a gun and started blastin'. That's when Kat and Desire made their break.

251

Andre Duza

"I don't know what we would've done if you two didn't come along," Kat said, as we sped away from the scene. Then she promised that they'd make sure to show us their gratitude. Desire got this expression on her face like she was pissed at Kat for including her without asking.

I was glued to the TV when Ace knocked on my door earlier this evening. Felt like I had been sitting there since 4:30 yesterday afternoon, when Channel 5 first broadcasted the funeral. It was an urgent kind of knock that woke me right outta the trance I was in while the TV told me what was going on around town. I guess I had dozed off at some point because I didn't hear the phone ringing when Ace tried to call "like 50 times." It was one of those things where day turned to night without my noticing.

I checked the two-way and discovered that the battery had died. And I had already packed the charger.

Shit!

On the TV, the Robogeeks were interviewing random guards in the street and mixing those spots with footage from the funeral. An older man reported the details in voiceover. They made Das Ramirez out to be a thug and a criminal. Even made mention of his ethnicity, as if that had something to do with his behavior.

Ace filled me in on what the television couldn't or wouldn't. He told me that Ramirez killed Chalk sometime before the funeral—dragged him outside and curbed him right in front of the tavern. It makes me sad that to think of Chalk's dying such a horrible death. He was a good guy. If he were here right now, he probably say "I told ya so."

I guess Linda Ludlow is sending a team here to investigate what happened. Ace said that the National News has people whose only job is to sit at a console jackin' broadcasts from communities across the country. Apparently, they had patched into

252

the feed from the funeral.

Ace also found out that Knox was using the morphine to deal with… he called it "an infection."

Artemus made a speech to the cameras after the funeral. He asked the public not to jump to conclusions and that they bear with him as City Council works to "reorganize and restructure." First on their agenda would be a full investigation into Mayor Knox's "as yet unknown condition," which Artemus claimed he knew nothing about.

Of course everybody knew he was lying, but they weren't willing to do more than bitch about it without proof. That came when one of Artemus' personal guards flipped on him during a street interview with one of the Robogeeks. It was like that one lie validated everyone's suspicions and, in their minds, tied the entire Rina government to a new and even greater conspiracy— the vampire takeover.

You'd-a-thought Christ himself had returned, only he was black or gay or something, the way people reacted. Suddenly, vampires were responsible for everything from the recent RS deaths to the war. People started holding secret meetings—members of the Brigade; former city officials; guards looking to defect; and random residents of Society Hill. Similar meetings were taking place off campus. The factions that began to take shape coordinated with each other via two-ways. They were talking about getting answers one way or another, even if it meant ropin' up folks lynch-mob style to get to the truth. And guess who was at the top of their list? If you said Artemus, you'd be right on the money.

"You ain't too far behind him," Ace added. "Your girl, too."

You know I've got it bad when I reacted more strongly to the mention of Desire than of my own tough-luck situation. At least that's what Chalk would say.

Lockdown was still in effect, but there were fewer guards to enforce it. Some of them left after the funeral. And they took the official Humvees with them. I'm surprised Ace didn't go with them. I asked him why he had stayed behind, knowing that he'd have to look for another vehicle.

"Because I keep my word," he said.

In my cynical mind, "word" came out sounding more like "weed," which is why I suspected he didn't run with the others and why he came knocking at my door.

People took to the streets with a vengeance on and off campus. The guards tried to contain the crowds with threats, then forceful shoving, then warning shots fired into the sky. Nothing worked.

They overpowered the guards and converged on City Hall, armed with their weapons and an assortment of old-school rabble-rousing paraphernalia—blunt weapons, Molotov cocktails, and torches. Artemus was holed up inside with the remaining city officials and some other VIPs. He ordered the remaining guards to form two groups: one to maintain a perimeter around City Hall and the other to assist the guards at the front gate. The guards at the gate were using rubber bullets to keep the off-campus folks from climbing over.

Large military vehicles stood between the guards and the crowd that surrounded City Hall like a post-apocalyptic wagon train. People were yelling and screaming and demanding answers. Instigators within the crowd were starting to rile.

Long story short, Ace was leaving early. "Like right now," he said. He started to go into how dangerous it would be: "We're gonna have to do this onna fly," and all that.

I told 'em I was in, that all I had to do was get his payment outta my safe. I warned him that it might take a minute. I knew the weed was the one thing he wouldn't mind waiting for.

Truth is, I wasn't exactly ready to go. I had most of my essentials in two backpacks. Had a duffel bag fulla weapons (two handguns, a sawed-off, knives, and a few concussion grenades) that I was planning on carrying in my left hand for easy access with my right, if need be. I'd wear the larger backpack on my back and the smaller one on my stomach. There were a few things that I still hadn't decided on, sentimental shit that Ace would say is only taking up space. But some of the things were really important to me for reasons that I'll get into later.

I had Ace's weed in my bedroom closet. But *he* didn't know that. I figured I'd use the time I spent "opening the safe" to make my final decision.

Then it went dark. I was in my bedroom, trying to stuff my favorite of Sabrina's wood sculptures into the large backpack, when Ace ran in and said, "They cut the power!"

You're probably wondering why I never mentioned that Sabrina was an artist. All I can say is that there are some memories that you keep just for yourself.

"Who are *they*?" I wondered out loud. "The crowd?"

"Yeah," Ace yelled from the other room. "Holy fuck! Looks like they're coming in."

The emergency lights popped on like red eyes waking from a bad dream. The red glow turned everything grim and creepy.

Ace appeared in the doorway, looking all worried. I'm sure I looked the same.

"We have to leave NOW!" he said.

He didn't say anything when he saw his weed sitting right there in an opened duffel bag on the floor of my closet. The backpack with Sabrina's wood sculpture sticking out sat right next to it. I was kneeling over it, looking all scared—which probably made me look guilty. But, like I said, Ace didn't mention it, so I didn't.

255

"Your payment," I said, as I zipped the duffel bag of weed and tossed it to him. He looped his arm through the handle straps and hiked the duffel bag up to his shoulder.

"Let's go," he said, disappearing from the doorway.

I grabbed my bags and followed him. Trying to get myself situated on the run was feat in itself, but I managed.

The crowds had cut the power to the entire building, so the hallways and the stairwell that we moved through were all daubed red by the security lights. We could hear the crowds coming up from the lobby as we headed down from the seventh floor. Ace had me by a landing.

Sixth floor. Fifth floor. Fourth. Third.

The second-floor door flew open just as Ace passed it. The crowd poured in and spotted his uniform right away. A few seconds later, and it would've been me. I was at the top of the staircase. All they had to do was look up to see me, but because Ace was so close, all eyes went to him.

Ace took off down the stairs. I ran up. I couldn't tell for sure, but it sounded like he ran right into the crowd coming up from the lobby. I'm still trying to block out his screaming. Sounded like he went down pretty quickly, at least.

I ended up hiding in a maintenance closet on five. I was headed to the roof (don't ask me why) when I heard angry voices traveling down from my floor like they had been coming after me specifically.

I was sitting there, entertaining the thought of being ripped apart by an angry mob, when I noticed that I was sitting on a bugsuit. It was the baggy kind that a lot of the construction workers wore. There was a 10-inch rip in the thigh, which was probably the reason it had been left on the floor of a maintenance closet. It was a little too big when I put it on, but I could manage.

I made my way down to the lobby. Bodies were sprinkled here and there as I made my way. Looked like they had been trampled or like they had fallen over the railing. Came across Ace—his body, I should say. He was lying at the bottom of a pile of dead men. Looked like he took them out with him. Good for him.

I took back the duffel bag of weed and said my goodbyes on the move. No disrespect to Ace, but I wasn't gonna just to let it go to waste.

The noise from the lobby ambushed me when I opened the stairwell door. It was coming from outside, through the plywood sheets, where the large windows used to be.

More bodies: guards and a few rioters.

I stepped carefully and made my way outside.

People were goin' apeshit. They were running around dressed in various bugsuit styles or wearing layered clothing wrapped in charcoal-covered blankets. It reminded me of the LA riots in '95 in that many of the participants seemed to have forgotten why they started rioting in the first place. I just stood there, dumbfounded, and took in the sights. I caught a whiff of the collective vibe. Call it a contact buzz—one that only lasted a few seconds.

I didn't really have a plan at that point. Coulda kicked myself for turning down Graham. On a whim, I fell in formation with a disorganized group that was headed for the front gate.

Among the bodies, which covered the streets and sidewalks, I saw that pervert Klimmick, still thinkin' he was invisible. He was beatin' off to some poor woman who seemed to have no idea that he was standing over her (naked except for a gas mask). He had lost a good 20 pounds since the last time I saw him, and his body was covered with open sores. It was disgusting.

The woman was slumped over a male body that was sprawled out on its back. It looked like she was crying. I assumed that the male body had been her husband.

There were explosions to the left of me. Debris fell violently to my right. The intimidating roar of the crowd came from all directions.

The front gates were hanging wide open when we got there. People were flowing in and out.

The off-campus streets were empty by comparison. There were people here and there standing in the streets, watching the activity at the top of Green Hill Mountain from afar.

I spotted a group of guards sneaking into a beat-to-shit maroon cargo van. The van was sitting in a lot with a bunch of discarded vehicles. Seemed like a stupid idea to me, hiding in a vehicle that looked like it couldn't move more than 20 feet. Especially with all these folks looking to do them harm. But then I noticed that their bugsuits looked... different. I could tell that the letters stenciled on their uniforms didn't say "Rina." I didn't have time to stay and investigate.

There were angry voices, but they were localized in one area, off to my right. I thought suddenly of Desire. I yanked the sawed-off out of my duffel bag and took off running at top speed. I was running across an intersection when a car came outta nowhere and nearly clipped me in my side. I had to arch my body sideways and roll to avoid it. Never knew I could move so quickly.

The car stopped a few feet away. The passenger door flew open. I did a quick check to make sure nothing was broken, then jumped to my feet and started running. I wasn't interested in listening to apologies... or threats.

"Roman!"

The voice came from behind—Graham's voice. I stopped, and turned around, and there he was, leaning across the passenger seat in that fucking hat and trench coat worn over his bugsuit. I was so preoccupied with getting to Desire that I didn't even notice the make of the car (Mercedes S-Class) until then.

He told me that he had a feeling something like this would

happen.

"Call it a sixth sense," he added. "I took off for Rina as soon as I heard about the funeral. Been hidin' out at the salvage yard since I got here. Been tryin'-na call yo' ass. Don't you ever pick up your phone?"

Oh yeah, the battery, I thought. Another fleeting thought: *How the hell did Graham know who I was inside this bugsuit?*

But then Desire started to dance.

Siren Dance

If there were a song for the way she moved, it would be something like sexualized violence, with its aggressive bassline and slurring guitars that came together like a Nine Inch Nails/ Alice in Chains deviant fuckfest.

The cassette in the old radio contained a mix of songs. "West End Girls" by the Pet Shop Boys was playing at the moment. The music that her movements suggested was much more complex.

Roman lay back on the old mattress, following every arch, sway, and thrust, as Desire danced over him. He was resting on his elbows, his torso sticking out of the baggy bugsuit (which was unzipped to his waist) like a half-peeled banana.

Desire shed her clothing like an artist wiping away layers of perfection with a turpentine brush. She was down to her bugsuit and hip-high stilettos. A large hunting knife was strapped to her upper thigh.

Desire pulled her mask off and whipped her head down and around to work her blackwater hair bone straight. Her skin was so fair that it made her seem to glow. Her hair was such a deep shade of black that it contrasted with her skin so as to make both seem unnatural. The result was beguiling in a gothic, earth-witch sort of way.

Liquid locks poured down from the top of her head and crashed against the slopes of her shoulders. It forked into streams of varying widths that continued down her chest and back. Fingerwisps dangled in front of her face. Eyes like orbs of emerald-green fire wrapped in polished glass peered out from behind them.

Desire's stiletto heels dug in and threatened to stab though the mattress. Roman expected to hear the fabric tear whenever she lifted her foot and spun and replanted it, or when she shifted her weight down to stabilize a gyrating squat, like she had just done.

Her slow-grind friction pressed Roman into the mattress. She timed her pelvic thrusts to maintain a steady flow of sensory swells that pulsed through his body like jolts from a defibrillator. Soon, Roman was on his back, looking up. Desire was on her hands and knees, chest to chest with Roman, their faces nearly touching. Her hair hung down and hid their faces behind an ink-fiber canopy. Roman was drunk on her scent, fragrant and feminine as it was. It affected him like a muscle relaxant. Her piercing eyes burned through his retinas and looked deeply into him. Their lips were so close that it felt as if Roman might not be able to resist the urge to steal a kiss.

Roman's thoughts became clouded and washed over in the echoed noised that evolved from the music of her movement. His body went numb. There was a hint of concern, the beginnings of a "wait a minute here" moment that eventually trailed off into some deep, reflective musing about her green eyes.

They watched together as she lifted her gloved hand between them and ran her fingertips down from his forehead to his stomach and back up to the bottom of his chin. Roman suddenly felt himself moving forward, as if guided by Desire's fingertips.

He couldn't explain how it was happening, nor did he care.

Roman sat upright now, eye to chest with Desire, who straddled his lap. He was dizzy, swooning to her addictive vibe. And he loved every minute of it. Even when he began to drown.

Desire unzipped her bugsuit to her sternum and parted it further with her hands. Roman was trying to look up and steal another fix of those burning green orbs, but she grabbed his head and held it against the sliver of bare chest.

She had a healthy embrace, maybe a little too healthy for a woman. At 5'11", Desire was a tall woman, but she was no Amazon. There were no bulging muscles, no squared jaw, no underlying masculinity. But damned if Roman found himself suffocating in her arms. He was on his way to losing consciousness when he felt his head being jerked to the side, as if to expose his neck.

A gunshot...

It took a moment for Roman to gain his bearings. It was as if the music had been cut off mid-song, yet it continued to haunt him. He knew Desire had been snatched from his arms by someone or something powerful, and now she was standing about five feet away, knock-kneed, and with a hole in her chest. She was facing the door to the shared bathroom, so that's where Roman looked.

Graham?

Graham was standing by the bathroom door. He had a shotgun in his hands. He was shirtless beneath his trademark blazer, exposing the salt-and-pepper hair of his barrel-chest. He had changed out of his bugsuit into a pair of black slacks. No shoes or socks. He wore a necklace with a silver crucifix pendant that Roman had never noticed before. For safety reasons, a lot of people wore their jewelry under their bugsuits.

Graham's face wore a look of smug satisfaction. He lifted the shotgun and fired three times. By the end of it, Desire lay on

261

her back, her head pushed upright against the wall in a way that looked unnatural. Her eyes were open and looking down. Her lips were parted slightly as her final breath left them. Her body was riddled with holes. A black puddle spread out from the back her torso like liquid wings.

"Goddamn bloodsucker!" Graham said, as if he were referring to a squashed insect. He lowered the shotgun and turned to Roman. His expression relaxed. "You all right?"

Roman's eyes whipped repeatedly from Desire's laid-out corpse to Graham, grasping for answers. All he could think of was *Why? Why? WHY?!!*

"You killed her," he whined. "You killed her! You killed Desire!"

Graham smirked knowingly. "She ain't dead, brotha. Don't let the possum act fool you."

Roman thrust his arm out into a rigid point.

"Whadayou mean she ain't dead? Look at her, for Christ's sake."

"Only two ways to kill a bloodsucker…"

"A wha…? Have you lost your mind? This is Desire we're talking about! *My* Desire! She ain't no fuckin'… fuckin'…" Roman paused as the options scrolled through his mind: bloodsucker, vampire. Both words were ridiculous.

"Vampire?" Graham interjected. "'Fraid so, brotha. How many regular people you know got black blood? Ol' gurl was fixin'-na sink her teeth into yo' ass. If anything, you should be thanking me."

Time slowed for Roman as he sat there on the mattress, wondering how to feel. Based on their interactions up to this point, he couldn't imagine that Graham would do what he did for no good reason. However, the reason that Graham had given was contingent on the fact that Desire was something other than the misunderstood, enigmatic beauty that he had come to know.

Maybe the information in front of him—that vampires were real and that Desire was one of them—was too much for him to accept all at once. Maybe Graham was just a crazy old man, and this was a sign of what was to come should their relationship continue.

Either way, Desire was dead. Roman's opportunity to recapture the feelings he had felt with Sabrina had died with her. What was it with him and women that they all seemed to die on him—the good ones, anyway?

Roman stared sheepishly at Desire's body. He silently willed her to wake up and tell Graham that he was full of shit. Of course, if she did wake up, that would mean...

Roman watched Graham reload his shotgun in slow motion. In that time, he managed to work up a healthy contempt for the old man. Maybe it was that his eyes were smiling or that he seemed too fucking calm and cool, like Desire was just another whore, like this whole thing was "nuttin' but a thang," as he would say.

The cassette deck was playing a song that Roman didn't recognize. It was hard, fast, and angry. The music worked as a sonic stimulant. It wasn't affected by the thickened reality that had Graham and everything else in Roman's field of vision moving in slow motion. The sonic surge intensified Roman's delicate emotional state and primed his thoughts for an explosion.

Graham was still reloading the shotgun.

Roman slid his feet beneath him. His fingers were curled for a sure grip around Graham's throat when he reached it. He planted his feet and shifted as he dug in for optimum thrust.

He caught the hint of something horrible. It was in Graham and Kat's room, on the mattress. Graham was standing in the way until Roman shifted his weight. He knew it was bad (at least as bad as what had just happened in here), so he hesitated to look up to verify his suspicion. He compromised by peeking over

Andre Duza

his upper eyelids and not committing to a direct face-off with whatever horrors awaited his gaze.

Roman's face tightened up the way people's faces do when they've witnessed a horrible accident. He sucked air through his teeth with a backwards hiss.

Kat lay on her back. Her head was turned to the side and was facing Roman, but it wasn't on top of her shoulders where it should have been. Instead, it rested at her side somewhere between her waist and her left breast. Her breasts looked much more firm than Roman thought they'd be. She had the same look on her face that she got when someone made fun of her voice. Loosely translated, it read, "What the frig did you just say?" Kat liked to say "frig." It was her thing.

Someone or something had cut or ripped her open from the chin down. Moist viscera bubbled up from the massive cavity. Plump intestinal tentacles reached over flayed skin flaps covered in red glaze and settled into a tangled pile. Her fingers were fixed in a death-clutch with the loose sheet. It was bunched into a mountainous cotton landscape all around her. Deep red stains were like territory markers on a topographical map. More blood pooled beneath her and soaked through to the second mattress.

Roman's eyes tracked over and up at Graham, who had just finished reloading the shotgun.

Reloading the shotgun...

Roman was on his feet and back in real time. He backed away from Graham. He held his hands waist high out in front of him, as if he thought he might be jumping to conclusions regarding Graham's intentions. But just in case...

"Hey! What the fuck are you doing?" he said to Graham.

"What do you think ahm doin'? I told you brotha, she ain't dead."

"Shit, man... You *are* crazy!"

"I'm crazy?" Graham snapped. "Why, 'cause I believe in

264

vampires? I think you gotchor proof on-nat one with the funeral, brotha. Is it because I had the *nerrrrve* to call your gurl out az-uh bloodsucker? I ain't the only one, brotha. Whydayou you think half the town was chasin' her ass in-na first got-damn place? But *I'm* crazy?"

Graham was talking with his hands while holding the shotgun. Roman was paying close attention to where Graham's aim landed at the end of every bounce and sway. It was nerve-racking.

"That's all right, though," Graham continued. "You say whatchu gotta say. I can take it. You'll feel better once you let out all that misdirected anger. Then maybe we can have an intelligent conversation."

"Feel better? Feel better? What the hell are you talking about, man? You just... you just fucking shot the woman I love—like it were nothing."

"Get a hold of yourself, brotha. You didn't love that whore."

Graham was pushing buttons like a motherfucker. Roman was sweating like he had just run a few laps. He was secretly eyeing his duffel bag full of weapons. He had put it on the floor a few feet from his bed.

Roman made a move toward the duffel bag... and another, while Graham's eyes were busy helping to illustrate his point. Roman had no idea what he'd do when he got his hands on a gun. Right now, he felt like he could empty a clip in Graham, but he knew that might change once he had the old man dead in his sights.

"You're thinkin' with your heart, brotha," Graham continued. "You know how it is out there, how fast we catch feelings for these broads that we wouldn't give a second thought to when the world was right."

"We're not talking about *some broad*, man! Jeezus, Graham! You *knew* how I felt about her. You *knew* what I've been going through since Sabrina."

Roman suddenly remembered that Kat was in the other room. He remembered how she looked.

"What about her?" Roman pointed toward the other room. "She a vampire, too?"

Graham looked over his shoulder.

"Who? Kat?" he asked. "Nah… that bitch was just annoying. 'Bout time somebody put her out of her misery. Your girl? Yeah, I knew you felt some kinda way about 'er. Why you think I warned you about them kinda broads? Your boy Chalk warned you, too. "Stay away from those broads," we said. But you had to follow your heart. Look where it got you—mixed up with a mothafuckin' bloodsucker. If I hadn't come in when I did, she'd be bleedin' yo' ass dry right about now. Bitch had you so dick drunk that you were just gonna let 'er, too. But that's what you get when you deal with shifty women, brotha. A whole lotta drama."

"You didn't know her like I did!" Roman yelled. "You didn't know!"

"Nah, brotha, it's *you* who don't know the half of it. This one here (pointing at Desire): her name ain't Desire. She ain't no hooker, either. That's just her latest disguise."

Graham's eye rolled over to Desire's corpse.

"Ain't I right, Mizz Mezerak—Mizz Mary Jane Mezerak?"

"Wha…?" Roman muttered, confused.

"That's right, brotha. You went and snagged yo-self the shiftiest bitch of 'em all." He turned to Desire's body. "Now get up off the floor and stop fuckin' around."

Nothing.

Roman had climbed the short ladder of suspense that Graham created, and now he was left hanging. To his surprise, he felt a little sorry for the old man.

Graham snatched his gun to a solid point and held it on Desire's body.

"Still playin' possum, huh?"

"She's not answering you because she's dead, man. Don't you get it?"

"It's like I told you, brotha. S'only three ways to kill a bloodsucker: sunlight, fire... or you can blow them apart like this here and scatter the pieces."

Graham pulled the trigger. The flimsy wall buckled but remained intact, save for a softball-sized hole speckled with dots like broken moons circling a misshapen planet.

Roman's eyes were too slow to make sense of the human-shaped blur that shot toward him when the gun went off. If they weren't, then he surely would've moved out of the way when the female vampire whizzed by him (running on the wall like an insect), knocking him off his feet.

A second later, Roman lay unconscious on the mattress, and the vampire formerly known as Desire; formerly known as Queen 'Bloody' Mary, evil zombie bitch; formerly known as Mary Jane Mezerak, wife and expectant mother, was pressed up against Graham's back with a hunting knife held to his throat.

"So, I *was* right about you." Graham said. The blade held against his throat affected his voice.

Silly old man. Now you can take that knowledge to your grave, Mary thought, as she slid the chip-toothed blade across Graham's throat.

Graham's aged skin wrinkled and snagged as the blade dug deep. At the same time, she palmed his forehead with her other hand and yanked it back and down until the back of his head was resting in the valley between his shoulder blades. It made a loud, crackling sound mixed with choking.

Instead of blood, a dark-matter goo poured and spurted from the jagged stump atop Graham's shoulders. It was a shiny black substance, the consistency of mercury, maybe a little thicker—just like the black blood that flowed from Mary's wounds.

Mary shoved Graham forward with her foot.

Graham staggered forward but managed to remain on his feet. Dangling upside down from the flesh-hinge at the back of the tender mound, Graham's head bobbed and bounced. Choking sounds gurgled from the wound. His mouth articulated the actions. He had a startled look on his face that quickly settled into a dead stare. His body relaxed. The dark-matter goo traveled down from the wound and lacquered Graham in a second skin. It soaked through his clothing and settled in the cracks and crevices.

A dark-matter geyser rose from the wound and stretched into a hand-like shape with rolling liquid fingers. The liquid hand-thing reached over Graham's shoulders and splashed down onto his chin. Shiny black fingers raced down his face and colored everything but the upside-down, fang-ridden smile that he flashed at Mary.

"You'd be surprised how effective this 'silly old man' get-up can be in disarming my enemies," Graham said. "I even had you fooled."

His voice was different. A rich, tangible baritone, like rolling thunder, replaced his smooth yet weathered drawl.

Mary was surprised that Graham could hear her thoughts—not by the act itself, as mind reading was a normal ability for vampires, but in the fact that Graham was... whatever he was.

Graham was completely covered in the dark-matter goo. It begin to expand and he with it. Along the way, he stretched and worked out kinks like he had just woken up from a long nap. He grunted and groaned like the experience kicked his ass in a good way.

Graham reached back and grabbed his head in both hands.

His new neck stretched like putty as he lifted his head off of his back and let it snap into place.

The seven-foot-tall, bald, black-lacquer vampire-thing turned and greeted Mary with a smile.

"Name's Onyx, baby. But you can call me Daddy." He spoke his name with pride, like he was relieved to finally be free of his human disguise.

Mary backed away.

Onyx had big, wide hands and long, bony fingers that ended in sharp claws, like human fingernails, but thicker and curved downward, like a cat's. His toes were clawed as well. His eyes (which were completely white with no eyeballs) and fangs stood out against his enigmatic, alluring, mesmerizing dark-matter glow. Silver hoops decorated his pointed ears and a crucifix dangled from his neck. His face was like an African mask hand-carved by a Eurocentric artist with a fair-weather interest in African culture. It was long, with hard-edged features that skewed both masculine and feminine. There was no color distinction between his skin and his clothing. It was as if the blazer and slacks (no shirt or shoes) was part of him.

"Don't fear the darkness, baby," he said. "It'll blow your mind if you let it. But then, I've got a feeling you already know something about that the way you've been tearing through this wretched place, trying to make soldiers out of these UV junkies. We wouldn't still be lingering between the lines if it were as simple as turning any old fool. Don't feel bad, though. It's a common rookie mistake."

All it took was a thought, and Mary was heading toward the front door so fast that she left spectral traces in her wake; so fast that she couldn't stop herself in time when she saw Onyx standing in front of it.

He shoved her backward, spectral traces racing to catch up.

"Typical!" he groaned. "You UV junkies get a taste of the Sanguinite Surge, and you think you can take on the world."

Mary landed on her hands and knees, sliding back.

"Besides, you can't run from what flows throughout that pretty little body of yours."

Mary was still sliding backward when she launched herself toward the bathroom. It was closer than the front door, so she felt confident that she could make it through before...

This time, she ran right into him. She saw it coming again. Onyx was posing antagonistically, as if to say, "Bring it!"

Splashing through layers of dark matter, Mary found herself stuck and being pulled under, like a large animal drowning in living tar.

Half-formed liquid arms reached out from the sides of Onyx' torso and writhed like snakes with deformed mammalian hands for heads. They wrapped Mary in slivers of darkness and melted together until most of her body was covered. Mary thrashed and bucked against their embrace as they constricted and pulled her deeper.

A sudden rush of endorphins commanded her body to relax. It was similar to the high that set her senses on fire upon drinking human blood, only this was much more potent. She fell limp as the dark-matter goo worked at swallowing the rest of her. Her head flopped to a bobbing backward slump. Her mouth hung open. Her eyes rolled back.

Onyx caressed her face with the back of his hand. The size of it made her head look small.

"Thaaaat's right. Ride it out, baby. Give in to the darkness like a good girl. It can take you higher than you've ever been, make you experience sensations that you never thought possible."

He grabbed the back of her head and pulled her close.

"Besides, baby... all the kids are doing it."

Leading with his snaking, black tongue, Onyx kissed Mary on the mouth. Dark-matter ribbons unfurled from his flesh and wrapped her head in goo. Familiar shapes became indistinguishable before finally forming into a mouth that stretched wide open. An oval, head-sized lump slid down its throat. The mouth closed and shrunk to its normal size.

Onyx made a swallowing motion. Satisfaction colored his peculiar features.

Chapter 15

Mary Jane Mezerak floated half-conscious in the dark-matter expanse. She was on her back, arms and legs dangling limp, hair lashing out in wild wisps. A fanged, white-eyed grimace oozed up and down dark-matter walls.

"Sexy bitch. Roman was right to obsess over you the way he did. I would've overlooked this place entirely if it weren't for his tireless pining. I personally detest listening to you UV junkies try to articulate your limited understanding of desire and loss. But then I began to wonder. I think it was the look in his eyes whenever he spoke of you that ultimately gave you away. The way his eyes swirled with irrational lust stunk of a Sanguinite spell."

The oozing grimace vanished and reappeared at different angles and distances from Mary, picking up syllables where it left off.

"It used to be that I could sniff out a single drop of my blood, but I'm afraid the years are catching up to me, reminding me that we, too, are slaves to time. That's what brought me here in the first place."

Mary tried to peel away the layers of catatonia, but she was virtually powerless to resist or struggle.

"What a coincidence that I should find *you* here as well," Onyx continued. "And masquerading as a hooker. I would've thought a woman of such... *principles* would be above that kind of thing. But you were counting on presumptions like that, weren't you? I've had people looking for you ever since you and your friends made your little rescue attempt on Market Street. Running out on us like that.... Your little brawl at the Club Adonis— I'm afraid your friends didn't fare as well, baby. I wonder what they'd think of this new army you've been trying to put together."

*   *   *

The Cemetery in the 'Hood

The full moon bore down like an angry Cyclops-eye reddened by cannabinoids. Trees twisted into curious shapes that grew more dreadful looking the deeper they stood in the cloak of nighttime. A mysterious fog bank blanketed the lumpy, dirt-and-grass-patch field. Improvised tombstones stood on tiptoes, peering over the haze.

The off-campus cemetery was like any other, save for the naked and broken-down soccer goalposts pushed off to one side, the distant vocal noise that polluted the surrounding air, the sounds of heavy machines rolling on squeaky treads, and, most of all, the bodies that clawed their way up from underground.

These weren't your garden-variety reanimated corpses. There was no melancholy discourse in the form of moaning, no calls for "brains" or "flesh," no ghastly wounds to indicate their post-mortem state to the naked eye. They didn't shamble drunkenly about, looking as if some important recollection lay just out of their memory's reach.

These were predatory beasts, complete with fangs, clawed fingers, eyes that glowed yellow-red, and faces that resembled Rina's recent wave of RS victims gone demonic.

Rising to their feet, they drank in the night with an impatient curiosity, steering with their eyes, all six senses firing. Something was making them angry. But this wasn't normal, "kick some ass" anger. It wasn't even "boil your bunny" anger. This was something deep-seated and raw. This was "torture you, then kill you, then eat you, and make toys out of the leftover parts" anger.

Along with the physical upgrade (depending on how you

look at it) and the thirst, the newborn vampires had also inherited a few human traits from their direct vampire antecedent, which just so happened to be Mary Jane Mezerak.

Acting on some unspoken command, the vampires directed their attention toward Mary's scent. It was faint, but they could smell it, taste it, and sense it in their clouded minds.

At the head of the cemetery, floodlights shot aglow with a loud, metallic clunk. The vampires turned away and hissed. The ones in front hid behind their arms.

A silhouetted formation of Sanguine Dawn soldiers (grunts) dressed in black-and-red bugsuits stood side by side in the light's direct path. They held long-barreled weapons (flamethrowers) down by their sides. A single tube ran from the butt of each flamethrower to a gas canister strapped to their backs.

Shining down from the tops of large armored vehicles, the floodlights cast a revealing glow on the pockmarked field and the vampires. They were starting to adjust to the sucker punch of brightness, creeping forward with aggression on their demonized mugs.

"Ready!" the Sanguine Dawn soldier at the far right of the formation yelled. "Aim!" The soldiers lifted their weapons simultaneously. "Fire!"

Liquid flames spit from the barrels in streams that bloomed into cackling, consuming walls of fire. The soldiers waved the weapons to cover a wide area.

The vampires shrieked and hissed as the flames rushed in and ambushed them. The pain taught a few of them to leap, but there was no escaping the flames.

*   *   *

"In case you were relying on your new army to save you," Onyx began, "let me assure you, baby… that *will not* be the

274

case."

Sudden heat overcame Mary. It was hot enough that it woke her from her near-coma. Her face contorted, fanged teeth clenching tightly. Her eyes, glowing yellow-red, flew wide open. Intense, burning pain was written on her brow. Her rigid body lurched, hands clawing at air. She groaned from deep down in her belly. This lasted for 30 seconds at most before she was once again lying flaccidly on her back, adrift in the dark-matter expanse, the oozing grimace materializing and vanishing all around her.

"All those lives wasted. And for what? Revenge?" he quipped. "Are you mad at me for breaking up your little family? It was nothing personal. You're just a means to an end, and after you've served your purpose here tonight, I'm going to make you my slave."

*   *   *

Mary woke up knowing only that she tasted dirt. That was all there was for the next few moments, but then it all came rushing back. She sprung to her feet and felt herself up like she suspected that the vamp makeover might have only been a dream. Just like the dream she thought she was having when she first begin to notice that her body was repairing itself.

It was the day after her knockdown, drag-out brawl at Club Adonis. Mary had been bitten so many times that she lost count. She refused to look at her reflection. She was afraid it would confirm her suspicion (that she was dreaming), and that confirmation would be the impetus for a wild ride back to the waking world—the kind of ride that would leave her dizzy and wanting to cry like a baby. Anyone who knew Mary knew not to bring reflective surfaces around her. She had had a falling out with her reflection back when she first saw the zombie with the ghastly, crooked smile staring back at her from a storefront window. She remembered it like it was yesterday. The sight brought her whole world crashing down around her. She fell to her knees and cried, but there were no tears and no tear ducts to produce them.

The ugly transformation came in stages. Her color was the first thing to go, fading from creamy white to corpse gray and finally to a desiccated brown color, where it stayed while other things degraded and decomposed. Her eyes shriveled up and fell right out of her face. Her joints stiffened. Her thoughts became less coherent; her mind swam in a strange, fanatical rage. The anger was there before she died, but this was different.

Over time, Mary learned to accept it, but it came at the expense of what little sanity she'd had left. In fact, if you had asked her how she felt about being a zombie back then, she would've said that she was fine with it and that she liked the power it gave her over people. Actually, she wouldn't have said anything, but that's what she would've been thinking.

The yearning to be pure and pretty again had waned over the years, but it was still there, buried so deep that she was unaware of it most of the time. It was a foreign feeling anyway, as she never appreciated her own beauty when she was alive.

Mary burst into laughter when she saw the final result of the vampire makeover. It was about a week after she was bitten. She must've stood there laughing for a half an hour. Then came the thirst.

Mary continued to feel herself up.
Taut, healthy skin? Check.
Long, silky hair full of body and shine? Check.
Eyes? Check.
She pulled her hands away from her face and watched them descend to about waist level.

You're standing in the middle of the street, her inner voice warned.

She felt as if she were being watched.

Mary's eyes scrolled up. Armed men dressed in black-and-red bugsuits appeared one by one. They materialized with a comical suction-pop sound that suggested a sound effect from a children's show.

She whipped around.

Surrounded.

Mary was the centerpiece of a big circle of Sanguine Dawn soldiers. They were standing "at ease," shoulder to shoulder. A caravan of fortified transport vehicles stood behind them on one side, facing Mary.

Unruly townsfolk had been herded into restless groups. People were shoving and yelling over each other, expressing their animal rage at the five-man units of soldiers who were bullying them. The nervous soldiers held their weapons horizontally with both hands to hold the crowd back. Piles of confiscated weapons formed behind the wall of uniforms.

Stoplights and lampposts and buildings materialized, and Mary now recognized where she was. It was the big intersection at Main Street and College Road. She was standing right in the middle of it.

Society Hill in flames illuminated the blackened horizon.

Mary backtracked and scanned a specific area of the crowd to her left, looking for something that she had noticed in a flicker on the first pass. It was something familiar, a metallic glint among the assorted limbs.

"Ahem!"

The voice came from above Mary's left shoulder, breaking her concentration.

Mary reached out with her leg and rolled a foot-long metal pipe underfoot. She kicked it up into her hand. Wielding the pipe like a baseball bat, she spun around. There were two soldiers standing behind her.

She heard the unmistakable crack of gunfire.

Something snatched the metal pipe from Mary's hand. The soldiers in front of her ducked and turned away. The pipe danced in the air between Mary and the soldiers—falling, rising, and flipping end over end. Tiny sparks and pinging sounds shadowed the pipe's motion.

Mary's yellow-red eyes tracked toward the source of the gunshots. They were still coming, one after another.

Three figures emerged from a dark crevice between two large vehicles. She knew right away who the one in the middle was. He was much taller than the other two and blacker than Africa.

To the left of the figure was another familiar sight. *Derek...*

Mary felt something warm in her chest. It was an unfamiliar sensation. Traveling up into her throat, the warmth swelled. Her mind surged with maternal happiness... and guilt.

"The most important thing is that you survive." That's what Mary had been taught since her teens, when her father unloaded all his "destiny" bullshit on her shoulders. She was only doing what she was told when she left Derek and the others behind. It was obvious that there was nothing she, alone, could do to save them. If she were going to avenge them, then she had to escape. She had to find a place where she could lay low while she came up with some kind of plan; she needed to recruit new soldiers. She needed supplies. She needed time.

Derek had grown since the last time Mary saw him. His face was different—longer, predatory, with prominent cheekbones, yellow-red eyes, and fangs. He twirled his guns before sliding them into holsters at his waist.

Mary didn't see any of that. If she had, she would've noticed how much his skills had improved. Derek had only taken

278

up gun twirling since discovering his connection to Deadwood Dick. Mary was busy trying to make sense of the upside-down torso that merged with Derek's at the waist.

Kagen?

Together, they were shaped like a scorpion's tail: Kagen was the shaft, and Derek was the stinger looming overhead. Kagen was walking forward on his hands. He held his body at a 45-degree angle, facing away from her. He was able to stretch his neck in a way that allowed him to look up at Mary. His face sported vampire features. A thick tangle of flesh and muscle bridged their torsos and served as a flexible joint that allowed Derek to lean and bob like a snake preparing to strike as Kagen walked on his hands. They wore a red-and-black bugsuit tailored to fit their queer shape.

"Secure her!" Onyx commanded.

The two soldiers jumped to the ready. One of them pointed his flamethrower at Mary while the other walked up and grabbed her by the arm. He pushed the barrel of his gun into her side and held it there. "Don't do anything stupid," he warned.

Dr. Lund approached from Onyx' right side, walking with his cane. His cloak swept the ground. He wore his trademark football shoulder pads and his blazing white hair worn spiky and stylishly unkempt. He was holding a microphone to his mouth and channeling the swagger of a game-show host.

"Isn't that something, folks?" he quipped. "Defiant to the bitter end."

He slid a knowing glance over his shoulder at the fortified delivery truck parked at the front of the mini-convoy. A large, flat, rectangular screen was mounted on the truck's side. "Applause" flashed repeatedly in a bright yellow font.

Silence...

Onyx leaned over and scolded Dr. Lund. He was speaking softly and in a language that Mary had never heard before.

Spectral white letters rained down an English translation that only Mary could see.

"I thought you said that you had these junkies under control," the subtitle read.

Dr. Lund scanned the groups of herded residents beyond the ring of soldiers that surrounded Mary. The crowd had grown calmer yet remained unruly and unpredictable. He singled out one of the guards.

"You there," he said, pointing. "Make an example out of someone. I don't care who it is."

The soldier grabbed the first person he saw.

"No! Wait!" A teenaged boy cried out. "I didn't do anything!"

The boy was wearing a bugsuit that looked like it was way too small for him, except for the hood and gas mask, which looked too big. He was reaching for his father as the soldier yanked him from crowd and shoved him forward. He fell.

"Dad!!!"

There was minor protest from the crowd.

A second soldier walked up and held his gun on the boy's father, who was pushing his way to the front.

"Hold it right there, *dad*," the soldier sniped.

"But that's my *son*," the father replied.

"*Was* your son…"

The first soldier raised his gun and aimed it at the boy's head.

"No, seriously, though… I didn't…" the boy started to say.

The soldier pulled the trigger as the teenaged boy lunged away. The blast chewed off the top of his head, leaving a wound like ugly teeth marks. Blood poured over the sides.

"Noooo!" the father yelled, as he watched his son flop to the ground and wriggle.

Others in the crowd tried to hold the man back, but the distraught father was determined to reach the soldier who shot his son. A number of guards fell upon him.

"That's my son, you motherfucker!"

"Let him go," the second soldier ordered.

Reluctantly, they let the man up.

He immediately charged at the first soldier.

The second soldier dropped the man in place with multiple rounds.

He turned to the crowd.

"Anyone else have something to say?"

There was no response.

The first soldier nodded at Dr. Lund.

Dr. Lund glanced over his shoulder at the screen. A word flashed repeatedly. He turned to the crowd and cupped his hand to his ear as if to say, "I can't hear you."

The night air filled with applause.

Mary was still staring at Derek/Kagen. She had given up trying to figure out what had happened to them and how they ended up alive despite their terrible deformity. She searched their eyes to see if there was any trace of the men she knew left in them. She was greeted with hostility.

"Don't act all upset now, MJ," Derek said. "None-a-this would've happened if you ain't run out on us."

"Plus, you of all people got the nerve to be judging somebody. Maybe you forgot about all that now that you got your looks back."

"You two: Shut your mouths," Onyx scolded.

The applause died down.

Onyx nudged Dr. Lund, who was still chasing the echoed leftovers.

"Huh? Oh..." Dr. Lund fumbled. A second later, he was back in character: "Good evening, ladies and gentlemen. I'd like to start by welcoming you, the citizens of…"

He glanced down at his hand. He had scribbled the name of the place on his palm.

"…Rina, Ohio, and those of you watching at home via satellite, to the first night of the rest of your lives. I am your host, Dr. Lund, and standing to my left is the man who made this all possible. Fear not his majestic exterior. He is here to help guide you on the path to salvation from the horrors that populate our world. Ladies and gentlemen… I give you your new master, the honorable *Count Onyx!*"

"Applause" flashed. The clapping came gradually, eventually giving way to wild cheering.

Onyx soaked up the surreptitious adulation. Still wearing a smile on his face, he leaned over and scolded Dr. Lund in his native tongue. The English translation rained down for Mary to see.

"Refer to me as a 'man' one more time, and I'll have you running with the grunts," the subtitle read. Onyx guided Dr. Lund's eyes around to the soldiers.

Dr. Lund covered the microphone with his hand.

"Dammit, Onyx! You broke the spell," he hissed under his breath. "I was just about to lower the boom."

Onyx brought his big face closer to the side of Dr. Lund's head. He spoke in his native tongue.

"And cursing me as well? You're pushing your luck, Sanguinite," the subtitle read.

"No. I… I didn't mean to…" Dr. Lund stammered. He was speaking out the side of his mouth. "I'm sorry, Onyx, but…"

"*Count* Onyx!"

"I'm sorry, Count Onyx. It won't happen again. Just bear with me, though. You must relate to these junkies on their level. You'll see."

Onyx pondered and decided to let it slide.

Dr. Lund exhaled and let the blood return to his face. He turned to face the crowd, sporting an affable smile.

"In the past, many have claimed to know the way. The Christians. The Jews. The secular human governments. The Ergeister cultists. Many have claimed to know the way, yet your species has been moving swiftly toward extinction since your ancestors first discovered fire. And here we are, at the precipice of your demise. In other words, you had your chance, and you blew it. What I am prepared to offer you tonight is a new beginning: a rebirth, if you will. Many of you are wracked with illnesses brought on by the poisonous atmosphere. You've lost family members and friends. You're frustrated, weak, and tired of hiding indoors under protective clothing. Tired of being lied to by your human leaders. Imagine an existence where you won't ever have to worry about that again. Where you have the power to overcome all illness. A world where you can live for centuries. As the Sanguine Territories expand, there will be a place for all of you who wish to become a part of the next evolutionary step in the history of this planet. But first, I challenge you to let go of your preconceived ideas about 'who' or 'what' we are. We are not the savage, bloodthirsty monsters of your human myths. We do not creep through windows at night and bite attractive women as they sleep, all the while spewing purple prose. We do not sleep in coffins."

There was sarcasm in Dr. Lund's tone now.

The large, flat rectangular screen flashed "Laughter."

The crowd fake-laughed.

Dr. Lund's face became serious.

"The truth is… we've been here longer than you. We've existed on the fringes of your culture since those first flames revealed our world to your ancestors. Frightened by what they found, they spread stories that painted us as devils and bogeymen. As your population grew, so did the threats to our way of life. Thus began the persecution of our species. Some of us

283

chose to integrate with the humans, to hide among them rather than live in constant fear of conflict and mob justice. Our interspecies mingling produced such infamous figures as Temüjin, Dracul, and Bathory, to name a few. Time has taught us the value of caution, discretion, and assimilation. Which brings me to our guest of honor. You're probably asking yourselves, 'Why us? Why choose a tiny, insignificant hole in the ground like Rina, Ohio to host your... official coming-out party?' Well, it just so happens that you have a celebrity in your midst, a bona-fide legend living right here under your noses. You know her as "the floating woman," or as Desire, the vampire-hooker who is single-handedly responsible for the wave of 'RS' deaths that have befallen this community in the past few months. In fact, she is much more than that. Allow me to educate you."

Dr. Lund pointed at the screen behind him. He was holding the microphone by its head, his hand muffling it. He leaned closer to Mary and whispered to the soldier who restrained her, and to the other one who held his gun on her, "Make sure you have her."

VIDEO:
Execution Chamber
Sanguine Dawn Headquarters, Sanguine City (formerly Philadelphia, Pennsylvania)

A room appears, with concrete walls painted black and pointed light fixtures glowing halogen white. A giant marble statue of Count Onyx standing on one knee looms over the room. The statue's arms reach down to the floor, hands upturned, knuckles resting against the painted concrete. A life-sized, black sarcophagus sits in each palm. On the left, a sculpted, feminine shape protrudes from the face of the sarcophagus. She has eyeholes carved into her sleek, featureless face.

She is the Iron Maiden.

The sarcophagus on the right is slightly taller and wider, in the shape of a man. His features are similarly smoothed over. Eyeholes are cut into his face.

He is the Iron Man.

A thick, steel door in the wall behind the statue swings open. A rusty squeal bumrushes the microphone.

Static ripples.

Light rushes in between the statue's legs. Two soldiers enter the room dragging a female prisoner between them—a youngish blond dressed in a loose-fitting, gray prison jump suit. They drag her to the front of the room and drop her on her knees a few feet from the camera. She kicks and screams the whole time.

The woman goes down hard. She makes no attempt to break her fall. She sits there on her knees and forearms. Her head is slumped forward, touching the floor. Her dirty blond hair hides her face. Her skin is raw and covered with ugly blisters and sores. Some of them are bleeding or leaking pus. There are bruises, too. They look grave.

The soldier on her right nudges the woman with his boot.

SOLDIER: Get up!

The woman uncurls vertically until she is kneeling upright. She lifts her head. He hair falls away from her face. More sores and bruises are revealed.

It's Rainah. She has lost a good 15 pounds, yet her face is swollen like a woman's twice her size. She has a busted lip. There is dried blood caked around her nostrils. Her blackened jaw appears to be broken.

She looks directly into the lens.

SOLDIER: Prisoner, state your name, your crime, and your sentence into the camera!

Seconds pass… a minute…

The soldier smacks Rainah in the side of her head with the butt of his gun. She falls over. The soldiers grab her by the armpits and lift her. They force her to kneel. She is still woozy from the blow.

SOLDIER (louder this time): Prisoner! State your name… your crime… and your sentence into the camera!

Seconds pass…

RAINAH (to soldier): My name is fuck you! My crime is fuck you! And my sentence is FUCK YOU!

She spits at the soldier. She starts laughing. She turns and points at the camera and laughs harder.

RAINAH (laughing): Fuck you, too, TV-land people.

One soldier grabs her by the hair and yanks her head back. The other cocks his leg to kick her.

CUT TO:

Rainah kneels with assistance in front of the camera. The soldiers hold her up by her armpits. She is holding her ribs on the right side and gasping for air between sobs. Tears form a moist, transparent layer from her eyes down.

Rainah's eyes give away the truth—that she has been broken.

RAINAH (crying): As a willing... a-co-lyte of the Ergeister Church and a founding member of the Revenant Clan, I am guilty of crimes against humanity and against... and against the progression of the new world order. These unspeakable crimes for... for which I am convicted show an utter disregard for life and further hhh-elp to illustrate the human species' appetite for self-destruction that has been made so evident with the war... and with the subsequent breakdown of society. Despite the hateful and racist human propaganda that commonly depicts San-guin-nites, or vampires, as bloodthirsty savages, it is humanity that had failed repeatedly to coexist peacefully with Sanguinites, the Earth, and even itself. As the new dominant species, we, the Sanguine Dawn, claim the right to this land, from border to border and coast to coast. This transition has already begun in communities like Lazarus, Aube Nouvelle, Sunrise, and now Rina, Ohio. Let the capture of me... of my associate, Griffen Elam... and of our l... leader, Mary Jane Mezerak, aka Bloody Mary, and our sub... sub-sequent executions at the hands of the Iron Man and Maiden serve as the definitive ending of the v... virus known as the Revenant Clan... *and* as an example of the superior power and intellect of your new leaders.

Rainah's face suddenly lights up.

RAINAH (Screaming): Don't worry about me, Mary! If you're watching... I'm not afraid! Run! Fight! Do whatever it takes! You have to survive! You have to su...

One of the soldiers steps toward her and yanks her back by the collar of her jumpsuit.

CUT TO:

The two soldiers are walking Rainah over to the Iron Maiden. She growls and thrashes.

RAINAH: You can't judge us! We're bigger than you! We're bigger than you!

The soldier standing by the Maiden unlocks a series of metal latches that runs down its side. He swings the heavy door away from its base. The inside of the Maiden appears solid except for a human-shaped impression that is carved into the complementary halves.

The other soldiers are trying to remove Rainah's clothing. One holds her around the waist while the other one tries to pull her shirt over her head. Rainah doesn't make it easy.

RAINAH: Git-your-hands-offa me!

———————————

"Ohhhhh my, I certainly wasn't expecting this," Linda Ludlow muttered to Mizz P., her bodyguard. She looked down at her prostheses. "Can you feel it, P.? S'like it all happened just yesterday."

To blend in, Linda and Mizz P. wore wool blankets over their bugsuits. Bug-eyed masks peeked out from the darkness inside improvised hoods.

P. was busy shooting figurative eyebeams over the shoulders of the people in front of her.

People were whispering. Adults and children alike were crying and whining. Others just stood there, mesmerized by the events on the screen and by the giant black vampire that stood in the middle of the street.

Onyx had just snatched Mary from the soldier who restrained her when she tried to look away from the screen. He held her close to him and forced her to watch. She was breathing heavily. Her nostrils were flared; her eyes were fixed angry slits.

It was all about not giving Onyx the satisfaction of seeing her break down. Linda used to wonder if Mary ever felt anything besides anger. Now, her despair was written all over her new face of hers.

In times past, the old Linda likely would have felt sorry for Mary. She might've even felt obligated to feel that out of some idea of gender loyalty. After all, Mary was a *mother*, and mothers were *angelic creatures* to be cherished and pitied. When they committed crimes, it was probably some man's fault.

She could just hear the excuses flying, as the usual panel of "experts" tried to explain away Mary's deviant behavior. Either she was raped by a man (father/step-father), or she was physically abused by a man (boyfriend/spouse), or she was constantly harassed and used and taken for granted by a man (boss/co-worker). Inevitably, someone would toss out that old, tired adage about hell and scorned women, and voilà—another criminal turned victim by the media. Ahh… those were the days.

Linda couldn't tell if P. was staring at Mary or the screen; they were both located in the same general direction. P. was off someplace where only she and her targets existed.

Linda had seen P. like this before, so she knew what was likely to come next. If she had hands, she would've placed one on P.'s shoulder to help reel her in.

"That's not why we're here, P.," Linda whispered at the side of P.'s head. "Just caaaaalm down, girl. I know the fantasy. I know you want to be the one to put her where she belongs. Especially now that we know she's alive."

Linda lifted her prostheses.

"It hurts me, too—trust me. But there's nothing we can do about it. Not at the moment. Right now, we should be concerning ourselves with getting the hell out of here. We have to get back and report this. Warn people..."

But Mizz P. was off on a rageaholic fugue. Linda's words made no impact.

Linda noticed awkward attempts at stealthy movement from the people around her. They were passing small, concealable weapons (handguns, knives, even grenades) back and forth behind their backs. No one was talking. Not even a whisper.

Linda worried that these people were planning to go for broke.

The entrance to one of Linda and P.'s planned escape routes (a manhole in the street) was only about 25 feet away. There was a food vendor cart that appeared to have been used as a flaming battering ram at some point parked on top of it.

Linda worried that people would follow them and create a scene. She worried about the rats that she'd probably encounter in the sewers. But mostly she worried that Mizz P. (whom Linda still called Tasha in her thoughts) would rather stay and fight.

VIDEO:
Execution Chamber
Sanguine Dawn Headquarters, Sanguine City (formerly Philadelphia, Pennsylvania)

The soldiers are attempting to force Rainah into the Iron Maiden. She continues to resist.

RAINAH: *We* are the new world order! *We* are! Ask anybody! They'll tell you! Ask anybody!

Rainah kicks her feet up, plants them against the Maiden's outer shell, and pushes off. The soldiers stumble backward but manage to hold onto her. The third soldier walks over and punches Rainah in the gut. She cries out and immediately stops struggling. Her muscles relax. She doubles over, gasping for air. Together, the three soldiers place Rainah inside the Maiden. One of them holds her in while the others close and lock the contraption.

CUT TO:

A close up of Rainah's face fills the frame. The camera, mounted at the top of the front groove, is so close that it distorts her features in a comical way. Her forehead appears big and bulbous. Her eyes, which dart in anticipation of something bad, are enormous. The rest of her face appears small and distant. Rainah tries to turn her head, but there isn't much room to move. Her eyes take over, rolling down and around to cover the small area.

RAINAH: You can't break me! You hear me, you stupid fuckers?

291

I said you *can't break me*! Kill me if you want to, but you can't have my...

Rainah hears a ticking sound somewhere below her feet. It startles her. Her eyes roll down. She listens. Another sound. This one sounds like the deep whoosh of an oven turning on. Heat ripples rise up and create a layer of movie flashback distortion between the camera and Rainah. Her face registers panic.

RAINAH: Oh my God...

She coughs as the heat fumes enter her nose and mouth, disrupting her breathing. Her eyes dart faster. Her arms and legs thump against the groove as much as they can. She lifts her feet one after the other. Her knees thump against the inside of the lid.

RAINAH: Oh God. Oh fuck! Oh fuck!

The temperature rises. Rainah squeezes her eyes shut to escape the intense heat. She is tired of struggling. She tries to meditate and visualize someplace nice, like Griff taught her to do, but fear won't let her concentrate. She groans at the heat and tries to turn her face away from it, but the hot air is everywhere. She explodes into a momentary fit of panic, moving as much as she can.

The temperature rises. Rainah's skin begins to flutter like a pilot's face during a zero-gravity dive. Her skin begins to bubble, tear, and slide from her face. The layer underneath is colored grayish-white like undercooked, skinless chicken. Her hair ignites.

Rainah opens her mouth to scream. Her voice is cut off by hot air rushing in and singeing her lungs. She groans. Suds push their way through the crevices between her eyelids. A milky white liquid seeps out and immediately begins to sizzle as it runs down her cheeks. Her eyes pop and force her eyelids open. They sink into empty eye sockets.

Rainah is shaking violently. The blood that garnishes her blisters has turned a sizzling black. The edges of the human-shaped groove begin to glow orange. The glow moves inward and colors the rest of the groove orange-hot. Rainah gnashes her teeth and groans. Her lips become black and rigid; they crack and tear and, eventually, curl back away from her teeth and gums like paper from a flame's touch. Her saliva sizzles inside her mouth. She tries to spit, but the saliva just opens a groove down her chin. Her skin ignites.

CUT TO:

The eyes of the Iron Maiden are glowing orange-hot. Inside, the thumping and groaning reaches a frenzied peak, and then goes silent.

The two soldiers exit the room through the heavy steel door between the statue's legs.

———————————

Onyx was still holding Mary close. His long, thick arms spilled over her shoulders and lay on her breasts. His massive hands were clasped together at her waist. As he watched the screen, Onyx was rubbing his cheek against Mary's, like a cat fawning over its surrogate human parent.

Mary's fake stoicism faltered under duress. She hated how the "Sanguine spell," as Onyx called it, put her in touch with her emotions like never before. No one would have ever mistaken her for sensitive back when she was alive in the traditional sense. In high school, they gave her nicknames like "Ice Queen" and "Cold Fish." Her husband Carl was fond of the latter when he was alive. As a result of her pokerface mentality, Mary never learned how to deal with things like the warm lump that climbed up her throat and camped out there as she watched Rainah—her adopted daughter, for all intents and purposes—die. She tried to ignore the tears that streamed down her face and the overwhelming urge to scream.

Together, Onyx and Mary looked like an interracial couple on the outs.

Onyx touched his lips to Mary's ear and whispered, "I know it must sting to watch your hopes and dreams come crashing down before your eyes."

The screen blinked "Applause." Half of the crowd responded—less than half. The others were preoccupied.

"Not to worry, though," Onyx continued. "Your fate…"

He lifted his head and peered angrily around the crowded intersection. He stopped on Dr. Lund, who was already reprimanding the crowd.

"We can do this the easy way or the hard way, people!" Dr. Lund said. "It's your choice."

The applause grew and grew until just about everyone was contributing. Onyx let his roving glare linger for a bit before returning his attention to Mary.

"I was going to say that your fate doesn't have to be so… extreme. As far as the rest of the world knows, you'll be dead, but if you play your cards right, you might just live a long life of servitude. In time, you might even learn to appreciate it."

The people standing around Linda Ludlow were using the applause to mask their conversations. She saw a man crouching and drawing up some kind of map in the air with his finger.

"You go here. You go here," she heard him say to the loose huddle of people who watched as they clapped. "The rest of us'll double dribble."

Linda figured that she heard the last part wrong. She broke it down in her head and came up with "The rest of us'll come up the middle." Made sense. If they were smart, they'd wait until Onyx did away with Mary. Maybe that was their plan.

The way Onyx held Mary against her will and made her watch what they did to Rainah put Linda back in her feminine-bond state of mind. There were people in the crowd who couldn't take the execution. They were covering their faces and turning away. A couple of them fainted. These were the same people who Linda had watched bludgeon and kick and stomp their own mayor (interim mayor) and a number of his guards to death less than an hour ago. Where the hell did they get off being squeamish?

Some of the people who watched the whole thing had looks on their faces that said "No one deserves to die that way." It was a look that Linda was very familiar with and a sentiment that she subscribed to until she lost her hands. Still, she saw no point in outright sadism, which is how she classified Rainah's execution.

They should have just killed her and been done with it. What they did spoke to their own wickedness.

She could have accepted such sadism only for Griff. Griff: His name gave Linda chills, but not the scary kind. These were like being stung all over by hot-ice jellyfish quills filled with 'roid-rage. It was then that she could really feel the phantom-limb sensations. She would swear that she was really opening and closing her hands. It was awful really, like a cruel joke.

Looking at the conjoined thing standing next to Onyx, Linda figured that Derek and Kagen, whom she knew the least of the old gang, had gotten what they deserved. It wasn't exactly death, so some people would say that they got off easily; that being made a vampire was a blessing.

Linda didn't see it that way. Drinking blood and running from the sun (if that's indeed what they do) were hardly benefits. There might be something to the eternal-life thing, but not if it meant spending it in the service of this Onyx character.

Mary's head whipped around like someone had yelled "Look this way!" She was looking right at Linda now, or so it seemed. Linda was immediately swept up in Mary's yellow-red eyes. Even glassed over, their shine was palpable. She spent the next few moments in what she could only describe as a trance state. It wasn't until someone tapped her on her shoulder that she snapped out of it.

"That woman's hands..." said a confused male voice from behind. "I... is she all right?"

He was talking about Mizz P. Linda thought P. was still standing beside her, but P. was about five feet away, walking through the crowd with her hand held up as if to guide someone's gaze. Mary fixated on her with her yellow-red eyes.

Linda filed through her extensive, internal database, like a good reporter, and stopped on the entry marked "Vampires." Thumbing through what she (and everyone else) already knew about them, Linda came to a minor detail from Mizz P.'s incident with a drifter in the wasteland a few months back.

It was nighttime. The drifter hid in the shadows and taunted P. before leaping out at her "like he had wings," P. told her. The taunts were, in fact, directly related to her thoughts, "like he was in here with me," P. said. She was pointing to her head. His voice made it throb in a manner similar to the way Griff's coaxing did.

The drifter wasn't wearing a bugsuit, yet there were no signs of RS. He wasn't wearing a shirt either, so P. got a good look at his body. She said that his face looked "demonic," that maybe he even had sharp teeth. She squeezed off a few rounds from her HK45C right into his chest. She put two in his head, to be sure. She swore she did. She said that she even saw the bullets punch through his skin and snap his head back. At best, all they did was slow him down a little. She said it took a grenade to stop him.

Of course, that whole thing got P. going on one of her "I'm coming apart" rants. "Maybe I was seeing things. Maybe I was hearing things," she said. "Maybe I completely missed him. Maybe there *was* no drifter. Maybe I should just pack it up and go rot somewhere. I'm just a liability to you!"

It was best to let her vent. Sometime during the silent afterward, Linda walked to the other side of the room and held her arm up next to her face. Her three-pronged, metal hand opened and closed. "How many fingers am I holding up?" she teased.

Linda couldn't see P.'s face beneath her helmet, but she recognized her lips twisting, trying to hide that haunted grin of hers, as she shook her head from side to side in response.

Linda trusted P. implicitly, so she had no doubt that she had killed the drifter. She didn't have an explanation for why the man was so hard to put down.

Now Linda had an explanation. She couldn't be 100-percent certain that the drifter was a vampire, but everything seemed to add up to that. P. had probably come to the same conclusion.

Mary's head whipped toward Linda, yellow-red eyes scanning the general area, then locking dead.

Linda replayed the image in her head. It was like someone had yelled, "Look over here!" Maybe that someone was P. Maybe she did it with her mind.

Linda turned to the man behind her and demanded, "What happened? What did you see?"

"Your friend—she took off her glove and held her hand up like that," he responded. The man was holding his hand up in front of his face, palm facing in, "...like she was showin' it to somebody. Ah... ah-could see down to-tha bone. She had something in her other hand, too. I saw it when she held it up. Looked like a grenade."

––––––––––––

VIDEO:
Execution Chamber
Sanguine Dawn Headquarters, Sanguine City (formerly Philadelphia, Pennsylvania)

An alarm sounds. The soldiers standing by the Iron Man and Maiden head toward the door to investigate. Another soldier enters the room and startles them. He is holding his gun at half-ready. Commotion from the hallway outside of the execution chamber follows him in.

SOLDIER 1: What is it?
SOLDIER 2: What's going on?
SOLDIER 3: Griffin Elam has escaped.

Soldier 3 hurries up to the camera, his body language projecting dismay. He swallows hard before speaking.

SOLDIER 3 (into camera): Uh... the prisoner, sir—he isn't in his cell. We're looking for him as we speak. Couldn't have gotten far.

––––––––––––

Onyx shoved Mary forward and turned toward the screen.

A spit-string of foreign words bellowed from his mouth. Mary tried to catch her balance.

Onyx hissed and slid his finger across his throat toward the controller of the video feed. The screen went black for a second and then came back to life.

"Applause"

The crowd responded, confused.

"No! No! No! No applause! There's been some kind of mistake!" Dr. Lund whined.

Onyx erupted with anger. He let out a passionate roar that sent an electric shudder through the suddenly transfixed crowd.

It got so quiet that you could hear the Geiger counters crunching away. Someone was laughing. It was a hearty, lunatic laugh.

Onyx, Dr. Lund, the Sanguine Dawn soldiers, and the crowd turned simultaneously toward the source of the sound.

Mary was laughing her ass off. She held her arm over her stomach and doubled over. She cackled upon seeing Onyx' squinting glare. She pointed at and taunted him.

Onyx balled his fists and rampaged toward her.

Dr. Lund sidestepped out of the way.

Venomous words in Onyx' native tongue rolled from his lips as he shoved the two soldiers aside with a single sweep of his massive arm.

White wisps spelled "Insolent junkie bitch!"

Mary stood and turned off her laughter as if she had flipped a switch. She extended her arm to the side and opened her hand to catch the tennis ball-sized metallic orb that zipped toward her like a line drive.

The grenade smacked against Mary's palm. Her fingers closed around it.

Onyx was only a step or two away. He thrust forward with single-minded rage. Mary seized upon Onyx' careless charge and lobbed the grenade in his path.

The grenade exploded right in front of Onyx, disintegrating his torso. The force reached Derek/Kagen and sent them reeling. It lifted the two soldiers off of their feet and deposited them five feet away. The soldier with the flamethrower squeezed the trigger in reaction as he flew back.

Derek/Kagen lurched out of the path of the flaming tongue and fell to the ground when Kagen's hands got tangled.

The flames licked Dr. Lund all over. He let out a high-pitched shriek and ran around in circles, flailing his arms.

The incendiary blast reached Mary as well. She let out a terrible wail as her bugsuit ignited.

Dark-matter legs staggered backward. A ring of gnarled tentacle-slivers hung like fleshy dreadlocks from Onyx's belt-line. Dark-matter flesh rained down from the writhing strands with wet, plopping sounds.

Mary took off running toward the crowd. She was completely covered in flames. The crowd parted abruptly when she reached them.

Screams jumped out in reaction.

The circle of Sanguine Dawn soldiers broke apart. Some of them dropped into defensive stances, training their weapons in the direction of the grenade blast. The soldiers standing near the convoy took cover behind the large vehicles.

"Heads up!"

A second grenade rolled beneath the delivery truck with the screen mounted on the side at the head of the convoy. The soldiers scattered.

The explosion was much larger this time. The delivery truck rocketed several feet in the air, then landed on its side. Its exposed belly suddenly burst into flames, spewing burning petrol. Another explosion from inside the trailer portion of the truck kicked the back doors off of their hinges. The truck shook the

300

ground when it landed and sparked a three-vehicle-deep chain reaction of explosions.

A team of Alpha Dogs wielding curved blades and showing teeth came running out of one of the trucks in the very back of the convoy. They leaped over the flaming vehicles and spread out to engage the crowd. The grunts who survived the truck blasts ran around on fire.

The crowd of residents had splintered into several small groups. Resident-group leaders kneeled by the piles of confiscated weapons and handed them to waiting hands.

The armed residents opened fire at the Alpha Dogs and grunts.

Bodies shredded. Pulverized limbs littered the air. Black-and-red blood was everywhere.

The Alpha Dogs hacked and slashed soft tissue, sinew, and bone, splitting heads in half vertically before severing them clean from shoulders.

Somewhere in the eye of the flesh-storm stood a pair of dark-matter legs, barefoot and clothed in black pants. Tentacle-slivers that emerged from the form swatted and pierced through anonymous human bodies and flung them away.

One of the tentacle-slivers sprouted an oval shape at its tip. The oval shape grew pointed ears and white slits for eyes. A long, fanged mouth formed at the bottom.

It was Onyx. He waved the plesiosaur-like neck of the appendage to his left, toward Dr. Lund's frantic shrieking. Dr. Lund was trying to smother the flames by rolling around on the ground.

Onyx looked to his right and saw Derek/Kagen, who had just regained their footing after the explosion. They looked dazed and were teetering awkwardly.

Onyx continued to scan the area. He spotted Mary in the distance. She was running down a side street, completely engulfed in flames.

He turned back to Derek/Kagen and ordered, "Go after her! Don't you dare let her get away!"

"P.! Wait!" Linda Ludlow yelled, as she watched her bodyguard run after Derek/Kagen, who were chasing Mary.

Linda knew her attempt was in vain. There was no stopping P. once she had made up her mind about something, especially with regard to family. Or enemies. Or her blood-sister, who was both.

Linda turned to the south and took off after P. The mob swirled around her, hiding her pursuit. She spotted a grunt who had joined the chase.

"Oh no you don't!" she said, lifting her right arm.

Her three-pronged hand folded back. A phallic rod extended from the base like a telescope and spit out an automatic hail of small rounds that tore into the grunt, knocking him to the ground. A pile of residents dead and alive collapsed onto the grunt, suffocating him.

Linda lowered her arm and disappeared quickly into the crowd.

The Parking Garage

"I got a friend named Mary Jane, and she makes me feel strange… so I got-ta call out her name…"

Derek's nasally B-Real voice echoed through the lower level of the enclosed parking garage. The place had a way of amplifying sound. Surprisingly, there were still cars parked where their owners had left them years ago. Most had been stripped and looted. Some were overturned and painted with silly tags; others seemed virtually untouched, sitting dormant under layers of concrete dust that had fallen from the flaking ceiling.

Concrete structural pillars stood every few feet. Most of them were bent into crooked postures, exposing rebar skeletons. Rusted pipes criss-crossed the water-stained ceiling. Toxic-looking puddles gathered in pockets on the uneven floor.

Mary was sitting with her back against the bed of a pickup truck that lay on its side. Her body smoldered but was otherwise intact. From afar, she appeared to be in the same condition she was in before she was bitten at Club Adonis.

A small, blue sedan rested upside-down next to the pickup, its rear windows broken.

Mary avoided looking at her reflection in the windows of the truck, but she could feel that something was wrong. She felt a sudden spike in anger and an empty feeling, a sensation that she hadn't felt since… She stopped right there, afraid of where that line of thinking might lead.

A tool bin spanned the width of the truck bed behind the cab. Mary leaned forward, carefully worked it open, and looked inside. It was full of hand tools.

Mary grabbed a crowbar and leaned back into the truck bed.

Derek/Kagen walked down the center aisle of the garage, scanning left to right. They moved with the grace of two men sewn together.

Derek was whistling the theme from *The Good, The Bad, and The Ugly* as he skulked.

"Knock it off, wouldya?" Kagen said. "This ain't no time to be shittin' around."

"You just keep your eyes on the road and let *me* worry about finding her," Derek replied.

"Oh, so you can take all the credit?"

"Now, how the fuck does *that* makes any kina sense, considering…"

"It makes a whole *lotta* sense considering that I'm the one who's gotta do all the legwork. You think I like hauling your black ass around?"

"Here we go…"

"Shit on yer 'here we go,' man. It's yer fuckin' fault that we're like this, Mr. fuckin' hero. And for what? Rainah's still dead. If you hadn't jumped on my fuckin' back, I mighta got me a piece-a-that fine ass before…"

"Who's the better shot, though?" Derek interrupted.

"Fuck you and your Deadwood Dick crap!"

"No, fuck you! Besides, you still didn't answer my…"

Intense pounding interrupted the moment, followed by the sound of shattering glass. The noise bounced from wall to wall.

Derek/Kagen moved to the right and spotted a figure about 25 feet away. The enraged figure was thrashing wildly and swinging a crowbar repeatedly, with savage force, into a blue sedan.

"No! No! No! No! No!" the figure roared. Her voice sounded painfully dry.

"Well, look what we have here," Kagen said.

Mary whipped toward them. Derek/Kagen recognized the terrible face. It was Mary. Zombie Mary.

"Damn, girl!" Derek quipped. "You look like shit!"

Mary swung repeatedly at Derek's face and head. The sound of metal meeting flesh and bones crumbling underneath echoed throughout the garage. Derek's head flopped from side to side, black blood spurting from fresh wounds. He was groaning and spitting out teeth. She stomp-kicked Kagen when he tried to reach for her legs and then started in on him with the crowbar.

Mary kept swinging, alternating between the heads. She

forced them back into a pillar and stabbed the tip of the crowbar deep into Derek's brow.

Derek flailed and swatted Mary away. She hit the ground hard and crawled out of sight.

"FUCKING BITCH!" Derek growled, as he extracted the crowbar from his head. "*See* if I don't make you pay for that shit!"

"See if *we* don't!" Kagen added.

Both of their faces were covered in black blood, but Derek's looked worse. Blood oozed from his nose and mouth and the hole in his forehead. Vagina-shaped gashes in his face leaked blood and pus.

Derek shook the blood from his eyes, wiped it from his nose, and spit it from his mouth (along with a few teeth). More blood poured down from the top of his head. It was clear that he wouldn't be able to stop the flow with just his hands. To a human, it would have been a fatal wound.

Kagen had a large, vertical gash down the right side of his face that opened and closed as he breathed. You could see the inside of his mouth through it.

Derek scanned angrily. He glanced up at the criss-crossing pipes and sent out a thought to Kagen.

Gimme a boost!

Derek grabbed the pipe directly overhead when Kagen pushed off of the ground. Using his hands, he moved from pipe to pipe like a monkey negotiating branches in the jungle.

Mary crouched behind an old Buick and waited for them to approach. She could hear and feel them coming. Suddenly, she sprung at them with her arm cocked, wielding a four-foot section of pipe.

Derek caught the pipe with his free hand as she swung. He snatched it away, still holding on the latticework of pipes above him with his other hand.

Just as Derek prepared to strike Mary with a vicious blow, the ceiling above him exploded. Derek's hands and forearms exploded with it. The force knocked Mary back.

Derek/Kagen toppled to the floor. The ceiling fell on top of them, burying them beneath concrete chunks. Ruptured pipes sprayed brown water.

Mizz P. shouldered her weapon (an AGS-30 automatic grenade launcher) and stood over the mountain of concrete. She was poised to shoot, but the pile remained still.

Chapter 16a

Hollywood Ending

P. whipped her head in Mary's direction...

She was gone.

P. pulled off her mask and threw it to the ground. It made a clicking sound when it landed.

Her skin was brown and desiccated. It stretched tightly over her feminine bone structure. Her eyes were hollow. Her stringy hair was pulled back and twisted into a single, thinning braid that dangled just below her collar. Her lips had receded slightly from her teeth, leaving a gummy smile.

"Goddamn you, Mary!" P. rasped. Her voice sounded terribly dry, like her larynx was lined with sandpaper. "I didn't save your ass twice just so you can run out on me! What's the matter, huh? You ugly bitch! You scared to face me like a *real* woman?"

"Hello, *little sisssterrr*..." came Mary's voice.

P. spun around and lifted her weapon. Her actions were immediate and simultaneous, yet Mary was still able to block her movement. Mary countered.

Slamming her palm up under P.'s chin, Mary shoved her head back. The gun went off and tore another chunk out of the ceiling 10 feet away. This time, the entire roof buckled.

Undistracted, Mary followed up with a flurry of wild clawing to the face.

P. raised her hands to deflect the flurry. Mary went low and tackled P. around the waist. She barreled forward and took the fight to the ground. The gun flew out of P.'s hand.

P. was overwhelmed as she struggled to defend herself.

She was used to being the aggressor, but this time, she had to adapt and react to someone else's game. Mary beat on P. mercilessly until P. thrust her legs straight and kicked Mary off of her.

P. climbed to her feet.

Mary just stood there, waiting.

P. was first to move. She thrust herself forward at Mary. They clashed and spun into a parked car. The pair were a whirlwind of hands, feet, knees, elbows, and teeth. They threw each other into cars and crumbling pillars. The ceiling rained dust all around them. Each combatant gained and lost the upper hand again and again as the savage battle brought each toward exhaustion.

P. found herself face down on the floor. She lifted her head. Mary was standing 15 feet away… waiting. P. spotted her gun on the ground to her right.

She planted her hands beneath her and used them and her feet to push herself forward toward the gun. Mary finally noticed the gun and made a delayed move for it.

P. grabbed the weapon with her right hand, rolled onto her back, and took aim at Mary from the ground.

Mary froze.

P. stood up slowly. She was careful to keep the gun trained on Mary.

Time stopped as the blood-sisters exchanged dead glares. Both women spoke volumes without uttering a word. The enmity between them was palpable.

Deep, wicked thoughts and feelings flowed like an electric current merging two super-conductors. The air around them pulsated and rippled with emotional energy.

P.'s hand began to tremble as she flashed back through her sorrowful life. All the reasons for her rage came to her in a flurry. She pictured Dana's smiling face, only for it to morph into his death grimace before her mind's eye. She reflected on all the physical and mental abuse that she'd endured at the hands of her sister; at the hands of Rainah and Griff; and at the hands of the police. Through a series of memories—her capture, her time alone at the Ries Institute for the Criminally Insane, her sexual abuse at the hands of Tarkington, and her pitiful suicide—she felt all at once her degradation and loss of dignity. Yet it was all based on a flat-out lie. Dana's birth, his death, and all the years in between: All of it was a lie. Part of her still couldn't accept that.

"Is it true?" P. asked. She knew that Mary would know what she meant. "Was it all a lie?"

Mary eventually nodded "yes."

P. looked down and contemplated.

"I remember when we were kids, Mary. I remember everything…. Most of all, I remember the look on your face when I left you."

She looked up and locked hollow eyes with her blood-sister.

"Whatever happened to you, whatever direction your life took: It wasn't my fault. I didn't deserve what you did to me, Mary. I DIDN'T DESERVE THIS!"

P. was holding her hand up in front of her face to display her rotten complexion.

Mary's dead expression hadn't changed one bit since P. started talking. P. could see that she wasn't getting through.

"I promised myself that I would be the one to put an end to your madness," P. continued. "This is where it ends for you, Mary. Here. Today. Right now."

Mary squinted, hollow eyes hovering above a sideways, skeletal smile that seemed to mock P. It was that exact expression, like the devil's joker-mask, that had been haunting P.'s thoughts and dreams since she first witnessed it.

"This is where it ends… *for you*… *little sissssterrr*," Mary hissed.

P. began to shake her head "no." It was slow at first, as if she were still in the process of convincing herself that killing Mary once and for all was the only option; that there was no other way to express the pain that she had endured because of her; that she couldn't possibly let this bitch get away with what she had done to Dana, even if he existed only in manufactured memories. Her anger filibustered away any reasonable thoughts and ideas concerning empathy for her blood-sister, who had lost a child of her own—a real child.

P. flexed her gun-arm rigid, reaffirming her murderous intentions.

Mary shifted her stance to prepare for evasive action.

P. squeezed the trigger and...

Something grabbed P.'s leg and yanked her backward. The grenade shot past Mary and landed behind her. The explosion destroyed a support pillar. A section of roof overhead began to collapse. More pipes burst; brown water was everywhere.

P. looked down and saw Derek trying to pull her close. He was growling like an animal. His yellow-red eyes pierced through the dark, wet layer that poured down his face, fangs jutting out of his mouth.

"You!" he groaned. "We shoulda killed you a long time ago."

"Killed you and ate you," Kagen added.

P. kicked and stomped at Derek's face. A concrete chunk fell down and clocked him on the top of the head, dazing him momentarily.

P. crawled backward and sprung to her feet.

Derek/Kagen spotted her and let out a unified roar.

P. continued to step backward.

Derek/Kagen dug in and proceeded to charge.

P. lifted her gun and fired.

The next thing she knew, she was covered in black blood.

Moist chunks slid down her body and plopped to the floor. A lump of twisted flesh wrapped in black-and-red fabric occupied the spot where Derek/Kagen stood a second ago.

The parking garage was coming down all around her. It was clear that time was running out, and that she had to escape quickly if she wanted to avoid being pulverized. As she ran toward an exit, her eyes darted around, looking for Mary, but she was nowhere to be found.

Chapter 16b

Bizarro Ending

P. whipped her head in Mary's direction…

She was gone.

P. pulled off her mask and threw it to the ground. It made a clicking sound when it landed.

Her skin was brown and desiccated. It stretched tightly over her feminine bone structure. Her eyes were hollow. Her stringy hair was pulled back and twisted into a single, thinning braid that dangled just below her collar. Her lips had receded slightly from her teeth, leaving a gummy smile.

"Goddamn you, Mary!" P. rasped. Her voice sounded terribly dry, like her larynx was lined with sandpaper. "I didn't save your ass twice just so you can run out on me! What's the matter, huh? You ugly bitch! You scared to face me like a *real* woman?"

"Hello, *little sisssterrr*…" came Mary's voice.

P. spun around and lifted her weapon. Her actions were immediate and simultaneous, yet Mary was still able to block her movement. Mary countered.

Slamming her palm up under P.'s chin, Mary shoved her head back. The gun went off and tore another chunk out of the ceiling 10 feet away. This time, the entire roof buckled.

Undistracted, Mary followed up with a flurry of wild clawing to the face.

P. raised her hands to deflect the flurry. Mary went low and tackled P. around the waist. She barreled forward and took the fight to the ground. The gun flew out of P.'s hand.

P. was overwhelmed as she struggled to defend herself.

She was used to being the aggressor, but this time, she had to adapt and react to someone else's game. Mary beat on P. mercilessly until P. thrust her legs straight and kicked Mary off of her.

P. climbed to her feet.

Mary just stood there, waiting.

P. took a step. The hinge in her left knee stuck and caused her to stumble into a lunge-type stance with her leg locked straight behind her.

P. checked her balance. She reached down and twisted a knob in the middle of the hinge, unlocking it.

P. was first to move. She thrust herself forward at Mary. They clashed and spun into a parked car. The pair were a whirlwind of hands, feet, knees, elbows, and teeth. They threw each other into cars and crumbling pillars. The ceiling rained dust all around them. Each combatant gained and lost the upper hand again and again as the savage battle brought each toward exhaustion.

At some point, Mary grabbed P.'s right arm and twisted. The hinge in her elbow snapped. A metallic clang, followed by a scream, echoed throughout the garage.

P.'s arm went limp. Her face changed. Suddenly, she bulled forward with her shoulder, and she and Mary spun to the ground. P. lifted her head. Mary was standing 15 feet away… waiting. P. spotted her gun on the ground to her right.

She planted her hands beneath her and used them and her feet to push herself forward toward the gun. Her right arm buckled and gave way. Mary finally noticed the gun and made a delayed move for it.

P. grabbed the weapon with her left hand, rolled onto her back, and took aim at Mary from the ground. P.'s hand was shaking.

Mary froze.

P. stood up slowly. She was careful to keep the gun trained

on Mary.

Time stopped as the blood-sisters exchanged dead glares. Both women spoke volumes without uttering a word. The enmity between them was palpable.

Deep, wicked thoughts and feelings flowed like an electric current merging two super-conductors. The air around them pulsated and rippled with emotional energy.

P.'s hand was trembling violently now as she flashed back through her sorrowful life. All the reasons for her rage came to her in a flurry. She pictured Dana's smiling face, only for it to morph into his death grimace before her mind's eye. She reflected on all the physical and mental abuse that she'd endured at the hands of her sister; at the hands of Rainah and Griff; and at the hands of the police. Through a series of memories—her capture, her time alone at the Ries Institute for the Criminally Insane, her sexual abuse at the hands of Tarkington, and her pitiful suicide—she felt all at once her degradation and loss of dignity. Yet it was all based on a flat-out lie. Dana's birth, his death, and all the years in between: All of it was a lie. Part of her still couldn't accept that.

"Is it true?" P. asked. She knew that Mary would know what she meant. "Was it all a lie?"

Mary eventually nodded "yes."

P. looked down and contemplated.

Her shoulders bounced as emotion poured out of her. She was sobbing nosily and sucking air in big gasps. Tears did not come, as she had no tear ducts to produce them.

"I remember when we were kids, Mary. I remember e-e-everything…. Most of all… I remember the l-look on your face when I left you."

She looked up and locked hollow eyes with her blood-sister.

"Whatever happened to you, whatever direction your life took: It wasn't my fault. I didn't deserve what you did to me,

314

Mary. I DIDN'T DESERVE THIS!"

P. was holding her hand up in front of her face to display her rotten complexion.

"Every day is a struggle for me not to end it again. E-v-e-r-y *day*. Do you know why I don't just do it? DO YOU?!"

Mary's dead expression hadn't changed one bit since P. started talking. P. could see that she wasn't getting through.

"Because I promised myself that I would be the one to put an end to your madness," P. continued. "This is where it ends for you, Mary. Here. Today. Right now."

Mary squinted, hollow eyes hovering above a sideways, skeletal smile that seemed to mock P. It was that exact expression, like the devil's joker-mask, that had been haunting P.'s thoughts and dreams since she first witnessed it.

"I don't *think* so, *little sisssster*," Mary hissed. "But you can try…."

P. began to shake her head "no." It was slow at first, as if she were still in the process of convincing herself that killing Mary once and for all was the only option. In the sad story of P.'s life, the chapter on avenging Dana was all that was left to write. Even if she now knew that her son was just a figment of her imagination, the feelings that she had for him were as real as they had ever been. The sorrow and yearning would never end.

I can't live like this.

P. flexed her gun-arm rigid, reaffirming her murderous intentions.

Mary shifted her stance to prepare for evasive action.

I can't.

P. relaxed her arm and lowered her aim. She relaxed her fingers and let her gun drop to the floor.

A bewildered look came over Mary's face.

"Goodbye, Mary," P. sobbed.

Mary's eyelids spread apart as she poised herself to lunge.

The last thing she heard was the sound of a pin skidding across the concrete.

The grenade hit the ground and exploded.

Dream

The footfalls of a thirty-something woman echo through the sterile hallways of a research facility. A crisp blouse pokes out from the collar of her neatly pressed lab coat. She is wearing glasses and carrying a briefcase in her right hand. She holds her body in perfect posture as she presses forward.

Military vehicles can be seen through the windows on the tarmac outside.

She comes to a reinforced steel door. She flashes a card and a wry smile.

The door slides open to reveal a steel-and-glass chamber brimming with high-tech equipment and security personnel.

She passes through the room and turns toward a long, white hallway. She nods to the guard standing by the reinforced door at the far end. The guard nods back and punches a code into a keypad on the wall next to the door.

The door slides open.

The room is cold, dark, and empty except for an enormous glass cylinder standing vertically at its center. The cylinder is filled with a green liquid. A light recessed into the lid of the cylinder hauntingly illuminates Mary Jane Mezerak's naked torso as it floats within. Her spine extends about a foot beyond her ribcage like a bony tail. Fibrous tentacles protrude from her head. A network of tubes runs from her chest and temples up and out through holes in the sealed lid. Her face is without expression.

317

The thirty-something woman enters the room with an older man who also wears a lab coat.

The scene jumps forward. The older man is walking toward the door with a briefcase in his hand and his lab coat draped over his left shoulder. "Remember, the guard is just a call away if you need anything. But there's no way she's getting outta there."

The woman cracks a thin smile. "Thank you, doctor. I'm not afraid of her…. Anyway, she's half the woman I am."

The older man laughs as he turns away. The door slides open, and he walks out.

The scene cuts to murky blur of dark colors. It is the view from inside the cylinder. The sound of bubbles is deafening. Slowly, the room comes into focus. A figure dressed in a white lab coat walks up to the glass. It is Griff.

A tear hangs from the corner of his eye. He lifts his right hand and touches his fingertips to the glass.

A dark shape from the other side moves to meet his touch. It is Mary's hand. She is reaching out to Griff.

The B Sides

She Swims with Corpses

What the hell was Audrey Keller thinking when she came to this place? Gerald York, her boyfriend, always warned her that her "dreams" would get her in trouble. Of course he wasn't talking about anything like this-swimming naked with two dozen corpses interwoven in a pile of anonymous limbs and cold, wet bodies laid out in various positions and beset with decomposition in all its stages that littered the stinking, maggot and fly infested burial pit, hiding from the little people who wanted to kill her and possibly molest her corpse. A few of the bodies in the pit were still clinging to life.

As Audrey lay there perfectly still, she wondered how it came to this.

It was all Gerald's fault. He didn't believe that Audrey could actually see the future, the past, or anything else that she claimed. By "trouble," he was implying that what her "dreams" were doing to her might affect her friendships or her job, even though he knew that being a receptionist for an auto dealership that specialized in RVs wasn't the career of her dreams. Although he was quick to deny it, Audrey got the feeling that Gerald secretly included their relationship in the warning.

What was she thinking when she bought the gun-a Derringer-and began spying on Joshua Ray and his family?

It was the dreams that led her here. They had been coming to her-more like attacking her, really-for months. They were never complete, leaping out of the cerebral darkness like pulse-pounding trailers for some nihilistic, hyperkinetic horror yarn put to celluloid, which made things worse, as they always left her with a feeling of dread. There were random scenes of violence and brutality: mushroom clouds, war scenes, and emaciated bodies hobbling along in the toxic aftermath, covered with blisters and open sores and plagued by crippling sickness.

And then there was that woman. She exuded elegant ferocity, moving with purpose in her own herky-jerky way even though she was clearly dead and considerably rotten. For some reason, Audrey knew her name: Mary Jane.

Strange that it was also the name of Joshua Ray's little girl, who never seemed to speak. She was the youngest of his three children, and the only girl. Audrey put her at about nine or 10 years old. Clothed in the kind of innocent-looking dresses that little girls usually wore, Mary Jane was a cute little thing, pale as a ghost, with traditional hill-jack, dirt-smudged markings, wispy strawberry-blonde hair that looked like it hadn't been washed in a day or two twisted into long, chunky braids that hung from either side of her head, and a stone-cold stare that was off-putting, even from afar.

There was something twisted beneath that indifferent expression, something angry and aggressive and hungry as a ghetto-mutt chained by the neck to a post in the backyard and forgotten for days at a time. Audrey could sense it; her flesh understood it in ways that made her feel like she needed a jacket or a blanket to both keep her warm and hide her. And that doll... *That fucking doll...* Mary Jane carried it with her everywhere she went. It was an ugly little thing, dirtier than she was, with thick, red hair that dangled a foot past its plastic feet.

The whole family was strange in a backwoods, white-trash sort of way. Joshua himself looked like a disgruntled veteran, the kind who hadn't quite let go of whatever war he might have served in, walking around in worn fatigue-bottoms and a flannel shirt with a shotgun strapped over his shoulder. A military-style cap turned backwards covered the bald spot encircled by dry, grayish-white hair pulled into a short, thin ponytail.

Although Audrey eventually got close enough to hear their conversations, which were usually about mundane things, she never got a good look at his face.

From what she could tell, Joshua Jr., who was about 12 or 13 years old, was somewhat of a disappointment to his father. He was a sweet kid who liked to joke around with his younger brother, Raif, who was probably around 11.

Audrey had been watching them-okay, stalking them-ever since she happened upon the old house in the woods when last week's "girlpower" joyride ended with a flat tire in the boonies off Route 20.

As she hid and watched them come and go, her gut feeling said *danger*…. Her "Audrey Sense," she jokingly called it, said that something lascivious was going on behind closed doors.

Still, she kept coming back. She told herself it was because she forgot to take down the license plate on the red Ford pickup that sat out in front of the house; then it was to make sure she didn't see what she thought she saw-Josh Jr. and Raif kicking around a human head like a soccer ball. She convinced herself that she was seeing things or, at most, that the head belonged to some kind of dummy or mannequin. Then it was to get a few photographs with her camera.

Despite the risk and the strange, ever-present stench of something big and rotten that polluted these woods, Audrey began to enjoy the voyeuristic rush. She felt that she was onto something big; what it was exactly was beyond her. Audrey was young and naïve enough to feel that despite what her intuition told her, she was never actually in any *real* danger.

There was a moment when that all changed, though. One day, little Mary Jane suddenly stopped walking on the way to the pick-up to retrieve something, turned toward the woods, and stared suspiciously in the general direction of where Audrey was hiding. She stood there, motionless, for a full 20 minutes.

This is it, Audrey thought. *I'm caught.*

And Joshua Ray definitely didn't look like the type to call the police.

Audrey took off running when Mary Jane finally tottered away.

Based on a feeling that chilled her through and through and a crisp memory of Mary Jane's face, her wide eyes cutting a path through the trees to find her, Audrey told herself that she would take what information she had and hire a private investigator.

She managed to stay away for a full month, until one day when the "Dear Jane" letter that Gerald left on the mantle when he up-and-split while she was at work prompted Audrey to take action. He cited her "psychic bullshit" as his main reason for leaving, so, in her mind, all she had to do was convince him that she was telling the truth about the dreams. And there was only one way that she knew of to do that. She had to go back to the house. She had to see what was inside. That was when she bought the gun.

Audrey waited all day for the Rays to leave. She wore dark clothing, for which she later chastised herself once she settled into a groove as she lay on her stomach in a patch of fallen leaves, partially covered.

Stupid. Stupid. Stupid, she thought. With the dreams and everything else that she was dealing with—like her relationship and her life in general, both of which were going to shit-she didn't think about the time of day when the subject of stealthy attire came up. She didn't even dwell on it, like it was a given: sneaking around = dark clothing.

Audrey lay there, daring herself to "Get up and go!" after

watching the red pick-up pull slowly down the driveway and onto the road. For one thing, she was sure that Mary Jane was looking right at her as the child sat clutching that ugly little doll in the back of the truck while Josh Jr. and Raif sat up front with their dad. She even saw her whisper something to her doll, then point in Audrey's direction. With her other hand wrapped around the back of the doll's neck, Mary Jane thumbed its head around to face Audrey as well.

Audrey finally coaxed her body out of tension and headed for the house.

She shook her head when she found the front door un-locked. Where she grew up-just outside Philly-you'd be a fool to leave your house unlocked.

The stench of church incense backhanded her when she entered. As she expected, the place was a white-trash paradise. There were clothes, books, old newspapers, and magazines stacked high next to each other. The walls were covered with old maps, blueprints, yellowed newspaper clippings from the Viet-nam era, covers of gun and mercenary magazines, and strange—most likely religious—paraphernalia. From another room, an old radio blared bluegrass music.

She crept around from room to room, stopping on little things that caught her interest. She made her way up the stairs to the second floor. She had just reached the top step when she heard the truck pull up out front.

Audrey panicked and ran to the first room she saw. She opened the door and screamed. Like the rest of the house, it was replete with clutter except for the queen-sized canopy bed upon which a woman, naked and strangely colored, like the hue of the recently deceased, lay with her legs akimbo. Audrey was about to ask for her help when common sense smacked her upside the head. This chick was dead as a doornail, and judging from the way she was positioned, it appeared that she was being used for sexual gratification for some sick fuck. Considering that this was the master bedroom, she most likely belonged to Joshua Sr.

Audrey ran to the next room and opened the door. Between the two twin beds that hugged the walls on either side of the room, there were comic books and action figures and other staples of pre-adolescent boyhood mixed in with a few hunting knives, a shotgun, and a long, complicated hunting bow propped next to a pile of arrows, a few of which were stained red. In the back, by the window, there was a closet.

Bingo.

Audrey hurried over to it and opened the door. She immediately gasped and leaned out of the way of the body that fell out and slammed to the floor at her feet. It was an older man, very Irish looking. He was completely wrapped in what looked like gauze, or ACE bandage from his feet to his biceps, pinning his arms down to his sides, like an Irish mummy.

Around his abdomen, there was a large red stain, darker at the center. From the color, Audrey could tell that the wound was deep.

"Oh my God," she cried, her hands covering her mouth. "Oh my God. Oh my God. Oh my God. Oh my God. These people are fucking crazy."

Audrey was so scared that she forgot about the gun that was stuffed in her sock; so scared that she couldn't tell if she heard the front door open or not, although when she thought about it, Joshua Sr. and the kids had more than enough time to make their way from the truck to the door.

Suddenly, at her feet, there were sounds, like someone stirring in their sleep. Finally, the Irish mummy coughed himself awake and began to choke on his own backwash from a balled-up rag held in his mouth with duct tape. Once the haze wore off, he whipped his head around and stopped on Audrey. At first, he seemed to think that she was one of them.

Realizing this, Audrey raised her hands and shook her head, "No." Then she pointed to the doorway.

"I think they're in the house," she whispered. "Just be quiet and I'll…"

But the Irish mummy was having none of it. He panicked, wriggling and pulling against his restraints. With a series of loud grunts, he demanded to be set free.

"Please, just be quiet," Audrey whispered, approaching mental collapse. "They'll hear you."

That only seemed to make him try harder. As he continued to fidget, Audrey, whose mind was a complete blank, noticed that the bandage had shifted around his abdomen, exposing the wound, which was much more serious than she imagined. He was cut way down to the muscle and sinew, opened from oblique to oblique. From inside, his intestines, which had been held in place by the bandages, began to ooze out.

The Irish mummy groaned, and began to breath erratically. He was as good as dead. There was nothing Audrey could do for him, not that she had a plan in the first place. His jutting organs slowed his fight for freedom and invited dementia to step in and have a go at him. His moaning grew louder and louder. He closed his eyes and began to thump the back of his head against the old wooden floor.

Please just die, Audrey thought. She needed it quiet to think.

"Goddammit! I said shut up," she whispered, but by now, he was shoulder-deep in shock and far beyond the reach of reason.

Oh God! I don't want to die, she thought, searching the room for an option that finally presented itself in the form of a pillow on the floor next to one of the beds.

Audrey ran over, grabbed it, and, after taking a deep breath, she looked up at the ceiling and signed the cross over her

chest.

"Please forgive me," she said as she kneeled down beside the Irish mummy and held the pillow over his face with all her strength until he finally stopped moving. It took longer than she expected, much longer than it did in the movies.

By the time Audrey caught her breath, there was someone standing in the doorway. Judging from the blur in her peripheral vision, it was too small to be Joshua Sr., which left her feeling slightly relieved, until she turned and saw who it was. Mary Jane's red-haired doll stepped awkwardly toward her. Its hair, which swept the floor for a foot behind it, was attached to a patch of dried, shriveled flesh, caked to hardened edges where it was sewn sloppily onto the top of its plastic head. It appeared to be a piece of someone's scalp.

The doll's joints weren't bendable, so it kicked its legs up like a Nazi soldier. Audrey fell to her ass and crawled backward to the wall beneath the window. The doll followed, kick-stepping around the dead Irish mummy and right up to Audrey's feet, where it stopped, pointed at her, and turned its head toward the door.

Audrey trembled, unable to move. She could only imagine what kinds of horrible things might happen next.

The doll let out a scream that caused Audrey to cover her ears. Its voice, like a little girl's, reminded her of what she imagined Mary Jane must've sounded like.

That was it. Fuck it. Audrey turned and looked up at the window. It was her only option.

As the doll continued to scream, Audrey climbed to her feet, closed her eyes, and dove through the window. Halfway down, she realized that she was probably seeing things before, and it was then that a realistic version of what just happened-Mary Jane holding the doll, and manipulating it-materialized in her mind. Sometimes the psychic shit had a way of fucking with her.

Audrey woke up in a daze. The back of her head and her right leg were throbbing like a motherfucker. She felt as if she had been lying there amidst shards of broken glass, dirt, and gravel for some time, yet she was still alive and in one piece.

As she limped through the woods, chased by Joshua Sr.'s voice reciting Julia Ward Howe's "Battle Hymn of the Republic" through a megaphone, she thought of Gerald and how he would feel if he knew what she had gotten herself into. If she survived this... *when* she survived this, she planned to use it to work his sympathies and bring him back to her.

Mine eyes have seen the glory of the coming of the Lord / He is trampling out the vintage where the grapes of wrath are stored / He hath loosed the fateful lightning of His terrible swift sword / His truth is marching on.

Joshua Sr. wasn't a child of God, but the song held a sentimental place in his heart, as it was one of his late father's perennial favorites.

The words echoed through the trees, the tops of which seemed to dance in testament, while below, Audrey limped as fast as she could away from the three tiny shapes that darted through the brush about 50 yards behind her.

When she turned, she could see Mary Jane clearly. She was carrying a large kitchen knife, and she was gaining on her, her dirty white dress bouncing around and lifting and occasionally giving her panties a peek at daylight.

There was something else.

Sometimes when Mary Jane's feet slapped the ground, Audrey saw... well she could only describe it as an echo, like a ghostly vision of Mary as an adult appearing and disappearing behind her with each heavy step. She had seen this woman before, all dead and rotten and moving in that herky-jerky way, her long dress flowing and snapping in a nonexistent wind.

After awhile, Audrey thought she had lost them. She could

still hear them coming, their distant rustling competing with Joshua Sr.'s voice as he continued to recite the Battle Hymn of the Republic.

Glory, glory, hallelujah! Glory, glory, hallelujah! Glory, glory, hallelujah! His truth is marching on.

Audrey knew that she was going the wrong way. Her car was north of the house, and she was running west. She kept on running anyway, and eventually came upon a cliff. When she looked down over the edge, she understood the strange smell that she had noticed but ignored every time she came through these woods. It was a pit, six feet deep, and full of bodies, all naked, bruised, slathered in blood, and stacked on top of each other. Ten feet across, on the other side of the dirt cliff, there was an old, rusted metal fence overrun by nature that stretched as far as she could see in both directions. It would take her too long to climb it.

Audrey would have to cowboy-up and hide down in there, amongst the bodies, if she wanted to live. It was the only way. The thought of it made her woozy, but she undressed, and climbed inside anyway.

Once inside, Audrey vomited at least twice before she lay down. Shivering and crying silently, she hand-painted her body with blood and dirt to look like she'd been there for a while, and snuggled with the crowd of dead strangers. She didn't expect to find that a few of them were still alive, though in the comatose but not-dead-yet sense, and not the thinking, feeling, able-bodied sense. She could tell that they were alive by the flashes of premonition that hit her like a locomotive every time she passed out, which was happening every couple minutes. She kept flashing to scenes from other people's lives that all had the same end: nothingness.

Audrey bit her lip to keep from screaming her lungs out. The dizzy spells came and went, and so did the visions. Readjusting slowly to minimize any contact with the dead and dying crowd that surrounded her, she noticed a lone eye deep down in the pile. It was looking right at her. She thought it was frozen in death until it blinked drunkenly and threatened to roll up under its upper eyelid.

Suddenly, a wet thud from her right caused Audrey to whip around. Standing over her, Mary Jane looked down and gave Audrey an angry squint, before raising the knife over her head and…

…Audrey flailed and knocked the knife from Mary Jane's hand. They watched it stick into one of the bodies and sway back and forth as the weight of the handle pulled it. Before Mary Jane could react, Audrey sat up and shoved her back onto her ass. Mary Jane stood up slowly, her dress stained with the various blood types, and flashed a full-on frown.

Man, did this little bitch have face.

Still, Audrey felt that she might have a chance against Mary Jane as long as she kept her cool. She was just a little girl.

Audrey tried to find a good position in which to meet Mary Jane's eventual charge when a deafening boom struck her in the chest like a hot fist and knocked her back. It took her a moment to realize that she had been shot, and another to trace the path of the bullet up to the edge of the cliff, where Joshua Jr. stood, silhouetted against the sky, with a hunting rifle. He lowered the rifle to his side and nodded to Mary Jane, who pulled the knife out of the anonymous corpse, stepped carefully from body to body over to Audrey, and raised the knife again. As the knife began its descent, Audrey put up her hands. She knew she was already dead, but what the hell…. In her right hand, she caught Mary Jane's arm, triggering a mental flash and another vision, which would be her last.

The Final Vision of Audrey Keller: *A Day in the Life of Mary Jane Mezerak*

The mental camera focuses. Blurry shapes chase clarity.

The low whistle of the wind first catches a female voice, muffled but rising in volume. Primal emotion weighs down the male voice that follows, deep and mocha-smooth. The man's voice has a slightly refined, ghetto-fied flavor that floats out from its source and induces a certain level of dread in all within earshot here in the suburbs. Even the scenery beyond the windshield seems to feel it—trees standing at attention, when moments ago they were swaying to the wispy songs of the wind, which has suddenly become reflective of the darker side of nighttime.

Snaking through the stately trees, Ridley Creek Road carries an expensive sports car on its tarred, two-laned back. Moving in tune with the anger and bad feelings swirling around the car's lit interior, the vehicle swerves in and out of the oncoming lane as the driver, Carl Mezerak, faces his wife, Mary Jane, who sits beside him in the passenger's seat. He has just finished yelling in defense of the unexpected accusation that she threw at him.

Eh... now, what was I going to say? Carl rolls his eyes and turns back to the road. His face relaxes into a look of smarmy satisfaction.

"Well?" Mary Jane seems to say as she leans in, face to profile.

He tries to ignore her, first by turning up the radio, which is playing "Dream On" by Aerosmith, then by concentrating on the single yellow line in the middle of the road and scrutinizing its crooked flaws as if it matters that it isn't perfectly straight. Neither strategy works.

Carl is nearing his boiling point, heated by Mary Jane's tenacity, her patience, and her refusal to back down. Doesn't she know that he could snap her neck like a twig? Not that he would. Part of it is that as big as Carl is compared with Mary, she makes him nervous when she gets angry, and lately she's been angry all the time. Carl developed insomnia as a result.

333

Without thinking, Carl stomps on the brake, reaches over, fingertip-flips the handle, and shoves the passenger door open.

"Get out!"

Mary Jane takes a silent moment to feel him out. She watches his eyes to give away his bluff as they usually do. Tilting her head, her eyes slit-squint as if to signify that he'd better fucking rethink his decision *or else,* Mary Jane massages her hip where she kept the .38 that she swore she'd use on Carl if he tried to deny that the baby was his.

Clutching her skirt to hike it up a few inches, and then a few more, she begins to think it through. It has been so long since she took a life, and she has been doing so well at suppressing the inner fire that her father had ignited in her. It takes all of her resolve to keep her hand still, to keep from putting a bullet between Carl's brown eyes. If he only knew that side of her—the one that she kept secret ever since she decided that she wanted to try her hand at a normal life. She wanted so much for them to be a family. She felt that this was her one shot.

"I fucking hate you," Mary Jane hisses as she backed out slowly, her eyes burning holes of resentment that Carl brushed aside.

Once she's out, Carl leans across the passenger's seat and acknowledges the additional space with a smile that he doesn't mean for her to see.

"You have a nice night," he says, and closes the door.

Screeching rubber interrupts the concentrated rage that bursts from Mary Jane's mouth in a scream. She jogs toward the shrinking taillights that now only peek through the darkness, firing her gun until it clicks empty.

Mary Jane stops and lets her head fall back as if the starless sky might offer her some comfort. She stares herself dizzy, swaying to its numbing, slightly nauseating allure.

From her left, blinking lights and ghastly sounds turn her

attention to the gaps in the sturdy trees that allow hints of the Halloween decorations to shine through from the neighborhood way at the bottom of the steep incline. She doesn't care about them one way or another. She is beginning not to care about anything again, the way her father had taught her.

Slipping in and out of "kill mode," she wages an inner war against the person that she knows she is destined to become.

She doesn't hear the van that comes speeding around the curve behind her until it is too late.

It wasn't so much the pain of being hit that bothered her as it was the driver, who morphed from some anonymous grease monkey to her father and back when the impact made her blink; not so much the shatter-pop of her ribs as the cold windshield that kissed her aggressively like Captain Kirk used to do to the ladies.

Sailing through the trees, Mary Jane goes limp and accepts the switch-lashings and blunt whacks of the twigs and branches that reach out to welcome her. She hits the ground with an "Umph!" that echoes through the long, tall shadows.

The slope of the hill gives her extra velocity and bounce. She tries not to anticipate the blacktop and the snarling faces and electronic cackling from the lawns on the other side. At the rate she is traveling, it looks like she might clear the road entirely.

Her father always told her that she would die young; in her twenties to be exact. Mary Jane was 24. To be honest, it was the one part of her father's ominous predictions that she didn't believe, until now....

I Eat Niggas Like Ramrod for Breakfast!

"Ooo-OOOO!!!!"

Winding in and out of houses packed tight for blocks and blocks, the concrete-jungle call echoed, reminding these fake-proud folks of what they both loathed and lauded about the 'hood. Single mothers called their children in for the night. Ghetto bastards longed for father figures.

The disembodied voice soaked into the background. Somewhere back there, Jimmie Too-Fly (Too-*Motherfuckin'*-Fly, he constantly corrected), the most delicious-dicked (so he claimed), most exquisitastical, mackadasical mack daddy mack, and the biggest, baddest P.I.M.P. in all of Philadelphia, hid beneath a small, termite-infested, wooden staircase in a modest backyard.

The yards around here (62nd & Osage, he guessed) were basically tiny, fenced-in cubes crammed together like an outdoor urban office space. One out of every six or seven cubes contained some intimidating breed of dog doing hard time in the name of security. In between yelps of sadness, each contributed their two cents to the network of neglected pets that spanned for miles.

Sixty-second and Osage was Southwest Gunnerz' turf. The call Too-Fly had heard belonged to them. He had provided girls for a party they threw for their leader, Omant Weeks (aka Down & Dirty), after he beat that murder rap. But that didn't mean that they would help his ass, especially now that he was public enemy number one.

This was Countess Mangela's turf as well. Mangela (a transsexual pimp) was known for catering to extreme fetishes.

Too-Fly had nothing against alternative lifestyles; however, some of Mangela's girls were downright scary.

Last week someone stole Too-Fly's pink stretch Escalade and drove around picking off hookers with a shotgun—first in King Rob's turf, then Mangela's, then Daddy Morebucks'—and returned it to his garage before anyone realized it was gone. Dem Hos was the only major player that she (Bloody Mary, the dead bitch from the news) didn't hit that night. The response was swift from all parties-girls killing each other, random drive-bys, hitmen sniping Johns and spreading fear throughout the general area, thus creating anarchy and clogging the wheels of opposing organizations.

The news was calling it a street war. It meant that the police would be nowhere in sight. To them, street war was like a code for "let the bastards kill each other." So far, the casualties included three pimps (King Rob, Daddy Morebucks, and Countess Mangela-all of whom were murdered in intimate ways and blamed on Too-Fly), dozens of hookers from each side (Too-Fly's organization was wiped out completely), and a few bystanders caught in the crossfire. Too-Fly managed to escape the violence until last night.

As he hid (the fact that he *was* hiding tickled his shaky manhood with feather-flicks of pussy-dom), Too-Fly thought about Ramrod, his surrogate mentor.

Vice Squad (and more specifically, Wings Hauser's portrayal of Ramrod, the killer pimp) was a perennial favorite of his ilk. Too-Fly was more partial to Willie Dynamite with Gordon from Sesame Street, but he was willing to give ol' Wings his props.

Debating which one was the better pimp was a favorite pastime when business was slow and he felt like honoring his bitches with his presence with a little socializing. In his opinion, Willie Dynamite had more style, but Ramrod... now that was a crazy motherfucker right there. "Almost as crazy as me," he'd

338

The persona of Ramrod had universal appeal as it began to work its way into their culture; "He's having a Ramrod moment," or "He got all Ramrod on that bitch."

Their reverence gave him a sense of realness, like some legendary figure in the pimp lineage. It began to rub Too-Fly the wrong way.

"Fuck Ramrod," he liked to say whenever someone questioned his pimp-hand (status), or pretended not to be afraid of him. "You think that nigga was crazy? Well, you ain't seen nothing yet. Ramrod is a pussy! I eat niggas like Ramrod for breakfast!"

Yet he crouched, wondering exactly how Ramrod would handle the situation he was in.

Too-Fly fought the urge to check his injuries, as there were too many to worry about. And without the visual punch, he was able to deny the pain more effectively. To that end, he quietly thanked the cold weather (it was the middle of December) for keeping him mostly numb until the shivers came around, as they had been doing more and more frequently.

Too-Fly was bruised and battered; covered with third-degree burns; soaking wet; and leaking blood from an assortment of wounds that were exposed and hanging open to various degrees. He clenched his teeth and growled.

"I SWEAR TO GOD, I'M GONNA KILL ALL YOU MUTHAFUCKAS!!!!! EACH AND EVERY ONE OF YOU!!!!"

He went down the list.

1. Mangela's girl for shooting him back at the Lavender Lounge and for killing Tony Ducketts
2. King Rob's girls (the one with the slicked back hair and the pig-nosed one) who plowed their SUV into Too-Fly and sent him tumbling at the burn-barrel in

front of the lot selling Christmas trees for $45 a pop. He didn't even have a chance to acknowledge the pain before the flames from the overturned barrel licked his flesh, then ambushed him.

3. Daddy Morebucks' blockheaded henchman, Maximillian (if he was still alive). Too-Fly had taken the plunge off of Pier 7 with him. They were entangled in each other's embrace, wrestling for a fatal choke, clawing, scratching, and biting until the water hit them and the struggle became who could keep whom under long enough to drown the other. That was the last thing Too-Fly remembered before waking up 20 minutes later floating face-up on the surface.

4. That bitch, Bloody Mary… the one who was supposed to be dead, but was not dead. She was responsible for most of Too-Fly's injuries.

5. The *Philadelphia Inquirer* for running that terrible picture of him

6. That nappy-headed young buck who flipped his car the bird as he drove past the other day. The little bastard didn't think he saw him.

7. His 9th grade gym teacher for throwing him down the bleachers. Back then, you could get away with doing that to a kid.

8. Delia Diaz, who laughed in Too-Fly's face when he asked her to the junior prom. It was one of the reasons he dropped out of school a week later.

9. That shifty-assed guard who got him shanked when he was in the Pen.

10. His father.

11. The muthafuckin' White Man.

Light came in a silent burst from the window above the steps, winking first, then settling into a sustained glow. Too-Fly could see it through the slivers of open space between the wooden planks. There were footsteps from above, as if someone was approaching the back door. Probably someone with a gun coming to investigate all the noise.

Too-Fly was well known throughout the city. To "decent" folk, he was one of the scourges of the black community. Down in the ass of society, where hope dangled out of reach, he was a god among Players. He exploited women—so what? He drove a pink stretch Escalade, wore a different full-length fur every day of the week, rocked ice like it was nothing, and controlled a stable of the best hos in the city. Too-Fly's hos came in every flavor.

Explaining things to whomever lived here would be too difficult and time consuming at this point. Based on his appearance, they were more likely to shoot first when the saw him, and Too-Fly had already taken a bullet or two tonight.

His shiny brown hue was singed onyx about his face, head, and hands; his tight cornrows frayed. The red velvet suit with the fleece collar that clung to his long, tall frame, exposing the drastic v-shape of his back, was spotted with smolder-smudge soaked in city water that formed a puddle underneath him. His right sleeve was torn away at the shoulder to reveal his wiry yet sturdy arm, the lithe musculature like a tight braid of cable.

Too-Fly didn't know how he made it to the top of the ten-foot fence that separated the yard from the alley, but there he was. He shifted his weight and fell to the ground on the other side. The CLING-CLANG of fence-links slapping vertical posts started a chain reaction of barking.

Too-Fly worked his feet beneath him and launched forward to the end of the alley and out into the neighborhood. He crouched behind a wall of bushes that bordered the property at

341

the mouth of the alley until the short, plump, female silhouette that stood at the top of the stairs he was just hiding under finally went back inside, then awhile longer until the barking died down. It took awhile—about an hour.

"Enough of this cat-and-mouse shit," Too-Fly groaned. All this running and hiding was started to weigh on his ego.

What would Ramrod do? he thought.

Too-Fly popped what was left of his collar and walked out from behind the bushes. The last time he saw a clock, about twenty minutes ago, it was around 10:00 pm. It was a Tuesday night.

The streets were empty except for suckers pulling over-time coming home late and third-shift street urchins who glued themselves to a corner in groups of three or more to talk shit.

Too-Fly made it about four blocks when he heard his name.

The women's voice was unfamiliar, shifting effortlessly from playful ("Tooooo-Flyyyy") to deadly serious ("You're gonna pay for what you did to the Countess") in a matter of seconds.

There was a pick-up truck stopped at a red light on the other side of the parked car coming up on his left. Too-Fly's first instinct was to jump into the flatbed when the light turned green, but there was the thing with his pride. It put a stutter in his step, which allowed the truck to pull away before he could possibly reach it.

Too-Fly was in bad shape, his vision falling in and out of focus, his reflexes muddled and lazy. More and more, he wanted to lay down and sleep.

Just for a minute, his body tried to convince him. *Shot, stabbed, beaten, hung, thrown from a roof, set ablaze, drowned, and hit by a car...*

He shunned the words as if to acknowledge their meaning would therefore make it true. And the truth was that with all

the damage he had sustained in the past 36 hours, Too-Fly should be dead by now.

He was, in fact, dying, and he knew it. But he had unfinished business. If he was going out, he damn sure wasn't going out like no bitch. That's what they were calling him (a bitch) for starting this whole war. Even in the underworld, there was a certain code of conduct. And Too-Fly had walked up and shit all over it in their eyes.

Too-Fly flexed his shoulders, his back, and his arms, clenched his fists, and turned. In the dark, steam rising from his broad shoulders, he looked like a monster. It caused the woman behind him (one of Mangela's girls) to hesitate as she aimed her gun at him and fired twice. She was an older woman (Mature Fetish) with droopy, U-shaped breasts wrapped in a leather bustier and pasty belly fat pouring over the waist of her tight leather miniskirt. She held the gun sideways like she'd learned to shoot from watching hip-hop videos and "in the 'hood" flicks. Too-Fly could've stood still, and she would've missed him each time. Instead, he ran in a zig-zag pattern down 63rd Street and rounded the corner onto Market without looking back.

Mature Fetish was wearing stiletto heels and shuffling along like a bloated Peggy Bundy as she chased him. When Too-Fly looked back, he saw the way her eyes squeezed shut, and her arm bucked with each shot.

What the fuck is your problem? Pride said to him. *You look just like what they're calling you, running from that slut.*

Change of plans.

Too-Fly hid between two parked cars waiting to jump out and wring the life from Mature's throat when she reached him. Then, at least he'd have a gun… again.

He shrank, ready to pounce as she rounded the corner searching for him. She held her gun out in front of her, her arm shaking, tears streaming down her reddened face. He was just about to spring when a car rolled past and slammed on its brakes. From inside, a young black man leaned out.

"You da man, Too-Fly," shouted the young black man. His tone suddenly changed when he got a closer look. Most of Too-Fly's facial features—his lips, nose, eyebrows, and much of his skin—had been eaten away by flames. "Oh Sheeyyit!"

Too-Mutherfuckin'-Fly, Too-Fly thought, even as he darted out from his hiding spot and held his arms up over his face in case Mature took another shot. He felt a burning sensation in his left shoulder and knew immediately that he'd been hit yet again. Funny that he didn't even hear her gun go off. Maybe his hearing was starting to go.

Yep. The sound of Mature's heels clicking the pavement faded in and out, as did the music from the young black man's car stereo.

Too-Fly zigzagged down Market Street toward 62nd. He ducked in and out of the El stanchions to further disrupt Mature's aim. Two blocks back on the incline that crawled from Philly to Upper Darby, an old, red-orange van painted with a 70s-style mural rocked to life. Its rear doors flew open and coughed out the fattest woman Too-Fly had ever seen (Fat-Chick Fetish). She was wearing a headset microphone that cut into the soft, ample flesh around her cheeks and threatened to pop right off her big fat head. Her body was a map of cellulite and bruises and excess skin that completely covered the tight halter-top she wore when she jumped down from the van, which caused her blubber to bounce. Her wide, flat ass tested the seams of the hot pants that barely covered it, hip-fat bursting out from the edges like peach-pink dough rising.

Behind her, an attractive blond (attractive from afar) in a cheerleader's outfit (Cheerleader Fetish) hopped down and reached back inside to retrieve an automatic weapon. Cheerleader tossed it to Fat-Chick and grabbed another for herself.

Together, they fired away at Too-Fly.

Too-Fly grunted at the overwhelming PING of multiple rounds ricocheting off the stanchion he hid behind. He heard a "God-DAMN!" in the distance. It was the young black man reacting to Fat-Chick, who stopped momentarily and turned to face him. She was sensitive about her weight. The young black man peeled off as she raised her gun and fired at his car. A spray of bullets shattered his back windshield, but he kept on going.

"You know you want it, bitch!" Fat-Chick screamed as the young black man's car vanished up the hill.

"Hey, stop fucking around," Mature Fetish growled. "We gotta get that fucker."

"Where is he?" Fat-Chick responded, breathing heavily.

"Like, I think he's still behind that pillar," Cheerleader said. Her voice was different, bubblier than the others.

Maybe it was his mind fucking with him as its facilities dwindled, but Too-Fly could've sworn that he felt the ground shake beneath Fat-Chick's massive feet. She was getting closer. The bullet-pings were getting louder, and the time between the gunshots and their impact on the stanchion was shortening.

Too-Fly waited for a break in the gunfire, then zigzagged away.

He rounded the corner onto 61st Street and headed east. Even in his weakened condition, he easily outran them. He could still hear them searching in the distance, though. The night was quiet, and their voices carried like a motherfucker.

Too-Fly came to the first person he saw: a thin, non-threatening looking man working on his car at the corner of Arch Street. The man saw him coming, but there was no time to run after he slammed the hood again and again until it stuck.

"Fuck!" the man yelled and threw his arms in the air. "Please don't hurt me."

346

"Move!" Too-Fly growled, his voice bobbling on saliva and blood. He dug in his pocket for the gun that he forgot he didn't take from Mature Fetish.

"No, please," the man pleaded. "Take my money, but I need my ride."

If he had a gun, Too-Fly would've shot the man when he jumped in the car with him and buckled in.

"Just go where you need to go," he said. "But I need my car, man."

Too-Fly turned and gave the man a good, hard stare, yet he was strangely unaffected by his appearance. *This guy must really love his car*, he thought. It was a Mitsubishi-a '93 or maybe a '94. It wasn't a piece of shit; didn't look like it anyway. But it wasn't all that, either—certainly not worth dying over. Nothing was, 'cept maybe Too-Fly's pink stretch Escalade.

The man stuck out his hand. "I'm Carlos, by the way," he said. "You're Too-Fly, right?"

You've got to be fucking kidding me, Too-Fly thought of Carlos' gesture, which he ultimately ignored.

"That's Too-Motherfuckin'-Fly," he rasped.

The engine kicked in after the third attempt. Too-Fly turned the wheel and stepped on the gas.

Neither of them saw the massive blur that ran up behind the car. The engine revved and the back tires dug in for a moment, then spun freely. The car rocked forward and before they knew it, they were sitting at a decline.

"Oh my God!" Carlos said, staring out the back window.

Too-Fly, who was still trying to pull forward, turned and saw the shoulders and head of a tall, extremely muscular woman (Buff-Chick Fetish). Her thick biceps flexed tight, plump veins and horrible striations decorating her shoulders and neck as she held the back of the car up off the ground. Her face was beet-red and twisted into a clenched-teeth mask, similar to the ones that all

347

the meatheads in the back of all the gyms Too-Fly had ever worked out in made when they handled heavy weight.

Too-Fly reached for his gun... *D'oh!* He fumbled around for anything hard and preferably sharp that his fingers came to-a photograph in an antique brass frame, the whole thing wrapped in ribbon. There was something inscribed on the photo. His eyes skimmed it and kept going to the back windshield where Buff-Chick grimaced, square-jawed and wild-eyed. Her big, permed hairdo was like a tribal headdress.

Too-Fly flung the photo at the thing in the rear window, causing her to flinch, turn her head, and let go of the car.

Buff-Chick let out a loud scream. She had regained her footing, shuffling her legs beneath the car as she held it, which left them right in the path of the rear bumper when it fell and snapped both her shins. The antique picture frame had only splintered the window, so he could see her fall to the ground, knees first.

A pitter-pat of bullets shattered the window and smacked the leather headrests.

"Aaaah! We're going to die!" Carlos yelled, as he and Too-Fly ducked beneath the seats.

The car shot forward and planted a hard kiss on a few of the cars parked closest to it before stabilizing. Fat-Chick and Cheerleader ran after them (well, Cheerleader did, anyway), pointing their automatic weapons and shooting. Fat-Chick was only good for a few steps before she had to stop to suck wind in deep, audible gasps. She used one of her breaks to comfort Buff-Chick who was curled into a fetal-like position, shaking and clutching her legs.

Carlos waited until they were out of the bullets' reach and surveyed the damage. "Dios Mio... I said I *need* my car, man."

Too-Fly was fading at the wheel, swerving into the oncoming traffic. He kept catching himself at the last minute before a potential collision. Carlos reached for the wheel, but caught a firm backfist to the nose for his troubles.

"Hey!" Carlos cried out through his hands, which covered his bloodied nose.

"I ain't dead yet," Too-Fly mumbled. "Not by a long shot."

Carlos fell into a sudden sneezing fit, nasal blood flying all over his shirt, his pants, the dash, and Too-Fly's naked right arm. Something about the way Carlos' wet shirt clung to his chest caught Too-Fly's attention. The contour was plump and rounded, large nipples semi-erect. Right away he thought of the photo (a naked male stripper) and the inscription, which read, "To Carlos, the biggest queen in Philly."

Carlos remained in character until he tracked Too-Fly's sight-path down to his tits. Carlos' face suddenly relaxed.

"They look gooood, don't they, Too-Fucked?" Carlos said playfully, tracing circles around his wide areolas with his finger.

Too-Fly slammed on the brakes and flung the driver's side door open. Before he could jump out, Carlos plunged a switchblade deep into his thigh.

Too-Fly hit the ground rolling. Carlos jumped out after him and began kicking him as he tried to come to a stand. He reached in his car and grabbed a crowbar from the back seat.

Too-Fly was saving his strength for just the right moment. It came when Carlos raised the crowbar over his head. He lunged forward and shoved Carlos into the oncoming lane. Carlos fell backwards and rolled in a way that looked as if it should've broke his neck. Too-Fly fell too.

"Yer gonna get yours, motherfucker," Carlos said in a slightly higher voice than he spoke with in the car. He sprung to his feet, stuck his pinky and his index finger in his mouth, and whistled in the direction that Buff-Chick's screams were coming from. "I got 'em! He's over here," he said.

Too-Fly lay on his back, looking up at the tops of houses and the clouds and the dots that danced around in front of his face like a boxer down for the count. For a moment, he didn't know where he was. Once he remembered, he wondered how Carlos was able to hide those tits from him. Clearly they weren't taped down.

Carlos had already retrieved the crowbar from beneath a parked car on the other side of the street and was tapping it against his free hand as he approached, grinning.

"Who'd have thought that lil'-old me would take out the great Too…"

A passing hoopty snatched Carlos from sight-gobbled him right up and kept going for fifty feet before the driver stopped, stepped halfway out, and looked under his car. He gasped at the sight and again when his eyes backtracked to the point of impact.

There was Too-Fly, all burnt and bloody, crawling into Carlos' car.

"Fuck this!" the driver remarked as he jumped back into his hoopty and peeled off.

Too-Fly took off driving in the other direction, swerving terribly. In the rear-view he saw the hoopty shit Carlos' body messily from it rear end. He smiled and broke left at the corner.

From the right, Fat-Chick and Cheerleader were running toward him, but they were too far to do anything but fire off a few wild shots, which is exactly what they did.

Too-Fly threw up a few times as he drove, on creep, like he did when he wanted to announce his presence, but there was no adulation, no fear-based respect thrown his way this time. He drove until the scenery turned pretty—prettier than where he had been, at least.

He ended up on South Street—right off of it on 6th, actually. The surreal atmosphere set by the deliberately gauche storefronts boasting multicolored signs topped off with fluorescent lettering, the tricked-out econoboxes that oozed in a slow procession from stoplight to stoplight blaring low-end hip-hop and cheesy dance music, and the eclectic crowd didn't quite reach where he was parked, but it was close enough to it that he leeched off the feeling of motley unity in the air and sense of safety that the heavy police presence instilled.

Sheree, his "real-world bitch," lived five or six blocks south of here. Her place was his intended destination, but his body implored him to stop and rest NOW!

Sheree was the one he called when he wanted a break from the hustle: somewhere to lay low "in the cut" and chill. She liked nice things and was willing to overlook how he acquired the money to pay for them. On the surface, she was all innocent and shit. One of *them* types: kinda light-skinned (but thought she was lighter than she was) with bone-straight hair. She was pretty, but not nearly as pretty as she thought she was; not underneath the make-up and the expensive clothes, and the weave, and the fake eyelashes, and the implants, and the stank attitude she exuded around people who she thought to be uglier than she was. Still, men fawned over her.

At her core, Sheree was smart and funny as hell. She had a calming aura that made Too-Fly feel as if he didn't have to put on any airs around her. Of course, he did anyway. This was Too-Muthafuckin'-Fly, for fuck's sake, the biggest, baddest, P.I.M.P. in Philly.

Too-Fly reclined his seat, closed his eyes, and let his head fall back to the cushion.

Floating just out of clarity's reach, a voice teased his foggy awareness. Too-Fly opened his eyes and squinted away sleep's residual funk. He hadn't even realized that he dozed off.

His pride quickly reminded him that, in the shape he was

in, he could very easily have not woken up from that nap.

But he did. He had to.

Too-Fly absolutely refused to go out "like a bitch." He had two reputations to live up to: his and Ramrod's.

Was that *his* name he heard being spoken in that annoyingly robotic newscaster tone, or was he just dreaming?

Too-Fly closed his eyes as if the momentary blindness might enhance his hearing. Sure enough, he heard his name again. It was coming from a radio or a television.

He opened his eyes and followed the voice. A large-screen TV looked out through a window in a house across the street. Too-Fly could see the back of the person inside (an older man) sitting with his remote held in perpetual channel-surf position.

The news was running footage from the security camera in the gas-station/mini-mart where Too-Fly and Bloody Mary (in caked-on, flesh-tone makeup, heavily tinted, bug-eyed ski goggles, and a black, Neoprene facemask that covered the lower half of her face from the tip of her nose down) squared off like wild dogs earlier in the night. The sight of her tweaked his sore muscles. Too-Fly had gotten in a few good shots, but she had clearly whupped him.

But how could that be? A chick? Whup *him*??? Whup *Too-Muthafuckin'-Fly*, the biggest, baddest, blah, blah, blah...?

The fight unfolded slightly different in his memory; hence, the reality was painful to watch. The camera hadn't caught what happened up on the roof at least, before his feet kicked through the front window of the place as he dangled from the rope that she strangled him with from behind. He managed to flip her off of him just as consciousness started to slip away. He got in a couple good kicks as she worked her way back to her feet. Despite his long, tall frame, Too-Fly had big, muscular thighs—"thick," he

352

called them. He claimed that they gave him a better thrust when he was "handlin' his bidness." What they did was send Mary flying with each kick.

In retrospect, it probably wasn't a good idea to stop, but Too-Fly needed to catch his breath and stabilize his double/triple vision. He thought for sure that he'd put her out of commission. He had kicked her so hard that it hurt his own leg, so hard that he felt her bones shatter.

Too-Fly looked up in time to see Bloody Mary coming at him fast. She was poised between horizontal and vertical, and she was baring teeth.

The next thing he knew, he was falling over the edge of the roof, watching the ground approach, and wondering whether or not he would be able to unravel the rope around his neck in time to….

Too-Fly awoke on the floor of the mini-mart coughing and gasping for air. There was glass everywhere. People ran when they saw him. The pain that radiated out from his neck was so intense that the quick jaunt down from its throbbing peak was almost orgasmic. Then he went numb.

He had wondered exactly how he broke the rope. The first thing he saw on the security footage was his feet dangling outside the window, then CRASH!

The way his body jerked just before he fell, it appeared that all his flailing must have caused the rope to break before he went unconscious.

Too-Fly never saw Bloody Mary enter. He was too dazed from his trip to the precipice of death and back. She just seemed to be there, standing over him, her chest heaving. In reality, her entrance was much less dramatic than that.

Mary met Too-Fly halfway between kneeling and standing and tossed him into the six-foot pyramid of Pepsi two-liters, then the rows of steaming coffeepots lined up like bleachers, then through the glass doors of the refrigerated bins—one after another after another.

Too-Fly climbed to his feet, glass raining down from his clothing, the rest embedded in the flesh of his face and hands.

Bloody Mary walked over, snatched a large knife from the bin behind the deli counter, gave the petrified deli clerk a condescending once over as he curled into a tight, quivering ball in the corner, and returned to her business with Too-Fly.

From where he sat, in his car, across the street, watching the footage unfold, Too-Fly counted 27 times that she stabbed him.

Hmmm... Seemed like a lot more at the time.

Too-Fly thought he was gaining headway when Mary's arm came off in his hands. But the surge of confidence was bittersweet.

Great. I'm getting my ass whupped by a chick...with a prosthetic arm.

He didn't expect the disembodied arm to wriggle in his grip, or the hand to flex, then clamp down on his balls.

Of course, the camera didn't catch that part. His back was to it. He was doubled over in pain trying to pull the severed arm off his jewels.

Bloody Mary stepped in from just off camera, kicked his legs out from under him, and pulled an entire aisle-full of convenience-store groceries and snacks down on top of him.

Pinned beneath the pile, Too-Fly watched the arm crawl out and up to her feet.

She reached down, grabbed it, and walked across the fallen aisle to the one next to it, where she grabbed a roll of duct tape. She tore it open with her teeth and taped her arm back to her shoulder. She was horribly encumbered in doing so, having to lean against the shelves, pressing her severed arm between it and her body. As a result, it hung at a strange angle. She looked

354

around, down at the fallen aisle that shook as Too-Fly struggled to lift it off of him, then right into the security camera. She turned away, unconcerned with being filmed, jogged toward the front window, and jumped through it like she was used to leaving scenes that way.

Too-Fly never bought any of this undead-killer nonsense. A few things *had* left him wondering, though. She was extraordinarily gaunt, almost skeletal. And she smelled like something had jumped inside her and died days ago. All the cheap perfume in the world couldn't hide it, even though she obviously had tried. And there was all that thick, waxy makeup she wore. It was caked on in sloppy layers, like a mortician might apply in haste to hide a large bruise or an ugly, gaping wound. Some of the makeup rubbed off during the melee, revealing sections that projected a grey, rotten hue. Her long red hair was twisted and unkempt, the color faded. Her eyes, which were supposed to be hollow, according to the story, were hidden behind those bug-eyed goggles, so he never got a look at them.

But c'mon… a living dead chick? A fucking zombie? Ri-i-ight…

She *did* seem to move differently than a normal person. And yeah, the arm *did* seem to move on its own when he ripped it from her shoulder. But she *had* beaten him near unconscious with that damn support beam, so maybe it was just his mind playing tricks on him. Watching from the camera's perspective, he couldn't be sure that it wasn't just a prosthetic or that all that other shit that he had noticed before was just a result of the power of suggestion coloring his reality.

Bloody Mary was all over the news lately. Tony Ducketts, Too-Fly's very own "Huggy Bear," informed him on the sly that Mary was the one in the back of the black van, which lead Too-Fly to surmise that she was behind this whole frame-up. Too-Fly and Tony used to hustle together when they were kids. Now,

Tony ran a dope ring out of the Lavender Lounge at 54th and Cedar. It was the last place Too-Fly expected an attempt on his life to go down.

It was another one of Mangela's girls: two of them, actually. Two raven-haired, Latin beauties, conjoined at the left bicep and hip (Girl-on-Girl Fetish). One wore a leather corset and assless chaps, and the other a tight see-through top, a mini-skirt, and high boots. Unless you were looking for it, Girl-on-Girl looked like ordinary twins who were strangely close the way twins usually are, walking around, standing, or sitting with an arm around the other.

One of their talents was lulling men into a daze, then going for the kill while their victims stared, mesmerized. They were sitting in a booth on the other side of the dance floor, sucking face like two lipstick lesbians, until they jumped up on the table and let their handguns flash.

Too-Fly was sitting right next to Tony Ducketts, who had just told him about Bloody Mary, when Tony's head blew apart. Too-Fly had been shot, too (in the right arm), but it wasn't until he got out of there that he noticed.

By then, he had been shot three more times. That was last night.

So, why him? Why T.M.F.?

He was asking the same question before he went to see Tony Ducketts.

It started about a month ago when the old, black van began trolling Too-Fly's turf night after night. The pretty blond inside finally stopped to chat with Jade, one of his prime girls. She said her name was Rainah, and that she and her friend (an older woman who always sat in the back, shrouded by darkness) were into pretty young girls like Jade. Jade was into it right off the bat, but she told them to come back the next night. She said she needed to talk it over with her pimp, only she referred to him as her "daddy." Too-Fly usually reserved Jade for his well-known, high-rolling clients, but Rainah was flashing big (stolen) money, and if she was freaky enough to play with hos, then maybe Jade could talk her into coming to work for him. He could get top dollar for a hot piece of ass like Rainah.

The next night, Too-Fly went with Jade to collect the money personally from Rainah. He tried to get a look at the woman in the back of the van, even smiled and gave her his best "Hey girl...," but she only nodded in response and turned away from him. He had his reservations about her, but the money was too good to ignore, so he sent Jade on her way with directions to "make daddy proud." It was the last he heard from her.

A month had passed. Too-Fly had the word out to watch for Jade. He went looking himself a few times, peering under cardboard tenements and in abandoned buildings where the crackheads languished like the living dead, scurrying from light like giant, flesh-covered roaches.

Eventually, one of Too-Fly's eyes in the street told him that they saw Jade hanging out with a pretty blond that sounded a lot like Rainah.

He found them out in Manayunk. He followed them for a while and watched them lure men into precarious situations, then rob them blind. They were actually quite good at it.

Fucking bitch, he thought. *How dare she disrespect me like that?*

Too-Fly waited until Jade was alone (at least he thought she was) and made his move. She was standing outside of a bar, puffing on a cigarette. To his surprise, she told him that she wasn't going anywhere with him; that she was with *them* now, that she was happy. There was something about an army and a lot of other bullshit about self-respect and not having to comprise her dignity, blah, blah, blah. Most of all, it was her confidence in the way that she blew him off that infuriated him.

A group of chivalrous college-types showing plumage filed out of the bar when Too-Fly got loud with her. Rainah was hanging all over one of them; her next victim, no doubt.

"Ayyight!" Too-Fly said, as he backed away to his car. "So, it's like *that*?"

He started the engine and tossed a "Suckas!" to the college-types. A few of them motioned as if they were going to give chase. Too-Fly slammed on his brakes and stared them down. "That's what I thought," he said, as he drove off.

The next night, Too-Fly hired a crackhead to take them both out: Jade for straight-dissing him, and Rainah for filling Jade's head with all that garbage in the first place. Those crackheads would do anything for a fix.

The crackhead told Too-Fly that his name was Bryan.

"I don't give a fuck what your name is," Too-Fly responded, as he dressed Bryan up nice and clean, just like the college boys that Rainah and Jade liked to rob.

The girls fell for the ruse hook, line, and sinker. When Bryan got them to his car (a rental that Too-Fly paid for under an alias), Too-Fly shot Jade in the head. He shot Rainah too, but she managed to get away.

The news flashed a photograph of a pretty man dressed in Sunday clothes. He had one of those fine, wrap-around beards that looked as if it was drawn on with a Sharpie. It was Dem Hos. Too-Fly almost didn't recognize him with hair and wearing "normal" clothes. Words screamed in bold lettering beneath the photo: **Another Pimp Murdered.**

Next came the newscaster tone that annoyed him so: "The war in the city's underbelly continues as 44-year-old Lester Banks-a local pimp known in the streets as Dem Hos-was found about an hour ago, murdered in his home in the Strawberry Mansion section of the city. Evidence has been found at the scene that links rival pimp, James 'Jimmie Too-Fly' Shockley, to the murder. Shockley is also the prime suspect in the murders of three other local pimps in what authorities are referring to as a street war."

Great. Now he'd have to deal with Dem Hos's people as well.

Suddenly, the crowd spooked him, floating in and out of the frame of buildings on either side of South Street like characters on a tall movie screen. The police... they were all suspect now. Too-Fly stewed in his anger and pessimism. *They know. They have to. How could they not see me?* Shit like that.

He'd have to cross South Street to get to Sheree's place. It wouldn't be easy, but Too-Fly finally felt well enough to maneuver, so he was going to try. His plan was to get some money from her and disappear for a while.

Too-Fly knew right away that something was wrong when he found Sheree's place ransacked. Well, maybe not right away... First, he had to wait for his vision to right itself. Maybe all the mess was just a result of double vision. It was happening so often that he stopped trying to differentiate between the two modes of sight, reticent to just *be*, and *do,* and live in the moment. There was a horrible smell, maybe... or maybe he smelled himself. *This* smell was like bad sex and sweaty ball-funk, like the worst body odor imaginable. Like human shit.

He kept the lights off, which made things more difficult, but Sheree's house was one of those places with a lot of windows—too many for Too-Fly's paranoid taste. And she refused to dress them with curtains or blinds.

Too-Fly was still wearing the trenchcoat with the hoodie lining that he used to get past the crowd and the police on South, which he "borrowed" from an old homeless man on 5th and

Bainbridge. Too-Fly lowered the hood and staggered over to the couch. Along the way, he kicked a few things—things made of glass, things made of plastic, and… something slippery. There was a note stuck to the TV. It was the first thing he saw when he reached the couch. Sheree had him position it (the couch) according to some Feng Shui bullshit so that the eye had a direct path to the opposite wall, where the entertainment center was located.

Too-Fly slipped and kicked his way over to the television and lifted the note from the bottom.

Watch Me!!! It read, with an arrow pointing down to the VCR/DVD combo that he got her for her birthday.

Too-Fly's eyes tracked back to the couch. He hadn't noticed until now that it was pushed away from the wall. Behind it, *his* video camera sat atop *his* tripod, facing him. He always fronted like he had some secret interest in filmmaking to seem more "intellectual" to Sheree, but really they were just toys.

Too-Fly wobbled where he stood. His head spun and made him nauseous. He was colder now than before, colder than when he was outside.

He dropped down to a crouch and waited for it to pass. He tore the note from the screen and pushed "play" on the VCR. He knew it was going to be bad.

*　　*　　*

FADE IN: Screams. King Rob's blockheaded henchman, Maximillian, stands over Sheree in the space between the couch and the entertainment center, clutching a mess of her thick black hair in his hand, his large, fat penis hanging out and glazed with something, maybe saliva. Sheree is naked, her nose bloodied, her left eye blackened and swollen shut, lip busted. Her face is damp and bloated as if she has been crying for some time. Her

360

mouth leaks a steady stream of drool laced with blood. Her pubic hair is matted and moist.

She cries out as Maximillian yanks her head and leans down closer to her. He licks her face and turns to the camera. "Casualties of war, motherfucka," he says into the lens.

In the background, six sets of legs standing in a sloppy semi-circle reach up into the darkness. They belong to a few of Dem Hos's girls, a few of Daddy Morebucks' and a few of Mangela's-Midget Sex Fetish and Schoolgirl Fetish, who wears Amputee Fetish's limbless body on her back like a bookbag.

"Bring em' in," Maximillian says to someone. We hear a door open and close off camera and the sound of feet shuffling. The camera zooms out to reveal three withered, lurching bodies (crackheads-two men and a woman) in various stages of complete rock-bottomness. They perk up when they see Sheree, who screams and bucks in Maximillian's grasp when she recognizes them. Apparently, they have a history.

"Hold em' there for a minute," he says, digs into the pocket of his leather jacket, and retrieves a crack pipe, a lighter, and a dimebag-sized baggie filled with crack. He exaggerates his movements to ensure that the crackheads see him put the pipe and the lighter on the floor. He holds the baggie up in front of the camera, then looks directly into the lens.

"She's already got a couple of these in her stomach, but I thought I'd give her one more just to refresh their memory. They'll do anything to get this shit, but I'm sure you know that."

"Please help me, Shock!" Sheree screams at the lens.

Maximillian reacts angrily. He yanks her head and slaps her. When she opens her mouth to scream, he shoves the baggie down her throat. "Be a good girl and swallow this," he says, and holds her mouth closed.

Sheree grunts in protest and shakes her head.

"I said swallow it," Maximillian roars and kicks her in the stomach.

Sheree crumbles to the floor, coughing and choking. Maximillian looks up at someone off camera. "Didju get the…" he starts to say, then motions to catch something. A metallic blur flies through the frame and into Maximillian's hands. He holds it (a butter knife) in front of the camera. "Nice and dull," he smiles, as he places it on the floor next to the crack pipe and the lighter and motions again to "throw it." A larger blur flies past. Maximillian catches it (a bottle of vegetable oil) and holds it out. He places it on the floor next to the knife.

"Don't forget to leave a note," he says, just as one of the girls tapes the note to the TV screen.

Maximillian disappears into the background where he and the girls watch the crackheads ambush Sheree. She screams and tries to fight them off, but they are in a frenzy. One of the men shoves his arm in her mouth and pushes with all his strength to reach down her throat. Sheree flails and bucks, choking on the frail limb. She manages to kick him off, but another one tackles her. The first one shakes off the blow to his abdomen and crawls over to her. Sheree is weak from almost losing consciousness. She moans and kicks pathetically, her eyes threatening to roll back. They fly open when the woman shoves her greased forearm up into Sheree's anus, invading her rectum with its aggressive probing, fingertips clawing and digging into its lining. Sheree opens her mouth, but nothing comes out. The first crackhead shoves his arm back in and down her throat. Her body begins to twitch involuntarily. While the others probe, the third crackhead grabs the butter knife and holds it close, as if its value might make him a target. He pushes the others away from her. The arm in her ass slides out with a squirty-pop, the one in her mouth with an awful, belching sound that precedes a wash of bile and a coughing fit. The crackhead with the knife kneels down beside her and begins to rub the dull blade against the soft, slightly loose flesh of her stomach. Again, it wakes Sheree out of near unconsciousness. She screams and bats his arm away. The others pummel and scratch at her. Sheree fights them off again. She gets up amidst the barrages of fists and clawed hands and stumbles in a hunch toward the bedroom. The crackheads chase her off camera.

*   *   *

Too-Fly followed the scene beyond the frame of the television, back down the hallway that led to the bedroom. He could hear the struggle. On the tape, it was coming from right where he was looking. The bedroom door was closed, and there were handprints of... something, probably blood, leading up to the doorknob.

Too-Fly pounded the "off" button with his fist (but hit "input" instead) and hurried down the hall. In the background, he noticed the theme music from Friday Night Fights on ESPN and realized what he'd done. Friday Night Fights was his favorite show, next to The Sopranos.

As he approached the door, Too-Fly's excitement made him lightheaded, so he braced himself on the walls at either side to keep from falling. The doorknob slid in his hand when he tried to

open it. It was wet.

He kicked the door open.

The smell of crack smoke stung his sinuses with its B.O. and sour blood-stank aftertaste. Sheree was propped against the dresser, not quite sitting up, not quite lying down. The expression on her face looked almost as if she went out laughing as a result of some swan song of endorphins that sparked up to mitigate the terror she must have felt. Her eyes were frozen wide open and looking down at the vagina-shaped wound in her gut and the tangle of intestines strewn in a pile between her legs. Indentations in the intestinal wall marked where one of the crackheads had tried to work the baggies along from the outside. At some point, they gave up and cut them out, or tore them out, or bit them out.

The crackheads sat close together, marinated in Euphoria. Their eyelids fluttered at the suggestion that someone else might be in the room with them but ultimately floated to a half-open, half-shut position, eyes looking straight ahead, but seeing nothing but their ordinary surroundings. Their hands and arms were covered with blood; the woman's hand was caked with dried feces. The crack lady had blood smeared all over her face and in her hair as well. Too-Fly guessed that she did the cutting/tearing/biting.

"Such a waste," said a female voice from behind.

Too-Fly whipped around. There was a tall, gaunt female shape standing in the darkness in the middle of the living room. Light from the television bounced off her left side, lending it slight detail. It was Bloody Mary. Behind her and to the left, Rainah sat on the old-fashioned radiator. She was dressed in dirty cargo pants and a fitted shirt. Her hair was in a messy bun on top of her head. She wore her right arm in a splint.

"Guys like you ruin everything you touch."

Too-Fly felt suddenly energized. This was the moment he'd been waiting for. It crossed his mind that he might be dreaming this as he lay dying somewhere. It felt real enough when he balled his fists.

"I should've had that crackhead hunt you down and finish your ass," he said to Rainah.

"Yeah. You probably should have. But you didn't. We won't make the same mistake."

"All this over a stupid bitch?" Too-Fly said. "All *this????*"

Rainah snatched a Balisong knife from her waist, flipped the blade, and hopped down off the radiator.

She lunged at Too-Fly and ran into Bloody Mary's extended arm.

"She was one of *us,* you son of a bitch," Rainah screamed, her voice cracking and primed to break. "She was... my friend."

Mary shoved Rainah back and hissed through her teeth for her to settle down.

Rainah surrendered her hands to the air and backed off. She was pissed.

Mary turned back to Too-Fly. She held her left arm out in front of her (the one that Too-Fly ripped off) and took it through its full range of motion, flexing her fingers and curling her wrists. She ended with her palm turned upward, fingers flexed. With her index finger she called him forward.

On the TV, Michael Buffer stood in the middle of a ring, leaning in to the overhead microphone that tumbled down from the ceiling, his hand caressing it from the bottom up and guiding it toward his plastic face. "LLLLLLET'S GET READ-EEE TO RUMBLLLLLLLLLLLLEEEE!!!!!!!"

It was as good a cue as any for Too-Fly to launch at her. He cocked his arm back, fist balled tightly, and charged.

Author photo: Darin Basile. Models (From left to right): Camille, BombRog, Key

ABOUT THE AUTHOR

Andre Duza is a member of the Bizarro movement, writing under the sub-style Brutality Chronic. His books include Dead Bitch Army, Jesus Freaks, and the upcoming Dead Bitch Army Graphic Novel. His novelette Don't F(Beep)k with the Coloureds! is featured in The Bizarro Starter Kit, and he has contributed short stories to Permuted Press' zombie anthologies Undead and Undead: Flesh Feast. In addition to writing, Andre is an avid bodybuilder and a certified instructor of Spirit Fist Kung Fu. Visit him online at **www.houseofduza.com.**

ABOUT THE ARTISTS

Published locally and nationally, **Fred Moore** is a freelance illustrator currently residing in Pittsburgh, PA. While working professionally as a motion broadcast designer, Fred maintains his creative eye on the side. His illustration endeavors include oils, pen & ink, pencils and digital renderings. Examples of Fred's work can be found at **www.illustrationwizard.com** or contact him directly at illustrator89@hotmail.com

Silverfish was born in Houston, Texas on March 10th, 1983. Currently living in Lake Jackson, Texas. Works largely in (sometimes macabre) surrealism, though available for illustration. Also does some clothing design. Materials used are primarily pencil, colored pencil, and ink. View online at: **http://www.angelfire.com/scary/silverfish370**

Bizarro books

CATALOGUE – SPRING 200

Bizarro Books publishes under the following imprints:

www.rawdogscreamingpress.com

www.eraserheadpress.co

www.afterbirthbooks.com

www.swallowdownpress.co

For all your Bizarro needs visit:

WWW.BIZARROCENTRAL.COM

Introduce yourselves to the bizarro genre and all of its authors with the *Bizarro Starter Kit* series. Each volume features short novels and short stories by ten of the leading bizarro authors, designed to give you a perfect sampling of the genre for only $5 plus shipping.

BB-0X1
"The Bizarro Starter Kit"
(Orange)

Featuring D. Harlan Wilson, Carlton Mellick III, Jeremy Robert Johnson, Kevin L Donihe, Gina Ranalli, Andre Duza, Vincent W. Sakowski, Steve Beard, John Edward Lawson, and Bruce Taylor.

236 pages $5

BB-0X2
"The Bizarro Starter Kit"
(Blue)

Featuring Ray Fracalossy, Jeremy C. Shipp, Jordan Krall, Mykle Hansen, Andersen Prunty, Eckhard Gerdes, Bradley Sands, Steve Aylett, Christian TeBordo, and Tony Rauch.

244 pages $5

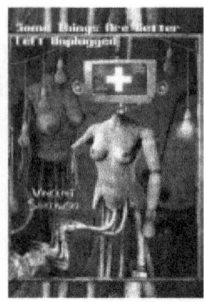

BB-001"The Kafka Effekt" D. Harlan Wilson - A collection of forty-four irreal short stories loosely written in the vein of Franz Kafka, with more than a pinch of William S. Burroughs sprinkled on top. **211 pages $14**

BB-002 "Satan Burger" Carlton Mellick III - The cult novel that put Carlton Mellick III on the map ... Six punks get jobs at a fast food restaurant owned by the devil in a city violently overpopulated by surreal alien cultures. **236 pages $14**

BB-003 "Some Things Are Better Left Unplugged" Vincent Sakwoski - Join The Man and his Nemesis, the obese tabby, for a nightmare roller coaster ride into this postmodern fantasy. **152 pages $10**

BB-004 "Shall We Gather At the Garden?" Kevin L Donihe - Donihe's Debut novel. Midgets take over the world, The Church of Lionel Richie vs. The Church of the Byrds, plant porn and more! **244 pages $14**

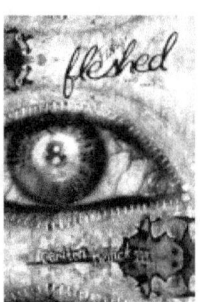

BB-005 "Razor Wire Pubic Hair" Carlton Mellick III - A genderless humandildo is purchased by a razor dominatrix and brought into her nightmarish world of bizarre sex and mutilation. **176 pages $11**

BB-006 "Stranger on the Loose" D. Harlan Wilson - The fiction of Wilson's 2nd collection is planted in the soil of normalcy, but what grows out of that soil is a dark, witty, otherworldly jungle... **228 pages $14**

BB-007 "The Baby Jesus Butt Plug" Carlton Mellick III - Using clones of the Baby Jesus for anal sex will be the hip sex fetish of the future. **92 pages $10**

BB-008 "Fishyfleshed" Carlton Mellick III - The world of the past is an illogical flatland lacking in dimension and color, a sick-scape of crispy squid people wandering the desert for no apparent reason. **260 pages $14**

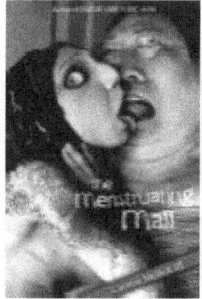

BB-009 **"Dead Bitch Army"** Andre Duza - Step into a world filled with racist teenagers, cannibals, 100 warped Uncle Sams, automobiles with razor-sharp teeth, living graffiti, and a pissed-off zombie bitch out for revenge. **344 pages $16**

BB-010 **"The Menstruating Mall"** Carlton Mellick III *"The Breakfast Club* meets *Chopping Mall* as directed by David Lynch."* - Brian Keene **212 pages $12**

BB-011 **"Angel Dust Apocalypse"** Jeremy Robert Johnson - Meth-heads, man-made monsters, and murderous Neo-Nazis. "Seriously amazing short stories..." - Chuck Palahniuk, author of *Fight Club* **184 pages $11**

BB-012 **"Ocean of Lard"** Kevin L Donihe / Carlton Mellick III - A parody of those old Choose Your Own Adventure kid's books about some very odd pirates sailing on a sea made of animal fat. **176 pages $12**

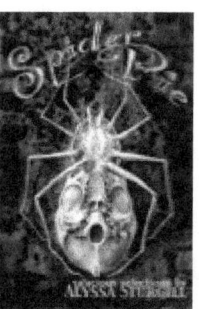

BB-013 **"Last Burn in Hell"** John Edward Lawson - From his lurid angst-affair with a lesbian music diva to his ascendance as unlikely pop icon the one constant for Kenrick Brimley, official state prison gigolo, is he's got no clue what he's doing. **172 pages $14**

BB-014 **"Tangerinephant"** Kevin Dole 2 - TV-obsessed aliens have abducted Michael Tangerinephant in this bizarro combination of science fiction, satire, and surrealism. **164 pages $11**

BB-015 **"Foop!"** Chris Genoa - Strange happenings are going on at Dactyl, Inc, the world's first and only time travel tourism company. "A surreal pie in the face!" - Christopher Moore **300 pages $14**

BB-016 **"Spider Pie"** Alyssa Sturgill - A one-way trip down a rabbit hole inhabited by sexual deviants and friendly monsters, fairytale beginnings and hideous endings. **104 pages $11**

 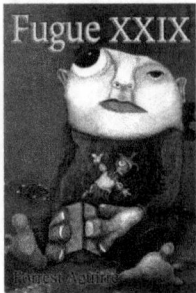  

BB-017 "The Unauthorized Woman" Efrem Emerson - Enter the world of the inner freak, a landscape populated by the pre-dead and morticioners, by cockroaches and 300-lb robots. **104 pages $11**

BB-018 "Fugue XXIX" Forrest Aguirre - Tales from the fringe of speculative literary fiction where innovative minds dream up the future's uncharted territories while mining forgotten treasures of the past. **220 pages $16**

BB-019 "Pocket Full of Loose Razorblades" John Edward Lawson - A collection of dark bizarro stories. From a giant rectum to a foot-fungus factory to a girl with a biforked tongue. **190 pages $13**

BB-020 "Punk Land" Carlton Mellick III - In the punk version of Heaven, the anarchist utopia is threatened by corporate fascism and only Goblin, Mortician's sperm, and a blue-mohawked female assassin named Shark Girl can stop them. **284 pages $15**

BB-021 "Pseudo-City" D. Harlan Wilson - Pseudo-City exposes what waits in the bathroom stall, under the manhole cover and in the corporate boardroom, all in a way that can only be described as mind-bogglingly irreal. **220 pages $16**

BB-022 "Kafka's Uncle and Other Strange Tales" Bruce Taylor - Anslenot and his giant tarantula (tormentor? fri-end?) wander a desecrated world in this novel and collection of stories from Mr. Magic Realism Himself.   **348 pages $17**

BB-023 "Sex and Death In Television Town" Carlton Mellick III - In the old west, a gang of hermaphrodite gunslingers take refuge from a demon plague in Telos: a town where its citizens have televisions instead of heads.   **184 pages $12**

BB-024 "It Came From Below The Belt" Bradley Sands - What can Grover Goldstein do when his severed, sentient penis forces him to return to high school and help it win the presidential election? **204 pages $13**

BB-025 "Sick: An Anthology of Illness" John Lawson, editor - These Sick stories are horrendous and hilarious dissections of creative minds on the scalpel's edge. **296 pages $16**

BB-026 "Tempting Disaster" John Lawson, editor - A shocking and alluring anthology from the fringe that examines our culture's obsession with taboos. **260 pages $16**

BB-027 "Siren Promised" Jeremy Robert Johnson - Nominated for the Bram Stoker Award. A potent mix of bad drugs, bad dreams, brutal bad guys, and surreal/incredible art by Alan M. Clark. **190 pages $13**

BB-028 "Chemical Gardens" Gina Ranalli - Ro and punk band *Green is the Enemy* find Kreepkins, a surfer-dude warlock, a vengeful demon, and a Metal Priestess in their way as they try to escape an underground nightmare. **188 pages $13**

  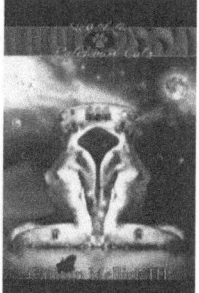 

BB-029 "Jesus Freaks" Andre Duza For God so loved the world that he gave his only two begotten sons... and a few million zombies. **400 pages $16**

BB-030 "Grape City" Kevin L. Donihe - More Donihe-style comedic bizarro about a demon named Charles who is forced to work a minimum wage job on Earth after Hell goes out of business. **108 pages $10**

BB-031"Sea of the Patchwork Cats" Carlton Mellick III - A quiet dreamlike tale set in the ashes of the human race. For Mellick enthusiasts who also adore *The Twilight Zone.* **112 pages $10**

BB-032 "Extinction Journals" Jeremy Robert Johnson - An uncanny voyage across a newly nuclear America where one man must confront the problems associated with loneliness, insane dieties, radiation, love, and an ever-evolving cockroach suit with a mind of its own. **104 pages $10**

  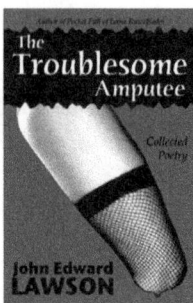 

BB-033 "Meat Puppet Cabaret" Steve Beard At last! The secret connection between Jack the Ripper and Princess Diana's death revealed! **240 pages $16 / $30**

BB-034 "The Greatest Fucking Moment in Sports" Kevin L. Donihe - In the tradition of the surreal anti-sitcom *Get A Life* comes a tale of triumph and agape love from the master of comedic bizarro. **108 pages $10**

BB-035 "The Troublesome Amputee" John Edward Lawson - Disturbing verse from a man who truly believes nothing is sacred and intends to prove it. **104 pages $9**

BB-036 "Deity" Vic Mudd God (who doesn't like to be called "God") comes down to a typical, suburban, Ohio family for a little vacation—but it doesn't turn out to be as relaxing as He had hoped it would be... **168 pages $12**

  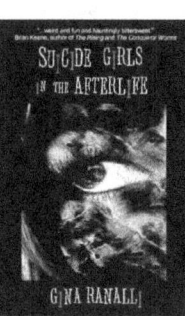 

BB-037 "The Haunted Vagina" Carlton Mellick III - It's difficult to love a woman whose vagina is a gateway to the world of the dead. **132 pages $10**

BB-038 "Tales from the Vinegar Wasteland" Ray Fracalossy - Witness: a man is slowly losing his face, a neighbor who periodically screams out for no apparent reason, and a house with a room that doesn't actually exist. **240 pages $14**

BB-039 "Suicide Girls in the Afterlife" Gina Ranalli - After Pogue commits suicide, she unexpectedly finds herself an unwilling "guest" at a hotel in the Afterlife, where she meets a group of bizarre characters, including a goth Satan, a hippie Jesus, and an alien-human hybrid. **100 pages $9**

BB-040 "And Your Point Is?" Steve Aylett - In this follow-up to LINT multiple authors provide critical commentary and essays about Jeff Lint's mind-bending literature. **104 pages $11**

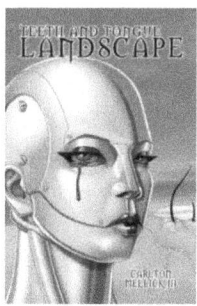

BB-041 **"Not Quite One of the Boys"** Vincent Sakowski -While drug-dealer Maxi drinks with Dante in purgatory, God and Satan play a little tri-level chess and do a little bargaining over his business partner, Vinnie, who is still left on earth. **220 pages $14**

BB-042 **"Teeth and Tongue Landscape"** Carlton Mellick III - On a planet made out of meat, a socially-obsessive monophobic man tries to find his place amongst the strange creatures and communities that he comes across. **110 pages $10**

BB-043 **"War Slut"** Carlton Mellick III - Part "1984," part "Waiting for Godot," and part action horror video game adaptation of John Carpenter's "The Thing." **116 pages $10**

BB-044 **"All Encompassing Trip"** Nicole Del Sesto -In a world where coffee is no longer available, the only television shows are reality TV re-runs, and the animals are talking back, Nikki, Amber and a singing Coyote in a do-rag are out to restore the light **308 pages $15**

BB-045 **"Dr. Identity"** D. Harlan Wilson - Follow the Dystopian Duo on a killing spree of epic proportions through the irreal postcapitalist city of Bliptown where time ticks sideways, artificial Bug-Eyed Monsters punish citizens for consumer-capitalist lethargy, and ultraviolence is as essential as a daily multivitamin. **208 pages $15**

BB-046 **"The Million-Year Centipede"** Eckhard Gerdes -Wakelin, frontman for 'The Hinge,' wrote a poem so prophetic that to ignore it dooms a person to drown in blood. **130 pages $12**

BB-047 **"Sausagey Santa"** Carlton Mellick III - A bizarro Christmas tale featuring Santa as a piratey mutant with a body made of sausages. **124 pages $10**

BB-048 **"Misadventures in a Thumbnail Universe"** Vincent Sakowski - Dive deep into the surreal and satirical realms of neo-classical Blender Fiction, filled with television shoes and flesh-filled skies. **120 pages $10**

 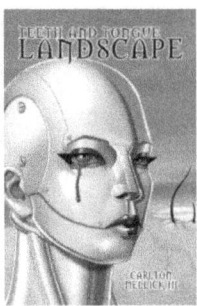  

BB-041 **"Not Quite One of the Boys"** Vincent Sakowski -While drug-dealer Maxi drinks with Dante in purgatory, God and Satan play a little tri-level chess and do a little bargaining over his business partner, Vinnie, who is still left on earth. **220 pages $14**

BB-042 **"Teeth and Tongue Landscape"** Carlton Mellick III - On a planet made out of meat, a socially-obsessive monophobic man tries to find his place amongst the strange creatures and communities that he comes across. **110 pages $10**

BB-043 **"War Slut"** Carlton Mellick III - Part "1984," part "Waiting for Godot," and part action horror video game adaptation of John Carpenter's "The Thing." **116 pages $10**

BB-044 **"All Encompassing Trip"** Nicole Del Sesto -In a world where coffee is no longer available, the only television shows are reality TV re-runs, and the animals are talking back, Nikki, Amber and a singing Coyote in a do-rag are out to restore the light **308 pages $15**

BB-045 **"Dr. Identity"** D. Harlan Wilson - Follow the Dystopian Duo on a killing spree of epic proportions through the irreal postcapitalist city of Bliptown where time ticks sideways, artificial Bug-Eyed Monsters punish citizens for consumer-capitalist lethargy, and ultraviolence is as essential as a daily multivitamin. **208 pages $15**

BB-046 **"The Million-Year Centipede"** Eckhard Gerdes -Wakelin, frontman for 'The Hinge,' wrote a poem so prophetic that to ignore it dooms a person to drown in blood. **130 pages $12**

BB-047 **"Sausagey Santa"** Carlton Mellick III - A bizarro Christmas tale featuring Santa as a piratey mutant with a body made of sausages. **124 pages $10**

BB-048 **"Misadventures in a Thumbnail Universe"** Vincent Sakowski - Dive deep into the surreal and satirical realms of neo-classical Blender Fiction, filled with television shoes and flesh-filled skies. **120 pages $10**

BB-049 "Vacation" Jeremy C. Shipp - Blueblood Bernard Johnson leaved his boring life behind to go on The Vacation, a year-long corporate sponsored odyssey. But instead of seeing the world, Bernard is captured by terrorists, becomes a key figure in secret drug wars, and, worse, doesn't once miss his secure American Dream. 160 pages $14

BB-050 "Discouraging at Best" John Edward Lawson - A collection where the absurdity of the mundane expands exponentially creating a tidal wave that sweeps reason away. For those who enjoy satire, bizarro, or a good old-fashioned slap to the senses. 208 pages $15

BB-051 "13 Thorns" Gina Ranalli - Thirteen tales of twisted, bizarro horror. 240 pages $13

BB-052 "Better Ways of Being Dead" Christian TeBordo - In this class, the students have to keep one palm down on the table at all times, and listen to lectures about a panda who speaks Chinese. 216 pages $14

 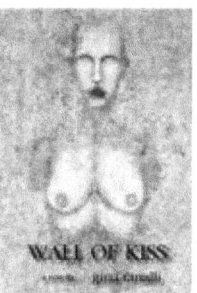  

BB-053 "Ballad of a Slow Poisoner" Andrew Goldfarb Millford Mutterwurst sat down on a Tuesday to take his afternoon tea, and made the unpleasant discovery that his elbows were becoming flatter. 128 pages $10

BB-054 "Wall of Kiss" Gina Ranalli A woman... A wall... Sometimes love blooms in the strangest of places. 108 pages $9

BB-055 "HELP! A Bear is Eating Me" Mykle Hansen The bizarro, heartwarming, magical tale of poor planning, hubris and severe blood loss... 150 pages $11

BB-056 "Piecemeal June" Jordan Krall A man falls in love with a living sex doll, but with love comes danger when her creator comes after her with crab-squid assassins. 150 pages $11

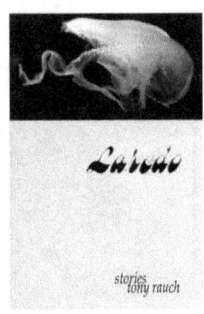

BB-057
"Laredo"
Tony Rauch
Dreamlike, surreal
stories by Tony
Rauch.
180 pages $12

BB-058
**"The Overwhelming
Urge"**
Andersen Prunty
A collection of bizarro
tales by Andersen
Prunty.
180 pages $12

COMING SOON

"Adolf in Wonderland" by Carlton Mellick III

"House of Houses" by Kevin L. Donihe

"Super Cell Anemia" by Duncan Barlow

"The Ultra Fuckers" by Carlton Mellick III

"Cocoon of Terror" by Jason Earls

"Jack and Mr. Grin" by Andersen Prunty

ORDER FORM

TITLES	QTY	PRICE	TOTAL
Shipping costs (see below)			
TOTAL			

Please make checks and moneyorders payable to ROSE O'KEEFE / BIZARRO BOOKS in U.S. funds only. Please don't send bad checks! Allow 2-6 weeks for delivery. International orders may take longer. If you'd like to pay online via PAYPAL.COM, send payments to publisher@eraserheadpress.com.

SHIPPING: US ORDERS - $2 for the first book, $1 for each additional book. For priority shipping, add an additional $4. INT'L ORDERS - $5 for the first book, $3 for each additional book. Add an additional $5 per book for global priority shipping.

Send payment to:

BIZARRO BOOKS
 C/O Rose O'Keefe
 205 NE Bryant
 Portland, OR 97211

Address
City   State   Zip
Email   Phone

www.ingramcontent.com/pod-product-compliance
Lightning Source LLC
Chambersburg PA
CBHW060927030726
47503CB00003B/505